MYSTIC ROSE

Patricia Gallagher

MYSTIC ROSE

ISBN 0 600 36341 4

First published in Great Britain 1978
by Hamlyn Paperbacks

2nd printing 1978

Hamlyn Paperbacks are published by
The Hamlyn Publishing Group Ltd,
Astronaut House,
Feltham,
Middlesex, England

Made and printed in Great Britain by
Hazell Watson & Viney Ltd,
Aylesbury, Bucks

To Nancy Coffey,
my good friend and editor,
with gratitude and appreciation.

PART I

Chapter 1

STAR LAMONT stood on the deck of the *Pearl* as it docked in Charleston harbor, her eyes searching anxiously for her father's carriage. He knew she was arriving today, home from Boston after a year in Miss Christian's Lyceum for Young Ladies. Her symbol of achievement, her diploma, tied with a blue ribbon, was in one of her trunks. She had graduated neither at the top of her class nor at the bottom, and she was glad to be done with formal education. She had not wanted to go away to school in the first place and certainly not all the way to Boston. But in that year, 1811, it was fashionable for the daughters of southern aristocracy to be "finished" in the North, a fad which the second Mrs. Lamont had taken quite seriously in order to be temporarily free of her stepdaughter.

Star had opposed Emily Wilson from the beginning when she had been hired as her governess, and she had never accepted her when she became her "new mother." Nor had she acknowledged Emily's children, Lance and Lorna, both older than Star, as her brother and sister.

She especially resented Emily's influence over her father and her interference into her own life. It seemed the creature could not be content as mistress of the manor, managing the domestic affairs. She wanted to control the master and his daughter as well—and while her husband was inclined to acquiesce, his child was not.

But where was pa now? Wasn't anybody going to welcome her home, not even a servant, after all this time away? Star tapped her foot restlessly on the deck, hands on hips, offended by this apparent neglect. But she did not blame her father. If John failed to meet her, it would be *their* fault, the three of them. Somehow, in their perpetual conspiracy against her, they would prevent his meeting her, just as they had persuaded him to send her away. In her history studies at the lyceum, she had read of kingdoms and governments ruled by a triumvirate, and she had immediately thought of her stepfamily. Her resentment of the tyrannical trinity that dominated the Lamont domain had become an intense obsession in which she suspected them of all sorts of tricks, schemes, and treacheries.

"Mauma."

She spoke to her servant, a middle-aged Barbadian woman in a starched calico gown and immaculate white tignon, who had been exiled to Boston with Star and had shared the slave quarters at the lyceum along with the servants of other southern students. Mauma was the name, taken from the Gullah dialect, for a black woman who took care of white children.

"Yes'm?"

"Do you see father anywhere?"

"No'm. But your pa be there, honey. He can see the boat comin' with the spyglass. Most probably he's been watchin' from his factory office. He'll be waitin' when we land, sure. And Lordy mercy, am I glad to get home! That was the worst year of my whole life."

"Mine, too," Star agreed.

Contrary to its glowing reputation the exclusive lyceum had proven to be a secluded institution with inflexible rules and regulations. High stone walls and locked gates guarded the campus, and though the school was centrally located, the students saw little beyond the towers and steeples of the other metropolitan religious and educational facilities. Governed by a stern old Puritan headmistress, it lacked only barred windows to transform the spare rooms into reformatory cells. Only the memories of Mystic Rose and the periodic love letters of Grant Russell had made Star's immurement there endurable.

"I ain't never goin' North again, Miss Star. I pretty near froze to death up there. If you want to get any more learnin' in foreign countries, you're gettin' it alone or takin' another woman with you. Draft mules couldn't drag me back to Boston."

"Me, either," Star murmured. She grimaced as she thought of those horrid dark poplin uniforms with the stiff white collars and cuffs that she had been forced to wear, and those long black capes in winter that had made the girls look like shadows as they moved through the silent corridors to the refectory or across the cloistered grounds to evening vespers in the chapel. Immediately upon graduation, when freed of Miss Christian's jurisdiction, Star had gone with Mauma to a chic shop on the mall and bought a complete new ensemble for the voyage home.

Now she raised her parasol to block the view of a leering sailor, one of the *Pearl*'s crew. She was conscious that the breeze was molding her thin green silk gown to her figure and that the bold sailor was frankly enjoying the voluptuous display of bosom and hips, now considered quite acceptable since the Empress Josephine had made the female form an important part–indeed, the essence–of feminine fashion. The flattering high-waisted, low-necked empire style was extremely popular in America that season, and enterprising modistes, quick to capitalize on a trend, imported other Parisian styles; less-constricting corsets, silk stockings, and high-heeled slippers, as well as rouge and carmine lip pomade, false curls, mascara, and beauty patches. A whole new era of comfort and freedom in dress was being introduced. The emphasis was on charm and femininity, and Star Lamont was generously endowed with both.

But her beauty was not typical of southern aristocracy, nor did it reflect the blood of English nobility. Her high cheekbones might have been Indian, her oblique eyes Egyptian, her mercurial nature Latin. She looked exactly as her mother had looked, and though it was never openly acknowledged in the genealogically conscious Low Country, it was obvious that Angelique Dumaine was not pure French. There had been a Romany somewhere in her ancestry, and evidently the strain had been a strong one, for the characteristics were inherent in both Angelique and her daughter.

To the drab Emily and her equally drab daughter, Star's vivid coloring and volatile spirits seemed excessive and somehow indecent. The fire of life burned too intensely in her dark, passionate eyes. Her wildly curly hair was too black, her ripe mouth too lush and inviting, her voluptuous young body too mature and promising. Such tempestuous beauty forbode trouble and heartbreak, but Star would have been the last to regard it as a misfortune.

"Miss Lorna goin' poke fun at your grade card, Miss Star, cause you never made high marks like her at that fancy school," Mauma predicted.

Star shrugged. "Who wants to be a bluestocking!"

"Miss Lorna, she's pretty smart, ain't she?"

"She reads a lot," Star allowed, "but there's not much good that books will do her when it comes to getting a man."

"Reckon she goin' to be an old maid?"

"She already is, Mauma. She's twenty and still single."

"The gentlemen don't shine up to her, do they? She's sure a wallflower at the balls and parties. I hates to say it, but Miss Lorna is downright plain-lookin'. I seen swamp hens with more charm than that poor gal. Goin' take a mighty big dowry to get her off your pa's hands."

"Hush, Mauma. You mustn't criticize the family in public, although I'm afraid it's true. Pa will have to be a shrewd horse-trader to marry off that bony nag. Why, she doesn't even have all of her teeth!" She sighed impatiently. "Well, the ship has docked! *Where* is pa?"

Sighting a familiar vehicle arriving at the dock, Mauma exclaimed, "Yonder he comes now! Ain't that our carriage, Miss Star, and old Lige atop the box?"

"Yes, that's pa!" Star called out to him, waving a gloved hand and fluttering her kerchief to attract his attention. "Pa! Here I am, pa! He sees us, Mauma. He's waving his hat."

Then suddenly she frowned. "He's alone. I thought Mr. Russell would be with him. I didn't expect Aunt Emily or Miss Lorna or Mr. Lance to meet me, but I thought sure Mr. Russell—"

"A year's a long time to be away from a man," Mauma said ominously. "Specially a man like Mist' Grant."

Star glanced at her irritably. "Mauma, you're such a crepe hanger!" Still, it was odd, Grant's not meeting her. . . .

"All ashore that's goin' ashore!" the steward bawled. He sounded a brassy gong, and the passengers filed toward the gangway.

The dock was pure pandemonium. Gruff voices bellowed orders about baggage, and great canvas bags of mail and parcels were thrown from the ship onto the wharves. Star feared for the contents of her trunks, especially the delicate pieces of china she had painted under exacting instructions. She had hoped to bring home something of which she could be proud, since her scholastic record merited no praise. Now those clumsy oafs would destroy all her painstaking efforts!

The docks were piled high with crates of goods, barrels of rice, bales of cotton, stacks of lumber, and drums of turpentine. Sailors bandied insults and profanities with the stevedores loading and unloading the vessels. A slave ship had just put in with a cargo of West Indian blacks, and the frightened, miserable men and women, in chains and smelling of bilge water and vomit, were herded ashore like so many trapped animals. Star knew they would be auctioned off the block at the slave market on Chalmers Street. Perhaps her father would bid on some—they would be fortunate to acquire such a kind and tolerant master as John Lamont.

"Papa!" she exclaimed. "Oh, papa! It's so good to see you again!"

She rushed into his waiting arms, and John Lamont held her close, kissing her pink cheeks that were flushed with happy excitement. "Welcome home, honey. Your old pa missed you dreadfully. But you look fine! The Yankees treated you well, I trust?"

Her effervescent chuckle bubbled up from a spring of mirth and vitality. "Like nobility, pa."

"And so you are," he said proudly. "Descended of English lords, no less!"

"Oh, pa! Titles don't mean anything in America now. You said so yourself, many times. Besides, the Yankees treat anyone with money well."

That was a thoughtless aspersion on her stepmother, but her father ignored it. Star was glancing curiously about, still expecting Grant Russell, thinking that he was teasing her, hiding behind the mountains of cargo on the wharves and intending to surprise her.

"Are you alone, pa?"

Sudden pain flashed across his face, and in that moment Star saw how drastically he had aged in the short time she had been away. So much new gray in his brown hair and beard, so many deep furrows in his face, even a slight stoop to his once tall and erect body. He was old, old beyond his sixty years. A fierce sadness gripped her. What had those monsters done to him?

"Quite alone, daughter. Come now. Let us go home. The family is waiting. They'll be so happy to have you back."

"Will they, pa?" she asked skeptically, for she did not believe what he said any more than he did. They were not her family and would not be glad to see her again. She suspected they had hoped and perhaps even prayed that she would never return—that she would fall ill in Boston and die or that the ship would go down with all aboard in a storm at sea.

They climbed into the landau, Mauma occupying the perch with the coachman, Lige, who grinned broadly at his young mistress. Two other muscular slaves wrestled with Star's heavy leather trunks, loading them onto a wagon that would follow. She heard the rattle of broken china, but it did not matter now if every last piece were shattered. Grant Russell had not met her, and it would not take the news long to circulate throughout Charleston and the Low Country.

Star could contain her curiosity no longer. "Where is he, pa? Why didn't Grant meet me? A girl would naturally expect her best beau—"

"My dear—"

"What is it, pa? Is he ill? Tell me, or I shall scream!"

"Grant is all right, Star."

"Then where is he? He knew I was arriving on the *Pearl*. You told him, didn't you? And I wrote him. Why didn't he meet me, pa?"

"Because, under the circumstances, it would not have been proper, daughter."

"Not proper? What are you saying, pa?"

John Lamont's facial muscles tensed and flickered under the neatly trimmed whiskers. "Grant Russell is going to marry your sister, Star. He and Lorna are betrothed."

Though his voice was low and guarded, Mauma's alert ears caught the incredible news, but Star scarcely noticed her backward glance of amazement and commiseration. Her face blanched, and for the first time in her life she experienced a sensation of giddiness, as though she might faint.

"It's not true," she whispered in disbelief. "It can't be true, pa! His letters never once—"

"I'm sorry, Star, but it's quite true. I wanted to write you, but the mail wouldn't have reached Boston in time. It was all so sudden and unexpected. I had no idea there was anything serious between them. Grant called at Mystic Rose during your absence, but I thought friendship and his interest in you brought him. He was kind to Lorna on several occasions but certainly did not appear to be courting her."

"When is the—the wedding?"

"Two weeks from tomorrow."

Shocked and bewildered, Star could only murmur, "So soon?"

"Much too soon in the eyes of convention, but Lorna will hear no counsel or admonition. I don't know what's come over the young folk nowadays; so many are flying in the face of tradition and decorum. Perhaps it's the uncertain times and the possibility of war with England."

"I think I know what prompted Lorna's haste," Star said bitterly. "She wanted the banns published before I returned. Grant will have to go through with it now."

"Try to accept this graciously, Star. I know it's a great disappointment, but these things happen. Try to understand and treat your sister kindly."

"Lorna Wilson is not my sister, pa."

"She's a Lamont now, Star. I adopted her, remember. And Lance, too."

"I don't care! You can change their names, but you can't change their blood. They're still Wilsons to me. Yankee Wilsons, all three of them, including their mother! And I hate them. You can't make me love or even like them, pa. I never have, and I never will."

"My child. My poor little girl," John said helplessly, unable to comfort or reassure her. He felt awkward and inadequate before the servants, though they pretended not to hear, and he shouted at Lige to drive faster.

The whip flourished over the team of matched bays as the carriage careened through the narrow cobbled streets, following King Street to the Old King's Highway, off which ran the Cooper River Road. Star stared straight ahead, her small gloved hands clasped tightly in her green silk lap. This was the end, the nightmarish end to all her beautiful dreams.

Chapter 2

THE FIVE MILES through the lush, languid Carolina Low Country to the Lamont plantation on the Cooper River seemed interminable to Star. Recent rains had roughened the dirt road, and she wished aloud that her father had met her in a boat. But John explained that the family riverboat was under repair and the rice barges, used to ship the crops to Charleston for export, were unfit for a white woman to ride in.

Like all great plantations, Mystic Rose was a community in itself. A sturdy log fence bordered the property on the roadside, while dense woodlands and the curving river formed the other natural boundaries. Beyond the split railings could be seen the century-old manor house, patterned in a minor scale after Lamont Castle in Kent, England. It was architecturally unique among its more conventional neighbors of Georgian and Colonial design.

Age and careful landscaping relieved the English austerity somewhat, though it still gave the impression of a feudal castle, an aspect heightened by the forest of chimney pots and weathervanes above the steep slate roof and the turrets, towers, and cupolas surmounting the corners. Indians, Barbary pirates, and British soldiers had been fought from its battlements, and the families of other planters in the vicinity had often sought refuge there, secure behind the solid walls. Secret underground passages led to the Cooper River where a boat was always moored for quick escape to the walled village of Charleston.

Some distance from the great mansion stood the rows of neat slave cabins, built of timbers felled on the plantation and bricks fired in its kilns. The doors and shutters of the cabins were painted blue to keep away evil spirits. The gray morning mists hovering about the dark walls and the shadows of dusk creeping furtively into the moss-hung gardens cast an aura of mystery and enchantment over the place, which was keenly felt by the superstitious Blacks, inspiring many awesome hallucinations of witches and "haints." The summer sun dispelled the "ghosts," but in the winter haze they often lingered all day, causing the youngsters to come in early from play and families to huddle close to the fire.

The plantation had been named for the lovely but strange white rose that grew and bloomed only in the family cemeteries. Brought from Lamont Castle, where it had flourished in the burial ground but had refused to grow anywhere else on the vast estate, it promptly rooted in the family burial plot in America, while defying attempts to establish it in other locations on the property. Nor would it thrive in the graveyards of other than blood or married relations of Lamonts. Neighbors requesting cuttings, only to have them fail, soon ceased trying to cultivate the mystic rose that had a peculiar affinity for the dead of this particular family. Intrigued botanists and flower fanciers traveled for miles to observe this rare specimen of unknown genus, whose beauty and fragrance were as fascinating as its culture was mysterious.

There was also a jail on the property, and it had two occupants this bright June day: a young man caught pilfering brandy from the liquor cellar and an old man caught molesting a pretty young wench in the hayloft. Both would receive extra duty in the rice fields when their sentences were served. But now they were sullen and grumbling, because they were not free to welcome Miss Star. They had hoped Master John would pardon them for the occasion, but they knew they were lucky to have escaped without the whipping Master Lance had recommended.

The hunting hounds, recognizing the blue and silver carriage as it entered the broad oak-lined avenue, ran yelping to meet it. Pigtailed, barefooted black children pattered after the dogs, and happy women appeared on the stoops of the cabins. The field hands paused in their labors to wave and shout greetings to the young mistress, whose return they had all been anticipating for weeks, aware that it would mean a sumptuous feast, of which they would receive the abundant overflow.

Nothing had changed. Mystic Rose was exactly as Star remembered it: the lawn as emerald green as the summer day she had left, the gardens in riotous bloom, and fruit hanging heavy in the orchards. As always, a crew of slaves was beautifying the grounds, mowing and rolling the sea-island grass, trimming the hedges in precise geometric patterns, raking leaves, and setting out new plants from the conservatories.

But no, it wasn't really the same. It had not been the same for eight years now, not since her mother had died of a strange fever and that New England schoolteacher had come to be her governess and remained to become her stepmother and mistress of Mystic Rose. Oh, if only her father had never advertised in those northern journals for a governess, if only Emily Wilson had never answered the advertisement!

Alerted for the occasion, the entire household staff waited on the brick terrace: Cicero, the venerable seventy-year old butler, stately in his plain black suit, ageless except for the tufted white brows and the cottony kinks of his hair; Pansy, Fern and Gullie, the white-turbaned, white-aproned maids; the head cook, Taby, whose corpulence attested to her culinary arts; the housekeeper, Big Lou; and Bobo, the liveried valet of Mr. Lance. These were the principal domestics, but there were many more: footmen, scullions, kitchen helpers, laundresses, seamstresses, and assistants in the offices.

Emily was present also, sedate in severe gray muslin, a statuesque woman much too slender for her height. Her eyes were light blue, pale-lashed and slightly protuberant, and her thick fading blond hair rested in a ponderous chignon on her swanlike neck. Beauty had escaped her even in youth, but she had compensated for her lack of physical attractions by being educated and having impeccable character. To Star she would always be a governess–prim and reserved, the firm hand and voice of authority.

Beside her, lounging against one of the gray stone pillars, was her son Lance. He wore British tweed riding breeches and hand-tooled Cordovan boots. His drooping lids half concealed his yellowish eyes, and a smile played about his mouth as he watched the approaching carriage. At twenty-four, Lance already had the appearance and manner of a jaded libertine. The sallowness of his pitted skin was due as much to careless health habits as to a malarial liver. Riding was his only form of exercise. Gambling, drinking, and wenching were his chief diversions, and to be master of Mystic Rose was his paramount ambition.

Star viewed him with contempt and disgust, wondering if her father had ever regretted adopting Lance Wilson. Surely he could not call this arrogant wastrel "son" with any degree of pride and confidence. What earthly use would he ever be to the family, the plantation, himself, or anyone else? They would be extremely fortunate if he did not shame and disgrace them all.

As John Lamont and his daughter, assisted by two footmen, alighted, Emily came forth, embracing Star with cool restraint. "Welcome home, dear. We've missed you."

Their eyes met briefly. "Have you, Aunt Emily?" Star had never called her mother, and she refused to lie by saying that she had missed her or any of them, except her father.

Lance affected a languid yawn, intended to convey genteel boredom. Since his return from Oxford and his European tour, Lance considered himself a polished gentleman and continental wit. "Bring out the fatted calf, father."

Star flipped him a negligible glance, as though he were some intruder she had just noticed. "I should think that would have been more appropriate on your return from abroad, prodigal son."

Lance grinned, undaunted by her swift parry. "I see the Yankees did not blunt your tongue, little sister, it's as keen as ever. But I find that refreshing and stimulating. Things have been somewhat stale and dull here in your absence."

Emily hastened to stem an argument between the two, whose antagonism had evidently been increased by the separation. "Let us go inside. I'm sure Star is anxious to see Lorna."

"Undoubtedly," Lance drawled, dipping snuff from a jeweled gold box, a habit he had cultivated in Paris and thought highly elegant. "And 'tis a meeting I don't wish to miss."

The servants pushed forward then, fearful of being ignored, and Star greeted them warmly, with a familiarity which Emily frowned upon. "Bless your old heart, Cicero! Still as spry and spruce as ever, eh? And what have you cooked for my welcome meal, Taby? All my favorite dishes? Pansy–Fern–Gullie–Big Lou–Bobo–did you all miss me?"

They grinned and blushed under her attentions, and the butler, as he was accustomed to doing, spoke for them all, his flattering speech obviously well rehearsed. Cicero was major-domo of Mystic Rose, not only by virtue of his seniority but by the prestige resulting from his having personally served President Washington upon his visit with John Lamont during his southern tour in 1789. Cicero had never forgotten the great honor nor allowed any other Black person on the plantation to forget it.

"Miss Star, Mystic Rose weren't the same without you. Seem like the sun never shine so bright while you was away, or the flowers bloom so pretty. Welcome home, little miss. We's glad to have you back. Yes'm, we sure is!"

Deeply touched, Star squeezed his gnarled black hand in hers. "Thank you, Cicero. I was homesick my entire time in Boston, and hope I'll never be away so long again."

"All right, now! Back to work, all of you!"

Emily clapped her hands briskly, and the group quickly dispersed. She knew they were curious to see the meeting between the daughters of the house, and that their sympathies were with Star—Angelique's precious child, who had inherited their loyalty and affections upon her death.

When Emily had first come to Mystic Rose, she had heard nothing but laments for, and glowing tributes to, the beloved Miss Angel. And she had made the unfortunate mistake, too late now to rectify, of not commiserating with them. They had never forgiven her initial coolness and formality, nor the sterner discipline she imposed on them, though they accorded her due respect and obedience. The household ran as smoothly as it ever had, for Emily was a competent manager, but without the easy grace and harmony that had prevailed under Angelique's reign. Smoldering resentment often could be seen in the eyes of the slaves, and their quiet mutterings were directed at Emily and her overbearing offspring.

Lorna had been advised to remain in her room until the preliminaries of the homecoming were over. The servants might gossip and speculate among themselves later, but they would not be permitted to witness any scene firsthand. For of course there would be a scene, and Emily dreaded the prospect as much as her son relished it. But she could think of no possible way to avoid it. The young women, never friends and now foes, had to meet sometime, and it could no longer be postponed.

They entered the house in expectant silence. The foyer was dim and cool, lighted only by the rainbow reflections of the Belgian stained-glass window on the landing. Lamont ancestral portraits in reeded mahogany frames personalized the walls, and ferns and ivies in jardinieres trailed onto the tesselated marble floor. A suit of polished armor, worn by a relative in the Wars of the Roses, guarded one corner; near it hung the family coat of arms with its motto, *Aut Vincere Aut Mori,* meaning, "Either to conquer or to die."

At the head of the ornate stairway, framed in the light of the mullioned window, Lorna stood poised and waiting, smiling down at Star from her superior height, no suggestion of shame or apology in her manner. Indeed, she was triumphant. It had been no small feat to steal the beau of the belle of the county!

She descended slowly, one hand gliding along the carved banister. Her pink voile gown, though in high style, did little to improve her willowy form, and Star thought with grim satisfaction of how surprised and disappointed Grant would be when he discovered that Lorna's hipbones protruded like an old cow's, her bosom was mostly lace puffs pinned to her shift, and those golden curls, bleached with lemon juice and tortured in wires every night, hung limp and drab in damp weather. But perhaps he had already learned these secrets and still wanted her, still preferred this homely bluestocking to any charmer in the Carolina Low Country, including herself.

Pain and anger raged in her breast, pain at her loss, fury at having been outwitted by one whom she had never considered any competition or rival. And as Lorna reached her, still smiling complacently, Star's hand lashed out and struck her across her face, freezing her triumph in a stinging blow. Then, lifting her skirts, Star sailed past her stepsister and up the stairs to her own chambers, slamming the door and turning the key in the lock.

Startled, Lorna gasped and touched her burning cheek. Her dignity crushed and her victory tarnished, she wailed in mortification. "Oh, how mean she is, and how unfair! A perfectly horrid and hateful creature! And I was going to ask her to be my maid of honor, too!"

Her brother laughed, rocking on his heels in gleeful amusement, while his mother glared at her husband, mutely demanding an apology from his little vixen.

"Try to understand, all of you," John implored quietly, "that she has had a terrible shock."

He had tried to love Emily's children as his own; he had given them his name, an education and every social advantage, even a share in his fortune. But it was only natural that Star was dearer to his heart. Remaining neutral in the many domestic conflicts of the past eight years had made a reticent and retiring man of him. Interludes of peace and harmony had prevailed in the house while the children were away at various schools, but now that they were together again under one roof, the walls trembled with anticipation of renewed battle. Feeling the trepidations, John retreated as usual to the safer ground of his own domain, the land.

At least once a week he rode over the ten thousand acres of his estate, generally with the overseer, Clem Jones, but sometimes alone. Lance rarely accompanied him on these tours of inspection and never concerned himself with the business side of the plantation, although he expected one day to be the master of it. He had no practical knowledge of agriculture and no interest in acquiring any. He knew something about the breeding and training of horses and dogs, but nothing about raising cattle, sheep, and hogs. He regarded the rice paddies, Mystic Rose's chief source of revenue, as dismal swamps that bred mosquitoes and disease, and he shunned equally the sunny green fields where the crops of corn, oats, wheat, rye, and vegetables grew.

Lance was no fit master for the plantation. He had no

love of the land, no sense of duty to the ancestors who had carved it out of the wilderness and fought and died for it, and no appreciation of the beauties and bounties a generous nature had bestowed upon the Carolina Low Country. To him it represented wealth and luxury, and he accepted these gifts as if they were his birthright, without gratitude or even wonder at his great good fortune. John Lamont was well aware of his stepson's ambitions and inadequacies, and whenever he thought of his own age and the future of Mystic Rose, despair and bewilderment rose in him.

The glow of the setting sun made a bonfire on the west rim of the pine forest, and the familiar evening dampness exuded from the dark swamps. Lights gleamed in the manor, and candles burned in slave cabins. Smoke spiraled from the multiple chimneys of the manor, a sign that supper was being prepared. The meal would be delayed because of him, but he could not pass the cemetery without pausing for a few minutes of meditation at Angelique's tomb.

Leaving his mount outside the iron fence, John walked through the arched gateway entwined with English ivy. Immediately a sense of peace mingled with sadness filled him. Her memory would never leave him. How could he forget her when she lived again in her child? Star resembled her mother even more now than when she had left a year ago; seeing her again, embracing her, was almost like having Angelique with him again.

"Sleep well, my darling," he whispered. "One day I shall lie beside you. It is so written in my will, Angel. Life parted us, but death shall not."

From the twilight shadows of the gardens, Lance watched his stepfather. There was a scowl of contempt on his face as John plucked a single perfect bud from the mystic rose, laid it at the feet of the white marble angel guarding the tomb, and bowed his head in reverent prayer.

Pity the poor bastard who couldn't forget a woman, even a young and beautiful woman! And you, Lance, he chided himself, why do you not forget Angelique's daughter? What is it about her you find so attractive and bewitching? Is it her beauty—or her portion of Mystic Rose? Damn it all, he thought, the little gypsy has cast a spell over me—the same, no doubt, that her mother cast over that old fool in the cemetery!

Chapter 3

STAR DID NOT APPEAR for supper and could not be coaxed out of her room. Her absence at the table did not affect the appetite of either Lorna or Lance, and Emily declared that Miss Priss would change her mind when she grew hungry enough. John said nothing, inclined to agree with his wife that Star would not perish of starvation. But Mauma, aware of the heartbroken girl's impetuosity and fearing she might react rashly, worried through the night. And when Star failed to come down to breakfast, she prepared an appetizing tray and tapped at her door.

"Miss Star! It's Mauma, honey. I brought you some vittles. Open the door and let me in."

"I'm not hungry, Mauma, and I don't want to see anyone."

"You can't shut yourself up forever, Miss Star, less you aim to live in one of the towers. And you got to eat, less you want to go early to the Promised Land. Come on now, open the door before this food gets all cold and greasy. Besides, I got news for you."

"News?" Star repeated on the other side of the locked door.

Leaning closer, Mauma whispered, "I got a plan how you can win back Mist' Grant. Are you listenin', Miss Star?"

The key rattled in the lock, the door opened a crack. "A plan? What kind of plan?"

Pushing the door open, Mauma bustled in and set the loaded tray on the bureau. "I'll tell you while you eat, lamb."

"Why, you scheming old she-bear! You're as bad as they are! You haven't any plan. You just used that ruse to get in here. I ought to put you on the block."

"Yes'm, but first hear me out. I got a plan for sure, and it will never fail." She whisked the silver covers off the steaming dishes to display a small banquet: tiny patties of hashed turkey, a thick sliver of pink sugar-cured ham, hoecakes of Indian corn flour with butter and syrup, and the inevitable porringer of light and fluffy boiled rice. "Everything you like, honey, and plenty of it."

"Oh, all right. But I'm not hungry." Star popped a turkey patty into her mouth, but for once food did not taste good to her. "Well, I'm eating. What's the plan?"

"It's a magic plan. Gullah magic."

"Gullah! Have you been discussing my private affairs with the slaves, Mauma? With that sorceress Tawn?"

"Honey, my people know all 'bout your private 'fairs and everybody else's. Don't nobody need to tell them nothing; they got ways of findin' out for themselves. Tawn she like you, Miss Star, and she don't like that uppity Miss Lorna. Tawn she wants to help you get Mist' Grant back, and she goin' do it with a black cat bone. Ain't no magic like a black cat bone."

Star gagged on the patty, her stomach revolting at the idea of Gullah magic. She had never watched the actual preparation of any voodoo charm, such rites being carefully guarded and their practice expressly forbidden at Mystic Rose, but she had heard about the black cat bone from an old granny on the plantation and would never forget the dreadful recipe.

"First you get a black cat. Got to be black as Satan hisself. Then you put on a pot of boilin' water, throw the cat in and boil him alive. Mustn't kill the cat, else you kill the magic. You must cook him alive till the meat fall off the bones. Then you fetch the pot and all to a stream of runnin' water and dump it in. The water will carry off the meat and bones—all that is, 'cept one bone. That's the lucky bone. You can work any kind of magic with that bone. Man can get any gal he want with that bone, and a gal can get any man she want, no matter who he belong to, and that's the gospel truth."

Star shuddered at the repugnant thought, and pushed the tray aside. "Oh, no, Mauma! Tell Tawn that I appreciate her interest in me and her offer to help, but I can't accept it. I'm a Christian and don't believe in such superstitions. And I wish you wouldn't either, Mauma. It's wrong. Evil. And sinful, the preacher says."

"Maybe. But wouldn't surprise me none if Miss Lorna worked some magic on Mist' Grant. That gal couldn't of caught that man with what the Lord alone give her; she had to have extra help, and Gullah magic is mighty powerful."

"Shh, Mauma! Not so loud. Miss Lorna would have you whipped if she heard such scandalous talk about her."

"She ain't here. Her and Miss Emily gone to Charleston to shop for Miss Lorna's hope chest. Gullie say her weddin' box is near bustin' with stuff, and it 'pears she started hopin' and fixin' for to marry Mist' Grant the day you left for Boston. The seamstresses is workin' like crazy on the bridal dress. Miss Lorna say she goin' have the grandest marriage the Low Country ever seen. The invitations been sent, most a hundred or more. The house goin' be full of flowers, and there goin' be a big reception with a barbecue and a ball and everything."

Star clamped her hands over her ears. "Hush, Mauma, hush! I don't want to hear about it. Oh, I can't bear to think about it! Have you unpacked my trunks?"

"How could I, when you wouldn't let me in the room?"

"Well, don't bother to unpack them yet. I may be needing them again, very soon. Right now, I want my gray faille riding habit and my boots."

"What for?"

"What for? I want to ride, of course!"

"Where to?" Mauma asked suspiciously.

"Just on the plantation—and I don't need a watchdog! Where's pa?"

"Somewhere with the overseer, I reckon. Miss Star, you ain't fixin' to sneak over and see Mist' Grant, is you?"

"Certainly not! Do you think I have no pride? That I would go chasing after him now? No, indeed. I hate him! I never want to see him again. Oh, Mauma, I do hate him!"

"Well, don't cry 'bout it, honey. Ain't no man worth cryin' over, specially one you hates. But I still think a black cat bone—"

A warning glance silenced her. "My habit, Mauma. And then tell Dink to saddle my horse. My little red mare, Flame—if Miss Lorna hasn't appropriated her, too!"

"Yes'm, but you be careful now. Don't go tearin' off like a cyclone, fall off, and break your neck."

"It's my neck, Mauma, and I'll ride as I damn well please! Just do as you're told, you hear me?"

"My, my! If Miss Angel could hear her cherub now, yellin' and cussin' like a field hand." A doleful shake of her head and a mournful clucking of her tongue shamed Star into remorse and an apology.

"I'm sorry, Mauma. I was angry, but not at you. Will you be a darling now and do my bidding?"

"Yes'm." Mauma started for the door, unable to resist a final admonition. "Just don't kill yourself."

Star had ridden since the age of five, learning on a Shetland pony and was now an expert equestrienne, although a bit too reckless and daring for her father's peace of mind. And when he saw her on Flame, galloping across the meadow, toward him, her long black hair flaring in the wind, he rode forward on his big gray gelding to meet her. No female should ride like that sidesaddle; it was dangerous, and he marveled that she could remain seated. But he did not scold or warn her, having learned long ago that it was useless. He smiled, tipping his hat.

"Good morning, young lady. So the princess decided to forsake her tower?"

"Don't tease me, pa, please. I'm in no mood for jesting. I've come to tell you something important."

Instantly his face sobered. "What is it, Star?"

"I want to go away, pa. As soon as possible. I don't want to be here for the wedding."

"My dear child, where would you go?"

"Virginia would be nice, pa. I could visit Aunt Charity in Richmond and take Mauma with me. Or Aunt Prudence in Baltimore. It doesn't matter, I just want to get away. Surely you understand, pa?"

John nodded sympathetically. "I understand, daughter. But I must say I'm surprised and disappointed in you. To think you want to run away from something you feel you can't face. That's a cowardly attitude, Star, and you're no coward. How could you be, with the blood of nobles and warriors and pioneers in your veins?"

Now he was going to relate again the oft-told saga of her forefathers, which always began with Lord Newton Lamont, patriarch of the clan. Ordinarily, Star was proud of her distinguished lineage, for one's genealogy was important in the Carolina Low Country, even more important than one's religion or politics. But today she cared not at all about her illustrious origins. What did it matter if she were a princess royal, when the man she loved and wanted preferred a common Yankee!

"Your ancestors were not soft or craven, Star. Your great-great-grandfather was one of the bravest of Britain's noble sons. He risked his life to fight for King Charles I, in the civil war between the Royalists and the

Parliamentarians. He lost his castle and lands in Kent, his London properties, and all of his family possessions and when Cromwell's butchers beheaded their sovereign, he went into impoverished exile with the king's son and other cavaliers. And then, fortunately still young and healthy, he challenged life all over again in a strange new country."

Disinterested, Star fidgeted in her saddle. "I know, pa. But the land was given to him, wasn't it, as a royal grant?"

"True. After the Restoration, Lord Lamont was unable to recover his confiscated properties except for Lamont Castle, and King Charles II, in appreciation of his loyalty and support, granted him a part of the then new province of Carolina. He was one of the original Lords Proprietors, Star. Think of that! But he did not remain in England, content to sit at a desk planning colonization and helping to outfit expeditions, as some of his peers did. He sailed for America himself, bringing a party of settlers with him."

By mute and mutual consent one chapter was always omitted: that of Lord Lamont's shipboard romance and marriage to a commoner, whereupon he dropped his title, relinquished his proprietary rule, and all of his lands except ten thousand acres on the Carolina coast. Here, on the banks of the Cooper River, he built Mystic Rose as a monument to his ancestors and became Mr. Newton Lamont, Southern gentleman, pioneer planter, and country squire.

His descendants, however, reluctant to relinquish their claim to nobility, continued to embroider the Lamont coat-of-arms on the household linens and the servants' liveries, to have the impressive crest painted on the coaches and perpetuated on the silver ordered from foreign silversmiths, abandoning the practice only a few years prior to the Revolution, when sentimental attachment to the motherland proved socially unpopular and politically inexpedient.

Fervently absorbed in his subject, John continued in

reverent tones, "Ah, but that was only the beginning, Star. There was a wilderness of hostile Indians to conquer. There were plagues, floods, hurricanes. And wars. Oh, so many wars for Lord Lamont and his sons after him to fight. The Spanish in 1702, the Spanish and French in 1706, the Yemassee Indians, and the Barbary pirates. The persistent Spanish again in 1740, the Cherokees in 1760, and the hardest fight of all, against the Crown in the Revolution."

"Yes, pa, I know. But that's ancient history, and you've told me before."

"So I have, daughter, and I tell you again. All this is your heritage, too, not merely the wealth and position, the good times and easy living. From such strong and courageous forebearers, you must have inherited some strength and courage, my child. Enough surely to carry you triumphantly through these next few trying weeks?"

What a sly rascal pa was! The family honor was at stake, and he could not have presented a more convincing or persuasive case in its defense. There was something of the lawyer, the preacher, and the politician in him. How could she brook this grand old tradition? Walk away from the first real test of her fiber, the first great challenge to her heritage and character?

She sighed resignedly. "You win, pa." A tear trickled down her cheek, and she hastily brushed it away. "But sometimes I wish Lord Lamont had stayed in England. I might be married by now or at least betrothed to a noble. An earl or duke or even a prince. What future have I this way?"

"Is there no other young man in these woods who takes my little fawn's fancy?"

"None, pa. I like the county boys well enough as friends, but there's not one of them I'd want for a husband. No, not if I wither on the vine like an unplucked melon."

"Ah well, cheer up, lass. 'Tis often darkest just before the dawn. You'll not be a spinster—on that I'd wager Mystic Rose. Now the sun grows higher and hotter, and you'd best return to the shade of the house."

"It's early yet, pa. Couldn't I ride awhile on the River Road? It's shady there."

"Alone?"

"Please, pa. I don't need a chaperon on our land! I can take care of myself. I'm a Lamont, remember? Brave and fearless."

John smiled indulgently, knowing that he was bested. "All right, minx. Just this once. But mind you stay away from the swamps and return by noon, or I'll send a posse after you, and you'll not beguile me so again. Understand?"

"Yes, pa." With a pert salute, she wheeled the frisky mare around.

"Try to ride like a lady!" her father called after her, his admonitions muffled in the thud of flying hoofs.

The trees grew thickly along the River Road, forming a dense canopy of shade impenetrable by even the intense Carolina sun. It was pleasantly cool there now, but by noon the sea breezes would be stilled, and a stifling humid heat would steam out of the nearby swamps and marshes.

Those lush green jungles had always fascinated Star, primarily because she was forbidden to enter them. Gorgeous birds–snowy herons, pink-stemmed egrets, scarlet ibis–nested in the tall, bald cypresses, and rare plants and flowers grew and blossomed in the inky waters. But the swamps also contained vicious alligators, venomous snakes, and treacherous quicksand bogs into which a body could disappear. Eerie sounds came from the dark interiors at night. Numerous weird legends surrounded the swamps, and Star was convinced, as were the slaves, that no human being could venture into the swamps and come out alive. Nevertheless, they intrigued her.

Turning off the lane into the pine woods, she rode paths familiar to her since childhood: old Indian trails she had often ridden with Grant–when she could escape vigilant Mauma, who was a poor and reluctant horsewoman at best. Grant had kissed her in these protective shadows and brought her to the brink of physical surrender. As she remembered those occasions now, her eyes moistened and all the generations of brave Lamonts could not lessen the ache in her heart. This had naught to do with wars, pirates, or plagues; this was unrequited love, the most devastating defeat a young girl could suffer. To a young girl whose most serious and baffling problems heretofore had been how to dress her hair and what to fear, this rejection was an enormous dilemma, painful, humiliating, frustrating, bewildering.

Perhaps, she thought, she could do something to make him regret jilting her. What if she threw herself in the river or got lost in the swamps and sucked into a mire or was eaten by an alligator? Or what if she hanged herself like that poor abandoned girl whose ghost now haunted the Mossbank plantation? All the slaves had seen her floating around at night in a filmy white gown and had heard her weeping and wailing.

The horse, pausing with perked ears and quivering nostrils, startled her. The animal sensed something other than the wild life inhabiting the woods. A runaway slave hiding from the law and his master's hounds who would think nothing of raping and murdering her and disposing of the evidence in the convenient quicksand? An Indian who lusted for revenge on a white man's daughter and would take her before scalping her? Suddenly she wanted passionately to live.

She heard hoofbeats and then leaves crunching and twigs snapping. Flame neighed and bolted, and Star tugged hard on the reins to calm her. She sat rigid with fright. Should she try to escape, or should she scream? Who would hear her? Mentally, she had surrendered herself to a thousand different tortures at the hands of some desperate character when a familiar white Arabian stallion came into view, the rider no stranger to her.

"Hello, Star." He greeted her amicably, as if a whole year had not passed since their last meeting, or as if she were only a friend he had chanced upon in the country.

"You frightened me, Grant Russell!"

"I'm sorry. You shouldn't be out here alone."

Finding herself safe, Star no longer remembered her fears. "Go away," she said sullenly, all her grievances against him rising in hostility. "I don't need your company or your protection."

Laying the crop on Flame's flanks, she put her into a run, uncertain as to where she would go. Deep into the forest, if necessary, to escape him. He must not touch her, lest she make a fool of herself. A year's separation had only made him more handsome and desirable and her more vulnerable. He was still the gallant knight of her girlish dreams; he had the same intense blue eyes, the same burnished hair like a helmet of bronze, the same stalwart physique with muscles as hard and strong as a suit of armor. Dear God, what had happened? How had she lost him?

He was pursuing her and enjoying the chase. Star knew his horse was faster than hers, for they had raced before, and that he would soon overtake her.

"Go away!" she shouted over her shoulder. "Leave me alone!"

But he only laughed and spurred his mount. Catching up with her, his hand grabbed her reins. Star struck at him with her crop, but he held the lines firmly and managed to dismount. Then he pulled her off her saddle and fell to the ground struggling with her. They rolled in the pine needles a minute or two before he subdued her, pinning her shoulders to the earth and crossing her arms over her heaving breasts. She stared at him truculently, her mouth petulant.

"What're you doing here, Mr. Russell?"

"I came to see you, Miss Lamont."

"By what right, pray? It's Lorna you should be visiting now, sir. And she's in Charleston, shopping for her trousseau."

He nodded, somewhat breathless from the tussle and her disturbing proximity. "I saw Lorna and her mother come into town. That's when I headed for Mystic Rose. I wanted to see you alone, Star. Your father said you were riding the River Road. I thought you might be here, at our place."

"It's not 'our place' any more, Grant. And I wonder that you have the nerve to face me at all, much less here!"

"Star—oh, darling, don't hate me! I think I could bear anything but that. I can't explain now about Lorna and me, it wouldn't be decent. I can only ask your indulgence and beg your forgiveness."

"Why should you? A man may marry whom he pleases, and I certainly had no prior claim on you. No betrothal ring or vows to bind you, only your false words and letters! Now let me up. This is no bed of roses I'm lying in, you know."

He released her with slow reluctance. Star sat up, shaking the leaves from her tossed curls. Grant watched her intently, a familiar light in his eyes, that eloquent blue glow which needed no interpretation.

"You're beautiful," he said softly. "Even lovelier, I think, than when you went away."

"Did you expect me to return an old hag?"

"No, but it might help if you had. Oh, Star! If only you'd never gone to Boston!"

"You talk as if I wanted to go, and you know better. Your letters, Grant—why didn't you tell me the truth? Why did you intimate things you didn't mean? And why did you let me come home to—to *this* without any warning? It was cruel, Grant. Worse, it was cowardly."

His head hung. "I know, darling."

Star stiffened, fighting to strengthen her defenseless emotions, for she longed to embrace him. "Never call me that again, Grant."

"You think I don't love you any more? That I love *her*? Oh, God, if you only knew!"

"I don't want to know," she said, denying her curiosity. "I must go now. I promised pa I'd return by noon."

"He won't worry if we're together."

"I doubt if that would comfort him much now," she

said tersely. "You're hardly to be trusted, Mr. Russell."

Without reply, he stood and reached down to assist her. But as their hands touched, his warm and lingering, Star quickly withdrew hers and began to brush her habit.

"It's not that easy, Star," he said, "for either of us. You still love me, too. I know it. You can't deny it."

"Did you bring her here?" she asked. "To our place?"

Hope flickered in his eyes. "Then you do still care? You must, if you're jealous?"

"Silly sentimentality, that's all. Like your flowers that I pressed and your letters that I saved. I'm going home now and destroy all my romantic keepsakes, tear them to bits, and burn them!"

"That's exactly what you should do, my dear. Shall I help you?"

She mounted Flame. "No, thank you, Mr. Russell. Just watch the smoke from my chimney!"

Chapter 4

IT REQUIRED THREE SLAVES to carry in Lorna's purchases. Star eyed the boxes and bundles critically. Just like Lance, she bought everything she saw! What right had they to spend her father's money so recklessly, as if it came from a mint or bottomless mine? All those lovely things and still Lorna was whining because a length of brocade she had ordered some months ago from Paris had not yet arrived.

"That stupid French war," she fretted. "I suppose those bonnets on order from that Rue de la Paix milliner will never get here, either."

Emily attempted to mollify her. "Even if they don't, you still have much to be grateful for, dear: a nice dowry and as fine a trousseau as any court lady. But you must be exhausted from all that shopping and fittings. We'll have tea in the parlor."

Star joined them, still loath to believe the wedding was so near, still hoping that she would wake and find it all a bad dream. But published banns were real and almost as binding as the ceremony; a gentleman could not possibly withdraw from the planned marriage, he would have to leave the region if he dared.

"May I have some tea, Aunt Emily?"

"Certainly, Star. But isn't there something you would like to say to your sister first?"

Star nodded reluctantly. Lorna did not deserve an apology, but she would make one for her father's sake. "I'm sorry about yesterday, Lorna. I reckon I lost my temper."

"I reckon you did," Lorna sulked. "But just to show how generous I am, I forgive you."

"Thank you," Star murmured, though it burned her tongue. "And if you still want me, I'll be your maid of honor."

"That's very gracious of you, dear," Emily said, hoping this signified a truce. "Accepting one's destiny gracefully is the beginning of wisdom and maturity."

"Or spinsterhood," Lance drawled, sprawled in a Louis XIV chair, mint julep in hand.

"Lance!" Emily cautioned, but Star ignored him.

"Well," Lorna hesitated, "I don't know. I've already chosen my attendants, and only this morning I asked Letty Clayton to be maid of honor. We went to town expressly to ask her, didn't we, mother? Naturally, after the way you acted, I didn't think you'd care to participate in the ceremony. I wasn't even sure you'd attend. But I suppose if you are truly sorry and want to be decent about it, Letty will bow out for you. But can I depend on you not to balk at the last minute and spoil things for me?"

"I give you my solemn promise, Lorna." Star raised her right hand as if taking an oath. "What color shall I wear?"

"Letty had selected pink."

"Pink would be lovely on Letty, but it's not my best shade."

"No," Lance agreed, his eyes raking her. "Pink is definitely not for you. Too delicate and insipid. Red would suit you much better. May I suggest a scarlet gown with spangles, and jingling bracelets and looped earrings?"

"A scandalous suggestion, indeed!" Emily rebuked him.

"Why, mother? I've heard you call Star a gypsy on occasion. Why not let her dress the part?"

Lance had long been a thorn in Emily's side, and lately the thorn had begun to fester. Her eyes warned him again. She was embarrassed for Star and for herself but relieved that her husband was not present. "Your impudence will not be tolerated, son. Control your tongue or remain silent."

"Come now, mother. I'm not a child to be seen and not heard or spanked and sent to his room."

"Behave like an adult, and you will be treated so."

During the brief, tense silence that prevailed, Star covertly observed her stepfamily. She could feel their indignation, their antagonism toward her, and she reciprocated with an intensity they could not help but sense. Moreover, she scorned her stepmother's feeble defense of her, for she neither wanted nor needed an ally in her war with Lance. They were all hypocrites, anyway. Emily resenting her because she was Angelique's child and because her father still loved her mother. Lorna jealous of her beauty and fearful that she might try to take Grant back from her. And Lance, desiring her in an unbrotherly way and coveting her fortune even more. What did they want or expect her to do? Eat humble pie at the wedding? Be humiliated to tears and tantrums? Make a spectacle of herself and a laughingstock of pa? Well, she wouldn't give them the pleasure and satisfaction!

"I thought I'd wear green taffeta," she said demurely. "And gardenias in my hair."

"Naturally," Lorna muttered, unable to suppress the edge in her voice. "Your most flattering color and Grant's favorite flower. Very well, though Ninon Devoe chose green to complement her titian hair. I suppose she could change to pink or blue. But where do you expect to find a seamstress at this late date? They're all engaged and have been since the invitations went out."

"Don't worry, Lorna. I'll find one, even if I have to pay her extra."

Emily frowned her disapproval. "Spoil her with a bribe and she'll never sew another stitch for you without one."

Lance scoffed at the advice. "You needn't preach thrift to Star, mother. She can afford any extravagance. She owns half of Mystic Rose, you know." Lance could not reconcile himself to John Lamont's will, in which half of his estate would be bequeathed to his daughter and the other half divided equally between his wife and adopted children.

"That's nothing compared to what I'll own as Mrs. Grant Russell," Lorna boasted. "I'll have a plantation on the Santee River, another on Edisto Island, and a fine town house on the Charleston Battery."

"*You* won't be richer," her brother retorted, envious also of his sister's good fortune. "Grant Russell will gain your stake in Mystic Rose, that's all. A wife's property belongs to her husband by law. You're so brilliant, such a *bas-bleu,* I'm surprised you didn't know that. But why he didn't choose Star when she has so much more to offer in so many ways is a mystery to me. How do you explain this enigma, my clever sister?"

Once again Emily intervened. Sometimes it seemed that most of her time was spent trying to promote and maintain peace in the family, with little success. "Children! Shame on you, bickering at tea. Such manners! Worse than when you were in rompers and pinafores. What must the servants think?"

"They're slaves, mother, and should be accustomed to our bad habits by now."

"You are excused, Lance. Pray join your father in his office. It's high time you learned something about the plantation, if ever you hope to manage it."

Flipping open his snuffbox, Lance carefully removed a small amount of snuff, inserted a pinch into each nostril, and sniffed delicately. His every action was languid and affected. But the languor and affectation were deceiving, for they masked a sinister energy that could be ruthless and violent when devoted to his own selfish interests.

"A successful planter needs only a competent overseer, a trustworthy factor, and complete mastery of his slaves," he said, returning the box to his pocket. "One does not have to learn these things, mother; one simply acquires the right people when necessary. As for joining my father—that's impossible, unless I depart this earth. I'm the son of Paul Wilson, Yankee carpenter, and I know not where he's buried. In an unmarked grave in potter's field, perhaps."

Emily shook her head sadly, her stern features softening and a sudden mist blurring her eyes. "Your father lies in a churchyard in Salem, Massachusetts. And he has a headstone, the best I could afford."

"Too bad you have no portrait to keep his memory alive," Lance said. "And too bad he sleeps so far away, where you cannot lay flowers on his bosom and weep." He paused for emphasis.

"Do you know what people say about Mystic Rose, mother? They say it's haunted by the ghost of the beautiful Angelique. They say she is still mistress here and you are just another slave. Some believe the noble Mr. Lamont married his child's governess out of loneliness and desperation. Others maintain he was suffering from swamp fever and proposed to the Widow Wilson with her readymade family in a moment of irrational delusion. Still others insist he was bewitched and in a trance at the time."

Emily's face blanched in horror and dismay. "Where did you hear all this prattle, Lance? Who has dared to spread these vicious lies?"

"I've been eavesdropping on the slaves, mother. They know everything. If you want to know anything about us or our neighbors, just ask them. But it's more than mere gossip, mother. You must realize that yourself. You can't be so blind and impervious to the truth."

"What would you have me do, son?"

"What you should have done immediately upon becoming mistress of Mystic Rose," Lance told her. "Remove the source and inspiration of such rumors. Demand the removal of that portrait in the drawing room. Demand either that he cease mourning openly at her tomb or have her remains transferred elsewhere. It's cruel and unfair to you, mother, like having another woman in the house. And it's indecent, almost as if he were physically unfaithful to you!"

An imperceptible smile touched Emily's thin lips. "A man cannot commit adultery with a dead woman, son."

Astonished at this kind of conversation in her presence, Star could only stare in shock and disgust. She wished she might run and hide, never to have to see or listen to any of them ever again. The hatred for them she had declared to her father yesterday was no fleeting reaction to her own misery; it was real, deep, and abiding. At this moment, she longed for the death or banishment of her stepfamily, for she felt that she could never know true peace or happiness while they lived in the same realm.

"Pay him no mind, mother," Lorna soothed. "His liver is acting up again. Can't you see the jaundice in his eyes and complexion? He needs some calomel and bile salts."

"At least I have an excuse for my yellow skin," Lance scowled at her. "But what gives you that waxy pallor, pray? Constipation? Better purge, sister. Gad, what a sorry bargain Grant is getting! I'm half inclined to agree with the gossip. You must've slipped him a love potion or conjured him with a black cat bone."

Star tensed at that, remembering Mauma's contention, and Lorna leaped instantly to her feet. "Listen to him, mother! Make him hush! If any such wild tale as that circulates the Low Country, I'll be ruined and ostracized!"

"What nonsense are you spouting now, Lance?" Emily

demanded. "Voodoo? If the slaves dare breathe such scandal off this place, their mouths will be hushed with the whip!"

"No, no, mama," Lance mocked, wagging an admonitory finger. "Papa wouldn't permit. There hasn't been a flogging at Mystic Rose since Obah raped his sister in the corn patch last summer."

Adhering to the Barbadian Code of Slave Treatment, John Lamont preferred incarceration to flagellation as punishment for crime and insubordination. Occasionally, however, a hostile or belligerent male had to be beaten as an example to others so inclined. But it was an ugly business, and John soon sold such men off the place. Obah had been severely flogged for his offense and, though a robust giant and valuable worker, he was put on the auction block. Lance considered this practice both weak and foolish and resolved that it would not prevail when he became master of Mystic Rose.

A grim expression crossed Emily's face. "Nevertheless, these tales will cease, and the slaves will show more family loyalty and respect, or there'll be sterner discipline on this plantation. I'll speak to Mr. Lamont about it this evening."

Her son's brutal revelation was a stunning blow to Emily. She had not guessed that the whole county suspected what she herself had known all along. But if it were true, as Lance said, then they had never really accepted her as one of them. Their friendship was only pretense and hypocrisy. And so the ladies whispered about her behind their fans and teacups, and their servants broadcast the gossip, via the grapevine, all over the town and countryside.

Well, she could understand their jealousy and resentment. Apparently they had never forgiven her, an impoverished widow with two children and neither youth nor beauty to compensate for her lack of other qualifications, for snatching an eligible man from under their haughty and elegant noses. And now her plain little daughter was about to repeat the performance! Lorna's marriage into one of the oldest and finest families in the Carolinas would be another Yankee victory over their southern pride and arrogance and tradition, and for that they would despise and criticize her even more.

Let them. Her future and her children's futures were secure. Paul's children would never know want, never suffer hardship and privation. Such security was worth any price she had to pay for it. She could ignore the slights and petty chatter. She could tolerate her step-daughter's animosity and insubordination. She could abide her husband's indifference and the few demands his waning passion made on her body. She could even endure his open mourning at Angelique's tomb and her portrait in the drawing room. For solace she had security and her dignity. Poor substitutes, perhaps, for love and devotion, but beggars couldn't be choosers. And as long as she concealed her hurts and frustrations, no one would know and feel them but her.

But how long must that be, her anguished heart cried out? Dear God, how long?

Chapter 5

STAR, tumbling sleepily out of bed and into the wrapper Mauma held for her, frowned at the clear blue sky and the chirping birds in the trees outside her windows. This was the day, and she had hoped for rain. Stormy weather would have been compatible with her mood and might have delayed the wedding or at least minimized the attendance. But no such favor was granted to her, nor were her desperate prayers answered.

The roads to Mystic Rose were dry and hard and the carriages arrived in a steady caravan. Some had traveled all night; others had been en route for several days or more, stopping over at the homes of friends and relatives or in taverns and inns along the way. Planters' boats, gaily decorated with flowers and greenery according to custom, came from the islands and the navigable streams. There were guests from the Piedmont region, from North Carolina, Georgia, Virginia, Maryland, and Washington.

Under Emily's supervision, a detail of fifty slaves labored in the kitchens, sweating at the huge brick ovens and over the long outdoor pits where savory meats roasted over hickory coals.

A gluttonous people, these southerners, Emily thought. They loved to gorge themselves on rich foods and rare delicacies. Every affair must be a royal banquet. Well, she would cater to their appetites with traditional dishes. Barbecued beef, pork, and mutton, succulent seafoods, stuffed turkey, baked ham, chicken pilaf, and mountains of their eternal, infernal rice. Floating island, both chocolate and vanilla, and charlotte russe. Gallons of syllabub, the South Carolinian's nectar, a delicious froth of whipped cream, wine and sugar. Choice liquors, wines, and crocks of fruit punch. And the crowning achievement, a wedding cake four feet high, elaborately frosted in spun sugar. Let it never be said that the second Mrs. Lamont did not know how to provide a nuptial feast!

With Emily thus occupied, the duty of greeting the guests fell to John Lamont and his stepson. Lance was swaggering and arrogant, and already drinking despite the early hour. Observing him from her windows, Star grimaced. He would be royally drunk before sundown and acting as if he were a direct descendant of Lord Newton Lamont and sole heir to the barony of Mystic Rose.

Mauma was quietly laying out her mistress's wardrobe for the day. The apple-green taffeta gown, rushed to completion by two Charleston modistes, bore the Parisian touch: low neckline, tiny puffed sleeves, and a graceful skirt attached to the bodice high under the breasts. It was elegant in its simplicity. With it she would wear green satin slippers, long silk gloves, and a wreath of fresh gardenias in her dark hair.

"Are all the bridal attendants here, Mauma?"

"Yes'm. They is in Miss Lorna's chambers, and their servants is helpin' to get 'em ready. Gullie, Fern and Pansy laborin' with Miss Lorna. I reckon you best be gettin' fixed, too, Miss Star. The ceremony at ten o'clock, you knows."

"Have you seen Miss Lorna yet?"

"I sneaked a peek," Mauma admitted.

"Does she look pretty?"

Mauma hesitated, assembling lingerie and stockings. "All brides look pretty, child. It's the clothes, I reckon. But I seen prettier ones by far."

Star gazed down at the grounds. They were packed with vehicles of every description, with horses and coach dogs, slaves and servants, and children, white and black, playing games.

"I see the Russell carriage and coachmen in the yard," she said. "When did they arrive?"

"Most an hour ago. Mist' Russell's tryin' to act pleased 'bout the weddin'. But Miz Russell's dressed all in black, like she come to a funeral, and she keep dabbin' at her eyes with a black lace kerchief. Her maid, Sara, is followin' her round with smellin' salts, spectin' her to swoon again."

"Again?"

"Like she did when Mist' Grant told her he was goin' wed Miss Lorna. Sara told me Miz Russell got plum hysterical. She cry out, 'Oh, Lord, son! Is you took leave of your senses? That Yankee gal is no fit wife for a Russell whose grandpappy was a Knight of the Garter!' And then she up and flop on the floor, and Mist' Russell shout at Mist' Grant, 'Thunderation, son! Are you tryin' to kill your poor ma? I've got a good mind to disherit you!' And then he up and got drunk."

But Star scarcely heard. For as she watched, a bright yellow barouche, the fringed top folded back, turned into the avenue of live oaks. It was packed with the groomsmen, merry young blades sporting new finery, and the morose bridegroom was among them. In the wake of the barouche came the somber black buggy of the rector of Goose Creek Church.

Star clutched the curtain, hiding her face in the folds. "Oh, Mauma! I don't think I can go through with it!"

"Yes, you can, lamb. You promised your pa, remember? Come on, now. Time flyin'. You be the prettiest flower of 'em all in this lovely new frock."

I won't listen to the minister read the service, Star decided. I won't watch Grant slip the ring on Lorna's finger. I'll pretend it's nothing to me, that I've never been happier in my life. I'll pretend–I'll pretend–

"I declare," remarked one Charleston matron to another, "she gives as fine a performance as any I've seen at the Dock Street Theater."

"Unfortunately, Edith Russell isn't nearly so accomplished an actress. Poor dear! She hasn't stopped weeping since the ceremony. And her clothes–is she mourning someone?"

"Her son," the other sympathized. "I suppose she feels he might as well be dead as married to that fallen soufflé. And can you blame her? A Yankee nobody with heaven only knows what kind of background! Odd, isn't it, the sudden turn of events? Everyone assumed that Grant Russell and Star Lamont– You don't suppose there's more to this than meets the eye, yet?"

"Oh, I hardly think so. Such impetuosity is usually covered by elopement, although the girls will be counting the months from this date. Besides, I always thought Grant Russell a perfect gentleman."

"No gentleman is perfect, my dear."

"Well, Star won't have any difficulty replacing him. She has been surrounded by cavaliers all day and teasing them to distraction. What a coquette!"

"Isn't every southern belle? It's part of their charm, the heartless creatures. I had my bevy of gallants at her age, and so did you, Elise. Oh, dear! I simply must have another cup of syllabub. I don't suppose it will matter, now that I've lost my figure completely. I might as well enjoy the food."

Only toward evening, when the slaves were lighting the colored lanterns and torches in the gardens and the musicians were tuning their instruments in the ballroom, did Star begin to feel the burden of her false gaiety. She was tired of sweet-talking when she wanted to scream, weary of smiling when she longed to weep. And her persistent swains, beaming at her with new hope now that their arch rival for her affections was safely removed, were beginning to annoy her. Nothing was so welcome as the brief respite when she retired to her room to freshen up for the ball. At least she did not have to pretend with Mauma.

"You is doin' fine, honey. Your pa is proud of you. The pride is stickin' out all over him. You is a Lamont, all right, through and through. And you is foolin' 'em all!"

"I wonder, Mauma. I wonder."

"Sure you is! Now I hear the fiddles scrapin'. Got to brush your hair and put in fresh gardenias. Just a few more hours and it be over, honey. All over."

"Yes," Star sighed. "All over."

Garlands of flowers and ferns, ribbon streamers, and white satin bells festooned the ballroom. The crystal chandeliers and silver wall sconces blazed with candle flame. Patches of waxed floor gleamed between the dancers.

Grant was dutifully dancing with his bride, and Star noticed that Lorna was showing signs of strain and wear: there was dust on the long train of her bridal gown which dangled from a loop on her wrist, a reddish-brown stain of barbecue sauce on the bodice, perspiration stains under the armpits of her gown, and a rip in the wispy veil where it had snagged a bush. She caught Grant's attention, saw his eyes deepen and glow in admiration. But as he smiled, pleadingly, she turned swiftly away, almost bumping into her father and a stranger who had apparently just arrived.

He wore a uniform of some kind, handsome garment of a rich dark-blue material, embellished with gold buttons and braid. A silver-sheathed sword glinted at his side. His hair was as black as her own, and only a man of the sea could have skin of that color and texture. His height was impressive as was his formidable build.

Who was he and what was he doing here? Some nautical acquaintance of her father, no doubt, whose invitation he had forgotten or neglected to mention. Pa was a great one for taking up with strange mariners!

John smiled. "Ah, there you are, my dear! We have a new guest whom you have not met. May I present Captain Troy Stewart? My daughter, Star."

The captain bowed easily, but did not take her hand. "My very great pleasure, Miss Lamont."

As he straightened, Star looked up into his face, a picaresque, sardonic and arrogant face, but attractive enough with regular features and narrow gray green eyes under bold black brows. She could not determine his age, but he was no boy. He looked as if he led an interesting life, adventurous and exciting, free of worries and entanglements.

Hoping that Grant was watching, she spread her skirt in a brief curtsy and bestowed a dimpled smile. "Welcome to Mystic Rose, Captain Stewart."

"The captain's ship put into Charleston yesterday," her father explained. "He has been at sea for several months. His home is Nantucket."

The interest and curiosity he had aroused in Star vanished swiftly. A Yankee sailor! Probably the son of a whaler or a pirate. What was pa thinking of, inviting him to Mystic Rose? Still, he appeared prosperous enough and well mannered.

"How nice," she said.

"May I hope to claim a dance with you later this evening, Miss Lamont?" His voice was deep, resonant, a voice accustomed to commanding and being obeyed.

"I'm sorry, captain. My program is filled."

"My misfortune," he said. "However, should you find yourself bored—your servant, ma'am." He bowed again from the waist, smiling to show strong white teeth in a wide and pleasure-loving mouth.

"Oh, I shan't be bored, captain," Star assured him, flashing a brilliant smile at the young man hurrying to claim his dance with her. "I'm having a wonderful time!"

But it was all bravado. She was wretched, distraught, desperate, unable to think of anything but Grant and Lorna and the inevitable moment when they would take leave of the ball and drive through the moonlight night to Charleston, to the Russell mansion on the Battery, and the nuptial bed in the master chambers. She glimpsed herself in a mirror as she whirled to a lilting waltz popularized at the European courts, and her expression was anything but gay. Her mask had fallen, and she was horrified lest she betray her true emotions. The air seemed oppressively close, sickening with the mingled odors of flowers and perfumes, sweat and candle smoke. The music, the dancing, the laughter, the jubilance—all were a mockery to her, a scourge suddenly beyond endurance. She had to escape.

On the pretext of a sudden headache, she left her partner and slipped into the gardens. The lanterns lighting her way, she wandered far down the paths of the sloping terraces, almost to the bank of the dark river. She paused by a small pool. Fragrant waterlilies floated on its surface. It was quiet and restful here, silent except for the familiar summer symphony of the crickets and frogs. Star dropped her guard, relaxing her tense body in the first breath of freedom she had drawn in hours. But her peaceful respite was shattered when she discovered that she was not alone. A voice spoke in the darkness, and a uniformed figure emerged from the shadows.

"Did you get bored, Miss Lamont?"

Startled as well as angry that he dared to follow her and intrude on her privacy, Star snapped, "Did *you*, Captain Stewart?"

"Frankly, yes. I don't care much for weddings. Perhaps that's why I'm a bachelor."

"You missed the ceremony, captain. It was at ten this morning and was most impressive."

"No doubt. Did you enjoy it?"

"Certainly! Why shouldn't I?"

He shrugged. "Have you known the groom long?"

"All my life."

"Then you must know he's in love with you? That's obvious even to a stranger. Did you refuse him?"

"You are presuming on short acquaintance, captain."

"A nautical habit," he said. "Leisure is a luxury a man in my profession can't afford, and there are few timid souls at sea. But you haven't answered my question, Miss Lamont. Did you jilt Mr. Russell?"

"That's none of your concern, sir."

"None whatever," he agreed. "But may an unbiased party offer a little advice? Don't ignore him so elaborately. It's breaking his heart and giving you both away."

"I'm sure I don't know what you mean."

"Well, no matter." He indicated a marble bench by the pool. "Shall we sit down?"

"I'd rather walk."

"A restless nature, Miss Lamont? Mine also, but it's heredity with me. My father was restless. He sailed the seas for forty years before gout forced him to retire to a cottage on Nantucket Island, where he now polishes shells and builds ships in bottles."

"I see. And how long have you been sailing, Captain Stewart?"

"Longer than you've been alive. Since childhood, in fact. My father's ship was home, school, church, playground–everything to me. I've been in every major port in the world, including the Orient."

"You must be quite old?"

"Ancient," he grinned. "Twenty-seven."

"Is that all? You seem older."

"The sea ages a man."

"And your mother?"

He hesitated, frowning slightly. "Dead," he said then, and Star wondered at the hesitancy and brusqueness in his tone.

"My mother is gone, too," she said softly. "Since I was nine. I'm seventeen now, almost eighteen."

"Is that her portrait in the drawing room?"

"How did you guess?"

"It wasn't difficult, seeing you. Was she French?"

"Yes. A native of Normandy. The revocation of the Edict of Nantes drove her Huguenot family from France in 1685. They took refuge in Holland for awhile. Then they came to America, landing at Savannah, remaining for some years in Georgia, and finally settling in the Carolinas. My stepmother objects to my mother's portrait," she added in a girlish confidence that instantly embarrassed her. Why should he care about her personal problems?

"That's understandable, and you shouldn't hold it against her. I should think any woman would resent her husband's first wife if she were extraordinarily beautiful, and your mother undoubtedly was. It's hard to compete with a memory."

"I suppose it is. Will you be in port long?"

"That depends on how interesting I find Charleston. I've been here before, but it's always struck me as a rather dull and ingrown place."

"Oh, but I assure you it isn't that way at all! Charleston is just—just not very friendly to strangers."

He smiled. "So I've noticed. And the Low Country?"

They had strolled to the end of the rose garden where a gazebo formed an impasse, and Star suspected that he had maneuvered her there intentionally. Trapped in a somewhat vulnerable position, she evaded his question with one of her own.

"Where is your crew tonight?"

"My dear innocent!" he laughed. "Where is any crew after a long hitch at sea? Out on the town, naturally."

"Apparently they don't find our city dull?"

"Give a tar a full bottle and a buxom lass, and he's happy. I'm not so easily pleased." His keen eyes considered her objectively, as if charting a difficult but interesting course. "However, I find nothing here to displease me. That gown must have arrived on the last boat from Paris, and it certainly does justice to your charms."

Her cheeks burned, for he was frankly admiring more than the gown. Suddenly Star felt immodest, her shoulders and bosom indecently exposed, and she wished she had a shawl to cover herself. More disturbing, she believed he had definite designs on her. She only hoped her father had not been hospitable enough to invite him to stay at Mystic Rose. "Are you to be our house guest, captain?"

"No. Aren't you relieved? I'm returning to my ship. It's really quite comfortable. Come aboard if you're in town the next few days, and I'll give you a twenty-one gun salute."

"Your ship has guns?"

"Of course. Most merchantmen are armed. I expect to use it as a privateer when the war comes."

"What war?"

"Why, the war with the British."

"Oh, that one. Pa thinks we'll have to fight England again, too, and soon."

"He's right. The warmongers in Washington and London won't rest until the *Chesapeake-Leopard* Incident is avenged."

Star had only a vague recollection of the incident to which he referred, for it had occurred in 1807, when she was only thirteen and even less interested in such matters than now. But she had often heard her father and his friends discuss the naval engagement between the United States frigate *Chesapeake* and His Majesty's ship *Leopard* in the waters of the Chesapeake Bay. Indeed it was a hostile act on the part of Great Britain and had created quite a furor in the Low Country at the time. Hot-tempered Carolinians were all for an immediate declaration of war on England, confident of a swift victory since the Crown was already involved in a desperate struggle with the ambitious emperor of France, Napoleon Bonaparte, who was madly bent on world conquest.

But while President Jefferson and then his successor, James Madison, vacillated, public opinion subsided and political meetings in the state lessened. Still, the British Orders in Council, imposing a severe system of blockades designed to choke off French supplies by sea, remained in effect, interfering to a damaging extent with American trade with Europe. Seizure of United States merchant vessels and impressment of American seamen continued until New England shipowners were forced to send their fleets out in convoys. Indians captured in the wars raging in the Great Lakes region were discovered with English arms supplied through Canada—one more irritant to neutrality.

But Star, a great admirer of the charming and vivacious first lady, was confident that Dolley Madison would persuade the president to keep the peace, lest war interfere with the social activities in Washington, of which Mrs. Madison was the recognized leader. Her feminine logic amused Captain Stewart.

"Congress, not the president, declares war, my dear. Madison could only recommend it, and I doubt if he would be influenced much one way or the other by the social aspects of the matter."

"And why not, pray? They say Washington is just beginning to come into its own as a world capital. It would be dreadful to have a stupid war set us back into obscurity."

"Dreadful, indeed. But you don't speak the language of your fellow southerners. Some of the most fervid war birds in Congress hail from the South, and they'll be joined this fall by the fire-eating Henry Clay of Kentucky, chief of the war hawks, and your own state's John C. Calhoun."

"You sound like a British sympathizer!"

"Definitely not, and with good reason. My ship has often been stopped by English vessels ostensibly in search of British subjects. This voyage an American-born sailor of English parentage was impressed, and another of Norwegian descent who could not possibly pass for a cockney. Even a birth certificate or citizenship papers are of no avail to a stubborn British officer. To me, that's tantamount to shanghaiing. I was angry enough to fire on the marauder, but it was a man-of-war and could've blasted the *Venus* clear out of the Atlantic."

"The *Venus* is your ship?"

"That's right. I named her for her beautiful lines. Quite seductive, my *Venus*. More than one seaman has fallen in love with her, and she has lured some to a watery grave." He paused reflectively. "Storms at sea, mostly. I lost two of my crew in a Caribbean hurricane last summer. They were swept overboard and never seen again."

"How awful," Star murmured. "Your log must read like an adventure story. I suppose you're bored to distraction on a calm sea or dry land."

"On the contrary. I welcome, as does any sane seaman, an uneventful voyage. And, at the moment, I am not in the least bored on terra firma. Wouldn't you like to get acquainted with the *Venus*? My invitation remains open."

A torch flamed nearby, reflecting in his eyes, but hers were veiled with lowered lashes. "I couldn't possibly accept alone, captain."

"Bring your Cerberus with you."

Star had turned to leave. "My what?"

"Never mind. May I go in with you?"

"Heavens, no! What would people think?"

"What do you want them to think? That you were in the garden weeping–or wooing?"

"Wooing!" Her eyes flashed dark fire. "You flatter yourself, captain. And you run true to legend."

"Legend?"

"That a sailor has a sweetheart in every port. No doubt your collection is a large one, but you needn't think to add me to it. I've no mind to such a romance."

He laughed softly. "Good night, Miss Lamont. I'll pay my respects to your father shortly. Right now, I wish to enjoy a peaceful smoke in your magnificent gardens. Truly, I've never seen a lovelier paradise, and I've seen a good many. You Low Countrymen live in the luxury and splendor of the French aristocrats before their heads rolled in the Revolution. There must be tremendous profit in rice and cotton. And slavery."

Much of what he said was true. Not even the perceptive Lords Proprietors had visualized the full possibilities of the Carolina provinces, the potential wealth that would accrue from indigo and sea island cotton and the golden grains of rice. For rice was king in the Low Country, thriving in the marshes along the tidal rivers. Each abundant harvest increased the fortunes and prestige of the planters. No finer homes and gardens could be found in the South, nor in all America. John Lamont had traveled in many states and had returned justifiably proud in the knowledge that Mystic Rose had few equals and no superiors anywhere, either in tobacco-rich Virginia, cotton-arrogant Georgia and Alabama and Mississippi, or the sugar cane kingdom of Louisiana.

But Troy Stewart tempered his compliments with criticism of, and even contempt for, any aristocracy, particularly one built on slavery. His attitude angered Star. If he did not admire his host's way of life, that was his privilege, but he need not be critical, sarcastic, and downright rude. And suddenly she wanted to escape him more than she had any of the others.

"Excuse me, captain," she said abruptly. "I came out for a breath of fresh air, but suddenly I find the atmosphere in the gardens chilly and most disagreeable."

"Your servant, ma'am," he bowed, his sarcasm and mockery matching her own.

Chapter 6

JOHN LAMONT had business with his factor in Charleston, and Star persuaded him to take her along minus her chaperon. Mauma, nursing a digestive upset occasioned by overeating at the slaves' special wedding feast behind the barns, was too ill to do more than protest, and Star rushed off wearing a summery gown of yellow tiffany with a stomacher laced in narrow black grosgrain ribbon. Her mother's cameo, fastened about her throat on a dainty gold chain, was her only jewelry, and she wore black lace mitts and carried a pagoda parasol of yellow tiffany ruffled in black lace.

She planned to pay an impromptu visit to friends on the Battery near the Russell town house to hopefully hear some neighborly observations of the newlyweds. Since they would not leave on their honeymoon to Virginia Springs for two weeks yet, it could not long escape Grant's attention if she were seen in the company of the dashing young captain of the *Venus*. He had said he would remain in Charleston as long as he found it interesting, and Star did not doubt her ability to make matters interesting, nor her finesse in using him as a balm for her sore heart and an irritant to her former beau.

The tall masts of his ship were clearly visible from Mr. Grady's office on East Bay. A handsome brig, carrying sixteen formidable guns, it was painted deep blue with a replica of Venus and a great deal of gilt carving on the bow. Observing it through Mr. Grady's telescope, Star was surprised to see such an impressive vessel and pleased, too, for surely everyone in town must have noticed it by now.

There was considerable activity on board, indicative of impending departure. The crew was busy swabbing the deck, examining the rigging, and mending a few seams with boiling pitch. The captain, in dark, tight breeches and a white shirt open at the throat, a small-billed sea cap cocked on his head, was inspecting the work. Star focused the glass on him, smiling in premeditated mischief, then put it down and went into the room where her father, Mr. Grady, and an assistant were seated around a heavy oak table spread with ledgers and papers.

The factor was the planter's right hand, equally as important as his overseer and his slaves, and he did far more than just market his client's crops. He acted in large measure as counselor, broker, banker, and slave trader. He purchased tools and supplies for the plantation and sometimes even personal articles for the mistress and other female members of the family. He arranged for the planter's travels and the education of his children. In the event of the master's incapacity or death he often assumed management or administration, or both, of the estate. His knowledge of law and finance must be accurate, his judgment sound, his honor and integrity unimpeachable. Samuel Grady was such a man. And as the new rice crop of Mystic Rose would go to market after the September harvest, there were many pertinent matters to be settled before consignment.

"Pa?"

"Yes, dear?" John murmured absently, concentrating on an invoice.

"May I leave for awhile?"

"Leave?"

"Just for a little while, pa. I won't go far."

"Don't bother me, daughter. Can't you see I'm busy? You promised not to bother me if I brought you along. Go into the anteroom and sit down like a good girl."

"I'm tired of sitting down. I want to go for a walk. May I, pa? Please?"

"Yes, yes. Don't bother me."

"Thanks, pa." She planted a kiss on his cheek, smiled at Mr. Grady and his bespectacled apprentice, whose polite nods scarcely concealed their annoyance at the interruption, and credited herself with great cleverness. Pa was always agreeable when taken unawares.

Several turbaned black nursemaids were out with their little charges, wheeling them in hooded wicker baby carriages, gossiping about their masters and mistresses. Star had a sudden vision of Grant's baby in a carriage and closed her eyes briefly, hoping that Lorna would prove barren.

"Mornin', Miss Star. Where's your Mauma, honey?"

"Ailing. She gorged herself at the wedding and hasn't recuperated yet."

"Does your pa know you is out alone?"

"Oh, yes. He's in conference with his factor. I'm just taking a constitutional."

"Well, don't wander too far, child. The docks ain't no fit place for a lady without a chaperon. The docks ain't no fit place for a lady no time."

It was unthinkable for a decent woman, white or black, to go unescorted to the waterfront, where the prostitutes solicited, and Mauma would have had conniptions to see her young mistress nonchalantly parading herself there, tossing pennies to the black children who danced and sang for passersby, and smiling at the vendors hawking their wares. Star loved Charleston, loved the sights and sounds and smells of it. Lance said it did not compare with New York or Boston, that it was a mere drab village beside London and Paris and the other great metropolises of the Continent. But Lance was a prejudiced fool and a Yankee to boot.

With a population of twenty-five thousand, Charleston ranked among the largest cities of the United States. Its architecture was cosmopolitan, reflecting the influence of many nations: massive public buildings with pillared porticoes and Gothic columns; quaint little houses of colored stucco reminiscent of Normandy and Acadia; the overhanging eaves and Dutch gambrel roofs of Holland; the West Indian piazzas with lacy banisters to furnish shade from the semitropical sun and catch the refreshing evening breezes off the sea; stately Georgian mansions of heavy brick with typical English gardens as secluded as monastery courtyards. For a Charlestonian's privacy, as strangers soon discovered, was as sacred to him as his ancestors and his rice, and he guarded it vigilantly with jalousied windows and high-walled grounds.

Chimney pots and church spires dominated the skyline, with the venerable spires of St. Philip's and St. Michael's rising above all others. Star listened to their melodious chimes pealing the hours. It was eleven o'clock, and she was to return to Mr. Grady's office by noon, whence they would go to the Planters Hotel for the midday buffet.

Approaching the *Venus*, she felt a sudden qualm. Her audacity could bear unwanted consequences, for it could ruin her reputation, put her father to shame, and even force the necessity of a duel upon him. She had an urge to turn back and forget her little scheme, but that urge dissolved in confident optimism. There would be no unpleasantness unless she herself provoked it, and anything short of her father's life was worth the risk to hurt Grant and humiliate Lorna.

Obscene remarks and frank propositions followed her as she passed a group of drunken, loitering sailors, but she imperiously ignored them. No man in command of his faculties could mistake her for a harlot, and all except the sots and derelicts kept a respectful distance and civil silence. Those of the longshoremen who knew John

Lamont took it upon themselves to protect his impudent daughter from any further indignities and bloodied a few noses in the process. The old gentleman couldn't possibly know his pretty daughter was exposing herself to such curs, and someone should inform him—but there were no volunteers. What a charming wench she was, and bound for the *Venus*! Lucky bastard, Captain Stewart. In port three days, and look what he'd attracted.

Star picked her way daintily across the dirty, cluttered wharves, to the gangplank of the *Venus*. The captain was no longer on deck, and the crew paused in their chores to stare and speculate. "Is Captain Stewart aboard?" she inquired of the man nearest her, a muscular brute in a striped jersey, with a deforming wad of tobacco in his mouth.

"You expected, miss?"

"No, I want to surprise him. I'm a friend."

"The skipper don't like surprises, miss."

"I betcha he'll like this one!" someone said, and they all joined in his ribald laughter.

Star was furious. Did they imagine she had come to an assignation? "Take me to him, please."

"Very well, miss. Foller me."

He led her across the deck and down a half-flight of stairs to the master cabin. He rapped briskly on the closed door. "Cap'n Stewart! A lady to see you, sir!"

His voice answered, "Come in," and Star's heart gave a sudden leap—too late to run now. He smiled at her entry. "Well, Miss Lamont! Dismissed, Finch."

"Aye, aye, sir."

"Leave the door open," Star said, freezing the nasty grin on the sailor's face.

"Yes, miss."

"A fine crew you have, Captain Stewart! A few eye-patches and peg legs, and they'd pass for shipwrecked pirates."

He laughed. "They're good men for my purpose. Not the handsomest crew afloat, perhaps, but one of the ablest. And they don't always look so salty; they spruce up a bit when there are ladies aboard."

Star was observing his quarters, which were neat and comfortably furnished. Maps and charts lined the walls. There was a large globe in a brass stand bolted to the varnished floor, a mahogany desk, several chairs and sea chests, and an ample bunk. She noticed a shelf of leather-bound books, some of whose titles were also in the library of Mystic Rose, while others were forbidden in respectable homes.

"Do you have many lady passengers?"

"Not if I can help it. The *Venus* is essentially a merchantman. Besides, women are notoriously bad sailors. They're constitutionally unsuited to the sea and go berserk in an emergency."

"Oh, we don't all scream at the sight of a mouse, captain. I had a white one as a pet when I was small. And if some of us didn't have iron constitutions, there wouldn't be many children born into this world! But don't worry. I haven't come to beg passage or to stow away on your ship. Are you surprised to see me?"

"Somewhat. But surely you didn't come alone?"

"Am I not safe on the *Venus*?"

His eyes swept intimately over her. In addition to her physical assets, she possessed other attractions. "You're a brave and venturesome lass, Miss Lamont, and I'll wager your father has no knowledge of your whereabouts. Would you like the twenty-one gun salute I promised you?"

Star laughed, stimulated by her escapade. "Mercy, no! The whole town would know of my indiscretion."

"I'm flattered that you've compromised your reputation to visit me, Miss Lamont. And though my facilities for entertainment may be limited, my hospitality is not. Please sit down. I have some excellent Madeira, which I understand is much favored in Charleston. Will you join me in a glass?"

"Thank you, no. But don't deprive yourself."

"I never drink alone, not even wine. Solitary imbibing is the pastime of either an old or unresourceful person.

What do you think of my ship?" he asked with the pride of a man seeking an opinion of his home, his possessions, his grand passion.

"Oh, it's very nice, and much larger than I expected. It would make a fine privateer, but it would be a pity to have it blown up by the British navy."

"Would that matter to you?"

She shrugged eloquently, as her mother might have, to indicate indifference. "Comme çi, comme ça."

"Spoken like a true aristocrat," he said, chagrined. "Oh, yes, I know your background. Every dock hand in these parts is aware of your family history. Noble blood, somewhat diluted, flows in your veins."

Her dark brows, like delicately spread wings, arched in surprise and indignation. "You've been discussing me on the waterfront, sir?"

"Not directly, my dear, and only discreetly. I indicated that I might do business with John Lamont and was interested in his character and reputation."

"I hope you're satisfied of both?"

"He's an honorable man, no doubt, but I wouldn't consider shipping anything for him, even if he or his factor approached me. It would be against my principles to transport the fruits of slave labor. I happen to be an abolitionist."

"Well, if you want to be received socially in Charleston, don't broadcast your politics, captain. Abolition is a lynching word here."

"So I understand. But where I come from a man is entitled to his opinions and convictions."

"Pa says two-thirds of the Negroes in the North are held in slavery. And there are white slaves in the factories and sweatshops. Washington households, including the president's are full of Negroes."

"Southern legislators bring them with them," he said. "And, of course, Madison is from Virginia, a state that seems to have a monopoly on the presidency. One wonders when, if ever, Virginia will run out of candidates for the office, and how Adams managed to slip into it before Jefferson."

"Would you have preferred Aaron Burr?"

"That's the standard southern rejoinder to any complaint about the Virginia presidential dynasty, and you are obviously quoting your mentors. But it doesn't make them political deities, Miss Lamont, nor give divine sanction to their slavery covenant."

"We acquired our chattels according to state law, captain! Pa has a bill of sale for every slave born off Mystic Rose."

"Is it signed by God Almighty? If not, the transactions are legally right but morally wrong."

"Oh, we've heard all those old axioms and arguments from the Yankee evangelists," Star rebutted. " 'Slavery is capitalizing on human flesh, than which there is no greater debasement of mankind.' 'Slavery is evil, because it subordinates the soul as well as the body and mind—' "

"And I've heard all the defenses," he interrupted. "Foremost, that it's necessary to the economic existence of the South. Well, if that's true, I pity your future. Because one day, as civilization in America progresses, the society built on such feudalism will inevitably collapse. There's no place for a caste system in a free country, and it must ultimately fail in any true democracy. Where will your aristocracy be then? And your castles on the Cooper and the Ashley?"

Star clutched at her frayed dignity. "I see we are at odds again, Captain Stewart. We have nothing in common. Absolutely nothing. It was a terrible mistake to come here, and I can't imagine what possessed me."

"Shall I tell you? Sheer mischief prompted you, milady, abetted by feminine curiosity. You wanted to see how I would receive you. You didn't consider our farewell in your garden of paradise final any more than I did."

"Possibly not, sir, but I shall make it so now. I hope you weigh anchor fast and that foul weather accompanies your every voyage from here to eternity!"

He stood grinning at her. A triangle of coarse, curling black hair was visible on his chest—he was a flagrantly masculine man unashamed of his virility. "You'd better go ashore, Miss Lamont, before word spreads that you're aboard my ship unchaperoned. I should hate to prolong my stay in this driftwood port because some impetuous gallant considered it necessary to avenge your honor with a challenge."

"Does the prospect of a duel trouble you, captain? I should think a Yankee could defend himself as well as any other man and that one of your caliber would have experienced many challenges by now."

"I have," he said grimly. "I've fought with pistol and sword but always with good cause, never over an imagined slight or injury. If any of your noble champions should challenge me, I will first give him sufficient reason. I never risk my neck just for the sport of it. This is the essential difference, perhaps, between chivalry and cowardice."

His implication was plain enough, so brutally plain that Star blushed in comprehension. He would have to disgrace her in reality before he would fight over her. Obviously, she had misjudged him. He was not one of her Carolina cavaliers, and he was not infatuated enough with her to discommode himself for her benefit. She could only hope that he had the decency to allow her a graceful exit.

"I regret that you have such an ill opinion of me, captain. Apparently you take me for an adventuress, and such was not my intention. I came aboard the *Venus* on your invitation, in the sincere hope that we might be friends. But your reception has convinced me otherwise. I'll go now, sir, and trouble you no more. Good day!"

She turned swiftly, surprised to feel his hand, warm and persuasive, staying her. "Don't go. Please. I'm sorry. We started off on the wrong foot, but that's no reason to continue out of step, is it?"

Her eyes accused, then questioned, him. "First you

ask me to leave, and then you stop me. What new approach is this, captain?"

"Only an apology for my bad manners," he said, smiling in a conciliatory way. "My friends call me Troy. May I call you Star?"

After some hesitancy, she agreed. "My full name is Mary Star, but somewhere along the years I lost Mary. At first I didn't like it, now I do. It's different. There must be millions of Marys in the world."

"There are millions of stars, too," he said. "But not one that could outshine you."

She smiled faintly, soothed by the balm of flattery. "A moment ago we were quarreling. Now I half believe you're making love to me."

A negative shake of his head shattered that illusion. "No, my dear. When and if I make love to you, you won't be in doubt. You'll know it."

"What a shark you are! But I suppose every sailor is, and any maid who dallies with one does so at her own peril."

"Are you dallying with me?"

"That's an ugly word."

"You used it first. Tell me the truth, Star, if the truth is in you. Are you just teasing me?"

"Well—" She glanced away. "Truthfully—"

"Never mind," he muttered.

His arms slipped around her, reminding her of Grant's arms, hard and strong with a gentle strength. It was a good feeling, and she did not protest or resist. She expected to be kissed, even anticipated it, but he did not oblige. Instead he released her, quite abruptly, and ushered her rapidly out of the cabin, as if the ship were afire and he wanted to get her to safety. Star was disappointed. In some vague way, she felt cheated.

"Your father will be anxious about you," he said. "Run along now. Perhaps I'll see you again. Someday."

"Troy—"

"Yes?"

"If I asked you not to sail today—"

"Are you asking me?"

She nodded, dropping her lashes, unable to sustain the expectancy in his gaze.

"Remember I said I'd stay in Charleston as long as I found it interesting? Well, I'll have to retract that statement, lest I be tempted to remain forever. And since I have definite commitments elsewhere, I must leave soon."

"But not today?"

"Not today. May I call at your home this evening?"

"You'll have to ask pa."

"I'll call on pa, ostensibly."

"You won't fool pa. Nor Mauma, either."

"Mauma?"

"My nursemaid when I was small, and now my dogged duenna. This is one of the few times I've ever been able to successfully escape her."

"And immediately managed to get yourself into mischief."

"She can blame pa. He was supposed to keep an eye on me. But he got absorbed in business, and I took advantage of the poor darling."

"Which proves that men, even doting fathers, are not fit chaperons," he said, escorting her to the gangplank.

Star had difficulty cloaking her triumph. He was only a man, after all, and as gullible and vulnerable to feminine wiles as any other. A pretty face, a pleasing figure, a dimpled smile, and fluttering eyelashes could lure and capture almost any male. Except the one she had wanted.

"Until this evening," he said at the plank.

"What? Oh, yes. Until then, captain . . ."

Chapter 7

THE CREW OF THE *Venus* were disgruntled. Some were at liberty on the town, others lay stretched out on deck, dozing in the sun, while the rest sat about whittling sticks or tying knots. They were restless, and as miserable as fish out of water. Their evenings were spent enjoyably enough in the Mermaid Tavern in Stolls Alley or in some bargained bed, but the days were long and boring. From the first mate to the cabin boy, all were beginning to grumble.

"A week we been beached here, growin' barnacles," Boatswain Briggs complained. "The weather's been obligin' and the sea smooth as a baby's buttocks, but here we camp while the skipper squires a fair maiden about Charleston."

"Well, what the hell!" the gunner growled. His name was Carl Bull, a great hulk of a man covered with tattoos. "He didn't sever our pay, did he? He made enough off that last cargo to retire, almost. And you got to admit Miss Lamont ain't no ordinary female. Man, what a delightful stem and stern! The *Venus* in full sail ain't no prettier sight. Let the cap'n enjoy himself. Get yourself a new whore and a bottle of rum–"

"I done swilled so much rum it's runnin' outta my ears, and there ain't no new doxies in this port."

"All cats are gray in the dark. I had a little yeller one in Jamaica once, as fine a treat as a man could want. Some of them mulattoes is mighty fetchin' and know tricks no white gal ever heard of, much less practiced."

Briggs hawked and spat, first testing the wind with a moist forefinger. "Somebody smells like a pig."

Blubber, the cook, roared with laughter. "Look who's complainin' of stench! A salt that only bathes when the skipper orders us overboard in the raw."

"Yeah? Well, you smell like a rotten whale yourself, Blubber! How do you think you got your name? And I guess we'd all stink to the high heavens and be crawlin' with vermin if the skipper didn't make it an ironclad rule for everyone to douse in that cattle dip once a week. First time I got dunked in that vat, I thought my hide was gonna melt right off to the bone. So help me, I think it's pure carbolic acid."

"Naw, it's mostly pine oil."

"You notice he don't bathe in it? Uses that fine Castile soap he buys by the gross in Spain, and that fancy English bay rum on his face. Real gentleman when he goes courtin', and I fear he's gettin' hisself tangled up in that female octopus's tentacles. Reckon he made port with her yet?"

"How can he, with that big black woman around? Her old man must not trust the skipper alone with her."

"She's a maiden, you fool, and they got to be chaperoned! You can't take 'em at your will and pleasure like a trollop."

"Well, if he was to marry her first, we'll probably dry-rot in this drab hole. Might as well sign on another tub."

"Aw, stop spoutin' bilge, Briggs! You wouldn't leave the *Venus*, and you know it. She's a fine ship, meets every single requirement of the Lloyd's Register, seaworthy and buoyant as a bride's bosom. A king's yacht compared to some of the leaky coffins I've shipped on. And there ain't no better skipper on the seven seas than Troy Stewart. Right, Blubber?"

"I ain't complainin', mate. Ask the crew."

"Aye, I will. Hey, Rusty, Joe, Finch, O'Toole, Hammer! All hands on deck!"

"Aw, stop roarin', Bull! And don't bother us. Can't you see we're gettin' our beauty rest? We ain't complainin' about the cap'n. Poll the Kid."

The Kid was the newest and youngest member of the crew, having just completed his first hitch on the *Venus*. Troy had signed him on in Boston under the name of Michael Longstreet, a slight and somewhat sensitive lad of sixteen, an orphan taken on out of pity, since he was hardly an able seaman. He had been listening to the conversation, but did not join in until Bull posed his question.

"Stewart's a good master," he agreed. "He knows his ship and his course. But I didn't think so highly of him when he clapped me in the brig for a week on my first offense."

"You deserved it, Kid, for falling asleep on watch. That's a serious offense on land or sea, and more so the first time, because you're liable to get in the habit. Men have been shot for less, and ships have been lost or captured because some sleepy bird dozed off in the crow's nest. Troy was lenient with you. And look at the sportin' chance he gave Hobson, even after he tried to incite mutiny."

"Sporting? He runs his sword through Hobson's belly, pulls it out, wipes off the blood on the victim's shirt, and calmly asks, 'Are there any more would-be mutineers among us?' "

"Sure he done that, we all seen him. But only to keep Hobson's blade from gutting him. Troy didn't have to offer to fight it out with him, you know. Mutiny is punishable by death. It was damned decent of the skipper to challenge Hobson and give him a chance to prove he wasn't the best man, as he claimed. And didn't he give him a Christian burial? Wrap his slimy body in a blanket and read over him from the Scriptures? I been on ships where mutineers was just hung from the yardarm and tossed overboard to the fish. You're pretty young, Kid, and you ain't been on no other ship. You don't know how cruel some captains treat their men. Why, Troy is like a brother to us, long as we behave. Course if you shirk your duty or get insubordinate, like Hobson, he gets tough. There has to be discipline on a ship and respect for the officers."

"Bull's right," Blubber nodded. "Believe me, Kid, you ain't got nothing to chafe about, unless that last mess I fixed stuck in your craw. We get good pay, decent food, and fair treatment. Half the seamen ain't that lucky. But if you ain't satisfied, ask Troy to release you. That's all you got to do, boy. Just ask him."

"Aw, lay off the Kid," said Briggs, his tone mellowing somewhat. "This was his first hitch, and you'll admit we had smoother ones. Hobson's guts don't bother me none, he'd have died for his crime in any court in the world. But the Kid was so impressed with Troy's performance, he got sick and ain't recovered yet. He's got the skipper pegged for a sea monster, and it's gonna take a heap of brotherin' on the cap'n's part to overcome that image. Lucky he wasn't with us the time we was on short rations and Bistro was caught stealin' from the galley and suckin' more'n his share of lemons to ward off scurvy."

The Kid's ears wiggled. "What happened that time?"

"Well, Bistro didn't need to worry no more about losin' his teeth. The cap'n knocked 'em out, all over the deck. What else could he do? Let the bastard steal all the good food and the rest of us starve on scraps and get black gums?"

"Where's Bistro now?" the Kid croaked, fearing to ask.

"He jumped ship at Lisbon and ain't been seen or heard from since, the lyin', thievin' scum!" Briggs spat again, in disgust at Bistro's memory. "But all this gab ain't takin' us to sea. I hope the cap'n ain't gone soft in the skull about that little magnolia blossom. What if he decides to tie the knot with her and plant rice?"

"Not Troy," Bull was confident. "He'll never desert the sea voluntarily. There's salt water in his veins. Why, he was weaned on hardtack and cut his teeth on the wheel."

"Whatever happened to his old woman? He never talks about her. You'd think he never had a mother, that he was just spawned somewhere and washed up on shore. She's supposed to be dead, but it's strange the way he looks when he says she's dead; like he knows she ain't, but wishes she was. Sort of gives me the creeps. And it ain't natural—a fella ought to love his ma and have kind memories of her. But he only seems to care about his old man."

"Maybe he's got reasons. But don't worry about that little baggage gaffin' him. Troy likes his women all right, but he likes his freedom more. I think he'd pull his seacocks and scuttle hisself before he'd anchor onto a helpmeet and put hisself in permanent drydock."

"I hope you're right, Bill. But he's sure actin' like a first class landlubber now. Ridin' around with a gal and her chaperon, sippin' tea at garden parties, sittin' in a theater box dressed up like a tame monkey, and canterin' over the countryside on a curried horse! All he uses the *Venus* for now is to sleep and change clothes. He's goin' to a masquerade tonight. Fancy that! A costume ball, and he ordered some kind of sissy suit to wear. Christ! If the cap'n ain't careful, he's gonna lose his reputation."

Briggs continued his carping, interrupted by dissenting or concurring opinions from the crew, until the irritated parrot, Neptune, mascot of the ship, began to squawk and flutter on his perch, rattling his confining leg chain. His vocabulary consisted of two intelligible words, "Pipe down!" and a lexicon of garbled profanity.

Chapter 8

CHARLESTON HARBOR shimmered under a full moon, and the tide could be heard lapping at the shores and islands. Lights gleamed in the forts as Captain Stewart told Star that, although the city was proud of its defenses, they were inadequate against a potential British invasion. He warned that expeditionary forces could be landed with little or no opposition a few miles down the unpatrolled coast while battleships shelled the harbor fortifications. The ramparts were poorly manned and ordinanced with obsolete equipment, and the citizens did not seem to be at all worried about it. Star, herself, was not concerned enough to take up the gauntlet. All her emotions were concentrated on the ball, which they had left temporarily at her suggestion, because Grant's masked eyes were following their every move, unable to conceal or camouflage his jealousy. They stood now on the third story balcony of the Ralston town house, just outside the magnificent ballroom.

Star wore a glittering gold tunic with a heavy gold cord binding her slender waist, golden slippers, and a tight gold-mesh cap on her dark curls. She was impersonating Juliet at the masquerade and had persuaded Troy to come as Romeo, though he had protested before agreeing. "I'm a little old for that role. And wouldn't we be somewhat out of character? Romeo and Juliet were lovers, you know."

This was precisely the impression Star wanted to give Grant, and the expression on his face when she and Troy appeared in costume was rewarding beyond her wildest expectations. He quite obviously did not like or trust this handsome stranger with whom Star was being seen, and he was hard pressed to extend him the customary courtesies. And there were others who shared his reserve and suspicions. The young captain of the *Venus* was received in Charleston mostly out of deference to John Lamont and his daughter, and no one knew this better than Troy himself. Let the esteemed planter frown on him or question his character, and he would meet with cold stares and stiff nods. I'm as out of place here, Troy thought wryly, as a plebeian on Olympus or a pagan in the Holy City!

Aloud he said, "The jalousied windows and walled gardens of this city are symbolic of its hospitality. I'm sure they would never accept me without your father's sponsorship."

"Well, you can't really blame them, Troy. No one knows who you actually are, not even I. You've told me so little about yourself, and nothing of your family. People like to know who they're entertaining in their homes."

"They're entertaining Captain Troy Stewart, of the merchant ship *Venus*. What more do they need to know? Doesn't my conduct speak for itself? Must I come bearing my genealogy and credentials in hand?"

"Has anyone been unkind to you, Troy?"

"Your choleric stepbrother cuts me cold, and Grant Russell is hardly the soul of courtesy. He seems to feel you still belong to him and apparently fears for your safety in my presence. He's a tormented man, Star."

No observation could have pleased her more. "You

mustn't mind Lance," she said. "His jaundice affects his spleen. He's surly to almost everyone, including his family. As for Mr. Russell—"

"He's jealous, naturally, and resentful of my attentions to you. And I'm beginning to develop an active contempt for him. Married to one woman, with his honeymoon still before him, and coveting another! His poor bride is nervous and miserable. What prompted their marriage, Star? Do you know?"

A vehement shake of her head betrayed her emotional disturbance. "No, and I don't care to discuss it! For better or worse, it's done and can't be undone, except by death or annulment. There's no divorce in this state, and only death is considered a proper marital severance in the Low Country."

"Then you would marry him if he were free?"

"I didn't say that, Troy."

"Stop pretending, Star. I know how you feel about Russell and that you've been using me to rile him. I'd like to think otherwise, but I'm not a fool. And you'd better find a replacement, because I'm sailing tomorrow. I must. I've delayed too long already. My crew is impatient, and I have a contract with an export firm in New York. A cargo is waiting on me now. Besides, I'm tired of playing second fiddle. And I resent being used in your little intrigue."

"That's unfair, Troy."

"You deny it?"

"Well, if I said I was madly in love with you, you'd know I was lying, wouldn't you? But I've enjoyed being with you, Troy, and that's the truth. Haven't we had fun together? And haven't I made Charleston interesting for you? What more did you expect or want?"

"A lot more than you're prepared to deliver, my dear. At any rate, I'm sailing at dawn."

"Would you like a memento, captain? A flower, a fan, a lock of hair?"

"I'm not likely to forget you, Star, even without a keepsake. But if you want to give me a more personal reminder—" His eyes focused on her mouth.

"A kiss? I'm not in the habit of giving farewell kisses to any and every sailor going to sea!"

"I'm not any and every sailor."

"But I daresay you have other girls in other ports," she accused, piqued. "You'll sail out of here tomorrow and forget all about me."

"You know better than that, Star."

"Well, if you really cared about me, you wouldn't go away so soon."

"Darling Star, I have no choice! I make my living on the sea and so does my crew."

"And you're in love with the sea, too—and your precious *Venus*!" She gave a plausible imitation of a jealous woman, jealous of his profession, his ship, the girls he might meet in other places. Pretense or not, she could tell he was pleased. Yes, he would return. And to encourage him, she would give him the souvenir he wanted. Why not, she would never miss it. She wouldn't even feel it, if she closed her eyes and thought of Grant Russell.

"Hurry," she whispered, "before someone comes."

"Hurry?"

"And kiss me if you still want to."

"You sound anxious?"

"Oh, you're impossible! And I don't care if I never see you again. You can sail off to—to Hades, for all I care! Or have you already been there?"

"Not yet," he grinned. "The scarcity of water in that region would impede navigation somewhat." Then, abruptly, he sobered and touched her arm. "Oh, Star! Let's not spoil this night, of all nights, with a stupid quarrel."

"It's already spoiled," she sulked, turning from him.

"No, it isn't, darling. Come here." He caught her hand and swung her about into his arms. "You can't escape me that easily. Not tonight."

She acquiesced without response, and as his mouth sought hers, Grant, looking every inch the knight of his costume, appeared in the doorway. Troy glared at him, reluctantly releasing Star. "If it's the Holy Grail you seek, Lancelot, you'll not find it here."

Grant ignored him, fixing his gaze on Star. "Every man has his own Holy Grail, captain. It is but a symbol. And to me, it's not the enchanted cup."

"To me it is," Troy muttered.

"And you were about to drink of it? Well, forgive my intrusion, Romeo, but I believe this is my dance with Juliet."

"I believe it is, sir," Star agreed, and without consulting her program replaced her gold satin mask. "Will you excuse us, please, Troy?"

His exaggerated bow mocked them both. "Good night, Miss Lamont, and goodbye. Unfortunately, due to sailing preparations, I can't stay for the midnight unmasking. I'm sure Mr. Russell will be pleased to hear that I'm leaving Charleston tomorrow."

"Good luck," Grant said curtly.

A wistful smile bloomed on Star's lips, fading swiftly. "Bon voyage," she murmured. She turned and entered the ballroom on her resplendent knight's arm.

PART II

Chapter 9

RAIN, BORNE on a furious gale, lashed at the windowpanes of the Russell mansion, blowing across the piazza where the jalousies remained open. Lightning veined the black sky, and thunder cracked and rumbled sullenly over the bay like ominous drums. When a brilliant flash illuminated the dark night, Grant could see the vessels in the harbor straining at their moorings.

The *Venus* was in port again, after an absence of five months. It had docked that afternoon, carrying a cargo of tools and farm implements from Bristol, England. Merchants and planters alike, his father's factor among them, would be vying for them on the market.

Where was Captain Stewart tonight? Being entertained at Mystic Rose? What did Star see in him? And how could a man of John Lamont's position and traditions receive an outsider so cordially? Worse even, permit him to court his daughter? Who the devil was this arrogant interloper, anyway? It was high time someone found out!

Lorna was in the dressing room of their suite, preparing to retire. Finally she emerged in a voluminous peignoir, her yellow hair screwed up in curlers, as it had been every night since their marriage.

"What terrible weather," she remarked conversationally. "I hope a hurricane isn't beginning."

Her husband drank from the snifter of brandy in his hand, preoccupied, brooding. "Hurricane season is over," he muttered. Then, turning slowly from the window, he appraised her thin body in its loose covering. Lorna clutched the garment closely about herself, aware of his scrutiny and mounting suspicions. These searching, calculating appraisals had been frequent of late, and Lorna pretended that modesty prevented her being nude with him, even in bed, where she insisted upon wearing full and opaque nightgowns.

"It's been five months since our marriage," he said quietly. "Five months, Lorna, and still your belly grows no larger. Where's the baby you were expecting? The child you said would have no name unless I gave it mine?"

At last it had come, the question she had been dreading and evading. And what answer had she? What possible answer but the truth? Or a facile lie.

"I was mistaken, Grant. I—I wasn't pregnant, after all. I only thought so."

She shrank before the accusation in his eyes, the ugly skepticism on his face. "Did you think so, Lorna? Or was it only a contemptible trick to get me to marry you?"

"It could have been true, Grant. You know that."

"But it wasn't! That's the point, Lorna. And you knew it all along, didn't you? That's why you didn't see the necessity of an elopement. You must have a formal wedding, to humiliate Star and parade your gullible fish before the county!"

"I merely wanted a bridal gown and reception like any other girl," she said.

"Ah, yes," he mocked. "The crown and veil, symbol of virginity. And the groom forced to the altar like a condemned man to the gallows, feeling that every adult present knew the spur that drove him. How could you do that to me, Lorna?"

Thus accused, she retaliated defensively. "What did you expect, Grant? That you could trifle with my affections, amuse yourself during Star's absence, and then toss me aside like a used plaything when she returned?"

"Don't dramatize, Lorna. And be honest. I went riding a few times with you at your invitation. I ate supper with you at the Desmonds' fish fry because you had no partner and I felt sorry for you. I danced with you at the balls for the same reason, because you were an embarrassed wallflower. I was not trifling with your affections. I was in love with Star and intended to marry her. Pity—yes, pity! —was the basis of any attentions I paid you, and certainly there was no thought of seduction in my mind. What happened that day in the forest was more of your design than mine, and I tried to protect you. I didn't believe I'd fathered a child, but you lied and threw that goddamn crazy fit a month later—"

Pain and mortification flamed in Lorna's wan face, but her flip tongue parried sharply. "Indeed? Quite the innocent lamb, weren't you, beguiled into your own slaughter by a ruthless witch? What were you doing in the woods with me, pray, if you were so in love with your precious sweetheart?"

"Don't you remember? I'll refresh your memory. You *asked* me to go berry picking with you. You even went to the pretense of bringing along the pails and gloves!"

"Well, and didn't we gather blackberries? I brought home a whole gallon of them, and Taby made a pie and cobbler, which you enjoyed at supper that evening!"

"You also managed to conveniently stumble over a bramble. You bruised your ankle, and I had to chafe it. You broke your garter, and I had to repair it."

"You didn't have to, Grant. You could've refused, but you lacked the strength and self-control. Why aren't *you* honest enough to admit it? Why blame me entirely? You were cad enough to take the liberties. You should be man enough to accept the consequences."

"There were no consequences, Lorna."

"But there might've been, and I was ruined just the same! Oh, Grant, don't look at me like that! Haven't I been a good wife to you? I know you don't love me now, that you still love and want Star. But you'll forget her in time, and we'll be happy and content together when children bless our union–"

"Children?" He smiled grimly. "My dear, you will find that trapping a husband is one thing, holding him quite another. I'm leaving you, Lorna."

Panic rose in her, but she tried to suppress it. "Don't be a fool, Grant! That won't help your cause with Star. You've lost her. That sea captain has her now."

"Has he?"

"All of Charleston thinks so."

"All of Charleston may be wrong."

"You're married, Grant. Remember that. You're not free to compete with Captain Stewart or any other suitor for Star Lamont. Her father would show you the door. Have you no pride, no honor, no sense of propriety?"

His eyes stared at her, glittering dangerously. Then he advanced toward her slowly, looking gigantic in his fury, and Lorna's courage faltered. She moved cautiously behind a rosewood rocker, steadying her nervous hands on the high carved back, sure that he was going to strike her.

"You cunning little bitch," he muttered between his teeth. "You dare to fling those words at me, after what *you* did? Great God! I've known trollops and tavern maids with more principle and decency than you!"

She winced visibly. "You can insult me, Grant. I gave you that privilege when I gave you myself in the bushes. But isn't it strange how critical a man can be of a woman's virtue after he has robbed her of it?"

"Robbed, hell! No treasure was ever more easily surrendered, nor of less value once acquired."

His thrusts grew keener, deeper, wounding her pride and vanity, laying bare her feelings of inferiority. And Lorna, fearful of defeat, grew more reckless and defiant and recriminative. "You paid a high enough price for it, Mr. Russell!"

"So I did," he agreed bitterly. "And perhaps I deserved it for being so weak and gullible. But I don't intend to go on paying, Mrs. Russell."

"You can't divorce me," she argued confidently.

"No, but I can get an annulment on grounds of fraud," he countered, to her surprise and fear.

"And go home to mama? Oh, how happy that would make her! And papa, too."

"Leave my parents out of this," he warned her.

"Why should I? What consideration have they shown me? Do you think I don't know why they moved out of this house before I moved in, even though the summer season was just beginning? Because your mother would rather risk the fevers at Avalon-on-Santee or Russell Hall on Edisto Island than live under the same roof with me, that's why! Her ruse of wanting us to be alone didn't fool me. It was as obvious as that black garb at the wedding and her endless weeping."

"Perhaps she realized, more than anyone else, that it was an occasion for tears and mourning."

"Of course! What a tragedy to have me in the family! The daughter of a humble Yankee carpenter and schoolmarm couldn't possibly be good enough for the grandson of Sir William Russell, Knight of the Garter! You Low Countrymen act as if you're God's chosen people. You have a society all your own, and membership in it is hereditary. Woe and betide the unfortunate soul born out of it. He might as well have a boulder fastened to his neck and be thrown into the rice-mill pond. The great planter-merchant aristocracy! Well, I'll wager there's many a son of a Newgate bird and daughter of a Bridewell felon among their hallowed ancestors. Perhaps even among yours, my fine husband."

"You're screaming like a fishwife," Grant said. "If you don't lower your voice, the servants will hear and broadcast our quarrel like seeds on the wind."

"Oh, I don't doubt they've been trained to spy on us

and report our every action, whether in bed or on the chamber pot!" Instantly she regretted the obscenity, amazed that she could have uttered it, and clasped both hands over her open mouth anticipating his response.

His scowl conveyed disgust, loathing, and contempt. "Your vulgarity bespeaks your background, madam. Coarseness is a common trait in Yankee women, I understand. I suppose it's true, that old adage about the silk purse and the sow's ear—"

They argued far into the night, their voices clashing like the thunder, their tempers as violent as the storm. Several times they came near blows, Grant restraining himself by a mere thread. Lorna, bordering on hysteria, shrieked and wept, threatened and pleaded. The last shred of her dignity had been stripped away, leaving her emotions naked and vulnerable.

Grant remained adamant, as impervious as stone. There seemed no way to break down his barrier of cold reserve. He was going to desert her, and abandon her to shame and scandal. She felt herself losing the battle and was terrified. "But I love you!" she cried frantically, wondering why he was too blind or stupid to realize it.

"Why should I believe that, Lorna, when you've lied to me about everything else?" He pulled a valise from atop the armoire and began to throw some clothes into it.

Desperate with fear and despair, and determined to stop him somehow, Lorna rushed into the dressing room and grabbed his Sheffield razor from the shelf, knocking off a decanter of cologne that fell to the floor with a splintering clatter. Through the open door Grant saw the honed blade flash. He shouted at her to put it down, but before he could reach her, Lorna had slashed her left wrist, and blood was pumping out, spattering her peignoir, and staining the tile floor. Then, either from shock or fright or sheer exhaustion, she fainted and crumpled helplessly at his feet.

Horror stricken, Grant forgot his anger. "My God," he muttered. "You little fool!"

Snatching a towel from the washstand, he wrapped it tightly around the wound to check the hemorrhaging. Fortunately, the trauma was not serious and, barring complications, would heal promptly. Lorna soon recovered consciousness but lay weak and dazed, her skin waxen, and a dull blue glaze in her eyes.

"Lie still," he told her. "Don't move and don't talk. You're hurt, Lorna. I'll send a servant for Doctor Draper."

"No, please. I don't need a doctor. He'll ask questions. He'll suspect—"

"We'll say it was an accident—that I left my razor open on the washstand, you got up during the night, and accidentally brushed against it."

"No," she insisted. "I'll be all right, Grant. I feel better already. The bleeding has stopped; some alum and a bandage will fix it fine. And I'll just pretend I dropped the decanter and cut myself on the broken glass."

"That was a wild and foolish thing to do, Lorna. It could have been fatal."

Tears surfacing, she averted her eyes. "Then you would have been free. Isn't that what you want?"

"Hush," he said hoarsely. "Let's forget it, Lorna. Just forget this night."

"You mean it, Grant?"

"Yes."

"And you won't leave me?"

"No."

"Promise?"

"Promise," he nodded, and though his hesitancy and reluctance were apparent, Lorna was relieved. Happiness lighted her plain face, momentarily transforming it.

"Oh, Grant, I do love you! I'm not proud of the way I got you, but I'm not sorry, either. Maybe it was wrong, shameless, deceitful, and everything else—but I loved and wanted you so desperately, I couldn't help myself. And if you'll only let me, I'll be the best wife in the whole world. I'll try so hard to make you happy. I'll—"

"Save your strength," he interrupted. "You lost a good

deal of blood, and you've none to spare. I'll help you to bed."

He lifted her frail body effortlessly, carried her into the bedroom and placed her gently on the canopied bed, the Russell marriage bed he had hoped to share with Star, to love in and beget children. Not a moment of true happiness or ecstasy had he known in it with Lorna, so tormented was he by his longing for Star. Now there would be duty without honor, guilt without remorse, and promise without purpose. And he doubted if ever a child of his would be born in this or any other bed.

"Grant, don't worry about Star. She's young and beautiful and will find someone else."

He only nodded.

"Are you coming to bed?" she asked.

"Not yet. I want another nightcap."

"Let's have one together."

"All right," he agreed. Maybe brandy would make it all bearable. Enough liquor could make almost anything bearable, even amputation. He brought the bottle and two glasses to the bed, served her, and filled his to the brim.

Chapter 10

STAR WAS IN THE PARLOR, ostensibly absorbed in a piece of petit point. But her interest was on the library across the hall where her father, stepbrother, and Captain Stewart sat in conversation. The sliding doors to both rooms were open, and by straining her ears she could hear most of what was said. Politics and war, naturally. What else did men discuss these days? It was spoiling all the social gatherings.

Captain Stewart, smoking a fine Havana cigar and drinking her father's best cognac, was denouncing Henry Clay, newly elected to the House of Representatives. The Kentuckian's brief career in the Senate was already well known, but it had not created the national interest that his new triumph was creating. For the Senate then was second to the House in political importance, and young Mr. Clay, just thirty-four, became Speaker of the House immediately upon entering it. No other member had ever attained this great honor literally upon initiation, and since his reputation as a war hawk preceded him, the nation quaked with dread.

The fact that in that same year South Carolina sent John C. Calhoun to Congress increased the trepidation, for Mr. Calhoun's war sentiments were no secret, either; he had made them manifest in the State legislature at Columbia, which he had just left. The New England states, opposed to war though their commerce was severely harassed by the British marauders, talked of secession, lest the impetuous southerners drag them into an unwanted and possibly disastrous conflict with Britain.

Star was piqued with Troy, for he had hardly done more than salute her upon his arrival, acting as if he had come all the way to Mystic Rose in this bitter weather just to visit the menfolk and discuss politics. Apparently he had not forgiven her for their parting scene on the Ralston balcony. Well, she hadn't forgiven him, either!

She caught Lance's rasping voice; in damp, cold weather he suffered from respiratory ailments in addition to his constant liver condition. "Do I understand, sir, that you question Mr. Clay's abilities as a statesman?"

"Not at all, my friend. What I question is his judgment in desiring war on England at this time. I consider it unsound and irresponsible. My reason for dissenting with him is quite simple: unpreparedness."

"We were not prepared for the Revolution, either," Lance argued. "But that did not keep us from winning it."

"Just barely," Troy said. "And a greater issue was at stake, then. War was inevitable and excusable, even desirable. This is not the case now."

"What do you mean, captain? Would you have England run us off the seas?"

"Hardly," Troy replied, and Star could sense the irritation in his bland voice. "I live off the sea."

"And make a handsome living, too," Lance observed with unmitigated sarcasm. "Our admirals wear no finer suits than the one you're sporting now."

Her father said, "Captain Stewart's uniform is not

your concern, Lance. Let us not enter into a wardrobe discussion; leave that to the ladies. However, I must agree with my son on the war issue. While I deplore the prospect of another conflict with England, when the scars of the last one have not yet healed, I can see no other course but that proposed by Mr. Clay and supported by Mr. Calhoun and many other knowledgeable statesmen. And since they represent the people in Congress–"

"If I may interrupt, sir–the war hawks represent the war element in the South. I don't believe their views and wishes reflect those of all Americans. Certainly New England doesn't ride on the Clay-Calhoun bandwagon, except for some merchants, ship builders, and owners."

"New England is stagnant with old line Federalists," Lance scoffed, "who seem unaware that their isolationism is as outmoded and impractical as was Mr. Jefferson's conservatism."

"Perhaps," Troy conceded. "But there are many who feel that Jefferson's level head would be a greater asset to the country now than Madison's vacillating one."

John inquired with serious interest, "What alternative, as a New Englander, would you suggest?"

"Conference and negotiation, sir."

"Ah, my boy! That shows your youth and inexperience in such matters. Conference and negotiation did not prevent the Revolution, nor any other war in which man's basic rights and freedoms were threatened. Britain threatens our freedom of commerce now, and surely you'll agree there's no more God-given right to man than that of the sea. It's elemental."

"Most assuredly, sir, and I've had some traffic of my own with His Majesty's fleets. Don't misunderstand. I don't condone England's actions, but neither do I see war as the only solution to the problem."

"I should think you'd welcome it," Lance drawled, stretching his long spindly legs on a velour hassock. "There's much legendary romance attached to privateering–or is it piracy?"

"Both," Troy replied curtly.

"Do you speak now from experience, captain?"

Again John intervened, apology in his tone. "Forgive my son, captain. His tongue is often impetuous." And frowning his displeasure at Lance, he said, "Kindly remember that Captain Stewart is a guest in this house."

"It was but an idle jest, father. I don't believe our guest took offense. Certainly the two professions are closely related, there being merely a letter of marque to distinguish the one from the other."

"And a flag," Troy added.

"Ah, yes! A flag. What colors do you sail under, Captain Stewart? American or British?"

John shouted, "Lance!"

A pungent cloud of smoke from the captain's cigar floated across the hall into the parlor. Star sniffed it appreciatively, enjoying the aroma of good tobacco. She listened intently for Troy's reply, hoping he would harpoon her stepbrother, but he ignored him.

Lance was silent, temporarily quashed. Her father used the awkward interlude to pour more brandy. Proffering the drink, John said, "You've just come from England, captain. Does His Majesty, with all his struggles on the Continent, seem better prepared to launch a new battle than the United States? We receive the British journals here, of course, but the news is rather stale by the time it arrives."

Troy swirled the amber liquid in the thin crystal goblet, warming it between cupped hands. "My personal observations this trip were limited mostly to Bristol, sir. But I did get to London for a few days, and the editorials in the liberal sheets indicate that the populace as a whole is heartily sick of war. Napoleon's name is anathema, the soldiers and sailors haven't been paid in months, food is scarce and dear in price, there are men out of work and families starving–none of which seems of much concern, however, to the Court of St. James. It's my opinion that Britain has her hands full with France and Spain."

"Precisely," his host agreed. "And so our victory should be swift and uncostly."

"Two unprepared fighters, neither strong enough to whip the other, can prolong a conflict to a wasteful stalemate, Mr. Lamont. Let us hope and pray that does not happen."

"Let us indeed, captain. But I'll trust the decision of our astute leaders. President Madison would not lead us astray, nor Clay and Calhoun. I wish you could've been here a fortnight ago, Troy. You'd have had the pleasure of meeting John Calhoun, who was my honored guest after his election to Congress. I believe you'd have found him to be a sincere and honest man, dedicated to his country."

"Unfortunately," Troy responded gravely, "cemeteries all over the world are lined with the bones of men put there by champions dedicated, not so much to their countries, as to personal fame and glory and conquest. Caesar filled his share, as did Alexander the Great, Hannibal, Genghis Khan, and William the Conqueror. I suspect that even Napoleon, in his madness, believed himself dedicated to France and destined to conquer the Continent and eventually the world. But I daresay his legions of slaughtered soldiers did not share that conviction, nor consider him a deity. Not that I place your Mr. Calhoun in Napoleon's category. If you subscribe to his character and integrity, sir, that's good enough for me."

"I consider that a compliment, captain. And now," he moved his chair back and stood up, "I don't flatter myself that you've journeyed to Mystic Rose expressly to visit me or my son. There's some other attraction here, eh? You'll find my daughter in the parlor directly across the hall, sir. Come, Lance. We must prepare the guns for the hunting tomorrow."

Passing the parlor, Lance glanced in at his stepsister. His hooded eyes partially concealed his jealousy, but still it was visible in the selfish, possessive way he looked at her. He had no more use or friendship for Captain Stewart than for Grant Russell or any other man who so much as looked at Star seriously.

"Good afternoon, Miss Lamont." Troy stood on the threshold, smiling. "May I come in?"

"You may, captain. Now that your talk of war and politics seems to have palled, perhaps you'll find visiting with me refreshing."

"A more modest invitation I've never had, Miss Lamont, and I'm sure I'll find your company delightful."

"I wasn't speaking in conceit," she retorted. "It's just that men get so engrossed in those subjects that they forget everything else."

"Not quite," he said.

"I trust you had a smooth and profitable voyage, captain?"

"Smooth enough, after we managed to outsail an inquisitive British prowler. And extremely profitable. Now that free trade is considerably hampered and hazardous, there's no more lucrative business than that of the merchant marine."

"I must say you look prosperous," Star said, admiring his handsome new uniform, which appeared to have been tailored in one of London's best shops.

Troy grinned. "Your stepbrother made the same observation, but I don't think he meant it as a compliment. That young cock has some mighty sharp spurs. Someone should dull them for his own sake."

Someone will someday, Star thought.

"Sit down, Troy," she invited and as he did so, she leaned forward eagerly. "Tell me, is it true that the wars in Europe are affecting styles? The fashion journals say the ladies' clothes are taking on a decidedly military air. Did you find this so in England?"

"Heaven forbid! I can't imagine anything less attractive on a woman than a military uniform. But I did notice that the jackets have straighter lines and broader shoulders and the capes and cloaks more braid and button trim. So there may be such an insidious trend abroad. Paris is losing its place as the fashion capital of the world, you know. Blockade running of guns and ammunition is dangerous enough; few seamen want to risk their necks to bring out a lot of feminine fluff and frippery. London is creating its own styles for the Englishwoman, and of course Beau Brummell, who is an intimate of the prince regent, has long set the pace for gentlemen at court."

Star already knew that. Thanks to Brummell, gentlemen had some years ago ceased wearing satin and velvet knee breeches, silver buckles on their shoes, and periwigs. The foppish garments, the ribbons, laces, and powdered hair, had given way to more practical and mannish attire: long trousers and less frivolous shirts, heads unadorned except by hats and caps, darker colors and heavier fabrics, handsome cravats and waistcoats, and sturdier boots.

"You read simply awful things about the British court," Star ventured curiously. "They say King George is quite mad and the Prince of Wales is a profligate wretch and unfit regent. They say the prince drove his father to insanity with his wild antics, that he has run himself deep in debt with his follies and dissipations, and that his—his amours are public scandals. London must be a dreadfully wicked and exciting place!" she finished hopefully.

"Not especially wicked or exciting for the commoner," Troy said. "How to feed and clothe and shelter his family, pay his taxes, and avoid debtors' prison is the average Londoner's primary concern. With wheat selling at sixteen shillings a bushel, bread is a luxury, and the poorest cotton cloth is priced like silk. The debaucheries are necessarily limited to the court. But since they make more interesting copy than poverty and suffering and sell more newspapers, naturally they occupy more space. Publishers must live, too."

Again Star detected an underlying bitterness and cynicism in his references to royalty and nobility. She wished she dared pursue her curiosity, for in some vague way she sensed that he himself was connected with that same coterie of which he seemed critical and contemptuous. But he was a very private person, resenting any intrusion into his personal life and affairs, and he either ignored meddlers or silenced them. He was something of an enigma and mystery, which intrigued Star, who could not bear unsolved puzzles.

A bright fire burned on the hearth, dispelling the damp December gloom outside. The gray spectral mists of winter hung in the air, enveloping Mystic Rose in swirls of illusive gossamer which played tricks on the imagination. On such dreary days the plantation seemed to Star a lonely isle in a jungle wilderness, and she longed to escape it. She still brooded over the loss of her beloved and despised Lorna for her treacherous theft of him and wished she could somehow exorcise her malicious stepfamily. She gazed wistfully into the flames, her dark eyes aglow in the reflected firelight, forgetting Captain Stewart and the abandoned needlepoint.

"That's mighty pretty," he said, touching the tambour that held the material firm and taut. "Is it for your trousseau?"

"No," she murmured, still deep in thought.

"You don't have a hope chest?"

Star thought of the trunks in the garret, filled with the finest of linens now yellowing with age and the loveliest of lingerie now out of fashion. She shook her head emphatically.

"I don't intend to marry."

"Oh? When did you decide that?"

"What does it matter? I just made up my mind to stay single, that's all."

"Celibacy can be very lonely and boring for a woman, Star, and I must say I never met one who seemed less suitable to it than yourself. Somehow I just can't picture you in a setting of cats and books."

"There are other settings for spinsters, captain. I expect one day to manage Mystic Rose; that will keep me too busy for cats and books other than ledgers."

"An old maid planter?"

The amused skepticism in his tone irked Star, for she was perfectly serious. "There are several widow planters in the Low Country–and good ones, too. An old maid is no different."

"Only in one respect," he grinned. "But surely there must be at least one knight in the realm who takes your heart and quests for your hand?"

"I thought I made my intentions clear," she reiterated, disliking the subject and seeking to change it.

"Ah, well. Perhaps there's none among them worthy of the beautiful princess of Mystic Rose? If war with England does not materialize, your father should take you to London and present you at court. I'll wager you'd catch the eye and fancy of any number of courtiers."

"I should like very much to visit England," she said, thinking that even the dismal London fogs could be no more depressing than the ghostly mists outside.

"And wed a courtier?"

"You needn't sneer when you use that word, Troy Stewart! What have you against nobility, anyway? You seem to harbor a personal grudge. A man can't help being born noble any more than he can help being born—" She hesitated, seeking a better word than common.

"Illegitimate?" he supplied, startling her.

Star glanced up, nonplused. "Why, no! That's not what I meant to say at all! And if you expect me to apologize for my ancestors, you'll be disappointed. I'm proud of them. Are you proud of yours, captain?"

Immediately she regretted the bold challenge, abashed at her audacity, for the expression that descended over his face, masking it, was almost tragic. He inclined his head toward the fire and appeared to ponder it, as if searching for something in the embers and ashes. His profile was clearly outlined; it was strong, regular, and handsome, as though molded in bronze. Star had seen such a head once, on an old English coin.

Why had he said that? He was not fatherless; she had heard him speak of the old skipper on Nantucket Island and his childhood on his father's ship. Oh, Lord! Did *he* have a nameless child in some port? If so, then he had a woman somewhere, one he cared enough about to—

He rose slowly, a different man from the one who had sat down. Still debonair in his nautical attire, but no longer cynical or accessible. "Your father invited me to spend the night and go hunting in the morning. Unfortunately, I am unable to accept his kind invitation."

"Why not, Troy? Quail and duck hunting is excellent in the marshes and rice fields this time of year. If you're a good shot, you'll enjoy it."

"My aim is steady enough, Miss Lamont. The South has no monopoly on marksmen. However, I find it necessary to sail sooner than I expected."

"You're angry with me," she accused.

"Nonsense! Duty calls."

"Aren't your men entitled to some liberty?"

"Yes, indeed. But they'd prefer it in some other port. New York, for instance."

"And their captain?"

"New York is fine with me."

"I suppose you have a lady friend there?"

"Several," he said, "and I have a pretty trinket for each of them."

"You always bring them gifts?" He hadn't brought her anything, not even a pin to prick her vanity bubble.

"Always. A bauble of some kind; it doesn't take much to make some women happy."

"And you make a lot of women happy?"

"As many as possible," he said.

"Well, captain, I shan't detain you. Go spread your happiness and your baubles! Good day."

"Our usual memorable parting." He bowed, strode to the door, and paused, smiling wryly. "Goodbye, Miss Lamont. Give my regards to Mr. and Mrs. Grant Russell when next you see them."

"I shall, captain. But if you stayed the night, you could do so yourself. They'll be here later, for Mr. Russell is joining the hunting parties tomorrow. Ducks and quail first and then foxes. Sure you won't change your mind? You could pit your sporting skills against his."

"You're riding to the hounds, naturally?"

"Naturally."

"Well, I'm tempted, my dear. But one distraction is

enough for your idol and your stepbrother. I wouldn't want to divert them too much in their games. I only hope they remember which vixen they're chasing."

"If you mean me—"

He smiled, shrugged, and left.

Returning from the hunt the next day, Star found that a gift had been delivered to her: an ornate gilded cage containing a pair of turquoise parakeets and a note from Troy. "If not cats, how about birds?"

"Oh, the darling little things!" she cried. "Aren't they sweet, Grant?"

"They carry lice and disease," he said.

"Lovebirds," Lance sneered. "What'll you name 'em?"

"Why, Romeo and Juliet! What else?"

"What else indeed?" he muttered, and Grant scowled and left to join the other men in their drinking.

Star went to the ladies' parlor, where Lorna, who had been the first to corner the fox, was giving a full account of her exploits in the field.

Chapter 11

OF ALL THE Christian feasts, the Negro children preferred Christmas. They adopted its festive customs as enthusiastically as their elders did the religious rituals. While Lamont slaves were never forced into Christianity, their innate spirituality was encouraged by the master and the circuit ministers, and Mystic Rose had a high rate of conversions. Abolitionists believed that religion satisfied some intrinsic and vital need of which slavery deprived them, but Star attributed it to the gospel about the Promised Land, which meant heaven to them.

She set out with Mauma and several youngsters from the plantation to gather Yule decorations. Two male slaves followed, driving a wagon containing axes to chop down a well-shaped pine and pruning shears to snip off clusters of mistletoe and branches of holly and red-berried haw. Christmas was a time of great joy and festivity in the Low Country. With the danger of the dread fevers relatively absent in cold weather, many planters left their town houses in Charleston for the more commodious facilities of their plantation manors, where they could gather hordes of relatives and friends in jubilant celebration.

Ordinarily, Star would have been as happy about the holiday season as the children, and just as eager as they were for the preparations. But today she was depressed, remembering her last Christmas alone in Boston, snowbound in the lyceum, surrounded by gifts from home and letters from Grant. Because her correspondence was censored, she had not been able to express her emotions as explicitly as her lover, but she was sure that he sensed and shared them and that the misery, longing, and frustration of their separation was mutual. She had expected to be his wife by this Christmas and perhaps carrying his child. Then she had come home to a wedding, but not her own!

Lorna was not yet pregnant, at least not according to the gossip from her servants; apparently the rumors that had circulated the county had been premature and groundless. Grant had married Lorna for one reason only, then: love. This conclusion was infinitely harder to accept than having the rumors proven to be true. The blow of infidelity was less crushing and defeating than the pang of rejection; one stung the vanity, the other stabbed the heart. And while true love could generously forgive such a masculine lapse, how did feminine pride survive the seemingly mortal wound of being scorned?

The cold flushed her cheeks vividly, and a fresh north wind rioted in her black curls, which she had half expected to be white with worry by now. What did the future hold for her? What could she look forward to in the new year?

Huddling in her black shawl, Mauma admonished, "Tie on your hood, Miss Star! You goin' have a earache and runny nose. And that goes for you children, too. Rastus, Prunsella, Gaby, Tartan! Pull them caps over your ears 'fore I takes a stick to you! Tawn got enough patients in the 'firmary with the grippe and chilblains as 'tis. No need givin' her more."

Tawn was the head nurse of the plantation clinic, and

she and her assistants had a full schedule. Influenza, croup and other respiratory ailments in winter; fevers and dysentery in summer; childhood diseases and childbirth all year around; perennial cuts, bruises, sprains, snakebites, boils, minor maladies, and accidents. Tawn had a definite calling for her profession, but she was given to practicing unorthodox medicine on the side, for she was the daughter of an Angola witch doctor. She was also prone, much to her master's disapproval, to sorcery. Tawn was in love with Obah and had hoped to marry him before he raped his sister and was subsequently sold off the plantation. She still met him secretly at night, somewhere in the swamps, keeping his desire alive with love potions concocted of bits of her hair and nail parings in whiskey pilfered from the infirmary medicine coffer.

The children obediently covered their ears, and Star, in a tractable mood for once, did likewise. Tying on the beaver-lined hood of her wool cloak, she murmured, "I wish pa would skip the entertainment this year. I don't feel like a tree and all that fuss and bother."

The little black faces fell and began to pucker. "Ain't we goin' have a Jesus tree, Miss Star?"

"Oh, darlings, I'm sorry! Yes—yes, of course, we are! A great big one with candles and tinsel, popcorn and candy, and everything! And there'll be a present for everyone under it."

"How come you tell 'em that," Mauma protested, "when you know their presents gonna be on the stoop of they cabins when they wakes up Christmas mornin'? Miss Emily ain't never let 'em tramp through the big house and get gifted like your ma done. You know that, Miss Star."

"I know, Mauma. But for a moment I forgot and wanted to remember the way it was, not the way it is now. Things were so different, then. So wonderful!"

"Yessum. But that a long time ago, and ain't no use moonin' 'bout it now. Ain't no use wishin' your pa ain't goin' partyin' this season, neither, cause you knows he is. And you got to go callin' with him, and most every place you goin' run into Mist' Grant and Miss Lorna. Ain't no gettin' round that, child." She motioned to the men trailing behind. "Come on here, you black bucks! Roll that wagon! We got work to do, and we ain't fixin' to do it all ourselfs!"

Emily supervised the decorating with about as much imaginative originality as she might have decorated a classroom. She would have omitted the mistletoe entirely except for her son's sarcastic insistence.

"Is your heart too old for romance, mother? What would the holidays be without the ritual of mistletoe?" He winked at Star, who longed to stick her tongue out at him. "Right, little sister?"

With misgivings Emily left them alone in the drawing room. She no longer knew whose side to take. Lance grew more belligerent and Star more provocative with each day, until it seemed that even the vastness of Mystic Rose must eventually become too inadequate to contain them.

"Twist some tinsel ribbon for the mantel," Star told him. "If you're going to hang around, you might as well make yourself useful."

The scent of the freshly cut pine standing sentinel in one corner, its spire almost touching the ceiling, was strong and invigorating. Lance began to twine the silver streamers while Star arranged autumn leaves in a Sèvres urn.

"What happened to your captain?" he asked. "Why didn't he come back? I thought that gift was intended as a calling card?"

Star thought of the parakeets, Romeo and Juliet, in her room upstairs. They had been intended more as a tease. "He's not my captain, and I don't know or care why he didn't come back! Perhaps because he couldn't bear bickering with you."

"He strikes me as a British spy. And I'm glad to hear he's not your captain."

"When are you going to marry, Lance? I thought you

and Letty Clayton were practically betrothed?"

He laughed. "So did Letty."

"Then you're not?"

"Gad, no! I'm saving myself for better things than bucktoothed Letty Clayton."

"She's mighty rich, Lance. And young, too." Unfortunately, wealth and youth were Letty's only charms. She was plump, her straight hair was thin and mousy, her face was freckled, and her big mouth was all teeth.

"Too young," Lance nodded. "That's the trouble. She might outlive me by a decade or more—and what good would her fortune do me then?"

"Your greed and arrogance are monstrous, Lance. And just what better things are you saving yourself for?"

He eased toward her. "You, maybe."

Star gasped. "*Me*?"

"You could do worse, Star. Much worse."

"Stop babbling like an addlepated booby! I never heard of anything so preposterous." She laughed at the sheer absurdity of it. Her laughter infuriated him.

"Why? We're not blood relations, Star. There are no marital barriers between us, physical, moral, or legal. It wouldn't be incest, you know."

Horror and revulsion filled Star when she realized that he was serious, that he actually dared to think of her as someone he might marry. Nausea seeped into her throat, and she retreated as he approached. She felt that her flesh would mold and decay if he so much as touched her. "You're insane, Lance! I don't even like you, much less love you. The truth is, I despise you and nothing on earth could induce me to marry you!"

"Am I not good enough for you, Miss Lamont?"

"You're not fit to be my lackey, let alone my spouse!"

"Ho-ho! Hoity-toity! I suppose you think I don't know that your great-great-grandma was a nobody, a commoner your noble Lord Lamont picked up on shipboard and married before he reached America? She might have been a bondswoman, a felon from Bridewell, or a London prostitute, for all you know. And your fine

French *maman* had gypsy blood in her. Yes," he grinned at her surprise, "I've read the diaries of some of your illustrious ancestors."

"How? By picking the locks?"

"Never mind. Listen to me, Star–"

"No, I've heard enough–too much! Get out of here, Lance! Leave me alone! Mauma!" she cried. "*Mauma*!"

Mauma, never far away, rushed in from the dining room demanding, "What's the trouble?"

Lance's guilty expression betrayed him, and Mauma warned, "Mist Lance, you stop botherin' Miss Star, or I's goin' have to speak with Master John 'bout you. Yessir, I sure is."

"You know nothing, and you'll say nothing, you daughter of a ring-tailed baboon!" Lance growled. "I didn't even touch her. Can I help it if she's got a nervous constitution?"

Glancing at Star, he said, "Forget what I said. I assure you it was just an idle jest. Any designs I may have on you are definitely not marital."

"What he mean by that?" asked Mauma suspiciously.

"He means he's a pig," Star said, as Lance departed. "And he's going to one of his wallows now. . . ."

Snow covered the ground for Christmas, but it did not hamper the festivities. The rivers were not frozen, and the pageant of handsomely detailed family boats along the streams rivaled the gondola traffic of Venice. It was an interlude of leisure for planters; the autumn harvest was past, and it was too early for spring planting. They put the hiatus to the most enjoyable use, that of rejoicing with friends and neighbors.

There were numerous entertainments, both in the city and the country, and Star had a new frock for each one. But the loveliest of all, a ruby velvet gown trimmed in ermine, she saved for the party at Mystic Rose. Had Troy beheld her in it, he would have scoffed even more at her decision to remain single, for no woman was ever better endowed by nature with the inducements necessary to arouse the male mating instinct. And if one thing could ease Grant's special agony when he saw her, it was the absence of the *Venus* in port. Captain Stewart's somewhat hasty departure a few weeks before had given him consolation and new hope, for he was still intensely jealous and possessive of Star and selfish enough to prefer her spinsterhood to marriage with another man.

Because of mutual acquaintances, they met at almost every social function and were elaborately polite and proper. When they danced together at the balls, Star held herself aloof and engaged in trivial conversation. Touching was the hardest thing to endure, and for this reason Star persuaded her father to dispense with a formal affair this year and have a simple old-fashioned fest instead, with caroling, games, and merry feasting.

A symbolic yule log cheered every hearth. The dining table and massive mahogany sideboards were laden with crystal bowls of punch and syllabub; fruit cakes and brandy-soaked plum puddings flamed before serving; stuffed turkeys, glazed hams, and a roast suckling pig with an apple in its mouth in the old English tradition; a cornucopia of fruits and nuts; and such Low Country confections as peach leather and benne brittle. Pine boughs and bayberry candles scented the house, and poinsettias bloomed in urns and jardinieres. Numerous slaves were in attendance, including a fire detail of slaves with handy pails of water to guard the candle-lit tree.

Regardless of age, married women were considered matrons who dressed and behaved appropriately, and Lorna, in a modest gown of lavender silk, retired to the parlor with the coterie of wives, widows, and elderly spinsters. Grant joined the gentlemen in the library to drink and smoke, play cards, and discuss politics and business. The young single folk monopolized the drawing room, taking advantage of the ancient custom of the mistletoe and the relaxed and indulgent chaperonage. Star offered her lips to some, turned her cheeks to others, and would have avoided them all if she could have. When Lance approached her, she pushed him away so vigorously he reeled and almost lost his balance, eliciting jeers and howls of laughter from his competitors.

He fumed for awhile, glaring at Star furiously, then proceeded to drink himself into a morose stupor. When he could no longer focus his eyes, organize his tongue for speech, or maintain his equilibrium, his personal servant was summoned to assist him to his chambers.

"Come on, Mist' Lance. The party over for you. We're goin' to bed."

"No, we ain't," Lance mimicked his valet. "Since when do we go to bed together?"

Bobo took his arm. "Now, Mist' Lance, be nice and—"

Lance interrupted violently. "Let go of me, you jungle savage, or I'll cut your black hide off with a whip! You take orders from me, Bobo, not vice versa. And I'll leave when I damn well please and not before! Understand?"

"Yessuh," Bobo obeyed, ducking his master's flailing fists while the guests watched in contempt and disgust.

Star was glad that her father was not present to witness the sickening spectacle. Lance was an acute embarrassment to the family, and his reputation as a drunkard, rake, and rebel was spreading through the state and even beyond it. Many among the gentility wondered at John Lamont's tolerance of his stepson's character and conduct.

The evening was waning when Grant entered the room. Star was seated at the spinet, playing a jolly folk tune to which several couples had joined hands in a lively reel. He came and stood silent beside her for a few minutes. Then, under cover of the music, he bent and whispered, "Come to your father's office."

"Why?"

"I want to see you."

"You're seeing me now."

"Alone, I mean."

Her hands faltered on the keys, and she missed a note. She shook her head vehemently, her dark curls gleaming.

"Please, Star."

"No," she murmured, playing louder, her nervous fingers actually fumbling now. "Go away."

"I'll be waiting for you," he said.

"You'll wait in vain."

Grant smiled confidently and left.

He had chosen John Lamont's office because he knew it would be deserted, just as he knew that Star would eventually come to him. But she made him wait, tormenting herself as much as him. It was almost midnight before Mauma became too sleepy to notice her escape, and, pretending to go upstairs, Star slipped away to the office instead. A single candle flickered on the mantel, dimly lighting the black leather couch, armchairs, and oak desk. There was no fire but, for the moment, they needed none.

Grant's arms swept around her, as warm, strong, and eager as in days past. Possessive too, as if no legal or moral barriers separated them. Star surrendered her lips to him, savoring the kiss for which she had longed, her sensuality as avid and reckless as his. They clung together desperately, until some sense of gratification was achieved, then drew slightly apart, breathless and trembling.

"I love you," Grant said urgently. "I've never stopped loving you, Star."

"And Lorna?"

"Haven't you guessed the reason for that yet?"

"I heard rumors," she admitted. "But I couldn't believe— Anyway, she's still flat as a hoecake!"

"Flatter," he said ruefully.

Star stared at him, breaking the embrace. "Oh, I understand now! Yes, I understand now."

"Darling," he pleaded, reaching for her again.

"Don't touch me, Grant!" Her eyes, hurt and bewildered, accused him. "You loved me so much you couldn't be true one little year! You cheated on me, Grant. You played with Lorna, hoping to get by with it. But you didn't. She was smarter than you, wasn't she? You stumbled into her trap like a blind cock. Now you're cooped with her for life, and it serves you right! What do you expect from me? Sympathy? Comfort?"

"You love me, Star. Your kiss told me so a moment ago, better than any words. You can't deny it. Nothing has changed between us and never will. Are you happy this way? Pretending we don't feel anything when we meet in public, when we dance together, or merely shake hands!"

"You want me to say it? All right, Grant. No, I'm not happy this way. I'm miserable, wretched. But it can't be any other way for us!"

"Why not, Star? I'm miserable, too. Why torture ourselves for the sake of convention? If we sincerely love each other and want to be together sometimes, what's to stop us?"

"Nothing except honor and decency," she replied, tears glistening in her dark eyes. "But you wouldn't know about that, would you, Grant? It didn't stop you with Lorna!"

His hand caressed the soft white fur edging the décolletage of her gown, while his voice, low and contrite, implored, "I know I did wrong, Star. I hurt you terribly, and I'm deeply, humbly sorry. I'd rip my heart out if it could change things, could win you back. I'd die for your forgiveness and understanding. I made a mistake, Star. A stupid, tragic mistake. Isn't a man entitled to one mistake?"

"A man, yes. But not so a woman."

"Oh, hang the goddamn proprieties!" Maneuvering her toward the couch, he coaxed her to sit down with him. "If you loved me enough you'd take the risk. Darling, I want you now, so much that I'm half wild!"

He began to make ardent love to her, kissing and caressing her, whispering intimately. His hand slipped into her bodice, groping her firm breasts, trying to expose them to his mouth. Star felt herself weakening, yielding to her intense passion and wanting to gratify his. But as he lifted her skirt, the blurred images of Lorna, her father, Aunt Emily, and Mauma appeared in her mind. And, inexplicably, Troy Stewart's picaresque face appeared also, grinning mockingly. Somehow, unwittingly, Star retrieved her straying virtue. She grasped feverishly at her clothing and leaped up from the couch.

"How dare you use me this way! As if I were a tavern wench or street slut panting for a cur!"

"Oh, my God! No such insult was intended, Star. I have only the highest regard and respect for you. Love drives me to take such liberties, nothing else."

"Love," she scoffed. "Lust, you mean! You're selfish, Grant. Thoughtless and callous, too. Forgive me if I seem surprised. It's somewhat disconcerting to discover so many chinks in your highly polished armor."

"I suppose," he ventured wryly, straightening his cravat while Star smoothed her hair and gown, "there's none in Captain Stewart's?"

"Troy has nothing to do with this, Grant."

As always, his jealousy took refuge in skeptical cynicism. "Hasn't he, my dear?"

Her anger flared. "I don't have to answer that!"

"You can't, truthfully."

"How would a liar and cheat know about truth?"

Grant flinched, his honor wounded. "Go ahead. Punish me, crucify me with your tongue. It only indicates that you still love me, Star. And I doubt that Troy Stewart is more of a gentleman, certainly not by birth! A genealogical trace of his ancestry would probably reveal the bend sinister in his shield."

Star turned abruptly. "I must return to my guests."

"No, wait! Please. I'm sorry, darling."

But she was gone, hurrying through the labyrinth of dim hallways back to the drawing room, grateful that the shadows hid the tears she could no longer restrain.

Chapter 12

WINTER WAS UNUSUALLY LONG and disagreeable. There was much rain, often mixed with sleet, keeping Star indoors. She wandered from room to room, avoiding Emily and Lance as discreetly as possible. Embroidery bored her, and she could not long sustain interest in books other than fashion or romance. On her visits to Mystic Rose, Lorna recommended poetry and classical literature to her, along with Mary Wollstonecraft's *Vindication of the Rights of Woman,* which a few advanced American ladies were reading and advocating, mostly in the North. Star suspected that this liberal treatise was an attempt on her stepsister's part to justify her premarital behavior, since the authoress claimed to have taken lovers before and after marriage. Her father advised Star to ignore it, but Emily considered it a brilliant, scholarly, and significant piece of work.

"For a woman," Lance allowed. "But it'll never catch on in puritan America!"

Star tried to resume china painting, at which she was fairly talented, but imported porcelain and even bisque were hard to obtain now, and she refused to waste her art on inferior products. She considered sketching, but oils and canvas were also getting scarce, because the wars abroad dragged on. Then Emily contracted the grippe and though Star offered to be mistress pro tem of the house, Emily chose to remain in full command, issuing orders from her sickbed. Star complained to her father, "Aunt Emily is afraid to give me any responsibility, pa. She's afraid the servants might like the change of management so much that they'd want to make it permanent."

"Now, Star, you mustn't take offense at the whims of a sick person. I'm sure Emily merely thinks the household could not function smoothly without her at the helm."

"It functioned smoothly enough before she took over," Star argued, though she knew this was not entirely true. Angelique's death had created confusion and turmoil in the domestic domain of Mystic Rose, and Emily had undeniably restored order and routine, if not grace and harmony. "Besides, I want to learn to manage the house, pa. And the plantation, too."

"The plantation, Star?"

Her dark eloquent eyes obviated any reference to Lance. "Someone has to learn, pa. And there's no unwritten law that says it must be a man, is there? Look at Mrs. Townsley and Mrs. Kingston. Are there any better run estates than Fairhill and Brook Haven anywhere in the Low Country? In the Carolinas or the entire South, for that matter?"

"Not to my knowledge," John said. "But Ida Townsley and Maude Kingston are middle-aged women, Star, and they had the advantage of years of experience with their husbands. Is it possible you want to devote your life to Mystic Rose? My dear, I want you to marry and have children. You must not let your disappointment with Grant sour you on all men. There's only one completely satisfying career for a woman, Star, and that's the one God and nature intended: marriage and motherhood."

"Would you recommend it without love, pa?" she asked succinctly.

He sighed ponderously. "No, not without love, my child."

Perhaps his daughter, even in her youth, was wiser in years than he. For of all the ingredients necessary to a happy and successful union, love was surely the most important and flavorful. Without it, marriage was an unsavory dish, tasteless as cold porridge.

He bent his head over the books and papers on his desk: the endless records and documents essential to the well-managed plantation. The office was lined with file cabinets containing factor's correspondence and overseer's reports, slave bills of sale, and copies of other business transactions. The ledgers of many years past packed the shelves on the walls and the adjoining storeroom. These carefully preserved volumes contained a documentary history of Mystic Rose.

Glancing over this month's record, the first of the new year, did not hearten John. And only this morning Clem Jones had handed him another list of absentees.

Mystic Rose Plantation
January, 1812

January 1st	Holiday
January 2nd	Cold and rain. All hands in cabins. Three sick. Rachel miscarried.
January 3rd	Sunday.
January 4th	Cold and wet. All hands in cabins. Four sick. Ned and Rincy confined in jail for fighting. Grandpa Blue sent to infirmary, sprained back.

January 5th	All hands turning land. Seven sick. Granny Mae scalded herself. Gullah Jack injured in fall on pitchfork.
January 6th	Clear. Men ditching. Women turning land. Six sick. Lily confined in childbirth. Alex chopped off left thumb.
January 7th	Men ditching. Women burning stubble. Three sick. Nellie reports herself pregnant, taken off hard labor. Father of child uncertain. Probably Atlas.
January 8th	Men repairing leaks in dikes. Women chopping banks. Four sick. Ruck kicked in head by mule, possible brain injury.
January 9th	All hands turning land. Five sick. Ben bitten by alligator. Kitty's child died of whooping cough. A dozen or more kids sick with sore throats.
January 10th	Sunday.
January 11th	All hands turning land. Nine sick. Louella cut herself with butcher knife. Marcy's child born with waterhead.
January 12th	Cold and rain. All hands in cabins. Fourteen sick. Lizette miscarried. Lulu reports herself raped, refuses to name attacker. Probably not forced.
January 13th	Freezing. All hands in cabins. Jince punished for hitting Old Tom. Seventeen sick.

January 14th Sleet and snow. All hands in cabins. Rose refuses to live with husband Ted. Chloe requests permission to wed Philander. Beck apprenticed as cooper. Twenty-three sick.

For the next two weeks the reports were mostly the same. Reading them over her father's shoulder, Star could understand his concern and anxiety. The food, clothing, doctor, and medicine bills were mounting.

"I noticed some of the slaves without oilskins, pa," she said. "They'll get sick, and the infirmary is already full."

"I know, Star. Mr. Grady ordered a shipment from Boston months ago, but you can't depend on receiving goods even from our own ports any more. There are a hundred cargoes for every available vessel. Much of the slaves' illness is due to lack of proper clothing and covers. Some of the men are still in their summer cotton work clothes when they should be in winter woolens. And the duffel blankets ordered from London over a year ago have never been received. I wish I could dress them all in flannel and woolen garments, but these must be reserved for the aged and infirm."

"More rain is threatening, pa. Are the dikes in the rice fields holding up?"

"They have broken in places, but a crew is mending them. The rains will slacken soon, God willing. Where's Lance?"

"Throwing darts in the game room. Has he really ordered a sport phaeton from the royal coachmaker of London?"

"He has, and a more useless extravagance I can't imagine. His gig is perfectly good, but it's not the latest thing in self-driving vehicles. What's more, I've just had word from Mr. Grady that the phaeton arrived and is waiting on the docks. Necessities such as oilskins and blankets are long delayed, but the frivolities seem to come in record time. What a strange age this is!"

"Master John?" One of the maids tapped on the office door. "Miss Emily is askin' for you."

"All right, Pansy. I'll come in a minute."

"She say come now, Master John, and I ain't got time to run back up there with no message. She sent me after some more hot bricks to warm her feet. Lordy, if that ain't the coldest person I is done ever see! Even the fever don't heat her much. Master John, you better get up yonder quick. Miss Emily in a pother."

Watching her father go, Star thought his frame sagged more each day, and she hated that Yankee despot upstairs who reduced him to this state. He should be walking tall and erect, with pride and dignity, as became the master of a great plantation. He had walked that way when her mother was mistress of Mystic Rose. She sighed, visualizing what he would find upon entering the master chambers.

Emily would be sitting up in the lovely French bed which he had shared with Angelique and in which their child had been born. Star could not imagine a more incongruous setting for her staid stepmother than that pink tufted satin bed with its headboard decorated with wreaths of carved roses and gilded cupids. Emily's grayish brown hair would be parted in the middle and hanging in two long thick braids, like hemp ropes, on her flat breasts. A knitted capelet would cover her shoulders, while a long-sleeved, high-necked flannel nightdress would conceal every vestige of flesh. If she were peeved, it would be a silent anger, much more to be dreaded than her rare temperamental outbursts. Her faded blue eyes would be dull and unsmiling, and she would probably greet him with an accusation: "Well, John! Have you finally found a moment to visit your ailing wife? I'm sure *she* was never so callously ignored and neglected. No doubt you kept a constant vigil by *her* bedside when *she* was ill." Emily always referred to his first wife as "she" and "her," as if Angelique had been nameless.

Well, if nothing else convinced pa of her wisdom in

preferring spinsterhood to a loveless marriage, his own experience with Emily Wilson should.

By the end of March, the azalea buds showed colors of scarlet, pink, salmon, and snowy white. Purple wisteria covered the gazebo and hung on the split-rail fences. Tulips and daffodils brightened the gardens, and the mystic rose put forth its first lovely white bud. The fruit trees, apple and pear and peach and persimmon, blossomed so impetuously they would be in danger if there were a late frost. Wild flowers bloomed along the River Road and in the woods. Irises edged the swamps, and water lilies floated on the murky waters. Spring had come at last, and it was time to plant the fields again and sow the rice paddies.

Star was as ignorant of these intricate processes as any other sheltered young lady in the Low Country. Heretofore, spring had meant a new wardrobe to her, outdoor picnics and barbecues, and the most thrilling social event of all, the Tilting Tournament. Only two years ago Grant, riding as the Gallant Knight of the Santee, had won the contest and crowned her Queen of Love and Beauty by lowering his lance at her feet, after she and her father, one of the judges, had presented him the trophy. This was tantamount to a declaration of love, and all the county had taken it as a public betrothal. The memory would keep her from the tournament this year.

Lance, however, intended to ride again as the Valiant Knight of Mystic Rose. His tailor was making him a splendid costume, and Lance was diligently practicing for the feat. "If I'm the victor," he told Star, half joking, half in earnest, "I shall crown you my lady fair."

Star scoffed at the dubious and undesired honor. "You won't win the tilt, Lance. You never have yet, and the competition grows keener every meet. But even if you should, I'll not be there to cheer you."

"Why not, little sister? Would the presence of the Gallant Knight of the Santee be too much for you to bear? Good God, Star! The man jilted you—everyone in the

Carolinas knows that! When are you going to realize it?"

"Oh, go to blazes!" Star cried furiously.

But tears stung her eyes, and she brooded in her room for several days, pretending to spring malaise. She frowned at the lovebirds billing and cooing in their cage and wished Troy had given her a canary instead, or a brilliant bird of paradise or even a parrot to amuse her. The parakeets just ate, slept and made love. But, of course, that was exactly why he had sent them to her. And she was silly enough to name them Romeo and Juliet!

A vile tasting elixir prescribed by Doctor Frazer, the family physician, soon forced her back to health and more practical thoughts of her future as mistress of Mystic Rose.

All she knew about rice was that it constituted the main course of every Low Countryman's dinner, and there was even a special long-handled silver spoon to serve it. To call rice "cereal," as Lance and Emily did, was sacrilegious, and to scorn or malign it publicly was to court social ostracism. In the Low Country eating rice was as much of a ritual as drinking tea was in the Orient. Star could not recall ever having sat down to a meal lacking it.

Of growing the crop itself, she had only the most rudimentary knowledge. She knew that it was sown in spring, usually April, and harvested in autumn, usually September. The yield, all except that required for family and slave consumption, was milled and sent in flatboats to Charleston where it was stored in warehouses to await shipment to many parts of the world. The factor handled the business details.

Her appearance on the fields this morning caused some excitement and speculation among the slaves and some consternation to her father and the overseer. Dressed in a blue bombazine frock piped in cherry red braid and wearing sturdy boots on her tiny feet, she walked along the banks observing the plowing of the squares, hearing the overseer shout orders to the foremen and they in turn to the hands directly under them.

John smiled indulgently, but he wished she would return to the house where she belonged. She was disrupting operations and, worse still, exposing herself to the harmful vapors of the marshlands. The air here was so polluted and dangerous that only the strongest female slaves were permitted to work with the rice crops, and then only because their sensitive fingers were more competent at sowing the seeds than those of the men. The damp ground promoted foot diseases, and even the mules had to wear special leather shoes to prevent hoof rot. And here was this brave but obstinate child of his defying all the perils! Surely she was not serious about this spinster business? He wanted grandchildren, and there was only one way to get them. He was disappointed in that young sea captain whom he had expected to bring Star out of her shell.

Still, John could not help admiring his daughter's interest in the plantation. Would that Lance, who was gallivanting about Charleston in his new phaeton, showed some interest!

"What happens after the plowing, pa?"

"The clods must be broken up and raked smooth as a garden plot. Then comes the digging of trenches, twelve or so inches apart, in which to sow the seed. This done, we'll open the sluice gates and cover the fields with water for two tides, or until the sprouts begin to fork."

"Fork?"

"Put on leaves. Three weeks later, the fields will be hoed and more water let in, covering the plants for several days to discourage grass and insects. This flooding—or long water, as it's called—will be slacked off and held until the plants stand erect. Then the trenches will be cleared of foreign growth and the long water drawn off. Are you absorbing all of this, Star?"

"Most of it," she nodded dubiously. "Well, some of it. I reckon you can't learn everything in one day, pa."

"I reckon not." He smiled. "Perhaps you'd best take it by degrees and phases. As the crop grows, I'll explain the various procedures to you. They are numerous, dear, and all important to a successful harvest."

The overseer, a raw-boned, angular fellow with a shock of fiery red hair and huge freckles covering his face, neck and hands, joined them. Clem Jones was thirty-nine and a bachelor. His contract with John Lamont gave him a yearly salary of three-hundred dollars, plus a neat cottage, a Negro woman to cook, wash and clean for him, and a boy to wait on him. Clem had heard of rare cases where an overseer was fortunate enough to marry the widow or daughter of a planter, but he was too sensible to hope for any such miracle for himself. He tipped his hat and bowed to Star, his efforts at gallantry hampered somewhat by his awkwardness and lack of formal education. Clem Jones was, in every respect, a self-made man.

"Mornin', Miss Star. We ain't accustomed to the pleasure of your company on the fields. Is this an occasion of some sort, ma'am?"

"An occasion of curiosity, Mr. Jones," Star replied pleasantly. "I wanted to see how the rice is planted. I may have need of the knowledge some day."

"Well, ma'am, you couldn't find no better teacher than your own pa. I reckon he knows all there is to know about the crop. He sure learned me the trade. I used to be a cotton man, you know, from the Up Country."

"A fine one, too," John returned the compliment. "Now that the Whitney gin is making cotton culture so highly profitable, Clem is anxious to try our luck with it."

"Any time you say the word, sir. We got a lot of land could be grubbed out and put under cotton cultivation. No reason why it shouldn't grow as well here as on them sea islands. The long stable variety, that is. The short does best on the Piedmont Plateau. What's your opinion, Miss Star?"

"My opinion? Oh, I think we should raise lots of cotton, Mr. Jones, and more sheep, too. Then we could spin most of our own cloth and wouldn't have to depend entirely on the New England and British mills. The shipments are so long delayed now, I fear war would cut us off completely."

Clem nodded, sifting a fistful of rice from one hand to the other. "About how many bales to the acre you figure we could make on virgin soil?"

The word "virgin" had only one connotation for Star; she never thought of soil or forests in that capacity, and Clem's reference embarrassed her. "Why, I should imagine about fifty or so, Mr. Jones," she surmised, unaware of the men's exchange of amused winks, unaware also that one bale per acre was considered extraordinary production. "What do you think?"

"I think your pa would be a millionaire fast at that rate, Miss Star."

"Well, I've never known a Low Countryman to object to more wealth, Mr. Jones."

Then she turned to her father. "Now that I've had my first lesson in rice culture, could I go into the city with Mauma to see the new spring millinery at Madame Toulet's? All the ladies will be flaunting new bonnets at church Sunday."

"And so shall you," John said, pleased at her interest in new spring fashions. "I'll drive you myself. You and Mauma may shop while I see Mr. Grady."

"Oh, thank you, pa! I hope they have that new French color, powder blue. Maybe I'll find some material I like, too. And some new slippers. Why don't you buy yourself a new hat, pa? And a bright silk cravat if you can find one?"

In town they heard disquieting rumors that the war hawks were demanding a declaration of war on England as a condition for President Madison's renomination in the fall. But her father vigorously defended Henry Clay and John Calhoun.

"I refuse to believe they would resort to any such blackmail! Nor would President Madison allow himself to be so intimidated and coerced. Lies! Vicious Yankee lies!"

Star scarcely heard him. Her eyes were scanning the

harbor, but the ship she sought was not there. Maybe she would never see the *Venus* or her master again. The thought was somehow more disturbing than the possibility of war. She lapsed into pensive, wistful silence, broken only when she reached the pink stucco boutique on Legare Street, and the proprietress greeted her.

"Ah, Mademoiselle Lamont! My new spring chapeaux have just arrived, and I saved a charmer for you in the latest shade, *bleu poudre*. One in fuchsia, too—an exact copy of a favorite of the Empress Josephine. And some exquisite fleur-de-lis fabric that is all the rage in Paris—"

"Wonderful, madame! Bring them out. Everything!"

Chapter 13

FROM THE EARLIEST DAYS of the Carolina provinces, the slaves were taught to bear arms and help defend the master's family and property in times of emergency. Several slave uprisings resulting from the Negroes' knowledge and possession of firearms had cost the lives of white men, women, and children, but the percentage of such rebellions was not large enough to preclude the necessary military training. The vast majority of slaves remained loyal, even though they could be easily influenced by one strong dissenter. For this reason, and because there seemed less need of it, military training was considerably curtailed after the Revolution. The Indians were quartered on government reservations, pirates no longer menaced the local islands, and the English warriors had been defeated. Twenty-eight years of peace had reigned.

Now it was threatened. Once again the Low Country was in danger of British invasion, and defense preparations were imperative. At the Mystic Rose plantation, guns were mounted in the turrets, and lookouts were posted on the taller chimneys. Well-oiled muskets were removed from the armory and placed trustfully in the hands of Negroes. Companies of slaves, commanded by foremen, took turns at target practice, and the orders of "Ready, aim, fire!" echoed over the countryside.

Star and Emily were brought to the range against a grove of pines and given loaded muskets and instructions. Emily's hand and eye were steady; in a few lessons she was hitting the target expertly. She fired coolly, deliberately, and grimly, encouraged by the compliments of her husband and her son. Soon she was training several of the black women. Observing their mistress's skill and accuracy with the weapon greatly increased the women's respect and awe of her.

Star's aim was terrible; it tried the patience of her instructor and drew laughter and ridicule from Lance. "Lucky thing you don't live in a log cabin on a wild frontier with Indians and wolves howling at your door," he jibed. "I fear you wouldn't survive long. You're no pioneer, honey. Here, let me show you what you're doing wrong."

He moved up close behind her. Feeling his steamy breath on her neck, Star's flesh tensed in loathing. As his arm came around her waist, she stepped adroitly aside. "I don't need your help, Lance! Pa is a sharpshooter. If he can't teach me, no one can. Get away from me!"

"Still high and mighty, eh? Well, if the war lasts long enough you may be damned glad to have me around. With your other suitors rushing to join the militia, I may be the only available escort for miles around."

"Naturally," Star sneered, "you'd never consider joining the militia?"

"There are already more volunteers than can be properly trained and equipped. One more would just be a nuisance, if not a hazard. Besides, I must remain at Mystic Rose to protect my interests. And if you wish to protect yours, little sister, better learn to handle that weapon with deadly precision."

"Pa will teach me."

"Ah yes! Here comes the Daniel Boone of the Low Country now." His mockery increased as his stepfather approached, and he asked, "How soon do you think those English pigs will attack us, sir?"

"As soon as they feel secure on the sea," John replied, ignoring the deliberate slur on his ancestry. "Naval warfare is one thing, ground battle quite another. Transporting men and material three thousand miles across water is their biggest problem, and undoubtedly their best troops and equipment are engaged in Europe. Even so, there's no assurance that they'll confine their activities in this country to the Canadian border. An expeditionary force might land on our shores with little or no warning. God knows we have precious little to stop them."

He gazed at his daughter with grave and worried eyes. "You must not, under any condition, leave the plantation without my knowledge and permission. You are especially not to go into the city. If there's anything you need or want, make a list, and Mr. Grady will attend to it. Is that clear, Star?"

"Yes, pa. But Mr. Grady has atrocious taste in ladies apparel. That last scarf he bought for me was hideous, a relic five years out of fashion. The riding gloves were the wrong size, and I wouldn't be caught dead carrying that ridiculous reticule! I should hate to have to wear a bonnet he selected. Why can't I go to town with you and do my own shopping? For the accessories, anyway?"

"Why? Great Scot, girl, I'm trying to explain! Enemy warships may be cruising off the Carolina coast at this very hour. It's no secret that the harbor forts are inadequately manned, and the militia still disorganized. A force of raiders, effectively landed and equipped, could easily sack and burn and ravish Charleston. Do you imagine I'd want you on the streets in the face of such peril?"

Lance grinned at her. "What he means, dear innocent, is that you might be run down and raped by a herd of British swine."

"That's enough!" John warned him. "Star knows what

I mean, and she'll be safer here than anywhere else. Let us resume target practice now."

Star thought she was in greater danger of being violated on the plantation by her stepbrother than in Charleston by a British soldier, but she did not tell her father so. He had enough problems on his mind.

"Must I, pa? I'll never be a crack shot. I couldn't hit the side of a barn with a blunderbuss! Can't I just practice loading muskets for others?"

"For shame, daughter. Your mother could hit the bull's eye at fifty feet; your grandmother successfully fought off two Cherokees with one charge; and your great-grandmother helped rout Stede Bonnet's buccaneers on one of their raids of Mystic Rose. Every woman should know something about arms and self-defense."

"All right, pa. I'll try again."

"Clear the fields for action!" Lance shouted. "And run for your lives!"

Oh, Star thought furiously, it would be a pleasure to shoot *him!*

For the first few months of the war, tension and anxiety gripped the state, especially the coastal region. Churches, traditionally the signalers of invasion or other emergency, ceased tolling bells for services or the dead. A lone post rider galloping along a rural route was often mistaken for a courier and halted, if possible, for information. An early curfew was imposed on all slaves and freedmen and rigidly enforced. Hysteria and its attendant rumors and exaggerations were rampant. It was difficult to distinguish between fact, fiction, and propaganda, for the journals were full of all three. And now, more than ever, a stranger was regarded with suspicion and almost immediately suspected of espionage, sabotage, or both.

Social life in the city continued with some restrictions but was severely curtailed in the country. With miles of wilderness separating the plantations and farms, even the old custom of neighborly calling suffered, for such visits generally required leaving one's home all day and frequently the night, and few families felt it wise to be away from home that long. The boundaries of Mystic Rose became to Star a very tangible wall, confining her as securely as a prison. Her windows might as well have been barred.

Emily, worried about Lorna, suggested that she come home for the duration. Lorna declined, replying that her husband had wanted her to go to Avalon-on-Santee and stay with his parents, but that she had chosen to remain in Charleston. Grant was a captain in the militia, subject to call on short notice, and his wife felt duty bound to remain at his side, however much he might have preferred her absence. Furthermore, Lorna wrote confidentially, she was feeling poorly and hinted that she might be in the family way. The rumor, already spread by her servants, had arrived at Mystic Rose before her letter. Star heard it from Mauma and brooded for days. But then another rumor squelched that one. Apparently Lorna wanted a child so much she was constantly experiencing false pregnancy.

Star's only contact with the outside world was a vicarious one. John went into the city once a week to consult with his factor and spend an hour or two relaxing at the Planters Hotel. This splendid new hostelry, near the Dock Street Theater, had replaced the Old Carolina Coffee House on East Bay as the fashionable club for men of fortune and leisure. Here, great merchants and prosperous planters animatedly and sometimes heatedly discussed business and agriculture, politics and economics. And the war.

South Carolina's political power was concentrated largely in the distinguished, aristocratic old families of the Low Country, and their influence was strongly reflected in Columbia and Washington. Their individual importance had been reduced somewhat by the state legislation of 1810, which had extended suffrage to all white men over twenty-one, but collectively their weight was still impressive enough to affect government policy, both local and national, and gain judicial and legislative favor. Indeed their influence in these matters caused considerable friction between the two principal sections of the state: the Up Country, which continually sought control of the senate in Columbia, and the Low, which obstinately refused to yield it.

Star always met her father eagerly on his return from Charleston, begging for news. News of the war, of friends, town doings—anything that might relieve the monotonous boredom of her present existence. She missed acutely the gay social life of the county. Her two accomplishments, china painting and the spinet, provided little diversion for her; and she had lost all interest in needlework now that she was no longer preparing a hope chest. Unfortunately, she had never accomplished the simple art of entertaining herself and did not even enjoy riding or walking alone. Thus she was lonely, restless, unhappy, and starved for change and companionship.

"What news, pa?" she cried, running out to meet him. "Tell me everything!"

Sometimes he teased her. "Well, rice has gone up fifty cents a barrel, Hiram Foster put up a new sign over his chandlery, and Old Toothless Joe painted his hardware store yellow."

"Oh, Pa! Don't jest. What of the war? Isn't it over *yet*?" It was November, not six months since the declaration, but it seemed six years to Star.

John dismounted, and a groom led his horse to the stables. And though reluctant to tell her the truth, he did not lie to her. "Not yet, child, and perhaps not for a long while. The campaign in the North is faring badly. Since General Hull's defeat at Detroit in August, we've done little but founder and retreat and surrender. There was bitter talk at the hotel today," he reflected somberly, slipping an arm about her small shoulders. "Some men said we were betrayed by the war hawks, that when Henry Clay boasted on the House floor that the Kentucky militia alone could place Montreal and Upper Canada at our feet, he talked like a backwoods braggart. And that our fine Mr. Calhoun, predicting victory in four weeks, was an even greater and more arrogant fool."

This was not the kind of news Star had wanted to hear; it was gloomy. And it made her a little angry when she remembered the celebrations that had accompanied the declaration of war in June: the jubilant march of the militia, as if returning from a smashing victory; the torchlight parade and dancing in the streets of Charleston; the high-flown rhetoric of the orators. She and John and Emily had been among the spectators, and Lance had participated in the activities, uproariously drunk and whooping like an Indian at a massacre.

"Everyone was so confident in June," she said. "Charleston was wild with joy."

"Most wars are launched in glory and confidence, my dear. Ah, but I should not criticize our statesmen. I was as blind and gullible as the rest, and as beguiled."

Lance, idling and eavesdropping on the terrace, joined them as they mounted the steps, inviting himself into the conversation. "I'll tell you the trouble. Our army is commanded by doddards left over from the Revolution, and the spirit of '76 is not only dead but decayed. Military tactics change like everything else, and old men lose their vigor and perception and incentive. Worse still, their courage."

"You didn't trumpet that tune at the barbecue at Fairhill last April," Star reminded. "You bragged that one general like William Henry Harrison was worth a dozen Redcoat officers."

"I don't include General Harrison among the graybeards of the Revolution; he was a baby in '76. And he certainly distinguished himself at Tippecanoe last fall. He's still young, in his thirties, and if he can slaughter the British as well as he did the Shawnees, he'll make a bloody fine showing on the Canadian border. But you can't win a war with one good general and a few thousand soldiers."

"For the record," John said, "Congress authorized an army of twenty-five thousand."

"And forgot to appropriate the necessary funds to support it! You can't win a war on paper, either. Nor depend on individual state's militia, except when their own state is in jeopardy. We need an army in the field commanded by intelligent young officers with something more to recommend them than family background and political influence in Washington. The gentleman soldier always was overrated, and his day is past. The common man, as is being proved on the western frontiers, makes a better fighter, and tougher, although he has less to lose than the aristocrat. If it weren't for the bold young blood in the navy, the situation would even be more desperate."

"Give our privateers some credit, too," John told him. "God knows they deserve it. Which reminds me of something that might interest you, daughter. I heard today that the brig *Venus* engaged a British sloop off Jamaica last month and captured her with a cargo worth over thirty thousand dollars."

Although this was more the kind of news Star had hoped for, she shrugged, pretending disinterest in the exploits of Captain Troy Stewart. "Really? How nice for the captain."

Lance scowled. "The rascal will be rich if he can hold out. And since we must apparently trust offensive action to the navy and privateers, it wouldn't surprise me to see Stewart cheered if ever his ship touches our shores again."

"Why not," Star snapped, "if he's a hero?"

"If he's a privateer, you mean," her stepbrother drawled. "I imagine the high seas swarm with pirates under the guise of privateers, and many a corsair has been accorded a hero's welcome when he brings his prize to port."

"Captain Stewart invited you to inspect his flag once," Star reminded. "Why didn't you?"

"Come now. You don't suppose the man is foolish enough to fly the Jolly Roger on his mast? Why take such a risk now, when the government will grant a letter of marque allowing a man to prey in honor upon shipping? He probably enjoys a prince regent's license as well."

"What's a prince regent's license?"

"A British letter of marque to American merchantmen. They're being issued wholesale to some of our loyal privateers. Stewart is probably ruthless and enterprising enough to take advantage of a practice by which he could plunder both sides with impunity, and honor be damned."

John cautioned, "That's a reckless and dangerous statement to make in public, Lance. A man's patriotism is as sacred as his paternity, and to slur either is to risk a challenge. Besides which, I don't believe it's true."

"Of course it isn't!" Star declared emphatically, more out of hostility to Lance than loyalty to Troy. "Captain Stewart wouldn't think of betraying his country."

"How staunchly you defend the rogue! Does the fire in your heart burn less brightly for Grant Russell now? Has it been replaced by a candle in your window for the wandering sailor?"

"Mind your own business!"

"This is my business. Maybe I don't like the idea of a privateer courting my sister."

"Your sister?" Star mocked. "I'm no such thing, Lance Wilson! Nor is anyone courting me." And with a petulant swish of her skirts, she turned and walked into the house.

John sighed. "The way you two fight, one would believe you really are siblings. Does it pleasure you to torment her, son?"

"It's she who torments me, father."

"In what way?"

Lance squirmed and reddened under John's scrutiny. "Not *that* way, sir!"

"Are you sure?"

"Positive! My God, what gives you such an absurd notion? She's naught to me but an annoying piece of baggage."

"She's my daughter, Lance. A lady. And you will accord her due respect in my presence and everyone else's.

You know that I've always been lenient with you. I've never laid down any laws to you and never punished you, although you've broken many rules of decorum in my house. I did not feel free to take you in hand, and apparently your mother was unable to cope with you. But I've often had occasion to regret my leniency and indulgence and to wonder if I did not do you an injustice."

"Injustice?"

"Yes, Lance. Perhaps I failed in my adoptive parental role and duties. You needed control and correction in the worst way. Perhaps if I had tightened your reins and thrashed you soundly when you deserved it, I might have made a better man of you. Now I am going to issue my first order to you, Lance. Never touch Star against her will. If you do and I learn of it, you will have to leave Mystic Rose."

Lance smiled contemptuously. "You sound like the Almighty warning Adam in Paradise. The archangel, at least."

"This is no joking matter, Lance. I am utterly serious. If ever you indecently molest my daughter, you will not only be ordered off this plantation but also disinherited. Stricken out of my will completely. Is that understood?"

"My understanding is quite adequate, father. Have you told my mother how you intend to treat me?"

"There's no cause to upset your mother, Lance. This is between us, you and me, and need never go further if you behave yourself. When I adopted you, Lance, I had a very fatherly affection for you, which I had hoped you would reciprocate like a true son. I had great plans for you."

He paused, drawing a heavy breath, forced at last to an admission that obviously distressed him. "Unfortunately, things don't always turn out as one hopes and plans and dreams. You resent me and everything I stand for. No, don't bother to deny it; your conduct speaks for itself. I've tolerated much disrespect and disobedience and insolence from you and shall probably condone much more. But I will not tolerate any wrong intentions toward my daughter!" His voice trembled with violent emotion, his facial veins swelling like cords, and his hands strained hard on his riding crop, as if to prevent its use on his defiant, impertinent stepson.

Lance had never seen him so angry, so uncontrolled. Star was his seed, his and Angelique's creation, and no other man's child ever could or would mean as much to him. The realization infuriated Lance anew every time he thought of it. He longed to strike out at John Lamont with his bare hands, to wrest the crop from him and beat him with it. Curse him and his daughter and all his goddamned ancestors! But he moved back a step or two, watching him warily.

"Yes, papa. Now if you're done with your tirade, I'll be leaving. I'm engaged to play poker with some fellows this afternoon, and then I'm calling on Miss Letty Clayton. So you see, your fears for Star's virtue are unwarranted. But I wouldn't be too sure she still possesses it, if I were you, sir. It's possible, you know, that the honorable Mr. Russell long ago deflowered her. And if not Grant, perhaps your nautical friend, Captain Stewart. It's common knowledge that pirates have no compunction about ravishing maidens."

"You have a keen wit and quick tongue, Lance. 'Tis a pity you employ them so uselessly. I've been blinded by your true character for years, but no longer. My eyes are wide open now. I see through you and ahead of you, and I warn you to be extremely careful. Go now to your pleasures and pursuits. But remember what I said, boy. Never forget it!"

Chapter 14

DURING THE SPRING OF 1813 the British invaded Ohio. Operating from Detroit and controlling Lake Erie, they succeeded in penetrating to the Sandusky River by summer.

"Well," said Charlestonians, "that's bad. But Ohio is far away, and Old Tippecanoe and Commodore Perry will stop the invasion somehow."

Then, closer to home, in Georgia and Alabama, the Creek Indians went on the warpath. Incited by Chief Tecumseh and enemy agents, they massacred some five hundred settlers, both white and Negro, at Fort Mimms. When the gory headlines appeared in the Charleston *Courier*, gloom and fear shrouded the Low Country. The Indian tomahawk was more dreaded than the British bayonet.

Where was the swift victory the war hawks had promised? What was going to happen when Napoleon's legions were crushed in Europe, as was predicted, and Britain was free to turn her full might on the United States? The armies on the Canadian border seemed bogged down in a morass of failures. The navy, so greatly outnumbered in vessels, could not possibly control the seas, no matter how heroically the courageous young men fought. The blockade grew increasingly effective and strangling, with British squadrons patrolling the Chesapeake and Delaware bays and raiders terrorizing the coastal towns in these regions. Doomsday seemed imminent.

And then, one afternoon, there appeared, a few miles off the Carolina coast, the white sails of the privateer *Venus*; and with her, limping into harbor, was the British sloop *Elizabeth,* carrying several thousand muskets, hundreds of suits of uniforms, many bales of cloth, casks of wine, rum and whiskey, drums, and trumpets—a military cargo worth upwards of forty thousand dollars. The *Elizabeth* was out of Liverpool and bound for Halifax when intercepted by the *Venus,* and British commanders in Canada were anxiously awaiting her arrival in the Nova Scotian port. She had put up a brave and tenacious battle, damaging the *Venus* to a crippling extent with her formidable armament of eight twelve-pound guns and four long six-pounders. But the brig's sturdier construction and sixteen barrels had finally subdued her. The victorious crew boarded, disarmed the British officers, and claimed their prize.

Charleston was hysterical with excitement. Public opinion, like a weathervane, changed with the wind, and now the wind blew fair. An enemy ship had been captured, some tangible evidence of a victory! For of the many ships the city had armed and commissioned, several had already been sunk, and only the *Decatur* was making an impressive showing against His Majesty's fleet. And though the *Venus* counted Nantucket as her home port, Captain Stewart was well enough known in Charleston to arouse admiration for his prowess at sea.

A brassy band blared on the crowded wharves, and a number of prominent citizens, including the mayor, were prepared to shake hands and make speeches. Pretty young girls, enthralled at the prospect of meeting a real live hero, held baskets of flower petals with which to shower the intrepid captain and crew. A troop of militia was ordered out, with Grant Russell sourly in command. He had considered begging off but knew it would occasion snickering and speculation among the men. Stores and shops closed, flags were unfurled, and banners and streamers floated and fluttered in the September breeze.

But the news did not reach Mystic Rose in time for Star to come to town, even if she had been able to persuade her father to take her. She had to hear about the celebration secondhand from Letty Clayton, after services the following Sunday.

Letty, Lance, and Star stood in the shade of a monarch live oak in the courtyard of Goose Creek Church, where the Lamonts had worshiped since its founding in 1706. There were other Episcopal churches more convenient to the plantation, but John had a special fondness for St. James of Goose Creek. Lord Newton Lamont had contributed much to its construction, in funds and labor, and the family still occupied his original pew.

Reposing in a garden of flowers, the chaste white chapel seemed to have been transplanted there from an English village. Star thought it odd that the royal arms of James I had never been removed from the chancel, but neither the rector nor congregation appeared to object to this persistent religious devotion to the Crown, nor consider it unpatriotic during the Revolution or present conflict.

"Oh, Star, honey!" cried Letty, preening for Lance's benefit. "You should've been there! It was the most exciting event in Charleston since Damon Devoe shot Gregory Masters in that silly duel over that New York actress, Hope Carson. And the *Courier* estimated that there were more spectators than at the last public hanging. I declare Captain Stewart looked so handsome and dashing I could have kissed him! A lot of bold girls did, despite their chaperons. Even the older ladies, who never paid him much mind before, were making sheep's eyes and simpering like school maids. Several invited him to soirees and promised to make him guest of honor."

"And you were as silly as the rest of them, Letty Clayton," Lance chided, toying with the watch chain dangling with gold seals and looped across his embroidered silk waistcoat.

"I was not, Lance Lamont! You're just jealous because Captain Stewart kissed my hand when I put a rosebud in his lapel. He did, Star! He took my hand and kissed it, gallant as any knight or noble."

"He couldn't kiss your lips," Lance drawled, "because your teeth are in the way."

Letty blushed furiously, raising a timid hand to shield her unattractive mouth. "Oh, Star! Isn't he mean?"

"The devil incarnate on God's property," Star agreed. "You should slap him, Letty. But tell me more about—"

"Her hero," Lance supplied in the pause. "Tell her about the three crewmen he buried at sea, the holes the British blew in the *Venus*, the rigging they shot off, and the fire they set in the hold."

"Yes, isn't it thrilling? But you should see the *Elizabeth*! She'll probably never sail again, and her officers and crew are quartered in the jail house and armory. The *Venus* will be in port for repairs, and Captain Stewart will be the toast of the town. Mama's planning to entertain him too, Star. Naturally, you'll be invited."

"I'm not sure I can come, Letty. Pa has notions about invasion."

"Oh, pooh! Colonel Drayton won't let them get past Fort Moultrie. Darling, you must be simply perishing of loneliness and boredom at Mystic Rose. You never attend any parties or barbecues or ride in the hunts. You missed the last two tilting tournaments and all the new plays. Why, you don't even come to town to shop any more. The only place you go is to church."

Star sighed, thinking of the hard pews and long sermons. "And Lord knows that's not much fun! Not that I mind going to church and praying—"

"I know, dear," Letty sympathized. "The benches are so uncomfortable, I'd as soon sit in the stocks. Pa says the benches must have been designed as penance for the wicked—though, of course, everyone knows there are no wicked Episcopalians. Well, mama's getting impatient to go home. I'll probably see you again next Sunday. And you too, Lance?" she asked hopefully, her timorous smile the best Letty could do in the way of coquetry.

"Maybe," he replied indifferently. "Your Sunday would be spoiled if you didn't see me, wouldn't it, Letty?"

"I reckon so, Lance," she admitted helplessly, in love with this wretched creature for no explicable reason. "I reckon it would. . . ."

Almost a week had passed since the *Venus* had put into port, and still Captain Stewart had not called at Mystic Rose. Star knew she had unwittingly offended him on his last visit, but she did not believe he was staying away on that account, for he was not so easily discouraged. Either he was too busy with his ship, too absorbed in other pleasures and pursuits to bother with her, or simply too obstinate and contrary. Perhaps he expected her to go to him? But surely he must realize that was impossible! She had done so once at a hazardous risk to her reputation, and she did not intend to repeat her mistake. Besides, pa had forbidden her to leave the plantation without his consent and would hardly escort her to Charleston on such a mission. Fathers did not take daughters to call on gentlemen, and a lady dared not call on one alone. It was unthinkable. Exciting, but unthinkable.

When one of the Clayton slaves delivered an invitation to Mystic Rose and John returned his regrets, Star felt she might as well be immured in a convent or dead and entombed with her mother. Never had she felt more lonely, isolated, dejected.

"Oh, pa! The British are not coming—and even so, we'd have plenty of warning!"

"We had no warning in the Revolution," he said. "We woke up one morning to find the countryside scarlet with Redcoats. Cannon fire and houses aflame were the first realization we at Mystic Rose had of their presence in the Low Country. I don't want to be caught dancing at some ball if it happens again. They are in Ohio now and threatening Virginia."

"Ohio and Virginia are far away."

"But Georgia is not so far away, and the Indians are rampaging there. And the British have a fleet of fifty ships in the Chesapeake Bay, sacking towns and plundering plantations. What's to prevent them from visiting our shores?"

"Why must we always expect the worst, pa? Why can't we forget the war for just one evening? I want to go to a party, have some fun. I want to dance! Why, I haven't been to a ball in over a year. I'll forget how to dance if I don't get some practice, pa."

"I doubt that, daughter. Dancing is as natural to you as breathing, and when the war is over, I'll give you the grandest ball ever."

"When the war is over! I may be an old lady by then, with naught but cats and books for company."

"Well," John teased her, "isn't that what you want to be? An old maid?"

"No," she murmured. "I just don't want to marry."

"It's the same thing, child."

"No, it isn't, pa. Most spinsters are not single by choice. And perhaps I won't be, either, if I don't get around any young bachelors. You keep me cooped up like a turtle in a cooter pond!"

John smiled, chucking her petulant chin. "Come clean, girl. What you really want is to see Captain Stewart again, isn't it? Well, don't fret. He'll be paying you a visit soon, I warrant."

"Who cares?" Star muttered. "Anyway, the Charleston ladies are keeping him quite busy, I hear. Strange, they didn't think so highly of him before he became a hero."

"War changes things, Star. Customs and standards, values and people. Not that I ever considered Captain

Stewart unacceptable. Don't forget, I introduced him to the Low Country."

"So you did, pa. And I've often wondered why."

"Oh," he shrugged, "perhaps I thought the old society needed a new face and personality. But I had no idea, then, that I was giving it a celebrity."

"And you won't attend the Clayton affair in his honor? It'll be at their town house."

"I'm sorry, Star. We'd have to be away from Mystic Rose overnight, and I prefer not to take that chance. Now don't sulk. I have a delightful surprise for you: a box of French chocolates that ran the English Channel blockade. I was saving the treat for your birthday, but you may have it now. If you won't cry," he added hastily, as her dark eyes clouded.

French chocolates, Star thought morosely, munching on the sweetmeats. I'm dying of boredom, and he gives me bonbons!

Still, there *was* a way to outwit pa, if she had the courage and audacity to use it. . . .

Chapter 15

LIKE THE SWAMPS, the tunnel under Mystic Rose had always been forbidden to Star. Unlike the swamps, however, it had never held much lure or fascination for her. She knew that it led to an opening a short distance from the Cooper River, which bound one side of her father's property, but she had no desire to explore it. She had heard of the times the secret passageway had saved her ancestors' lives in sudden Indian and pirate raids, and of their escape from the British through it to Charleston in the Revolution, but she had never had the temerity to venture into that dark hollow herself. She had gazed curiously into its black mouth, unable to see anything; she had felt and smelled its dankness and heard what she imagined were snakes and other alien inhabitants and had quickly closed the heavy cypress door, bolted it, and rushed back up the stairs and through the concealed entrance in the basement. She was afraid of that tunnel, and nothing but the desperation of acute loneliness and boredom could have enticed her into it now.

Even so, she could not attempt the adventure alone. She would need assistance, a boat and someone to row her to Charleston. A strong and courageous slave, one who was more loyal to her than to her father. Dink was the man. She had defended him once when he had been accused by Lance of raiding the chicken coop at night and blaming it on the foxes. His innocence had later been proved when the fox was caught in the act, and Dink was eternally grateful to his young mistress for her faith in him.

"They ain't nothing I wouldn't do for you, Miss Star," he told her after listening to the plan she presented to him. "And you know it. You done me a good turn once, and Dink ain't forgettin' it. But this here plan you is got now is mighty dangerous, Miss Star. Plum crazy, in fact. And if your pa gets wind of it, he'll lock me up in the jail house or sell me off the block, if Mist' Lance don't whip me to death at the post first—"

"I can manage pa," Star assured him. "And Mr. Lance would not dare take a whip to you. He's not master of Mystic Rose yet, you know. Please, Dink. You must help me!"

The man scratched his shaved head. He was a tall sinewy Bantu, pure African, strong and agile as a lean black panther. He had been both baptized and confirmed, and his fine bass voice rose above all others in the spirituals. Star had never had the great fear of him that she had of Obah and some of the other slaves, but it still required considerable courage to entrust her life to him. And though he was at first reluctant to accommodate her in this wild and foolish adventure, he finally agreed after much persuasion and reminding of the favor she had once done for him.

Star swore Dink to secrecy and did not anticipate any difficulty with Mauma, for she had not dared confide in her. That simple soul put duty to her master above all other domestic traits and, Star was sure, would foil her plans, even if she'd had to lock Star in a closet to do it. In matters concerning Star's health, safety, reputation and virtue, Mauma could not be coaxed, coerced, or compromised.

Star retired early that evening. For Mauma's benefit she went through the bedtime ritual, disrobing and donning a white cambric nightgown, washing her face, and scrubbing her small white teeth with orrisroot. But she was nervous and wary, afraid the perceptive woman would sense something.

"You got a fever comin' on, honey?" Mauma asked, brushing her hair. "You looks flushed and acts jittery."

"It's hotter than usual," Star said, taking the hairbrush from her. "That's enough of that."

"It ain't fifty strokes even!"

"It's a hundred. I counted them. And I'll tie my own ribbon, thank you."

"My, my! You's snappy tonight! Must be that turtle-soup you had for supper."

"Good night, Mauma." Affecting a sleepy yawn, Star crawled into bed. "Never mind the candle. I'll blow it out."

"Yessum. Sweet dreams, lamb."

Mauma said that every night, but Star could not remember when last she had had a pleasant dream; not, in fact, since she had ceased dreaming of Grant and their courtship. Lately her dreams included Captain Stewart, and they were mostly stormy experiences, rarely tender, sometimes violent, always exciting. Why should that be, she wondered, when she still loved and wanted Grant Russell with all her being?

She stretched sensuously on the deep feather mattress, thinking how luxurious it would be if she could sleep naked in summer with only the cool scented sheets on her warm body. Did Lorna lie nude with Grant? The thought made her breasts taut, her thighs tense, and her pulse quicken. What was it like to be really intimate with a man? She had no realistic knowledge of the male-female sexual relationship, no actual initiation into the dark mysteries that had intrigued her since puberty when she was told only the essential facts about her maturing body and its disagreeable monthly process.

She knew something about animals in that respect—as much as a curious adolescent could learn on a plantation with a vigilant chaperon on guard. Nevertheless, her lascivious stepbrother had managed to lure her to the stud pasture to watch the blooded stallions service the brood mares; to the kennels where the pedigreed foxhounds performed the same function for the bitches in heat; and to the cattle breeding pen, where the bulls kept all but the milch cows with calf. She had heard frenzied cats cauterwauling at night and the bull alligators roaring in mating season. And she knew that the slaves, married or not, engaged in sexual relations, for there were always a number of pregnant wives and single girls. Some planters, though not her father, actually encouraged such promiscuity to increase their chattels, which were inventoried in their estates along with the livestock.

But a virginal young lady was not supposed to be aware of these natural instincts in human or beast, much less in herself. Should nature disturb or distress a decent maiden, she must promptly and effectively suppress her curiosity and inclination to experiment. Star had done this with Grant, time and again, and suffered afterwards with wonder, torment, and frustration. Lorna had not been so mindful of admonitions, so timid and fearful of the challenge of life. She had met it headlong, won what she wanted, and Star had hated and envied her for possessing the courage she lacked.

Satisfied that Mauma was safe in the servants' quarters, Star rose, dressed quickly and quietly, took a shawl, and slipped into the hall. The house was dark and quiet except for the muted voices in the master suite, the alternating low and high tones suggesting a marital quarrel. Remembering the soft laughter and intimate sounds that had emanated from those chambers when her mother was alive, Star sighed and rushed on, tiptoeing down the stairs, creeping and feeling her way to the basement, where she had hidden some candles, a small brass holder, and oxymuriated matches.

She refused to consider what she would do if Dink were not waiting at the other end of the tunnel, but she wished now she had told him to meet her at the entrance instead. The distance between the beginning and end of that dark cavity seemed suddenly formidable, and for the first time since she had conceived the plan, she was truly frightened and apprehensive. She lit a candle hurriedly, then set it on the floor while she opened the cumbersome door. The creak of rusty hinges sounded loud enough to wake the household, and she thought she heard shuffling noises in the cellar. Footsteps? She hesitated a moment, the blood surging in her ears, then shrugged it off as fantasy and fright. But she mumbled a hasty prayer before proceeding. Mauma said the Lord protected children and fools.

The tunnel was six feet wide and eight feet high, beamed with oak and lined with cypress and pine in some places, rock or brick in others. The floor was graveled. The candle, fluttering precariously in Star's nervous hand, revealed rotting boards and partial cave-ins where the earth had sifted through. If pa was so concerned about invasion, why didn't he repair this deathtrap? But of course he intended to, as soon as the labor could be spared from the fields. She hoped Dink had the sense to keep the outer entrance open so that the candle would receive sufficient air to survive.

Cobwebs hung from the ceiling and draped the walls. Brushing against them, Star imagined she felt a spider crawling on her. It was only a damp pebble that had filtered through the roofing, but she clawed at it frantically with her free hand. Her teeth began to chatter, a hard chill shook her, and perspiration flowed in her armpits.

Coward, she chided herself. You had the audacity to embark on this mad journey, and now you're going to complete it if you die in the act. Go on! Dink is waiting for you.

She ventured some fifty feet, paused, and listened. The thump of her heart was deafening. Still, she detected another sound, the sound of water dripping. A small slimy pool, fed by a miniature spring, glistened in her path. Where it seeped through the walls, the rocks were green and slippery. Either she had to ford it or jump it.

Deciding against wet feet, she lifted her skirts and leaped. The candle blew out, and the intense blackness enveloped her. She cried out in terror, hoping that Dink would hear her. But there was no answer from him, only her own eerie echo. Terrified, she managed to relight the candle.

She progressed some distance and stopped short, paralyzed by the sight of a huge coiled moccasin. She could neither scream nor move. She knew the lethal venom of the water moccasin, the swift death it dealt its victims. Plantation records listed snakebite as the cause of many a slave's demise, for the creatures abounded in the rice fields. And, unlike the rattler, which gave some warning and preferred to avoid humans, moccasins had been known to pursue and attack. There was only one recourse and that was retreat. Make her way back as rapidly as possible, crawl into bed, and hope no one had missed her.

At the sudden roar of a bull alligator, the viper slowly uncoiled and slithered away, disappearing behind some loose boards in the wall. The agitated alligator roared again, filling the hollow with a thunderous rumble. Star screamed and turned to run. The monster was not yet visible, and perhaps she could beat him out of the tunnel.

"Miss Star, Miss Star!" It was Dink calling to her. "Miss Star, don't holler no more and don't run! They's a bull 'gator in here with us, but I'll get him. I killed gators before, and I kill this one, too. Miss Star, you there?"

"Yes, I'm here, Dink! Where are you? I can't see you. I can't see the alligator, either. Tell me what to do!"

"I's right here, Miss Star, but the gator's between us. He's headin' your way. Now listen to me! Put your candle down and step back aways. I's goin' light a torch. Gators scared of fire. He won't come near me, and he won't foller you if there's fire in the way."

"All right, Dink. I hear you, and I'll do whatever you say. Only please hurry!"

Dink lit a torch and staked it. Star set her candle down. Now she could see the bulging eyes of the alligator, the fierce teeth in the gaping mouth. There was panic in his bellowing. He could be driven mad by the fire, frightened into stampeding. She watched him in fascinated horror.

With the swiftness of a jungle cat, Dink leaped upon the animal, holding a razor-sharp knife between his teeth. His prey fought back, roaring, lashing his powerful tail, snapping his monstrous jaws which could sever an arm or leg in one bite. Man and beast thrashed and rolled on the ground, and Star wondered what she would do if Dink lost.

The alligator was clumsy, frenzied. Dink was agile, cool, skillful. He wrestled his foe into a vulnerable position and plunged the blade into his throat. Blood gushed, staining Dink's clothes. A last agonized bellow escaped the animal, and then he lay on his back, dead. The victor retrieved his weapon and pulled the carcass out of the way.

Star hurried to the grisly scene. "Are you all right, Dink? Did he hurt you?"

Dink, panting hard, managed a proud grin. "Take more'n a gator to hurt me, Miss Star. I's strong as that fella in the Bible what pulled down them temple walls, named Samson."

So you are, Star thought. And here am I, alone in a tunnel with you—

"Dink, what about the dogs? Did you lock them in the kennels like I told you?"

"Yessum. I done everything you told me, Miss Star. The hounds no problem, and tomorrow I goin' drag this old boy outta here and bury him by the river. I only hopes I don't have to wrassle none of his cuzzins tonight. Come on now, missy. If we's goin' to town, we better make tracks!"

Chapter 16

THE BOAT Dink had waiting was a pirogue, a light, swift craft modeled on the Indian canoe. In Gullah patois, it was a *pettyaugah,* and so the slaves referred to it.

"The pettyaugah all ready, Miss Star. I got it tied over here in the weeds."

"How long do you think it'll take to reach Charleston?"

"Depend on how my wind hold out. Maybe I got to slow up sometime, but I go fast as I can. The pettyaugah's easy to handle, that's why I picked it. Careful now, missy, watch your step. They's mud everywhere. Better hist your skirts."

Star obeyed, the damp reeds stinging her ankles and legs. She slapped at a swarm of mosquitoes, aware that she should not be out in the dangerous night air. Dink assisted her into the pirogue. After the dark tunnel, the full moon seemed dazzlingly bright, like daylight after a dungeon. And it was fortunate that there was moonlight, for a lantern would have attracted the attention of the sentries atop the roof of Mystic Rose and any night patrollers in the vicinity.

As Star settled herself in the pirogue, Dink began stripping off his shirt. She sat up straight, demanding sharply, "What are you doing?"

"Shuckin' to the waist, so I can row faster. That how slaves rows in the galleys, you know, while a time-keeper beat out the rhythm with a mallet on a wood block, and the guards lash 'em with a whip if they fall behind."

"Not any more, Dink. I mean, galley ships are no longer in use. They're gone now."

"But not the whips, Miss Star. And the big boat I come here on kept us niggers in chains below the whole trip."

Oh, pa! Star thought with sudden poignancy. It *is* wrong! Slavery is wrong, and nothing can make it right. Not the economy of the South or the climate unfit for white labor or the goodness and mercy of the finest master in the world. . . .

These thoughts disturbed her as well as making her question her loyalty to her father and their way of life, as well as her qualifications as the future mistress of Mystic Rose. Slavery was the foundation of the plantation, and a successful planter had to believe in its necessity and rightness to survive. There was no room in his mind for doubts and qualms, and she was sure her father never felt any; nor had she until the advent of Troy Stewart. Born and bred to plantation life, she accepted the system as natural, fundamental, and pleasantly functional. She did not like to feel otherwise; it was like distrusting one's own faith and principles, and it upset her.

She tried to distract herself. But her eyes kept reverting to Dink's broad bare chest, the lean black muscles sweating in the moonlight as he worked the oars. He was doing so at her wish, her request, her *command*. Was she any different, basically, from the galley drivers? Was pa? What about the other kingly planters? Poor Dink. If caught, he would be severely punished, possibly banished from Mystic Rose, while she, the instigator and commander of the operation, would get off with a scolding.

She could only pray that he would not be caught.

The river rolled before them like a great gray python weaving through the jungle. Only when they passed the wharves and docked boats of other planters on the Cooper was she aware of civilization. Here and there the trees arched overhead, trailing long veils of shimmering moss. The sounds of night, which never bothered her safe in her bed at home, rose ominously on all sides, none so fearsome as the roars of the bull alligators. Never would she forget that monster in the tunnel!

A flock of white herons, disturbed from their roosts in a grove of bald cypress, fluttered overhead, soaring in the silvery sky, etched briefly and gracefully against the pale gleaming disk. Then they disappeared into the dark forest. Suddenly a pitiful wail, almost human, emanated from the spectral shadows. Dink promptly explained that it was the cry of a drone—a dead child lost in the woods. Her nerves already taut and thin, Star impatiently rebuked him.

"Hush that kind of nonsense, Dink! I don't want to hear any tales of ghosts and witches. Didn't the missionary tell you that such things do not exist?"

"Yessum, but they does. I seen 'em both, real witches and haints. This here country full of 'em."

"It's all imagination, Dink. Nothing more." But she realized that a few years of religious training could not eliminate centuries of superstition. "I'm sorry, Dink. I didn't mean to snap at you. I'm a bit on edge."

"Yessum."

Star felt so helpless against the night and the river that a tremor ran through her.

"Is you cold, Miss Star?"

"No, I'm not cold, Dink. Why?"

"You is shiverin'. Is you scared?"

"A little," she admitted.

"Of me, Miss Star?"

"You? Of course not, Dink. Why should I fear you?" But her body tensed as his arms eased on the oars. "What're you slowing up for?"

"There's a log in the way."

"Oh. Yes, I see it."

Dink pushed the obstacle aside with a paddle. "Don't be scared, Miss Star. Ain't nothing goin' hurt you. I's here to protect you."

Relieved, Star relaxed her grip on the sides of the pirogue and chafed her numbed hands. Bless Dink, he sensed her apprehensions and sought to reassure her. She wished to reward him some way and wondered if it would be fair to increase his food and clothing allotments from the next distribution. No, that would be slighting the others and certain to arouse suspicion and protest in some. Favoritism was keenly felt and resented.

"Thank you, Dink," she said gratefully, feeling a genuine affection for him. "How much longer before we get there?"

"Not much, missy. You just rest easy and don't fret. Old Dink'll have you there, safe and sound, in two shakes of a coon's tail."

They rounded a bend in the river, and the imposing silhouettes of the churches came into view. Soon Star could distinguish buildings, familiar roofs and chimney pots, and lights gleaming in the homes of friends. The sight of the city, after so many dull months in the country, thrilled her, and the night itself became a part of her adventure. Every sound and movement excited her, the slap of the water against the wharves, the scraping of a fiddle in a waterfront tavern, the laughter from a passing carriage. This was life—and living!

Dink skillfully maneuvered the pirogue past the vessels in port, finally arriving at the berth of the *Venus*. Near her captor stood the ruined hulk of the *Elizabeth*, her tattered sails draped in mourning, stripped of her possessions—a naked lady challenged and raped at sea. And despite visible evidence of a fierce and tenacious battle, the conqueror looked proud, noble and invincible. Almost arrogant, Star thought. Like her master.

The bells of St. Michael's had already rung the curfew for the slaves, and Dink would have to be extremely careful. Star cautioned him to remain in the pirogue, beneath the tarpaulin brought along for that purpose, while she boarded the *Venus*.

"When you figurin' on comin' back?" he whispered, tying the boat to a support under the pier.

"I don't know, Dink. Maybe soon, maybe not. Captain Stewart may not even be aboard." Suddenly it occurred to Star that all her pains may have been in vain. Troy might be kicking up his heels at some ball!

"You sure must set a store by that man, to go to all this here bother to see him."

"He's just a friend, Dink. Shh! I hear someone coming—"

They ducked under cover. A team of uniformed guards carrying muskets passed overhead, their boots clumping on the boards. Dear God, if she should be discovered in this peculiar situation, there would be no explaining it to anyone. She would be disgraced, ruined beyond salvation. But it was too late for any pangs of conscience to deter her.

She had to hurry. The guards would probably return shortly, making periodic checks of the waterfront. With Dink's assistance, she mounted a makeshift ladder on one of the slimy, barnacled posts and climbed onto the pier, glad that her clothes were inconspicuous enough to blend with the cargoes on the docks. She had expected to encounter at least a few derelicts and drunken sailors on shore leave, but fortunately it was that time of evening when such men were more likely to be patronizing the saloons and brothels, and she saw only two grizzled old reprobates propped against a bale of cotton and snoring in alcoholic stupor, empty liquor bottles beside them.

Hoping the crew of the *Venus* would prove no embarrassment or impediment to her, Star was disappointed to find one of them on watch. As she started up the gangway, her shawl concealing her face, he thrust a musket with fixed bayonet at her. "Halt and state your business!"

"I have a message for Captain Stewart," Star whispered like a scout giving the password to a sentry.

"Who from?"

"That information is for the captain!" she replied sharply. "Let me pass, you varlet!"

"Aha!" He grinned, recognizing her voice. "So it's you, is it? Suppose I told you the skipper ain't here?"

"Is he?"

"You really got a message for him, Miss Lamont?"

"Yes, I have, Finch! Now will you cease this chatter before I'm seen? Where's the captain?"

"In his quarters, ma'am." He lowered the weapon. "I don't suppose I have to announce you—"

Star had already brushed past him, guided by memory across the deck and down the short stairway to the master cabin. Aware that Finch was eavesdropping, she made a ceremony of rapping on the door, three quick brisk knocks, as if in prearranged code. She smiled secretly, enjoying her escapade, exhilarated by it, and hoping that Troy would respond in the proper spirit.

He opened the door and stared incredulously, as if seeing a vision. "Miss Lamont?"

"Good evening, captain."

He glanced swiftly about. "Are you alone?"

Star nodded, amused at his astonishment. For once she had succeeded in surprising him, disarming his complacency, knocking his aplomb awry.

"What did you do, escape a party?"

"Does this look like a party costume?"

His eyes considered the simple gray challis gown and soiled slippers, the dark scarf draped peasant fashion over her mussed hair. He pulled her into the cabin and closed the door. "All right, tell me about it! What happened? And why did you come to me, of all people, at this time of night? Are you all right?"

"I'm fine, and nothing's wrong, Troy."

"Not yet, you mean. There'll be plenty wrong if you're found here!"

"Aren't you glad to see me?"

"My dear, of course. I'm delighted! But where did

you come from, and how did you get here?"

"I'll tell you later. I wasn't sure I'd find you in, captain. I hear you're very popular in Charleston now, guest of honor at all the soirees. Quite a hero."

Cynicism quirked his mouth. "I'd rather have been entertained when I wasn't a 'hero.' But why haven't you attended any of the affairs in my honor? You were invited, weren't you? I assumed your absence meant you didn't care to see me."

"No, it wasn't that, Troy. Pa just hasn't let me off the plantation since war was declared; I guess he remembers the Revolution too well. Mystic Rose is under guard, and we have a small army of slaves."

"How did you get away?"

She told him about the tunnel and the hazardous flight down the river. He listened in amazement, marveling at her courage, her audacity, and her folly.

"Holy Jesus," he muttered. "I can't believe it, Star. You went through all that just to see me?"

"You wouldn't come to see me," she said simply. No need revealing that lonely, restless boredom had provided some incentive. It might disillusion him, and he looked so happy and handsome framed in illusion.

"You humble me, Star. I hardly know what to say or think. Perhaps I've been a blind fool. I wanted to call on you, believe me. But all along I thought—well, that's not important now." He took her hand, kissed the palm, then smoothed it against his cheek. "Darling, I'm afraid for you. You know you shouldn't be here. You're brave and impetuous and very foolish, and I love you for it, but—"

"Troy?"

"Yes, you heard me. I never meant to say it so unromantically, but it's true. I love you, Star. I have from the beginning, but it's no good—"

His declaration affected Star more than she had believed possible. Yet he seemed dubious and unhappy about it. "What's no good, Troy?"

"My loving you. It's all wrong, Star. You're a Lamont, with generations of proud Lamonts standing behind you.

But I can't boast of such a proud heritage."

"Do you need family support? You seem to do quite well on your own."

"It's not money I mean, Star. I don't need financial assistance. I have plenty. I've taken some valuable cargoes, and I'll take more when I go back to sea. My share from these prizes is on deposit, in gold, in banks here and abroad. Boston, New York, London, Liverpool."

Star's father was buying United States bonds, in response to Treasury Secretary Gallatin's urgent pleas to the people to help finance the war. According to the *Courier*, the South was far ahead of the North in answering the appeal, and she felt a sudden resentment toward Troy Stewart and all Yankees for shirking their patriotic duty.

"Don't you believe in federal bonds?"

"Yes, and I've bought some. But I don't believe in putting all my ships in one harbor."

"Nor all your faith in one country, apparently! Why are you depositing gold on both sides of the Atlantic? Playing it safe so that no matter who wins, you won't lose completely?" An ugly suspicion entered her mind. "Or is it possible that you don't really care which side wins, Captain Stewart, because your loyalties, if any, are equally divided? That you have a prince regent's license in addition to your American marque?"

He looked at her, his eyes the calm gray-green of a sea before a storm. "You didn't think of that by yourself, Star. Who put it in your head? Grant Russell—or that slimy stepbrother of yours?"

"Lance suggested it," she admitted, "and I quarreled with him defending you. Was he right, Troy, and I wrong? Are you a scavenger feeding on the spoils of both lands?"

His jaw tightened, and a tense nerve flickered at one corner of his mouth. "Is that what you think?"

"I don't know what to think! I'm asking you. Tell me the truth, Troy!"

A rueful shake of his head. "And only a moment ago

I thought you were in love with me and had risked all sorts of dangers to come to me. Obviously I was mistaken. You came to question my loyalty and patriotism. Are you a government spy? Or did the high tribunal of Charleston society send you? That's an old trick, employing a beautiful woman to charm information out of a suspected traitor. But if that's your mission, you're wasting your time. And mine." He laughed shortly. "My God! It almost worked. I was about to confess all my deep dark, ugly secrets to you."

"Confess? Secrets? Then it's true? You do have something to hide?"

"No, goddamn it, it's not true! I've nothing to hide and and certainly not of that nature."

"What nature, then? There's something troubling you, Troy. I've sensed it before. Can't you tell me what it is?"

He turned away from her, ostensibly straightening some papers on his desk. The whale oil lamps fastened to the cabin walls struck his swarthy face, etching harsh and bitter lines about his eyes and mouth. He spoke hoarsely, "Go home, Star. You should never have come and under such circumstances, yet! You're lucky you got here at all."

"If you mean Dink, he's more civilized than some white men I know."

"That could include me. You'd better leave."

Star hesitated. Again she had erred in visiting him. What could a girl expect but insults when she threw herself at a man? Well, it would never, never happen again!

"Goodbye, captain."

"I'll see you to your boat."

"That's not necessary, thank you. What time do those guards pass here?"

"Every hour. Perhaps you should wait a few minutes more. Sit down if you wish."

Star declined. Noticing a half-filled sheet of stationery and a quill on the desk, she asked, "You were writing a letter?"

"To my father," he nodded. "And to the families of the

men I lost in that last engagement. One was just a boy, not yet twenty. I'll miss the kid. I had to punish him once, and I don't think he ever forgave me for it. But I couldn't have been fonder of him if he had been my younger brother. You see, I have no brothers or sisters."

"Nor I," Star said. "No blood siblings, anyway. I'm sorry about your men, Troy. How long will you be in port?"

"I don't know. Some of the guns are out of commission, and replacements are difficult to obtain. But fortunately the masts escaped severe damage, and the sails can be repaired. I could try some other port for the armament and may do so."

"You're engaged in such a hazardous business. Your father must be terribly concerned about you."

"I suppose so. He was a privateer himself during the Revolution. But, of course," he added with grim sarcasm, "he didn't possess a prince regent's license. Why, all I do is flaunt the magic paper, and the British immediately surrender. I haul my prize into port, dispose of the cargo at a handsome profit, and sail away with the gold. I can't understand what went wrong this time, why they blasted me broadside, killed several of my crew, and damn near sunk me in the Atlantic! I had every intention of giving the prince his share of the spoils."

Star was abashed at her own obtuseness. "Oh, Troy! I'm sorry. How stupid of me not to realize that for myself. I'm as bad as Lance. And much too naive and dimwitted, you can see, to be a spy." She paused, chewing her lower lip like a contrite child hoping for forgiveness. But he only gazed at her, one dark brow raised in apparent wonder at her next move.

"Did you mean what you said awhile ago?" she asked. "About–about being in love with me?"

"I meant it, Star. The hell of it is, I still mean it."

"Then why do you just stand there? I came five miles to you. Can't you come five feet to me?"

"Star–"

"Oh, never mind! You're such a proud and stubborn mule, and I don't honestly care if—"

His arms enveloped her, his mouth silenced hers. He drew her close against him, as if his body could somehow absorb hers, his hands eagerly seeking, finding, caressing. "Sweet," he whispered, his tongue tasting hers. "Sweet." And his mouth moved to her throbbing throat and the soft swell of her breast, burning through the thin material of her gown.

"No, no," she murmured, "you mustn't." But her protests were weak, feeble, forgotten in a kiss or endearment.

Soon she was meeting his advances, and her ardor, in its first true awakening, transcended his. Her lips flamed under his, her arms strained him to her. She felt herself rushing toward surrender with no inclination to stop. Never, not even with Grant, had she experienced such precipitous emotions and sensations, such consuming weakness and desire, and such reckless impulses to submit. Oh, God! Was she about to be released from the limbo of one love into the hell of another?

"This longing," he said, "this terrible torture—do you feel it, too?"

She clung to him, whimpering as if in pain, distraught with passion. "I hurt all over."

"Darling, darling." She felt his tension, the violent tremor of his muscles, and heard the fierce thunder of his heart against her bosom. "Do you love me, Star?"

"I think so."

"Enough for marriage?"

"I don't know, Troy. But I've never felt this way before, so it must be love."

"Not necessarily, Star. It could be infatuation or impetuous passion. And that's not enough to overcome the other obstacles in our relationship."

"What other obstacles?"

"I can't really offer you my name, Star, because I have none, and you can't give something you don't rightly possess." She gazed at him mutely, waiting for enlightenment. "I was born out of wedlock, my dear. I'm illegitimate."

Star had never known anyone before who was admittedly illegitimate. The mere presumption of bastardy was a social stigma as ostracizing as leprosy, and the accusation of it was cause for duel. She was at once shocked and curious. "But the letter to your father—"

"I'm his natural son. My parents were never married, simply because my mother wouldn't have my father. That's a switch, isn't it? Usually it's the man who jilts the woman. But my mother happened to be the daughter of an English earl, and my father only a Yankee sea captain. Still, a young and handsome one, exciting enough for a lover—but not good enough to wed, even when she found herself with his child. She hied off to the country, bore me in some farmer's cottage, and left me with the cottager's wife until my father could take me to sea with him. Soon after my birth, the honorable lady married a lord and is now very much a part of the Court of St. James."

"She's alive, Troy? Then why did you tell me the night we met that your mother was dead?"

"That's how I think of her," he said, "and may God have mercy on her soul. Not only for what she did to me but to my father. He loved her, and she made him unhappy. On an island of lonely, embittered old men, he's the champion of them all. Strangely enough, he still loves her and spends hours staring at the sea toward England and his lost love. The 'ancient mariner' with his own tenacious albatross."

Tears glistened in Star's eyes. "I wish you hadn't told me, Troy. I wish I didn't know—"

"How could I not tell you under the circumstances? I was afraid it might make a difference, but I had to take the risk. It complicates matters, doesn't it?"

"Of course! I doubt if pa would consent to our marriage if he knew. Family is important in the Low Country, Troy. Oh, you don't know how important! It's not what a man is that counts here, but *who* he is! More important, who were his parents and his grandparents and so on, all the way back to Adam and Eve!"

"I thought Shintoism was practiced only in the Orient," he said wryly. "Is it also the religion of the Low Country?"

"Call it what you will," Star said, "ancestry counts here. And you—you are—"

"A bastard," he finished grimly.

"Don't say that word!"

"What other is there? Ironic, isn't it? We both have noble blood in our veins, but yours is legitimate. That makes a great difference, doesn't it?"

So many hazy things were clear to her now. "That's why you hate nobility, isn't it? All nobility, legitimate or otherwise. And yet, you could frequent court if you wished."

"Oh, yes, and probably be welcomed. God knows a bastard is no novelty at court. Such indiscretions are the privilege of kings and queens and lords and ladies." He paused abruptly. "What about us, Star? Will you marry me now?"

"How can I answer that? I'll have to think about it, Troy, and consult pa."

"I see." The familiar mask of cynicism descended, distorting his features. "I imagine my mother gave essentially that same excuse to my father."

"Don't compare me with your mother, Troy! I haven't taken you as a lover."

"No, but maybe you'd have no objection to it? You were willing enough awhile ago. Oh, don't bother to protest, Star. You know damned well I could have taken you to my bunk. Maybe you find me interesting in the same way my mother found my father? Maybe she slipped down the Thames to visit his ship, too. And enjoyed his lovemaking, but not enough to make it legal or permanent. She was English nobility, and he was a Yankee commoner. Perish the thought of such a misalliance!" He jerked her roughly to him. "Do you want that kind of excitement, Miss Lamont? Is that why you have twice visited me unchaperoned?" The steel traps of his hands bit into the soft flesh of her shoulders. "Is it? Answer me, damn you!"

"You're hurting me, Troy."

"And you like it. I can play rougher, and I think you'd like it even more."

"Let me go," she muttered.

He grinned, tightening his grip. "What a fascinating little gypsy you are, Star Lamont. All you lack is a red skirt and some baubles. Maybe I'll give you some. Real gold and jewels. I have a chest of gems."

Unwittingly, he had touched her most vulnerable sensibility, the one on which Lance so viciously harped. "Pirate's loot, no doubt! We don't favor freebooters in these parts, captain. Stede Bonnet and his bullies were hanged here, and my great-grandfather helped send them to the gallows!"

"Hurrah for your great-grandpappy! Would you like some jewelry, Star? In exchange for certain considerations?"

"I'd answer that if my arms were free."

"Oh, stop pretending, Star. You're as much a hussy as my dear mother."

Star tried to free herself but failed. "Let me go, Troy. Take your hands off me!"

His mouth was poised over hers, his gray-green eyes searching her face. "I want you, Star, and you want me. Yes, you do. If not for life, then just for tonight? It'll be fun, I promise, even if you're a virgin—"

"How dare you!"

"Use that word? A bastard is a bastard, a virgin is a virgin. What kind of euphemisms do you use in the Low Country? Do you ever speak the truth about anything?"

"Lance and Grant were right about you," she said. "You're a terrible person."

"Naturally. I'm a bastard, the son of a whoring bitch."

"I hate you, Troy Stewart! I hope your ship is sunk! I hope you fall overboard and sharks eat you. I hope—"

"Never mind. I get the message."

He pressed her body against the desk. Her hands touched hard cold metal: it was a pistol. Unconsciously, her fingers closed around the ivory stock. She let him kiss and fondle her, even responding until he dropped his guard. Then swiftly, her dark eyes blazing with angry passion, she wrenched out of his embrace, pushed him back a few paces, swung the weapon forward—and fired.

The flash blinded her momentarily, and the brimstone stung her eyes and nostrils. Troy groaned and caught his left side. As if through a mist, she saw him stagger, clutch at a chair, and fall to the floor. She screamed, panic-stricken, and dropped the pistol. Then she grabbed her shawl and rushed out of the cabin.

"Hey!" Finch shouted, starting after her. "Stop! Where're you heading in such haste? What was that shot?"

"Captain Stewart was showing me his pistol and accidentally shot himself. I'm going for a doctor. Go to him, please. Hurry!"

Finch ran off, muttering to himself. Star caught up her skirts and fled to the waiting pirogue. A slick black head poked over the pier.

"You all right, Miss Star? I heard a shot?"

"Quick, Dink! Help me into the boat, and then shove off. Get me home as fast as possible. Oh, Dink! I—I think I've killed a man—"

Chapter 17

NIGHTMARISH AS THE TRIP to Charleston had been, the return was more so; the incident on the *Venus* had merely climaxed the fantastic adventure. While Dink rowed the pirogue up the Cooper River, his passenger sat shivering and sobbing, pouring out the whole wretched story to him.

"I knowed they'd be trouble," Dink frowned worriedly. "I knowed it when I heard that whip'will callin'. That mean bad luck every time."

"What shall I do, Dink? That sailor, Finch, saw me, spoke to me. He could identify me—"

Dink counseled silence. "You's goin' get back home, Miss Star. Get to your room and into bed and swear you never left it. It be his word agin yours, and ain't nobody goin' doubt the word of a Lamont agin some white trash sailor. One thing for sure—old Dink ain't goin' betray you. The law can torture me, break my back and stretch my neck, but they won't drag nothing outta this here nigger. I promise you, Miss Star."

I'm a felon, Star thought, horrified, as the enormity of

her act finally penetrated her confusion and bewilderment. I shot a man, but I didn't mean to do it. I thought he was going to force me, but I don't think so now. He was hurt and angry, and he wanted to hurt me back, but not to that extent. He'd have stopped himself in time. Oh, Troy, I'm sorry! Forgive me. Please, darling, forgive me–

"I shouldn't have run away," she lamented aloud. "I may not have killed him. He may only be wounded, and I could help him. Take me back, Dink!"

"Miss Star, you is hysterical! You don't know what you is sayin'. I ain't gonna take you back there! They catch you and put you in jail and maybe string you up. No'm, I ain't takin' you back to Charleston! This one time Dink ain't obeyin' his mistress." He bent harder on the oars, sweating and blowing, forcing the craft along the tidal stream.

"Turn around, Dink! Take me back! I order you!"

Dink ignored her.

Star stood up, rocking the pirogue perilously.

"Sit down, Miss Star! You goin' spill us into the river!"

Star lunged at him, attempting to wrest a paddle. The boat tipped and began to take on water. Dink acted swiftly, murmuring, "I sure hate to do this, missy, but I got to protect you." His doubled fist silenced her frantic cries and subdued her futile struggles.

River water being splashed in her face woke Star. She lay motionless, one arm flung over her head, her face pale and puzzled. Her body ached from the cramped position in which she had lain, and her jaw was sore and slightly stiff from Dink's blow. He was bending over her now, anxious and clumsily tender.

"We is home, missy. At Mystic Rose. Soon's you get back into the house, you be safe. Is you all right, Miss Star?"

Weak and dazed, reluctant to wake from the merciful oblivion, Star could only nod. Dink lifted her out of the pirogue and carried her through most of the tunnel, careful not to ignite her clothing with the candle he had lighted.

"Lawd," he prayed practically, "don't put no gators or snakes in my path now—I ain't got time to whup 'em. And, Lawd, don't let the law catch my poor little mistress, cause she dint mean to shoot that cap'n. She told me so, and she powerful sorry now she done it, and we got to protect her, you and me. Is you listenin', Lawd? Then please help us. Amen."

Star regained enough of her strength and stability to make her way to her room, although her legs were unsteady and her head still whirled giddily. But at last she reached her chambers and slipped in, leaning wearily against the closed door.

A voice spoke, a familiar voice, and she saw a familiar figure rocking in the moonlight that spilled through the windows. "Where you been, child, and what you been up to?"

"Oh, Mauma!" Star ran to her, falling on her knees and laying her head in the black woman's lap as she had done in childhood. "Something terrible happened—"

A skillfully blended soporific of claret and extract of henbane administered by tender black hands had allowed Star to fall into a dreamless sleep, and Star opened heavy-lidded eyes on a golden morning with a hint of autumn in the air. She sat up, hugging her knees to her chest, smiling at the mimics of a mockingbird in the live oak outside her windows and Romeo and Juliet cooing in their cage. The busy sounds of the plantation came to her, soothing her. There were slaves singing and wagons creaking on the way to the fields, children romping and shouting at play, and the house servants commencing their routine chores.

For a few blissful moments, before the last effects of the sedative vanished, Mystic Rose was a bright and wonderful world, and she was a happy, carefree resident. There was no war with England, no hated stepfamily, no lost love in Charleston, and no shot captain in the master cabin of the *Venus*. Only the sun dancing elflike on the floral carpet, the pine-scented breeze fluttering the curtains, and the appetizing aromas of breakfast.

Then, into this pleasant reverie, entered Mauma and grim reality. A tray rattled in her usually calm hands, and her round dark face reflected fatigue and worry. Star's fantasy crumbled like the walls of Jericho.

"Mauma?–"

The woman nodded tragically. "Yessum, it happened. It weren't no dream. You told me all 'bout it last night. And we goin' do what Dink say. We goin' stick together in this, you and Dink and me. I brung your breakfast, honey. You goin' eat it just like any other mornin'. Then you's goin' go downstairs and act like it's just another day and you ain't got no more cares than a puppy with no fleas."

Star stared at her in surprise. "You didn't feel that way last night, Mauma. You were shocked and horrified, and you threatened to tell pa everything."

"Yessum, I say that. Then I got to ponderin'. I never sleep all night ponderin'." She set the tray on the bed and reached into the pocket of her crisp white apron, extracting a large red bandanna to blot her moist eyes. "They ain't no use tellin' your pa, Miss Star. It would just break his heart and lay him in the grave, side of Miss Angel, was he to learn the truth. And I ain't cravin' to see that happen."

"Oh, I know, Mauma, and that's what worries me most! The first blot on his name, and I put it there. Poor pa. You're right, Mauma. I fear it would kill him to learn that his daughter is a common–"

"Shh!" Mauma cautioned. "The walls got ears. You has got to be careful, child. Oh, Lordy, I dreads to die and get to heaven and meet Miss Angel! What is I goin' tell her when she ask, 'Mauma, how come you let my little gal get herself into such a heap of trouble? Didn't I ask you to watch over her, and didn't you promise me faithful you would?' How I goin' explain to her, Miss Star?"

The pathetic pleas wrung Star's heart, impressing the

full horror of her folly upon her as perhaps nothing else could. She had brought tragedy not only on herself and the shining shield of Lamont, but on two loyal slaves. She had involved Dink and Mauma in her predicament and made liars and cheats of them, accomplices to her crime.

Accomplices. Crime. Murder?

The dreadful words reverberated through her mind, echoing in every nerve and fiber. And while mental chaos wracked her emotionally, still another thunderbolt crashed upon her.

Hoofbeats!

Pushing the untouched tray aside, she jumped out of bed and ran in her nightshift to the windows. A party of men on horseback came thundering up the driveway, scattering gravel, and a pack of lean bloodhounds on chains accompanied them.

Mauma came to her side. "Who that? Look like a posse!"

"It is, Mauma! The sheriff and a posse! Oh, Mother of God! He's dead, and they've come after me! I'm going to prison, Mauma! I'm going to hang!"

"Hush!" Mauma commanded in a hoarse whisper. "Hush that kind of jabber! Yonder go your pa and Mist' Lance to meet 'em. Keep quiet, now. Maybe we can hear what they say—"

John Lamont, courteous and hospitable to all callers and strangers, no matter their purpose, greeted Sheriff Osborn and his party cordially. "Good morning, sheriff. Morning, men. What brings you to Mystic Rose this fine day?"

Star had never paid much attention to Will Osborn's appearance before, but now she noticed his hard-bitten brown face and uncompromising eyes, his heavy black mustache, and the frontier costume of buckskin breeches and coonskin cap he liked to affect. The executioner himself could not have looked more formidable and ruthless to her. The sunlight glinted on his silver badge, and she touched her throat apprehensively, visualizing the gallows and noose.

Osborn tipped his tailed cap to show his respect for the gentry and spoke in the nasal twang of the native Blue Ridge mountaineer. The two women in the bedchamber above strained their ears and crossed their fingers.

"A couple of runaway slaves, Mr. Lamont. They escaped from the Briarwood plantation four days ago and ain't been seen nor heard of since. The hounds was set on 'em, but lost the scent in the swamps. One of 'em was a former slave of yours, sir. Name of Obah. Have y'all seen him around here lately?"

"No, we haven't, Will. And I doubt seriously that Obah would ever set foot on my property again."

"Yeah, I heard about your trouble with him and that you had to get rid of him."

Lance said, "We sold him off the block! Mr. Petty's factor bought him for Rosedale. What was he doing at Briarwood?"

Osborn shifted his tobacco quid, forming a grotesque bulge in one cheek, and spat the excess juice onto the ground. He wiped his grim mouth on the fringed sleeve of his shirt and leaned forward in his saddle, resting his hands on the horn.

"Mr. Petty was forced to sell him, too. He's a mean fella, that one. Ungovernable. Real trouble. That kind of man could cause a mighty lot of trouble if allowed to run loose. Don't know how much truth there is to it, but I heard he's the son of a Zulu chief. Probably a headhunter and cannibal to boot and resents civilization and captivity. Them slave traders ought to know better than to bring men like that to this country; they breed rebellion like a privy breeds flies. But all this mouthin' ain't finding them, and that's my job. Sorry to have bothered you folks."

"Not at all, sheriff," John said. "If we see or hear anything of them, we'll get word to you immediately."

"Thank you, sir. I'd be much obliged." Osborn gave a farewell salute. "Well, we got a lotta territory to cover, men. Let's ride!"

They wheeled their mounts and galloped off, yelling as if on a coon hunt, the nervous hounds yelping and straining at their chains.

"Hallelujah!" sang Mauma, clasping her hands prayerfully. "Praise the Lord!"

Star almost fainted with relief. There was an intense and painful constriction in her breast, as if she had held her breath too long under water. They hadn't come for her! Not yet. Not this time. Maybe he was still alive and chivalrous enough not to tell Finch the truth. Or perhaps, before dying, he had declared it an accident of his own misfortune. Then she would be safe. Safe from the long arm of the law, safe from the bleak gray gibbet, safe from shame and disgrace and scandal. Safe from all but her own wretched nagging conscience, which she could never escape.

Of course, if caught, she could plead self-defense. Defense of her chastity, which women were supposed to cherish above all else in life and preserve intact until marriage. "Protecting her virtue," Dink and Mauma called it. But their loyalty and devotion overlooked her own willful role in the debacle, her provocation. And her guilt. How could any sensible judge and jury, in possession of the facts, conclude that she was a virtuous maiden defending her honor? Who but a tramp, a wanton slut, would go skulking through the night unchaperoned and uninvited to a man's ship? How could she convince anyone, pa most of all, that she was not what she appeared?

The suspense was the worst part, an agony transcending her despair and bewilderment. Not knowing whether he was dead or alive or dying. Knowing that deserting him might have meant the difference between life and death. Listening for hoofbeats, holding her breath at the sight of the sheriff, and living in the shadows of the scaffold. She was in much the same position as Obah.

Obah. Where was he? Tawn might know. But Obah was not her worry now; he was Sheriff Osborn's problem today. Tomorrow it might be John Lamont's daughter.

Chapter 18

SOON AFTER the posse's departure, Lance ordered his phaeton and drove to the city. He returned late that afternoon with some news he was especially eager to give his stepsister.

Star was in the rose garden, spectacular now in its fall finale, cutting long-stemmed blooms for the house. The pleasant task occupied her restless hands and gave her less time to brood, but still the day seemed endless. She had just about decided to send Dink down the river again that night to see what he could learn from the black freedmen stevedores, but Lance made the risk unnecessary.

"They had some excitement in town last night," he drawled, flicking a particle of dust off the sleeve of his new fawn-colored sport jacket. "I thought you might be interested in hearing about it."

"Did the British land an expeditionary force?"

"No, nothing quite that exciting. It was more or less confined to the waterfront and concerns a special friend of yours. Captain Troy Stewart."

"Oh? Don't tell me he was honored at another soiree. That's not news!" Her nonchalance surprised her, for she was quivering inside, every nerve tense with expectancy.

"His party days may jolly well be over."

Star snipped off a yellow damask rose, the size of a small cabbage, and laid it carefully in the wicker basket. Naturally he would taunt her curiosity, prolong his cruel advantage to the limit. "What happened? Did he insult someone and receive a challenge?"

"Not to my knowledge, though he couldn't have fared much worse in a duel. He was critically wounded."

"Wounded? How?"

"Bullet from a pistol."

"How terrible! Who shot him?"

Lance smiled faintly. "I didn't say anyone shot him."

"You said a bullet from a pistol! How else?–"

"His own pistol. He claims to have shot himself, accidentally."

"Claims? Then he's still alive?" Star knew she had made a mistake the moment she uttered the words, but it was too late to rectify her error. She guarded her eyes, concentrating on her task.

But Lance had caught the clue. "Why, yes," he said. "He was only wounded. Did you expect him to be dead?"

"Why should I expect that?" Star protested. "I didn't even know anything about it until you told me!"

"Didn't you, little sister?" He paused dramatically, his tawny hooded eyes never once leaving her face, which Star feared was naked in guilt. "Dock rumors say Captain Stewart's story is not the whole truth. A crewman, Finch, who happened to be on watch and unfortunately was the only one of his men present, bears him out, but is probably lying at the captain's request or command. Lying to protect someone. A woman, possibly. They say if Stewart dies, Finch might spill the rice, and some young lady might find herself in a highly embarrassing situation. What a juicy scandal that would make in holy Charleston! Especially if the lady should turn out to be of hallowed ancestry."

Star pricked her finger on a thorn but pretended not to notice the sharp pain and oozing blood. How much did Lance really know? Had Finch talked to him? Surely he wouldn't dare do so while his captain lived, nor divulge anything if ordered to silence. How gallant of Troy, protecting her reputation after what she had done to him! It wasn't true that all Yankee men were cads, without honor or chivalry. Southerners misjudged them, thank God.

"I suppose that would furnish considerable grist for the gossip mills," she agreed.

Lance plucked a French rose and deliberately destroyed it, the crimson petals fluttering to the ground like gory feathers.

"It would furnish more than mere gossip, my dear. Can you imagine the notoriety of such a trial? The lurid details of a clandestine affair that finally ended in murder aired in court for everyone to hear and judge. I warrant the war wouldn't rate an inch of space on the front pages of the local rags. I should think the unfortunate lady would prefer almost any fate, even suicide, to such exposure."

Star tightened the leash on her straying emotions. He might be only fishing, hoping she would naively swallow his bait. She must be calm, interested but not unduly curious, concerned but not overly so. Otherwise, she might as well wear her guilt like a scarlet banner across her breast.

"I don't see why, Lance. If there were no witnesses other than this Finch person and Captain Stewart maintains he shot himself accidentally, even if he should die, it would be Finch's word against the hypothetical lady's. They would need a lot more substantial evidence to make a case against her, wouldn't they?"

Lance twisted off another rose and proceeded to mutilate it with perverse pleasure, as if plucking a chicken. "Evidence often turns up in the most unexpected places. Witnesses, too. Both can be acquired if the price is high enough and just as easily suppressed for the right compensation."

"You studied law in England, Lance. It's a pity you never passed the bar. You might have defended that woman, if indeed she exists. But she may be only a myth, a figment of rumor's imagination."

"Oh, I doubt that. It's inconceivable that a man of Stewart's experience with weapons could accidentally shoot himself. And he would hardly be shielding a man. If he dies, the police will undoubtedly *cherchez la femme*. If I were *la femme*, I should immediately try to establish a convicing alibi for myself the night of the—er—alleged accident. Incidentally, where were you on the night in question, Miss Lamont?"

The challenge, flung at her so unexpectedly, gave Star an involuntary start. Obviously Lance suspected her, although she could not imagine how or why, and if she could not master her control, she might as well confess. Lance was shrewd and relentless; he would pursue her like a bloodhound baying a scent, torment and rile her in the hope of forcing self-betrayal. He would have made a brutal barrister. She must be patient and vigilant and, above all, keep her wits about her.

"I suppose you think that's very clever, Lance. You know I haven't been away from Mystic Rose alone since the war; anyone here can testify to that. So if you're through playing prosecuting attorney, please go and leave me in peace."

"You seem upset?"

"Certainly I'm upset! Captain Stewart is a friend of mine and pa's. Unlike you, it doesn't pleasure me to hear he's been hurt."

"Seriously hurt," Lance said. "Doctor Homer says he may loose a limb, if he doesn't die of gangrene. The ball grazed his chest and pierced his left arm. A sloppy aim, typical of a woman. Rather typical of yours, little sister."

Star winced imperceptibly. "I should like to visit him. I wonder if pa would grant me permission."

"Probably not. But if you really want to see Stewart,

I'm sure you'll find a way." A significant wink, a taunting grin. "Where there's a will, there's a way. Eh, cherie?"

Her eyes dropped to the basket of roses. "Perhaps it would not be fitting for me to visit him. I'll ask pa to go instead, and I'll send him the roses."

"Permit me," Lance offered. "I shall be glad to take him your bouquet and message of well wishes."

Star glanced at him suspiciously. "Why?"

"I just want to do you a favor, that's all."

"You never have before."

"Primarily because you wouldn't let me, Star. But I have no ulterior motives now. Give me the flowers. I'll take them to him this evening, since I'm going to town, anyway. Do you want to include a note?"

"No. Just say I wish him a rapid recovery."

The roses were not delivered to Captain Stewart, nor any of the subsequent gifts and messages Star naively entrusted to her stepbrother. On his fourth trip to Charleston, Lance returned with the spray of bronze chrysanthemums and ferns that Star had sent with him to Troy. He brought it to Star in the parlor, where she was painting Indian designs in bright hues on a leather cigar box she intended to send Troy in the next day or two. Lance's face was long and grave.

"Captain Stewart is dead," he announced solemnly.

The brush slipped from Star's hand, the indigo oil color staining the carpet. "No," she whispered, her face ashen. "No, it isn't true. It can't be true! Don't fool me, Lance. Don't frighten me."

"Captain Stewart is dead," he repeated tonelessly.

"I don't believe you, Lance, You're lying!"

He was affronted, indignant. "Would I lie about a thing like that?"

"Then you've been lying to me for a week! Telling me Troy was improving, that he thanked me for the flowers and my solicitude and—"

"I wanted to spare you any unnecessary grief and anxiety, Star. I know you were fond of him. But I was fibbing about his improvement. He wasn't faring well at all. Yesterday, gangrene set in. Doctor Homer amputated this morning, but it was too late to save his life. I'm sorry, Star."

Helplessly, her hopes crumbled about her. Star began to weep. Soft tears, tender, remorseful, futile.

Cynicism crossed Lance's face. "Don't take it so hard, my dear. The scoundrel wasn't worth your sorrow."

"How can a worthless person judge another's value, Lance? You're not in Captain Stewart's caliber or category and never will be! So please keep your vile mouth shut!"

Lance closed the parlor doors. He contemplated his stricken stepsister a few moments before speaking again. "Get hold of yourself, Star. It's too late for tears, and a river of them won't bring him back. Stewart's suffering is over, he's out of his misery, and no doubt he'd have preferred death to disability. Pity the poor creature who shot him, her agony is just beginning. That crewman, Finch, is sure to talk now."

Star raised wet and guilty eyes; she had never felt less like sparring. "Well, what if he does? Justice will be done, that's all."

Lance scowled impatiently. "Stop this maudlin pretense, Star! Don't you realize your precarious position? I know you were in Charleston that night. I know you went to the *Venus*, and I know how you got there. Yes, my dear sister, I was in the basement when you sneaked out to your lover. I followed you there and saw you enter the tunnel. I saw you and your black confederate get into the pirogue and go down the river. Do you deny all this?"

"Yes! Yes, I deny it!"

"Try to deny it under oath in court. There's a stiff penalty for perjury, Star."

"You can't prove anything, Lance. You have no confession, no positive proof, only suspicion and circumstantial evidence. And this isn't England! Here, remember, the accused is innocent until proven guilty."

"I could beat proof out of Dink with a whip! I thought there was something brewing between you two in the stables that morning when it took Dink so damn long to saddle your horse. I started to investigate, then, because I simply couldn't believe you had any personal interest in that stinking ape. I decided you must need him in some conspiracy. When he took particular care to lock the hounds in the kennels that evening and stash that pirogue in the reeds, I had an idea what you were about. The tunnel was the logical explanation. And I must say it was a brazen adventure, Star. Too bad it boomeranged."

Star said nothing but sat in complete dejection. The symbolic designs she had been painting on the gift for Troy blurred and swam before her eyes.

"My testimony could convict you, Star, and you know it," Lance resumed. "But that's not why I'm telling you all this now. Stop your sniveling and listen to me, girl. If Finch talks, your rice is boiled, unless you can establish a satisfactory alibi. And that's where I come in. You little fool! Don't you understand? I want to help you!"

"Help me onto the gallows?"

"Help you establish an unshakable alibi! We could say we were together that night, Star."

"Who would believe that, Lance, knowing us? Knowing we fight like cat and dog!"

"We could make people believe it," he insisted. "Make them believe we were together because we're in love."

Her jaw fell. "In love? You're daft, Lance!"

"If so, my lunacy is exceeded only by your stupidity. Don't you know that a husband can't testify against his wife? And what better proof of love can any man and woman furnish than a marriage certificate? We could elope, Star. Tonight."

"Elope?" she cried in horror. "Why, I'd rather hang than marry you, Lance Wilson!"

His complacency did not lessen, for her impulsive rebuff was a veritable admission of guilt. "So you admit the possibility of such a fate?"

"I admit nothing."

"Come, come, Star. Your lack of guile and subtlety

is almost pathetic. An intriguing woman should be better equipped with the arts of her trade. Any half-witted constable could trick you into a confession."

"You forget, Lance, that Troy himself called it an accident at his own hand. To carry any weight with a jury, Finch would have to swear he witnessed it otherwise. Suppose he couldn't do that without perjuring himself?"

"Could he, without perjuring himself?"

Star shrugged, regaining some of her composure and defiance. "How should I know? I wasn't there. You'd have to ask the mysterious lady, if there was one. But I'm inclined to believe she's a phantom of your own creation or some drunken sailor's illusive Lorelei. You don't frighten me with your threats, Lance, nor fool me with your offers of aid and protection. As for your ridiculous proposal–the real reason you want to marry me is to get my share of the plantation!"

"Your density astounds me, Star. Wouldn't it profit me more to have you hanged?"

"Hardly, since you and Lorna would then share equally with your mother in the estate. With me as your wife, you'd add my half to your third. You see, Lance, I'm not so stupid, after all. I understand your game well enough. Too well."

"If you won't consider yourself, Star, consider your poor old father. If this scandal breaks, it'll kill him."

"Much that would grieve you, provided his will was made in your favor!"

"You won't be so flippant, my dear, when Sheriff Osborn comes for you."

"Let him come," Star muttered.

It was a convincing bluff, because it lacked fear. Except for her father, she did not really care what happened to her any more. She wondered vaguely when her own life had lost its importance to her. Perhaps when she had lost Troy.

"You still refuse to marry me even to save yourself?"

"I still prefer the scaffold, if such is to be my destiny.

So sic the law on me, Lance; it doesn't matter. But one thing I do know: my death or imprisonment wouldn't profit you any. Do you imagine for one instant that pa would love and praise you if you helped to convict his daughter of murder? Why, if I told him how you've threatened me today and tried to coerce me into marriage, he'd probably throw you off the place! Certainly he would disinherit you, and you'd be extremely fortunate if he did not kill you."

All these possibilities had occurred to Lance, but he had hoped they would not occur to Star. "I underestimated you," he said slowly. "No, you're not dense or stupid, Star. You're a crafty little gypsy. Well, it's good to have an alert and formidable opponent–it sharpens one's wit and skill. Just remember this, Star. Each of us holds a trump card. If I play mine, the Lamont name will suffer throughout the South. If you play yours, I stand fair to lose my inheritance. Obviously, neither of us has the advantage."

"Not at present," Star agreed. "But if I know you, Lance, you'll cheat somehow. Employ some scheme or treachery to outwit me. You can't be satisfied with a draw."

"Possibly not," he smiled unctuously. "Then again, such efforts may not be necessary. You may tip your hand, sister."

"Will you leave now, or must I summon Mauma?"

"Summon whom you please. I have no fear of Mauma or any other of your trained monkeys, including Dink. But before I go, I may as well tell you that your lover still lives."

"He is not and never has been my lover."

"No matter. He's not dead."

"More of your lies and tricks, Lance?"

"You want an affidavit? He was alive enough to sail with the tide and against the doctor's orders. The stevedores say he was a mighty sick man, running a high fever, so he may have died at sea by now."

"With both arms?"

"I'm not sure about the amputation, but that's the usual cure for infection, isn't it? At any rate, you're safe, Star. You can relax temporarily."

It was not personal relief Star felt so much as happiness and gratitude that Troy was not dead. She had not killed him and perhaps not even maimed him. But her overwhelming anger against Lance mitigated her joy.

"So you wouldn't lie about a man's life? Oh, Lance! You *are* rotten!"

"You're not exactly the essence of purity yourself, cherie. That's why I think we'd make a good match. It's a shame you don't agree."

"Bastard," Star murmured uncontrollably.

"Bitch," he countered between his teeth. "That's us, bastard and bitch. Wizard and witch. Two of a kind, ideally suited to each other."

"Someday, Lance, I swear I'm going to–"

"Kill me? You'll have to improve your aim, sugar."

Star leaped out of her chair, her dark eyes glittering in violent rage. "Get out of here, damn you!" She stamped her foot and reached for a vase.

"Careful, little sister. You're exposing your hand. That Romany temper of yours is a great liability."

"But not so great a liability as your Yankee greed! That's the thing that will lose this game for you, Lance. Greed!"

"You want to bet on it? Winner take all?"

She hurled the porcelain vase at him, and missed; it crashed against the marble fireplace.

Lance grinned at her aim and left laughing.

Chapter 19

IN THE MONTHS that followed, the seclusion of Mystic Rose bore heavily on Star. She hoped in vain that the post rider would bring her a letter from Troy saying that he had recovered completely and forgiven her. But his fate remained a mystery to gnaw at her heart and conscience.

She searched for mention of the *Venus* whenever a newspaper fell into her hands and was disappointed to find none. Either his ship was no longer afloat or his exploits at sea were eclipsed by those of the navy and other privateers. Perhaps some of the vessels that called at Charleston could give her news of Captain Stewart, but she could not go into town to inquire, and she dared not send Dink.

In desperation she wrote a letter to Troy's father in Nantucket but lacked the courage to mail it, fearful of inadvertent incrimination. She burned it, weeping as the pages curled and blackened in flame, gazing forlornly at the dark ashes. Finally, she concluded that Troy was probably dead and buried at sea these many months, and she must try to forget him.

But there was no forgetting Lance. He continued to menace and intimidate her, and Star knew her armed truce with him was no more inviolable than one with Satan would have been. A sly glance or grin from him could prickle her flesh and set her teeth on edge and her blood boiling. They were mortal enemies, each waiting and hoping for the other to stumble into a pitfall. They were equally matched in obstinacy and defiance, but Lance's arrogance exceeded Star's audacity. He became ruthlessly oppressive in his attentions, insisting on riding with her and accompanying her on her strolls, though they quarreled and insulted each other every wretched minute they spent together. He badgered Star into playing various games with him, including darts and cards, and entertaining him at the spinet. Then he taunted her when she missed the target, cheated her at loo, and criticized her musical renditions. If she protested, he would refer to Captain Stewart's accident in her father's presence and hint at the convenience of a secret tunnel for wayward and impetuous lovers. Although fiendishly clever and furtive in his campaign, he eventually made the mistake of nettling Star before Mauma and Dink.

"That boy goin' find hisself face down in the swamp one day," Mauma predicted to Dink in a whisper, "and ain't nobody goin' know how he got there."

Dink nodded. "They's more'n one way to skin a skunk."

Star would have been alarmed to hear them, for though she longed to be free of Lance's yoke, she had never contemplated any such drastic or violent solution.

One evening a week later, Star was alone in her room listening to the slaves singing spirituals around a bonfire. It was the Easter season, and an evangelist had passed through the community a few days previous, preaching the death and resurrection of Jesus Christ. John had granted him permission to hold a revival at Mystic Rose, inviting the slaves of neighboring plantations to attend, and many conversions and baptisms in the Cooper River had resulted. The Holy Spirit, still very much upon the Negroes, was naturally expressed in song, some joyously jubilant, but most sad and mystical. Mauma's fine soprano and Dink's deep bass were clearly distinguishable. Familiar with many of the hymns, Star sang along with them, voicing her own melancholy and despair.

> Lord, I can't help from crying sometime,
> Lord, I can't help from crying.
> Since the day my mother died,
> That's the day I begin to cry.
> Lord, I can't help from crying sometime.

Angelique's memory brought a sob to Star's throat, and she could only hum as the slaves took up the second verse.

> Oh, my mammy boarded the train,
> Full many years ago.
> I promise I meet her on Canaan happy shore.
> Since the day my mammy die,
> That's the day I begin to cry.
> Lord, I can't help from crying sometime.

Suddenly Lance entered her room without knocking, the boldest act he had yet ventured. Star, who had been leaning wistfully on the windowsill, steeped in the poignant lyrics, turned on him in astonished fury. But though his lust for her was great and brooding, she realized it was not the purpose of his visit now. His face, inscrutable upon his entry, contorted with rage as he thrust a small object at her.

"Look at this! I found it in my room—under my pillow!"

Star stared at the tiny wax figure fashioned in his image, which Lance held in his trembling hands. There were no visible marks of violence on it, no cord strangling the neck, or pins puncturing the anatomy. Obviously, the charm had been placed in his room merely as a warning, and the thing that surprised and puzzled Star most was that she had no knowledge of it. She suspected that it was one of Tawn's creations and that either Dink or Mauma, or both, had had a hand in it. The vendetta between Lance and herself was serious, but Star had not expected it to reach these hideous proportions.

"Why," she whispered, "it's voodoo!"

" 'Why it's voodoo,' " Lance mimicked her. "You think I don't know that, you sly gypsy? That Angola witch, Tawn, made it; I've seen her handiwork before. But who prompted her? You?"

"No, Lance, I didn't! I swear I didn't! You know pa has forbidden black magic at Mystic Rose!"

His mouth twisted in a skeptical scowl, and his yellow eyes regarded her contemptuously. "Pa has forbidden a lot of things to which no one pays any heed! Didn't he forbid you to leave the plantation? You're lying about this, Star! You've been conniving with Tawn. You think this is the way to call me off, don't you?"

"Believe me or not, Lance, I had nothing to do with that charm! I don't believe in such nonsense."

"Then who's responsible? Mauma? Dink? It was one of you three. I'd take oath on that!"

"Why? We're not the only ones around here who have no fondness for you, Lance. You've mistreated some of the other slaves, too; any one of them could wish you dead. What about your valet? You've cuffed Bobo plenty for not tying your cravat just so or for forgetting to shine your boots. And you're always hinting that Cicero is too old to be a proper butler, though you know he's the best butler in the Low Country. And Tawn herself hates you, because she was in love with Obah and you caused him to be beaten longer than pa intended. He ordered ten lashes, and you increased them to twenty."

"He deserved fifty! But Tawn has more reason to despise your father than me. He sold Obah off Mystic Rose, not I."

"You'd have kept him and flogged him fifty times a day," Star said. "It was better to sell him, Lance. Anyway, he's gone now. He must be, the law never found any trace of him. But I don't think Tawn has ever gotten over it or forgiven you."

"If she had a grudge against me, she'd have sought revenge long ago," Lance argued. "You're a cunning little bitch, Star, but you haven't convinced me of your innocence in this plot. And I'd better not find any more of these dolls in my chambers, or I might be tempted to practice some sorcery of my own."

His eyes indicated the parakeets, whose cage Star was now covering for the night. She had developed a great affection for these little feathered creatures, a fondness which Lance considered a transference of her feelings for the giver.

"It'd be a pity if Romeo and Juliet suffocated some night, wouldn't it? Or their cage was left open, and the cats got 'em!"

"Don't press your luck, Lance! That figure is purposely unmarred, intended as a warning, but the next one may not be so subtle. You have an enemy at Mystic Rose who would not hesitate to remove or destroy you, and the ways of the black man are many and devious."

"The ways of the white man are just as many and devious, my dear. I realize that you have two aces up your sleeve in Mauma and Dink, but perhaps I have a couple up mine, too."

A chorus of voices, passionately fervent in praise of the Lord, floated up to them.

> Sweet Heaven, sweet Heaven!
> Dear Lawd, when shall I get to Heaven?
> To see the bright, the glitterin' bride,
> Close seated by her Savior's side.
>
> Oh, may I find some humble seat,
> 'Neath my dear Redeemer's feet;
> A servant as before I've been,
> And sing salvation to my King.

Lance slammed down the window. "What do they know of God? The word is blasphemy on their lips, and hell is too good for them!"

"They have souls like everyone else," Star said. "Or do you have a soul, Lance? Sometimes I wonder."

"Nigger lover," he spat at her. "Good night, little sister. The bugles blow truce for awhile."

Star did not reply, but the birds twittered as he banged the door. "It's all right, darlings," she quieted them. "He wouldn't dare harm you. Go to sleep now."

The next morning Star questioned Mauma and Dink about the charm, but both denied any connection with it. And whether the conjurer had decided against further action or was merely tormenting his victim with wonder and suspense, Star did not know, but a month passed without the appearance of another figure. And to her immense relief, Lance was hounding her less, although she was not superstitious enough to believe the black magic of witchcraft had transformed him. Apparently, for the present at least, he was occupied with more interesting matters, and he went about his business so stealthily that Star suspected him of some new and nefarious scheme.

Spying on him one night, she discovered that he was putting the tunnel to use. How strange! Lance was not confined to the place by parental order but was free to come and go as he pleased, and he had never attempted to conceal his actions before. His peccadilloes—gambling in the taverns and whoring in the city brothel—were no secret. Often, too drunk to drive home, Lance spent the night under a saloon table or in some harlot's bed. What need had he to escape to town through a tunnel? Star did not think it likely he was romancing some local belle or matron on the sly, for she knew of no decent girl other than Letty Clayton who gave a fig for him, and no wife who would jeopardize her marriage for him. The scoundrel was up to something, though she could not imagine what. She considered informing on him, but the whip he held over her head tied her tongue. Moreover, her father was not well enough to cope with both Lance and the plantation. A recurring ague sapped much of his strength and energy, and he was obsessed with the war.

The French wars in Europe ended that spring. Defeated and disillusioned, Napoleon was exiled to Elba, and France was in a state of anarchy comparable to that at the height of the French Revolution.

The full might of England had been felt in America, and hard. The conquest of Canada had failed most ingloriously; only one American victory of consequence, the Battle of the Thames, was won on Canadian soil, and that through the combined efforts of General Harrison and Commodore Perry. The British retaliated with a vigorous blockade, concentrating primarily on southern shipping and permitting only clandestine trade bound for English or Canadian ports to pass. As fast as the navy sent one British vessel down, another rose to take its place. Complete strangulation appeared imminent and inevitable.

Gloom and despair pervaded the nation. The people looked to the president for encouragement, and Madison had none to offer. The once gregarious war hawks were strangely silent. Secretary Gallatin, scraping the bottom of the Treasury barrels, declared that the country was on the verge of bankruptcy. New England again threatened secession. Mrs. Madison's fabulous balls were said to be political intrigues frequented by Yankee traitors, foreign agents, adventurers, knaves and opportunists, all hoping to wrest something of value for themselves before the ultimate collapse. They descended on Washington like vultures to pluck at a fallen carcass even before rigor mortis set in.

The invasion of Port Royal threw a great scare into the Low Country. Plantations were plundered, livestock and provisions carried off, and a few harbor craft burned before Admiral Sir George Cockburn's raiders withdrew to harass the Georgia coast. Similar attacks and pillage occurred on Caper's Island and Hilton Head, and Charleston held its breath.

The meetings at the Planters Hotel had the atmosphere of wakes. The harbor forts, inadequately manned and equipped from the beginning, called for volunteers and additional weaponry. The militia increased its maneuvers, rattling aimlessly through the streets. When a lantern appeared late one night on St. Michael's steeple to signal a fire in the east end of town, pandemonium reigned until the excited populace could be convinced that it was not of British origin. The few enemy prisoners in Charleston, brought in from captured warships and privateers, were clamped in irons under double guard. His Majesty's fleet was expected with every tide.

Memories of the Revolution haunted John Lamont as he relaxed on the plantation terrace. Defeat now would negate that terrible struggle and mock the brave men who had sacrificed themselves on the altar of independence.

A light cape was thrown over his shoulders, for though it was late May and so warm the camellias and jasmine were blooming, his feverish bones ached with intermittent chills. Star ministered to him, checking to make sure he swallowed the prescribed pills and tonics. She was worried and anxious over the rapid decline in his health. His once handsome face was gaunt, his skin almost transparent over the bones, his eyes sunk deep in dark sockets. He was so thin and frail that Star feared for his life.

"Shouldn't you be in bed, pa?"

"Bed is for invalids," he said stubbornly. "And I feel no better confined."

"But you could rest easier."

"My body, perhaps. Not my mind."

"Oh, pa, I know you're worried about the war! But making yourself sick won't help any."

"My child, you're too young to realize the gravity of the situation. It's not just my future or your future or the future of Mystic Rose that's at stake now, but the future of America and generations yet unborn. With every battle we lose and every ship that goes down, our liberty draws closer to an end. Do you realize what that means, Star?"

"I think so, pa. We might be British subjects again. Our homes might be burned, our property confiscated, and the Declaration of Independence just so much blood-stained scrap paper. Then there would be unbearable taxes and oppressions and more conspiracies and another revolution—"

John nodded ponderously, satisfied with her comprehension. "I fought in the last one, and turning against the mother country was one of the most difficult decisions of my life. Before declaring myself, I prayed for hours in Goose Creek Church for Divine guidance. Many another parishioner did the same, tediously examining his conscience to decide where his duty lay, how his God and his country could best be served and his honor maintained. And though our religious mentor, Reverend Ellington, counseled allegiance to the king and remained a Loyalist himself, the great majority of his flock found it in their hearts and souls to disdain his advice. My only explanation, when I sought to rationalize it to myself, was that my desire for freedom was stronger than my loyalty to the Crown."

"Have you ever regretted it, pa?"

He was silent a moment, reflecting on the past. "No," he said, "I would do it again, if necessary. I suppose the need for freedom is inherent in every human being. It has driven men to take up arms against their rulers, slaves to rebel against their masters, and children to strike out against their parents. But generally the rulers and masters and parents were tyrants."

Not always, Star thought. No one could accuse her father of tyranny. Yet she resented her confinement to the plantation, waiting for an army that might never come. It had driven her to sneak into Charleston where she had shot and possibly killed a man.

She glanced across the wide emerald velvet lawn to the green cornfields where the slaves bent over hoe and rake. How many of them, given the opportunity and proper inducement, would fight for their freedom? Kill for it?

"I wonder what happened to Obah?" she asked suddenly.

"Sheriff Osborn has ceased searching for him," her father answered. "He may have gone North or left the country as a stowaway. I hope so, and I hope he makes his way back to his people. I would never have bought him had I known his history, that he was a chief in his own right. Nor would I have purchased Tawn, aware that she was the daughter of a witch doctor. Those born to rule rarely make good subjects."

"Tawn hasn't been up to any mischief, has she?"

"Not to my knowledge," John said. "She's a fair nurse and a hard worker. But she was mighty fond of Obah. I believe she is still grieving for him."

"Apparently Mr. Vance hasn't given up hope of finding him. He's still advertising for Obah in the runaway slave columns, and offering a big reward. Couldn't he be hiding in the swamps, Pa? The Santee or the Pee Dee? Lance says either one is large enough to conceal an army —and impenetrable, too."

"That's true, Star. But Obah would have to be part muskrat and alligator to exist under such conditions. Still, if he built himself a tree house and subsisted on the fish and game in the swamp and on edible leaves and berries, it's possible. If so, he will eventually expose himself to capture. Obah is a man of passions and I doubt if his nature could keep him away from a mate indefinitely."

"You mean Tawn?"

"Tawn or any other woman he happens upon," John said frankly. "Even his own sister wasn't safe around him, you know. Poor girl. I think her brother's attack induced and aggravated the epilepsy that finally cost her her life. That's just one more reason why I don't like having you out of my sight, dear. Keep off the River Road and out of the woods."

Star sighed. "Yes, pa. I'll be careful. And do you really think the British will be here soon?"

"Unless the navy can prevent them, daughter. Perry made an admirable attempt on Lake Erie. But the English are a stubborn race, and the capture of the *Chesapeake* off Boston last fall left us only two frigates on the sea." He shook his head gravely, and Star noticed that his hair, like his beard was completely gray now. "That's not enough to stop a determined nation."

Chapter 20

THE SAFFRON TINTS of the sky, the stillness of the trees, and the molten blaze of the sun gave every indication of a long, hot summer. Flies and gnats, bred by the millions in the stables and privies, buzzed in and out of the screenless windows of the house and cabins. Servants armed with swatters constantly shooed the pests, and a meal could not be peacefully eaten without a slave continuously swinging the overhead fan in the dining room. Even more annoying were the big, fat bloodthirsty mosquitoes. A prolific crop of them, fostered by the mild winter, hatched in the swamps and marshes and made the lives of the rice workers a living torment. They invaded the house at night, so the beds had to be swathed in netting, thus shutting out most of the few evening breezes.

It was that time of year when Low Country planters and their families left the plantation manors and went to live in town houses in Charleston, to summer cottages on the islands, or to lodges in the foothills of the mountains, in the hope of escaping the mysterious fevers that thrived in the country in hot weather and almost miraculously vanished with the first hard frost. Some even fled the state entirely, traveling north to the delightfully cool Virginia Springs, the New Jersey resorts of Long Branch and Cape May, and the fashionable New York spas such as Saratoga and Balston-on-the-Hudson. During these virulent summer months, the plantations were managed by overseers and Negroes who were either immune or less susceptible to the ravages of heat prostration and tropical diseases than their white masters.

This season, however, the war prevented any mass exodus. John Lamont, himself the victim of a perennial ague, remained as always at Mystic Rose. His first wife's death there of an undiagnosed fever and his daughter's desperate struggle with one in early childhood still had not convinced him that the plantation in summer was any more unhealthful than any other place. People died all over the world of one ailment or another, and epidemics of some sort were constantly raging somewhere. But some years were naturally worse than others, and this he believed would be one of them.

"There'll be much sickness this season," he predicted worriedly. "Dysentery, typhoid, tropical fevers. Already malaria has started."

Star sighed disconsolately. "It's the same every summer, pa. Pests and heat and fevers. If only yellow jack doesn't come, too. Oh, papa! Sometimes I think that, for all its beauty and abundance, this is an evil land. Floods in spring, fevers and hurricanes in summer—"

"The sea brings the hurricanes, daughter."

"And what brings the fevers?"

"You ask me a question even the physicians and scientists can't answer," he said.

An idea struck Star, a possible means of escaping the scene for awhile. "Why don't we spend the season in Charleston, pa, like other planters and their families?"

"You know I don't believe in prolonged absenteeism, Star. It is not in the best interests of the plantation. Nor do I believe the air is any healthier in the city. If anything, it's more polluted because of ships arriving from all over the world, bringing disease along with their cargoes. Charleston has had its share of plagues—smallpox and cholera and all the rest. Besides, we have no town house."

"We could lease one on the sea wall. The old Devereaux mansion is always available for the right price. Think of the wonderful breezes at night!"

"And the wonderful view of the ocean?" John smiled. "The sun and moon on the water, and the ships' sails on the horizon? You must stop thinking of the *Venus*, daughter. I fear Captain Stewart and his ship are both gone. There are perils enough on the sea without warfare. There are reefs, gales, fog, and pirates. If Troy survived his wound, he could have met any of those other fates in addition to a British cruiser or frigate or privateer."

"I suppose so."

"You cared more for him than you realized, didn't you? Was it serious, Star?"

She dropped her lashes. "I'm not sure, pa. If I could see him again, perhaps I'd know."

Hopefully he asked, "Have you forgotten Grant?"

"Grant was my first sweetheart," Star murmured. "I—I reckon it's kind of hard to forget your first love, pa."

"I reckon so," John agreed, his gaze wandering to the cemetery.

Changing the subject, he said, "I heard a droll story at the Planters Hotel last week about our first lady. 'Tis said that after the capture of the *Macedonian* by the frigate *United States*, one of our officers was dispatched to Washington with the enemy's flag. As it happened, a ball was in progress when he arrived, and the bold young cock marched straightaway to Mrs. Madison, knelt at her feet, and presented the Union Jack to her. Miss Dolley was embarrassed to blushes, giving lie to the gossip that she uses paint, for the guests saw her cheeks change color. And now the ladies in the capital are discarding their rouge pots for fear of being considered frivolous and artificial."

Star smiled, though she had already heard the story from Lance. She wondered who the bold young officer was. Troy Stewart might have resorted to such an extravagant gesture, mocking gallantry. Could he have lost his ship and accepted a commission in the navy? Stop clutching at straws, she chided herself. Let go of the memory. Forget.

As they lounged in the shade of the terrace, a pitcher of mint-flavored lemonade on a wicker table before them, Dink came running up from the river bottom. Some distance behind him trudged two other slaves supporting a prostrate man between them. Dink arrived at the terrace wild-eyed and panting.

"Master John, come quick! Mose he flop down in the rice! Mose he mighty sick! Look like the black vomit!"

"Oh, no!" Star cried, jumping to her feet.

"God have mercy on us," John intoned. He rose, reaching for his wide-brimmed Panama hat. "Tell them to take him to the infirmary, Dink, and fetch Tawn. I'll send for Doctor Frazer."

But long before the doctor rode out from Charleston in his racing gig, the diagnosis was obvious. Mose's face was flushed crimson under its darkness, his eyes congested, lips and tongue and nostrils scarlet—all characteristic symptoms of that most dreaded of swamp fevers, yellow jack. The Negroes called it black vomit and feared it more than evil spirits. Once it appeared, they must be persuaded and often driven or threatened to get them to work in the rice fields.

Mose was confined under Tawn's care, but neither her nursing nor Doctor Frazer's medicines could save him. He died the next day, and a new plot was unearthed in the slave cemetery. While the slaves were chanting the funeral dirge, another rice hand dropped to the ground.

Within three weeks the infirmary was full, and a crew of carpenters was busy making pine and cypress coffins for new victims. Row upon row of fresh mounds rose in the graveyard, small wood crosses at the head bearing the single name of the occupant, the date of birth if known, and the date of death. The journals of Mystic Rose recorded a death a day, sometimes two or three. Mose, Jonah, Grub, Teeter, Monk, Prophet, Socrates. Most of them had been exposed to the miasmas of the rice paddies, but soon the cases spread to include women from the uplands and children who had never wandered near the river. This established the contagiousness of the disease in John's mind, and he suggested that a ship from the tropics may have brought it to Charleston. Perhaps it was in that last shipment of sugar he received from Cuba?

Doctor Frazer was dubious about his theory. "Then why isn't Charleston infected, too?'

"Because I purchased the entire cargo," John reasoned. "It was unloaded directly from the Cuban vessel onto my flatboats and brought to Mystic Rose. Perhaps there was yellow jack there, and the sugar was contaminated."

"Perhaps," the doctor conceded. "But I'm more inclined to blame the swamps, John. Some of my colleagues attribute yellow jack to the parasitical growths, moss or mistletoe. Others contend it's caused by the dangerous vapors of rotting leaves or corn smut or manure. But I think brackish waters—"

"No matter the cause!" Lance interrupted, panic-stricken. "It'll kill us all if it isn't checked! Can't you do something more than rationalize, doctor?"

Frazer clawed his ginger-colored beard, peering at Lance through the thick lenses of his spectacles clamped onto his bulbous nose. He was by temperament a kind and patient man, short and plump as a rice-fed partridge, but it bristled him to have his medical skill so rudely questioned and challenged. After all, he had studied in London, Paris, and Vienna, and if this impertinent pup did not respect his age and person, he might at least respect his profession and credentials.

"My boy, I'm doing all I can, everything within my power and knowledge. We have the powdered bark of the cinchona tree to control malaria to some extent, but no discovery half as effective against yellow jack. The cause is unknown, the treatment largely experimental. Fortunately, there are no recorded cases of reinfection among those who have recovered from the malady. One attack seems to provide lasting immunity."

"That's little comfort to me, doctor! I've never had yellow jack. Malaria, yes, but–"

"Well, you may have developed a natural immunity after all these years. Exposure to plague does not necessarily mean contraction. Many people escape even in the fiercest epidemics. About the only advice I can offer is fumigate yourself daily, purge regularly, and try not to worry." He turned to John. "How many of your slaves have had yellow jack to your knowledge, sir?"

"That's difficult to estimate, Charles. Those from the Antilles seem to recall a fever which in description resembles it. The Africans can describe a malarial sickness. Perhaps fifty percent have had some form of tropical disease, but that still leaves around five hundred without immunity. I've lost thirty of my best rice hands already! Surely you don't think–"

Doctor Frazer spread his hands in a gesture of supplication. "Don't ask for miracles, my friend. I am only a physician. Your entreaties will have to go much higher, I fear."

"You sound more like a parson," Lance snorted. "Since when does medical science depend on supernatural assistance?"

"Since Hippocrates discovered that 'art is long and life is short,' " replied the doctor laconically. Picking up his black satchel, he proceeded to the infirmary.

"Charlatan!" Lance muttered under his breath, stung by Frazer's wit. "We face certain death, and the old empiric tells us to pray! If prayer could heal, we'd have little need of his services."

A quarantine sign was posted over the arched entrance to the property, and Mystic Rose became a giant pesthouse isolated from the community. A flock of buzzards took up roost in the trees, and no matter how often they were driven off with rocks they returned, drawn by the odor of death, circling low over the infirmary or just perching patiently in the branches like hunched black figures at a wake.

Brimstone candles burned in the cabins and every room of the manor, befouling the air with an acrid stench that smarted the eyes and nostrils. Star and Emily breathed through kerchiefs dipped in cologne, while Lance resorted to clove pomanders and the black superstition of a protective amulet fashioned by Granny Mae of a rabbit's tail and the fangs of a rattlesnake. The shriveled old woman, so old her age was a mystery even to herself, attributed her longevity to this repulsive charm, and Lance was desperate enough to try it.

John Lamont, who had experienced many strange agues in his life, moved like a wasting shadow between fields and barns, infirmary and cemetery. Watching him, Star was alarmed. Pa's as sick as any of them, she thought. He's dying on his feet, but he won't give up. What a stubborn clan we Lamonts are!

Saws scraped and hammers pounded in the carpenter shed. The carpenters made crude boxes now, not even painted, for the bodies must be quickly interred in the terrible heat; decay was rapid and the odor unbearable to all but the carrion crows. Star wept at each solemn procession of creaking wagon and chanting mourners, and so often had John read the burial service he could recite it from memory.

"My poor people," he lamented over and over. "What have they done to deserve this cruel punishment?"

Emily replied quietly, "They are my people too, John, and I want to help them. I want to help Tawn and the other women nurse them in the infirmary."

"That's noble and unselfish, my dear. But you've never had yellow jack, and having you sick would only complicate matters. Who would run the house? I can't allow it, Emily. I need you here."

His wife looked at him. "You *need* me, John?"

"Of course I need you, Emily," he answered brusquely, his patience short these days. "What makes you think otherwise?"

"I don't know, John. You never told me so before." Her voice and expression softened and became tender and almost maternal. She touched his shoulder briefly, the first gesture of affection Star had ever witnessed between them. "I'm glad you need me here, John, but just now I feel the slaves need me more. Your daughter can manage the house well enough."

Star glanced up in astonishment. Aunt Emily must be taking the fever to make such a statement!

"Star?" John asked, as surprised as his daughter.

"How many daughters have you, pray? Of course, Star. She's a grown woman now, John, and ready for responsibilities. Tell him so yourself, Star."

"I could manage, pa," Star assured him. "But I, too, want to help in the infirmary. Big Lou is the finest housekeeper in seven counties–she and Cicero and Mauma could run the house as smooth as new churned butter. Let Aunt Emily and me nurse in the infirmary, pa. Please?"

"Thunderation!" John exclaimed in puzzled exasperation. "What's come over you two? Haven't I problems enough to worry and confuse me already? The slaves are dying like flies, Emily. Like flies! The crops are wasting in the fields, weeds are choking the rice, and fruit is rotting in the orchards. Even the animals are sick. Contagious abortion is spreading among the cows, and the hogs have cholera." Tremors of despair and bewilderment shook his thin frame. He was so slight and brittle now it seemed a strong breeze might blow him away. "Oh, God!" he cried in an agony of pleading. "What shall I do? What *shall* I do?"

"Let us help," Emily urged. "What else are a wife and daughter for, John, if not to assist in crises and emergencies? If you deny us the right, you deny us all reason for existence. You make of us useless dolls!"

"Emily, can't you understand? The disease is contagious. Deadly! I might lose you both!"

"Trust in the Lord, John. If it be His will that we should fall ill, this house cannot protect us nor can any earthly creature or thing. Faith, John. It's the only weapon we have left."

He stood irresolutely, caught between the logic in Emily's argument and the cajolement in Star's. And the two women, no longer enemies though still not friends, exchanged nods of mutual alliance.

John, no fatalist, would not have yielded except that he was desperate. Doctor Frazer had become ill suddenly and was returning to Charleston. This left John dependent upon a witch doctor's daughter. He was morally responsible for the health of his slaves; he owed them every possible chance for survival.

"I'll send medicines and supplies by your factor," Frazer told him. "Perhaps your wife and daughter can assist—"

John nodded resignedly. "God's will be done," he said.

"Or the devil's," Lance muttered.

Chapter 21

THE INFIRMARY was well constructed of solid timbers, whitewashed inside and out, but it simply was not adequate to meet the emergency. Narrow cots, most of them sheetless, stood side by side. One corner was blocked off as a dispensary, and pine screens separated the men from the women; whenever possible, ill children were nursed in their cabins by their own mothers. The few windows were open, and flies swarmed over the patients, tormenting them to frenzy. Sulphur candles discouraged the mosquitoes somewhat, but could not conquer the formidable odors of vomit, feces, urine, and sweat.

Star all but fainted on entry. She pressed her cologned kerchief to her nose and mouth. Waves of nausea nearly overcame her. But Emily seemed not to notice. Star gazed at her wonderingly; either she had no delicacy, as was said of Yankee women, or a mighty strong constitution, as was also said of Northern females.

Emily immediately assumed management, and Tawn, reluctant to relinquish authority, turned sullen and arbitrary, especially when Emily rejected and forbade her jungle practices. "Get those spiders off the beds instantly!" she commanded. "They have no magic powers! And remove those knotted strings from the waists of the patients!"

"Spiders is got healin' juices," Tawn protested. "And a string with sixteen knots tied round the middle cures malaria."

"Voodoo nonsense! Besides, this is yellow jack, not malaria. What's that stinking concoction on the stove?"

"Ague weeds. I's boilin' a potion."

"A witch's brew, no doubt!" said Emily, ordering the contents of the cauldron poured out. "I'm in charge here now, Tawn, and you'll obey me—or go to the fields!"

"Yessum," Tawn muttered, with no touch of servility in her low, languid voice.

She was a handsome bronze-skinned woman, tall and stately, her features more Arab than Negroid. Tawn had unusual oblong eyes, and she wore her thick brown hair in a massive bun like a crown. She and Obah would have made a magnificent pair, and it was of her lover that Tawn thought now, glowering her resentment at her mistress, remembering the twenty lashes Emily's son had caused to be laid on Obah's smooth black back, striping him like a tiger.

Out of Emily's hearing, she grumbled to Star, "Miss Emily don't belong here. The patients goin' get sicker just havin' her round."

Incredibly enough, Star found herself defending her stepmother. "Miss Emily is mistress of Mystic Rose, Tawn. Of course she belongs here. And so do I, as the master's daughter. We should have come before, but pa was afraid for our health, since our race is even more susceptible to yellow jack than yours. But our people are sick, and they need our help and comfort and cheer."

"Powerful little comfort and cheer Miss Emily dispense. I ain't never seen that woman smile big enough to show more'n two tooths. But the spirits knows we needs help, all right. Goin' need another grave before sundown. Old Tip givin' up the ghost. Won't last much longer."

Tip gave up the ghost within an hour, and while his cot was still warm his wife Mossie was placed on it. She was great with child, and the disease made swift progress in her. Soon she was vomiting black blood, the most ominous symptom, and each racking hemorrhage shook her belly so violently Star feared the fetus would be forcibly expelled. Mossie died the next day, and Star watched in sickening horror as the captive life in her grotesquely swollen body ceased its feeble struggles.

The coffin was too shallow to contain her bulk, and Tawn suggested that the baby be "cut out of her." But Emily refused such surgery and ordered two men to sit on the lid while the box was nailed shut. Just before dusk, as the chimney swallows skimmed low over the ground, Mossie joined her husband in the graveyard. Less than a year ago John had bought the couple for a high figure in the slave market, because he did not like to separate mates or families.

Star tried not to count her father's loss in money as well as lives and labor, but she knew each male slave represented at least five hundred dollars, the young and healthy ones often much more. With so many hands gone and the crops wasting in the fields, Mystic Rose would go into debt and perhaps bankruptcy. Many a planter had lost everything, the work and savings of generations, through one prolonged misfortune. The finest land was worthless without labor to work it.

Worse, the food supplies in the barns, smokehouses, and larders were dwindling. The slave allowances of rice, dried peas, and side meat had to be cut. There were fewer hands to harvest the gardens, grind and store grain, make hominy, and preserve fruits and vegetables. Unless matters changed shortly, they would face famine in winter.

But the expenses increased. The medical lists sent to the factor grew longer and more costly, and some items were difficult to obtain: paregoric, laudanum, niter, magnesia, borax, alum, camphorated Dover's powder, coal tar expectorant, and castor oil, none of which accomplished much. Some, croton oil and calomel, increased vomiting and induced delirium and spasms. Emily discarded their use, resorting instead to common sense and old remedies from the family pharmacopeia. She brewed teas and blended tonics from herbs and medicinal plants: sassafras, figwort, camomile, lobelia, dogwood berries, bark of wild cherry, mullein leaves. She kept brandy and whiskey in a locked cabinet but doled portions of cider and sarsaparilla freely. And if they did not cure the malady, at least they did not aggravate it or hasten the victim's death in unbearable agony.

Emily moved among the cots and pallets on the floor, serene and competent, and Star envied her equanimity. She spoke little to the Negroes, but there was gentleness in her tone and touch, anxiety and concern in her countenance, and she worked as hard as any of the dozen black assistants. She complained neither of the heat nor stench nor pests. She spooned gruel and broth down parched and swollen throats, emptied chamber pots and urinals, mopped up vomit, sponged sweating bodies, and administered enemas with equal dexterity.

Star retched each time one of her patients vomited or evacuated in bed and was grateful that her youth and innocence prevented her nursing the men—a restriction which John had imposed, lest his virginal daughter be exposed to shocking sights. The men were generally more difficult to handle than the women, who were accustomed to the nausea of pregnancy and the pain and discomfort of menses and childbirth.

"Well," Lance drawled, as Star walked wearily into the house one evening, her hair hanging in damp skeins on her drooped shoulders and her gown stained with filth and perspiration, "have you had enough of playing the Good Samaritan?"

Star had had more than enough, but would not admit it. "There's a plague on Mystic Rose, Lance, and you dare to jest about it! Don't you realize that no plantation can long support the losses we're suffering? Remember this, Lance. If pa goes down, we all go with him, including you!"

That sobered him somewhat. He puckered his sandy brows in a selfish frown, but he shrugged and temporized, "We won't go down. We can buy more slaves."

"With what?" Star demanded.

"There's a rice crop due in September."

"There may not be anyone left to harvest it by then. The best rice workers are already dead."

"The epidemic will run its course before long," Lance said with renewed confidence. "Epidemics usually do. But if you don't get some rest, you may not survive it. You look ghastly, Star." Protected by his pomander and amulet, Lance felt secure from the disease, though he still would not venture near any of its victims nor assist in the burial rites.

"Your solicitude is touching," Star mocked. "But I'll survive, Lance—if only to spite you!"

Exhausted, Star bathed and retired immediately after supper. Too tired to sleep at first, she tossed restlessly, finally falling into fitful slumber interrupted by nightmares. Premonitions, perhaps, for when she awoke in the morning and uncovered her parakeets' cage, she found them lying on the bottom of the cage, feet up. She stared fixedly, horrified and incredulous.

"They dead, honey," Mauma said gravely. "Something happen to 'em during the night."

Instantly Star blamed Lance. "He killed them," she wept. "That ogre did it!"

"Probably," Mauma nodded. "Maybe he creep in here while you was sleepin' and strangle 'em or put something in the feed and water. But he ain't nowhere on the place now, Miss Star. He slip out again somewhere through the tunnel. Slippery as a soaped snake, that man."

"Monster, you mean, Mauma. Monster!"

Star put the tiny corpses in the leather cigar box she had painted for Troy and asked Dink to bury them in the forest under a nice big shady tree. And when next she saw Lance, she demanded accusingly, "What did you do to my parakeets?"

"Nothing! Are they sick?"

"They're dead."

"Maybe they caught the plague?"

"I suspect *your* plague, Lance! Your evil touch."

"You would, naturally. But I wasn't near your precious pets, Star. And I'm sorry they're dead." Then he smiled faintly. "Perhaps they committed suicide–and what more appropriate death for a pair of birds named Romeo and Juliet?"

"You're going to be punished, Lance. By God or someone else, but your wickedness won't thrive forever! Frankly, I hope you get the fever and die in agony!"

"Thank you, little sister. And the same to you!"

The pestilence raged through June and July. The heat raged with it, searing the untended patches of vegetables, parching the unhusked corn in the fields, browning meadow and pasture. A few scattered showers fell, hardly enough moisture to settle the dust; in places the dehydrated earth cracked and split open, like overbaked bread. Grass was planted on the new graves, but it did not prosper, and the bare, dark mounds increased daily. A crew was detailed to chopping and hewing lumber to build more coffins. The scarcity of rainfall was in itself a curse and evil portent, for drought was rare in the Low Country. The Negroes said the spirits were angry at Mystic Rose, and Star believed it herself. God had forsaken them and had left them to wither and die.

Messages of sympathy and concern were delivered by anxious friends and neighbors to the box at the gates of the plantation, and not even the law dared venture past the quarantine. Sheriff Osborn merely scribbled a note: "Runaway slave believed hiding in Santee Swamp. Could be Obah. God deliver you and yours from this scourge. Will Osborn."

Lance evinced no surprise at the sheriff's message. It was as if he were aware of Obah's whereabouts. Star had an uncomfortable feeling that the plague had interfered with some nefarious scheme of his, but she was too weary and dismayed to pursue her suspicion. She wondered at the kind of justice that struck down decent and innocent people while sparing rogues and demons.

The note was of small import to John Lamont. Even the war had lost its interest for him. He was overwhelmed by the immediate tragedy, so the war seemed remote and far less crucial. Mystic Rose was itself a besieged fort valiantly fighting a losing battle, and the master was resigned to defeat. An army of Redcoats could inflict no more damage or punishment, if, indeed, they could be induced to defy the quarantine. Smallpox and yellow jack were two enemies all soldiers respected.

There were more recoveries than in the first stages of the disease, due largely to better nursing under Emily's supervision, but still the death toll mounted. Star had believed she would eventually become accustomed to the drama in the infirmary and regard it with the same calm efficiency that blessed Emity. But placidity was not inherent in her nature, and she could not resign herself to this calamity any more than she could to the loss of Grant Russell or the shooting of Troy Stewart. She hurried through her duties, exhausting herself, and carried memories of stricken faces and pitiful voices to bed with her at night.

"Miss Star, hold my head so's I can puke in the bucket."

"Miss Emily, I's burnin' up. Wet me down."

"I's dyin', Tawn. Conjure me back to life."

"If I die, Master John, please, suh, don't let 'em bury me deep, cause I want to get to Heaven fast."

The tension and horror mounted until one day Star could endure it no longer and rushed from the building, screaming hysterically. Emily caught her as she reached the veranda.

"Let me go!" Star cried frantically. "I can't stand any more, Aunt Emily! Let me go!"

"Hush, Star. Hush."

Emily shook her firmly, and Star gave another piercing shriek. She struggled desperately, babbling incoherently. A stinging lash across the cheek finally subdued her, jolting her back to rationality. Several of the black nurses had edged out on the gallery and were gaping curiously. Emily turned on them sternly.

"Get back inside, all of you! How dare you leave your patients! Do you want to be whipped?"

They obeyed, muttering sullenly, reluctant to return to their distasteful duties. But the mistress was not to be brooked, wheedled, or outwitted.

Star stood trembling, weak and confused.

"I'm sorry I struck you," Emily apologized. "You had lost control of yourself, and it was the only thing I could do. You must never panic before the slaves, Star. They may not admire self-discipline, but they respect it. And they may resent authority, but they recognize and obey it."

Star rubbed a tremulous hand over her moist face. Her palms were clammy, her clothes drenched in sweat, and she imagined she looked and smelled as bad as the most slovenly slave. "That's easy for you to say, Aunt Emily. You have no feeling, no compassion. You're made of stone. I've watched you, day after day—nothing affects you. You're an automaton! Well, I'm not. I'm flesh and blood, heart and soul. I'm weak and human and—oh, I can't take any more!"

A wan smile crossed Emily's face. "You are also young and vulnerable and romantic, my dear. Remember your Homer? The Trojans inside the wooden horse were supposedly human, Star. But they would never have accomplished their mission without that protective armor. As you mature, you will find it helpful to employ some kind of shield in your battle with life. Not that it will effectively ward off all blows and wounds; some will pierce the armor and penetrate deeply. But unless you cry out your pain, you alone will know and feel it."

For a moment the allusion eluded Star's distressed

mind. Then, slowly, its significance penetrated. "You mean, I'll still have my equanimity? My pride and dignity?"

Emily nodded sagely.

"Suppose I don't care about such things, Aunt Emily?"

"You care, Star. We all care about our image, including the slaves. What do you think makes some of them so resentful of their masters? They resent being owned and governed primarily because it deprives them of personal pride and dignity, even though they may not realize that this is their essential objection. They only know ownership makes them feel inhuman, like animals or possessions, and their humanity rebels at such emotions. I dare say flogging doesn't hurt them nearly as much as the knowledge that they can be flogged at their owner's will or whim, that they can be mistreated with impunity. Much of their loyalty is fear, even of the kindest master or mistress."

Star doubted that. Certainly Mauma wasn't afraid of her; she had been bullying her mistress since birth and expected to do so until her death.

"Now I think perhaps nursing is too strenuous for you," Emily said. "Your father has maintained so all along. But it's nothing to be ashamed of, Star. On the contrary, I understand that physical delicacy is traditional in southern womanhood. Quite admirable too, in masculine eyes. Return to the house, Star, and assist with the management if you wish."

Star considered the suggestion gratefully, as a prisoner savoring parole. How good it would be to return to the manor, to the peace and quiet, the clean rooms and healthy smells! But that would be admitting defeat and, infinitely worse, deserting her people in need. She lifted her chin resolutely and straightened her shoulders.

"I'm all right now," she said. "And I'll stay."

"Are you sure, Star?"

"Yes. It was just temporary release of tension."

"Very well. Shall we have a cup of tea first?"

"I'd like that very much, Aunt Emily."

Harmony entered their relationship, and the perceptive Negroes were quick to sense it. Not that either of them underwent an immediate metamorphosis, turning years of bitterness and resentment into sweetness and love; two such vastly different temperaments and personalities could not be so easily reconciled. Never flippant, or demonstrative, Emily made no physical overtures, and neither did Star. But it was good to feel friendly toward her stepmother, to have someone to converse with over a cup of tea, and Emily seemed to appreciate the relaxation and companionship as much as she.

I never understood her before, Star thought. Maybe because I never tried and never wanted to understand her. She's as proud and stern as a Spartan. But she's lonely and unhappy, too, and as hungry for friendship as I. Lance is a disappointment to her, she knows pa never really loved her, and even the slaves resent her. Dignity is her barrier, and affected imperviousness her shield against these hurts and frustrations. All those years of friction and antagonism—was I as much to blame as she and Lorna? I gave nothing of myself and got nothing in turn. There was no sharing, hence, no reciprocation.

"I received a letter from Lorna this morning," Emily confided as she prepared tea. She proceeded to tell Star what her daughter had written.

Star listened eagerly. The city and its people and pleasures seemed far away, as unattainable as the sun or moon. Oh, would she never dance at another ball! Never see another play at the Dock Street Theater. Never attend another musicale or supper or soiree or exciting tilting tournament!

"You miss Charleston, don't you, dear?"

"Oh, yes, I do!" Star cried passionately.

"Well, if this dreadful scourge ever passes, perhaps your father will take you to town with him sometime." Her tone implied that she might take a hand in the matter.

"Thank you, Aunt Emily."

"I'm not promising anything, mind you," Emily cautioned, "because there's still the threat of invasion. So don't set your heart on it."

Star smiled her understanding.

Suddenly Emily frowned and confided, "I've been quite worried about Lance recently. He has been defying the quarantine and leaving the plantation at night. I imagine he sneaks into the city to gamble and visit the wenches." Emily was sometimes astonishingly candid. "But I suppose that's better than frequenting the cabins."

Star wanted to tell her that Lance did that, too, and had since puberty, probably forcing the pretty young girls to submit to him; some little mulattoes on the place bore a remarkable likeness to him. But this was not unusual in the system, and there were many adulterations of the race by plantation masters and their sons. Star knew, in fact, that Lance had been in Tawn's bed often since Obah's absence, and not likely by invitation.

"I suppose," she murmured.

"It's not uncommon, you know," Emily continued. "There's something about black women that intrigues white men. Perhaps it's the lure of forbidden fruit. Whatever the fascination, it's a rare white man who hasn't been intimate with one, at least of mixed breed. In these parts, anyway. And to many masters, their female slaves are tantamount to concubines."

"Well, I don't think pa ever—"

"I didn't mean to imply that," Emily interrupted. "I'm only saying that many masters do visit the cabins at night. How else could all the mulattoes, quadroons, and octoroons have been born?"

Star could not argue the issue. She nodded.

Emily rose, her features once more composed in austerity. "Now I think we've idled long enough. There's work to be done. Oh, so much work!"

"So much," Star sighed. "And here comes Dink with another patient for us. Dear God, it looks like poor old Granny Mae! I guess her amulet finally failed."

PART III

Chapter 22

A SEPULCHRAL GLOOM hung over Mystic Rose. The healthy slaves, ever dwindling in number, no longer sang on their way to the fields. They were solemn with sorrow and apprehensive with the constant fear that tomorrow or the next day the funeral dirge might be chanted for them. Even the children seemed to sense the gravity of the situation and respect it; an hour might pass without the cry of a baby or the uninhibited laughter and shouting of youngsters at play. At times the quiet was encompassing and eerie, as if all sounds of life had been silenced, even in the kennels, coops, barnyards, and stables.

During one of these ominous interludes, Star sought a brief respite on the infirmary veranda. Her stepmother had suggested the pause, and Star was sensitive of her concern. But Emily need not worry that she would panic again. She was mistress of her emotions when she determined to be, a newly developed control that puzzled and disturbed Lance, and for which she had his mother to thank. Star had learned more about self-discipline from Emily these past few months than she had in all the years under her tutorship in childhood. And if the new serious mien lessened her verve and vivacity that were so much a part of her natural charm, she appeared either unaware or unconcerned about her loss. Emily believed the mantle of spinsterhood was settling on her stepdaughter's shoulders.

The shadows of the trees were lengthening in the gardens. In the nests under the overhanging eaves of the manor, which had sheltered countless generations of birds, the songsters were tuning up for their regular evening serenade. Smoke curled from the chimneys of the slave cabins and the house kitchens, either drifting lazily upward or merely hanging stationary in the stifling air. Mauma would be summoning her and Emily to supper soon.

Star leaned her head against a column. A spray of wilted honeysuckle brushed her cheek, imparting its welcome fragrance. She tried to ascertain from the setting sun if there were any possibility of desperately needed rain. But it was clear and blood red, without a touch of the haziness which, according to the almanac, indicated moisture in the atmosphere.

Across the ruby horizon, the silhouettes of the slaves and wagons, homeward bound, moved slowly, silent except for the jingle of harness and the creak of wheels, like pantomime figures on a giant stage. A day's work over and done, with victuals waiting in the cabins, was no longer a cause for rejoicing. A short distance behind them John and the overseer followed on horseback. Her father rode his favorite gray gelding, but the slump of his shoulders would have identified him on any other mount.

Church bells pealed, faint but distinct in the evening solitude. Vespers, Star thought absently. And then she remembered that the churches had voluntarily suspended tolling the bells except to warn of imminent danger or disaster: fire, flood, hurricane, riot, rebellion, or invasion.

She leaped off the veranda to survey the sky. No flames visible over Charleston or the countryside. No rain to indicate swollen streams, no wind or fury from the sea. Perhaps a riot in the city streets or a slave uprising somewhere in the vicinity?

The bells continued to ring, rapidly now, as if relaying an urgent message to neighboring parishes. Star's heart pounded, fluttered, and raced wildly to the most ominous conclusion.

Invasion!

The British are coming!

"Aunt Emily!" she cried excitedly, forgetting her poise and promises. "Come outside! Hurry!"

Emily appeared in the doorway, a tall spare figure in plain dark muslin and white apron. Her face, though pale and gaunt under the white mobcap, was carefully composed for the patients' sake if not her own. "What is it?"

"Listen! Church bells!"

"Yes, I hear them. Don't be frightened, Star."

"But, Aunt Emily—"

"Don't be frightened before the slaves," Emily cautioned in a whisper. "I think your father is coming off the fields. Go meet him, why don't you?"

"Yes. Thank you, Aunt Emily."

Star started off, walking as demurely as excitement would allow. But once out of Emily's sight, she broke into a run across the cane field, leaping over the furrows with raised skirts, swearing as she twisted her ankle on a stone or pierced her skin on some stubble. The British were coming, and dignity be damned!

John galloped toward her, kicking up a storm of dust and trampling stunted shoots of the precious feed. He drew rein so swiftly the horse reared and almost stumbled.

"What's the trouble, daughter?"

"Church bells, pa! Can't you hear them? The British must be invading Charleston!"

"Calm yourself, child. I hear the bells, but no cannon or musket fire. Surely they could not conquer Charleston without firing a shot; we're better prepared than that."

"Maybe the militia surrendered, and the city is being sacked and burned? They'll be here next! Oh, papa!" She began to cry and murmur incoherently, as undignified as any terrified young girl. The long weeks of suppressed tensions and anxiety had been too much for her, and releasing it all now did her more good than Doctor Frazer's tonic of aloes and licorice or Emily's exhortations to composure.

"There, there, baby." John dismounted to comfort her. "I see no flames and smoke over town, but I'll alert the plantation. And if such be the case, Mystic Rose will be the last place in the Low Country to feel enemy boots. No sane commander would deliberately march his men into a plague. Now go home and tell Emily not to wait supper on me. I'll ride down the River Road a piece and see if I can learn anything. May not be serious at all, honey, so don't fret. Dry your eyes now and watch that stubble lest you tear your stockings."

Star wasn't wearing hosiery, for it was as scarce and hard to obtain now as linen and silk lingerie. "I'm not wearing stockings, pa, nor fancy petticoats, either. And this old gingham gown is so faded it should be sent to the cabins!"

"Well, why don't you freshen up in a nice cool dimity or voile frock for supper," John suggested. "You still have plenty of clothes, Star. And pretty slippers. No need to look like a ragamuffin. Fix yourself up for your old pa this evening and pass the word to Emily. I'm going to spruce up a bit, too."

Did he expect the British and want his family to look their best, to meet them as ladies and gentlemen?

The household was already in a state of alarm when Star arrived. The servants rushed about aimlessly, chattering like hysterical magpies, accomplishing nothing. Even stately old Cicero, remembering the unwelcome foreign visitors during the Revolution, had much ado to maintain the dignity of his position. Chaos reigned until Emily entered the house. A few brisk commands quickly restored order. Star, admiring her martial abilities, had the comforting feeling that any British officer encountering the mistress of Mystic Rose would swiftly retreat out of range.

"Pa said not to wait supper on him, Aunt Emily."

"There's no hurry," Emily said, examining a yellow stain on the otherwise immaculate tablecloth; she must speak to the laundresses. "We shall wait. Where is Mr. Lance?" she inquired of the butler.

Cicero peered into the gathering dusk. "He comin' now, Miss Emily. Ridin' like a spirit after him and yellin' his head off. Master John comin' behind him. Hear what Mist' Lance say? Hear that? The British done burnt the capital! God almighty! We lost the war!"

Details were few and sketchy, gleaned from a post rider Lance had hailed on the River Road. "Why the church bells?" he had asked.

"Ain't you heard, man? The British put the torch to Washington! Burned the presidential mansion and the government buildings. Some John Bull admiral sailed his fleet right up the Chesapeake Bay and landed a bunch of raiders!"

"Who said so?"

"A courier rode into Charleston not an hour ago. It's true all right."

"Have we surrendered?"

"Don't think so. Not yet. Leastwise, the courier didn't know, but then he left Washington in a mighty big hurry, and we've just had relays from Richmond and Raleigh."

"Did they capture President Madison?"

"No, him and the missus fled across the Potomac to Virginia. But the mansion and the Capitol are burnt out, and lots of houses and commercial buildings, too."

"Where was the army? And the navy?"

"The navy blew up our gunboats to keep 'em from falling into the enemy's hands. The militia went out to meet the bastards but high-tailed it into the woods after a few shots. Only a handful of marines from the destroyed gunboats stood their ground and fought like men. The

British have got some kind of secret weapon, rockets that hiss and spark like hell, and they scared the pants off our farmboys and city clerks. If you ask me, mister, we might as well surrender."

And with that he spurred his frothing pony and thundered off down Old King's Highway, along which the Redcoats had marched and camped in 1780 when Charleston had surrendered and nearly all of the Continental troops in the Carolina provinces were captured.

So Lance related the story. But facts and figures were either lost in the telling or exaggerated or belittled in the repetitions of the news from Washington, and not until a week later did the Charleston *Courier* print a reasonably accurate account of the incident as witnessed by a correspondent on the scene.

The surprise raid on the capital had been eminently successful from a military standpoint, and it was a damaging blow to the country's morale. Washington was in ruins, Congress disrupted, the president and his cabinet trying to govern from Colonel Taylor's home. Mrs. Madison, receiving only an hour's notice before the actual invasion, had managed to escape across the Potomac Chain Bridge to a friend's home in Virginia, taking with her a hastily packed trunk containing the Declaration of Independence and other historic documents, Gilbert Stuart's portrait of George Washington, some state silver, and the precious Lowestoft dinner service she had bought to replace Jefferson's Cantonese china. It was said that Miss Dolley's courage and sense of history surpassed that of any man on the scene, including her husband, who had been on the verge of distraction. The magnificent Mrs. Madison was hailed as the greatest first lady of all time.

The British fleet still menaced the Chesapeake, eyeing heavily fortified Baltimore. But surrender was nowhere mentioned or hinted, and there was a ray of hope in the announcement that commissioners of the United States and Great Britain were about to sit down at a peace conference in Ghent, Belgium.

Reading this news, John felt little optimism. How could honest men discuss peace without at least a temporary truce on the battlefields? "A shame and a mockery," he declared to his wife and daughter, his only audience now. "If the British were sincere, they would first cease hostilities, then talk peace. I'm skeptical of the whole business."

Emily promptly agreed. "Yes, that's the sensible procedure, isn't it, dear? I suspect some Merlin maneuvers, too."

Her tone was placating and soothing. It was the first time Star had heard her stepmother use an endearment to her father. Perhaps Emily was mellowing, too.

It was late September before the plague finally lifted its curse from Mystic Rose. And if John could count any blessing or mercy in the relief, it was that the members of his immediate family had been spared. Lance, of course, had never willingly exposed himself. But Star and Emily had, and some miracle had protected them; John could only attribute it to prayer and divine intervention. Yet it was hard, a test that taxed every vestige of his faith, to view the filled slave cemetery and the scores of convalescents, mere scarecrows incapable of manual labor, and see any kindness done him. These living skeletons must eat, though they could not help to provide their food, creating a new quandary for their master.

"They'll be a pack of lazy, shiftless slaves, the way you're pampering them," Lance predicted.

"Well," said John, "a fine example of industry you set for them, Lance."

"Give me free use of the whip, and I'll show you how to get some work out of them."

"Such permission you will never receive from me."

Lance shrugged. "Then break your own back to save theirs. I'll not bend mine."

John virtually broke his back, for he wrenched it severely performing tasks too strenuous for his age and condition. But the potatoes and root vegetables had to be dug and stored in straw in the cellars.

The cabbages were lost, and most of the orchard crops had shriveled unpicked on the trees or rotted on the ground. Without Emily's supervision in the house, little preserving had been done and few jars of fruit and vegetables and conserves appeared on the depleted pantry shelves. There was no denying the need of a mistress over the best housekeeper.

Sugar, tea, and coffee—blockade luxuries now, dear in price and almost unobtainable—were kept under lock and key, as were the equally scarce liquors and wines. Salt, selling at eight dollars a bushel, was reclaimed from the brine-soaked earth floors of the smokehouses, which were dug up, strained through hoppers, and boiled down. And all slave rations were sharply cut and carefully doled out by the mistress on Saturday afternoons, so that none should feel slighted.

The slaves, tiring of cow peas, turnip greens, and corn pone, set traps for possums and coons and feasted on these animals roasted with wild yams. They relished catfish stew and would sneak down to the river and bait a hook on a cane pole or a trot line at every opportunity. At night they hunted wild pigeons by torchlight in the glades. And no stray deer, turkey, goose, duck, or delicious little rice bird was safe around Mystic Rose. Inventive and resourceful, they brewed tea from the dried leaves of blackberry vines and coffee out of parched okra seeds. They sweetened both with honey or molasses whenever they could manage to purloin a pint or so of either of these precious sugar substitutes from the manor.

Satiated with boiled rice and succotash, Star longed for a nice soft-shelled hen-crab, a creamed oyster patty, a bowl of turtle soup, or a slice of fresh roasted pork or lamb or barbecued beef. But the smokehouses, heavily padlocked, were low even on ham and bacon and dried meats and could not be replenished until the winter slaughterings.

A lean season was in store at Mystic Rose for both man and beast. John doubted if enough grain had been gathered to tide the stock over, and the fowl might have to scratch long and hard for a living.

For the first time in the history of the plantation, the rice crop was not harvested at the peak of perfection. Frost was on the pumpkins and haycocks before the last field was thrashed, and John knew that this crop, or what he could afford to sell of it since the lion's share must go into the bellies of hungry slaves, would win no ribbons in world exhibitions and bring no financial rewards in the market. His factor, viewing samples of it, shook his head dubiously.

"I've seen better, John. In fact, I've rarely seen worse. There's a lot of volunteer grain mixed with it, and you know that lowers the grade and asking price. You'll do well to break even this year."

"Break even? Sam, I've lost nearly fifty thousand dollars worth of slaves! I haven't the money to replace them even if I could find that many for sale, and I can't work all of my land without replacements. Write that in my books, Samuel. On the debit side of the ledger, fifty thousand dollars. In the credit columns, nothing."

Clem Jones, accompanying his master and the agent on tour of the plantation, took the blade of grass he was chewing out of his mouth. "Maybe we ought to plant cotton next year, Mr. Lamont. It's healthier to cultivate than rice and just as profitable. That little patch near the pines I been experimenting with has done mighty fine, sir."

"I know, Clem. But Mystic Rose was founded on rice and indigo. It's hard to change family tradition after a century. I'll have to reflect on it."

Samuel Grady grunted. "If you can believe what you read in the papers, a royal governor might be telling us what we can and can't plant next year. By Jove, the rascals seem to have us on a rack."

"Oh, we been in tight quarters before and wriggled out," Clem drawled, hooking his thumbs in his back pockets and rocking on his heels. "One thing I learnt in the Up Country, treein' a possum don't always mean he's caught. I had a few get away from me when I could already see their hides dryin' on the barn. Reckon it's gonna take a backwoodsman to teach them British varmints a lesson they won't soon forget. Too bad Daniel Boone's gettin' so old. But we got a fella borned in our own mountains, though Tennessee likes to claim him, that's a close ringer for Boone. Name of Jackson. General Andrew Jackson."

The factor nodded somewhat skeptically. "Newly appointed to the regular army. Yes, we all know of Jackson. But I wouldn't put much faith in a man who was a friend of the treasonist Aaron Burr, even defending Burr's murder of the honorable Alexander Hamilton."

"Mr. Hamilton was killed fair and square in a duel, sir. Andy knows about duels; he fought plenty of 'em himself. But that don't mean he's a traitor like Burr and sweet on the British. Why, he was only a lad when he fought 'em like a mad bear in the Revolution and was took prisoner. Hear tell an officer marked him with his saber because Andy refused to black the devil's boots, and you can bet your tobacco pouch old Andy ain't forgettin' that scar on his face. I reckon he showed them Creek Indians in Georgia and Alabama they was fightin' on the wrong side, didn't he?"

"It was his scalp or theirs," Grady argued. "And he had the help of an experienced Indian fighter, David Crockett. You may bet on the army and Jackson, Mr. Jones. I'll put my trust, shaky though it be, in the navy and men of Commodore Perry's ilk. Gentlemen, married to ladies."

Clem grinned, scratching the tip of his stubby, freckled nose with a blunt finger. "I see you heard about Mrs. Jackson's pipe and bare feet and cuss words. And since she's a fifth cousin, once removed of my maw's, I'll have to own it's true. But maw says one day Cousin Rachel might be first lady of the land and set a whole new style for the gals."

The other men chuckled at the absurdity of such a notion, and John said, "Your mother's a woman of some imagination, Clem. But I hope you're right about Andrew Jackson. Perhaps he's the man President Madison has been seeking and praying for. Somebody to stand and fight against any odds or secret weapons, not only a general but a savior. Now, if you please, Samuel, let us proceed with the inspection and inventory. Except for the year of the Great Hurricane, when all the crops were destroyed, I assure you Mystic Rose has never been in worse straits. I'm near bankruptcy, Sam."

Chapter 23

THE FIRST VISITORS to Mystic Rose following the plague were Lorna and Grant. Emily welcomed them happily, pleased to see that her daughter had gained weight and some color in her cheeks, although she was still far from robust.

Star noted with wistful envy Lorna's fashionable new gown of French-loomed brown jacquard which had run the blockade, and her chic cloche of beige velvet swathed in malines.

How mean of her, Star thought, to come strutting her finery, when she knows I haven't been to town in two years! My wardrobe is as outmoded as the farthingale and bongrace.

"Oh, Mother dear," cried Lorna, and she embraced Emily all the way from the carriage into the house. "I'm so happy you're all right! And you too, Star. That dreadful plague—I was so worried about all of you! Grant was anxious, too—afraid it might spread to Avalon and Edisto. Weren't you, darling?" She smiled at her husband, naked adoration in her faded blue eyes.

Grant was as handsome as ever and well tailored in gray broadcloth. He answered his wife's smile, but his gaze flickered across the parlor to Star.

"I'm glad your family escaped," he said, sitting down and crossing his long legs, thick with saddle muscles. "But I know what terrible losses your father sustained. If I can be of any assistance—"

Star interrupted, outraged at the thought of charity. "No, thank you. We'll manage."

"I'm sure you will." He glanced at his mother-in-law. "Where is Mr. Lamont?"

"He and Lance are attending a slave auction in Georgetown. We lost so many rice hands, and John hopes to replace a few." Emily did not add that any such purchases would have to be made on borrowed money.

"I doubt if he'll succeed," Grant said. "Planters are holding on to their good workers. Only sickly women, orphaned children, and old men are going on the block now. The slavers are having a difficult time getting past the British sea hawks. The few young males who reach our shores are readily snapped up. The bidding often takes place on shipboard, and it's astronomical. Five and six thousand dollars per head."

"You speak as if they were animals," Star said.

"Oh, no," he smiled affably. "They're much more valuable than animals now. Pa wouldn't part with one of his able young men for a king's ransom. But I know he would be more than glad to lend your father an experienced rice crew from Avalon next spring."

Star's humiliation was almost suffocating. The proud and mighty Lamonts reduced to borrowing money and help!

But it was true that the war had affected slave trade. Long coffles of Negroes being herded from coastal plantations to inland markets, once a common sight, were rare now. Sturdy field hands and skillful house servants were at a premium. Few notices of slave auctions appeared on posters or in the papers, and if a planter learned of one somewhere he would travel many miles to attend and would often endanger friendship by bidding against friends and neighbors. Now John Lamont was in this sad and embarrassing predicament, and his daughter, her pride rankling, rushed to his defense.

"Pa would insist on paying for any such favor, Grant. But it may not be necessary to borrow any rice hands. We're figuring on planting cotton next year," she said on sheer impulse, for no one had told her so.

"That's fine. The cotton from Edisto nets pa more than the rice from Avalon, but unfortunately it's almost impossible to market either crop now. You wouldn't recognize the harbor any more, Star. Ships are few and far between."

"The war won't last forever," Star said with more confidence than she felt. "There'll be enough merchantmen, then."

"Sure," Grant nodded. "Probably one on the sea for every star and planet in the heavens. Jupiter, Mars, Mercury, Pluto, *Venus*—"

Hot pink suffused Star's face, and her dark eyes glowered, for she considered his gibe deliberate. Cruel and petty. So he was still jealous of Captain Stewart?

Lorna twisted her hands nervously, sensing the mounting tension between her husband and stepsister, and sought to distract them. "I suppose you've heard that new song everyone in Charleston is singing, Star?"

"Why, no, Lorna. What song?"

" 'The Star Spangled Banner.' A fellow named Key—"

"Francis Scott Key," Grant interposed.

"Yes, dear, I know his name. And he composed the ballad during the bombardment of Fort McHenry, Maryland. The British shelled the fort all night, and the next morning, seeing the Stars and Stripes still waving, Mr. Key was inspired to write 'The Star Spangled Banner.' "

"Sing it for us," Emily urged.

Without further prompting Lorna rose to her feet, drew a deep breath and launched into the song as if she were a prima donna leading a patriotic rally on a flag-draped stage.

"That's beautiful," Emily said when Lorna had finished. "Truly inspiring."

Star agreed, though she thought the squeal of a stuck pig had more melody than Lorna's owlish screeching.

"That's only the first stanza," Lorna said, returning to her seat. "I haven't memorized the others well enough yet to sing them, but everybody in town is humming the tune. They say it's more popular than 'Yankee Doodle' was in the Revolution. The militia will be marching to it soon, won't they, dear?"

"Possibly," Grant said. "But it's not a military tune. 'Yankee Doodle' is much better."

"How do southerners manage to march to 'Yankee Doodle?' " his wife quipped, her sarcasm indicating that there was still some friction between them on this score.

His smile suggested some obscenity. "Oh, we have our own version of it, my dear. Tell Star about the ball."

"Why? Pa wouldn't let her go anyway."

"What ball?" Star asked eagerly.

"The militia ball," Grant said. "Three weeks from next Friday. In the armory."

Star glanced hopefully at her stepmother.

"We'll see," Emily said, promising nothing. "Now I'll go tell Taby to prepare something special for supper—"

"Please don't bother, mother," Lorna told her. "I'm sorry, but we can't stay for supper. There's a new play opening at the Dock Street Theater this evening. The entire cast is fresh from a recent triumph at Park Theater in New York, and we're engaged to attend with friends."

Emily was plainly disappointed. "I had hoped for a few private words with you, daughter. We haven't seen each other in so long. Do come along, then, and help me prepare tea. I'm sure Star and Grant will excuse us?"

"Of course," Star murmured, and Grant bowed prompt assent, ignoring his wife's suspicious frown.

"Poor mother," Lorna sighed, reluctant to leave the parlor. "Still preparing your own tea? I should think you'd have trained a servant by now to use your recipe?"

Emily removed a ring of keys, containing the one to the pantry, from the pocket of her gown. "Tea is precious in this house now, and the servants are inclined to waste it."

"And steal it, too?" Lorna added, departing the room with a warning glance at her husband and stepsister.

When they had gone, Star moved from the Queen Anne settee to the window. The gardens had been neglected by both nature and master that season, but hardy chrysanthemums and asters bloomed bravely in the borders, and sweet alyssum in its final effort edged the pebbled paths across which autumn leaves were already drifting. An elderly slave, too feeble for field labor, was raking the debris into neat piles. Another carried pails of water from the well to refresh the tender camellias beginning to bud, Star's favorite flower next to the gardenia.

"You look pale," Grant said, observing her anxiously. "Have you been ill, Star?"

"No, I'm fine. But we had a hectic summer, Grant. Even the gardens suffered."

"So I see, and I'm sorry. But now I think you're entitled to some pleasure and relaxation. Will you attend the ball, Star?" He came to stand beside her, close enough to touch, and his arm ached to circle her small waist and draw her tenderly, protectively to him.

"Perhaps, if pa can be persuaded. But I'm not sure I'd enjoy it without a new gown or escort."

He smiled. "I can't imagine you without either. Is there a shortage of dressmakers?"

"In the country, yes. And pa wouldn't allow me to go to Charleston for fittings."

"But surely there's no shortage of escorts? You can't have been foolish enough to annihilate all your old beaus?"

"The war is the villain that binds me."

"Well, there's always your stepbrother. Lance would be delighted, I'm sure, to rescue you."

Star grimaced. "I'd rather stay bound."

"Until your hero returns? Are you still not convinced that he is no hero at all, but as devilish a rogue as ever sailed the seven seas?"

"You speak riddles, Grant, and I'm in no mood to try to solve them."

"Spare me your pretense, Star. Everyone in Charleston has heard of Captain Stewart's accident in our port. But I happen to know it was no accident."

Star was surprised, but her face did not betray her emotions as easily as it once had; the ingenue was an accomplished actress now. "Indeed? How do you know?"

"Never mind. I just know, that's all. I know what happened that night, and some day Stewart will die for it. If he is not dead already, I will kill him."

"By challenge?"

"Yes, although he doesn't deserve such a gentlemanly consideration. A duel is an affair of honor, and Stewart has none. A man who forces his attentions on a woman should be shot like a mad dog."

"You're presuming, Grant. Hasn't it occurred to you that whoever gave you such information may have been in error? Even lying?"

But Star knew the informer well enough. Lance had betrayed her, aware that Grant would keep his confidence and also avenge her honor if ever the opportunity presented itself. Thus he might eliminate his competition, both past and present, in one expediently provoked contest. She ought to tell Grant a thing or two about Lance! His lies, coercion, threats–and murder of her parakeets, for she was convinced now that he had suffocated Romeo and Juliet simply to show her how easy it would be to sneak into her room and smother *her* some night.

"Nothing you say can dissuade me, Star. I intend either to kill Stewart or be killed by him."

"And so you may be, Grant. I understand he is skilled with both pistol and sword."

"Cutlass, too? Most pirates are."

"He's not a pirate."

"He behaves like one. Capturing vessels and ravishing maidens!"

"He's a privateer," Star insisted. "And he did not ravish me."

"You would defend the scoundrel?"

"Oh, Grant, don't be a benighted fool! Please? I don't want you to fight him for any reason, least of all that one."

"Do you fear for my life or his?"

"Both," she murmured. "Grant, if ever you loved me–"

"*If*?" He smiled wryly. "You still doubt it, Star? You want proof? You'll have it in Stewart's corpse."

"Aren't you forgetting someone, Grant?"

"No." His eyes guarded the door. "Lorna's a good woman and has tried to be a good wife. But I haven't been much of a husband. If I should lose, she would be a wealthy widow. That should be some compensation. And consolation."

"And just what reason would you give for your quarrel with Captain Stewart? How could you publicly defend my reputation without jeopardizing my character?"

"I'll arrange a private meeting."

"And let folks draw their own conclusions? I won't allow it, Grant! Do you hear?"

His jaw set firmly. "You can't stop me, Star."

"Not even if–if I could give you assurance that Troy did not harm me?"

"There's only one way you could prove–" He broke off, staring at her.

Star nodded, swallowing hard, for the prospect of such an intimacy with him still excited and intrigued her. "Would that satisfy you, Mr. Russell?"

His eyes narrowed, and Star saw the quickening of blood in his darkly flushed face. His voice was a hoarse, tense whisper. "Do you realize what you're saying?"

"Oh, don't act so surprised and shocked! You suggested as much yourself once, in pa's office. Remember?"

"I remember, Star. And you wouldn't consent then,

for love of me. But you would now, to save Stewart?"

"Do you want me or not?"

"No," he said fiercely. "Not if it's a bargain for Troy's life! And probably a trick to boot, to show me I'm no better than he, that I'd do the same thing with half a chance. I'd rather kill the bastard."

"If you do, you'll never know the truth, Grant. Because I swear I'll never speak to you again."

"I'll have to risk that, Star. Besides, he may already be rotting in Davy Jones's locker. You wouldn't want to make the supreme sacrifice in vain, would you?"

Voices in the hall and the rattle of the tea cart prevented Star's answer. She merely smiled at him, that coy, secretive tilt of her eyes and mouth that he had never forgotten. She still tempted and tormented him. She had lost none of her charm and coquetry, nor her ability to tease, taunt, and haunt him. Suddenly he wished he had not rejected her offer in such proud haste. Still, the possibility gave him something to relish and dream about and live for. God, how he loved and wanted her, and how long he had waited!

Chapter 24

STAR NEVER KNEW what arguments or persuasions Emily employed on her behalf and did not really care. The important thing was that her father had agreed to take her to the militia ball, and Emily was actually remodeling a gown for her to wear. Would Grant remember the last time he had seen her in the ruby velvet costume, the night he had attempted to seduce her in her father's office? Would he regard the gown as a symbolic gesture—or a provocative flag to tease an already disturbed and angry bull?

Apprehension tempered her enthusiasm as the ball approached. Suppose Grant had changed his mind and preferred diddling with her to dueling with Troy? After all, she was available now, and Captain Stewart might never be. It would take a strong and pious male to resist such a temptation, and Grant was not exactly a pillar of piety. Her challenge had ignited a raw flame in his eyes that could not deny either his love or lust for her. Only his pride and jealousy of Troy and his reluctance to buy his rival's life with her flesh had held him in check. Was he afraid he might find her virginal, and then Stewart would be in the position of avenger?

Star considered the ramifications of such an act. Certainly, after Lorna's treachery behind her back, she owed her no loyalty and should enjoy flaunting her husband's infidelity, yet deep down she knew she would not. She wasn't even sure any more that she loved and wanted Grant as desperately as she once had, for the thought of his belonging to someone else now caused her less pain and suffering. An affair with Grant was a fascinating prospect in fancy, but Star had qualms about experiencing it in reality.

Damn Lance! His insidious betrayal of her secret had forced this new anxiety on her. Now that he thought he had an ally in Grant, he was more arrogant and insufferable than ever. If only there were some way to extricate herself from his vicious web before it entangled and strangled her.

I've got to do something, she thought desperately. Throw a scare into him somehow. Perhaps if he found another image in his room?

Taking a shawl to guard against the October chill, she went out to the infirmary. One of the slaves was confined there with a huge boil on his neck, and Tawn was preparing a poultice of bay leaves, which was supposed to bring the angry red bulge to a proper head. Emily had suggested a paste of warm flaxseed, but Tawn preferred her own remedy. The patient was lying on a cot in a corner, moaning in pain, when Star entered. She paused on the threshold, still appalled by the memory of the mass suffering and death so recently there.

"Poor Joseph," she said. "What ails him?"

"Bad blood," Tawn diagnosed, "and it comin' out on him. Leeches could help suck it out, but your pa and Miss Emily don't believe in 'em, so I's fixin' a magic cure of bay leaves and swamp water. Is there something special you wants, Miss Star?"

"Yes, Tawn. I'd like to talk with you about something and perhaps ask a favor."

"Yessum?"

"After you tend your patient," Star deferred.

Tawn took the basin of slimy leaves to the cot, drained a few, and placed them on Joseph's neck. He groaned and flinched at her touch.

"You ain't got nothing to holler about, nigger," Tawn rebuked him. She considered her caste far superior to the average Negro's and had little to do socially with the men of the plantation. Only the son of a Zulu chieftain was worthy of the princess daughter of an Angola witch doctor! "Wait till you feels the whip on your raw hide and gets the hounds set on you. Then you is got troubles, black man!"

She referred to Obah, of course. And Star heard, as she was intended to hear. She was convinced now that Obah was hiding in the local swamps and that Tawn had been in contact with him all these months. Her devotion to her lover was boundless, and one glance at her sullen lips showed that she had not forgiven the master who had sold him away from her. Wrath and vengeance were strong in her nature, as deep and abiding as love and devotion could be.

"Tawn, if that carbuncle needs lancing, don't try to cut it yourself. Pa will summon Doctor Frazer."

"Doctor Frazer charge mileage for comin' out here and money to operate. I's just as good a surgeon and don't cost Master John nothing. But this old buckra ain't goin' need no doctor. Ain't I done treated boils before? That lump'll bust by mornin', and the core pop out like a cork." Snorting in disgust, she slapped another leaf on the patient and left him writhing and moaning on the cot. "What you wants to talk to me about, Miss Star?"

Something in Tawn's manner—her sly movements and the way she avoided her mistress's eyes—made Star wary. This woman was not to be trusted. Caution and finesse would be required in obtaining her assistance against Lance, but before she proceeded in that direction, she must be certain that Tawn was involved in the other incident.

"Well, I was just wondering if you have any beeswax I could borrow? We're out of it in the house, and I need some as a dip for the paper flowers I'm making." The hastily invented lie was clumsy, and Star did not think it fooled the perceptive woman.

Her coffee brown face was bland. "Wax? No'm, Miss Star. I ain't got no wax. I seldom uses it."

Liar, Star thought. You can model it with the skill of a sculptress! You made an image of Lance in beeswax and somehow slipped it into his room, but you didn't follow through. Why not? Was Lance instrumental in changing your mind?

"I understand, and it's not important. Liquid wax just protects the crepe paper from dust and fading. I'll have Dink fetch me some from the hives."

"Yessum."

Returning to the manor, Star felt a strange forboding. Her mind dwelt on Lance, and her thoughts raced back to the night she had observed him sneaking down to the tunnel. The plague crisis had lessened her interest in him temporarily, but she recalled again his lack of surprise at Sheriff Osborn's message concerning a runaway slave in the Santee Swamp, possibly Obah. There was little doubt that he was lurking somewhere in the vicinity and that Lance also had been in contact with him. Perhaps the three of them had decided to join forces against her and pa? Star shivered, unable to imagine a more terrible alliance.

Tawn had been her friend once, offering to help her charm back Grant Russell with a black cat bone, but apparently Lance had succeeded in undermining and possibly destroying that friendship. Tawn had not been glad to see her just now; she had been tense, cagey, and suspicious. Compromising her had probably not been easy. Certainly Lance had promised her something, something she valued above friendship for her mistress or loyalty to her master. Freedom to join her lover? Tawn would cast in with the devil himself on such a promise!

Star hailed Dink on his way to the apiary, and he hurried over. "Dink, you have charge of the hives and honey, don't you?"

"I sure does," Dink said, grinning proudly, for it was a broad and enviable trust.

"Did Tawn ever get any combs from you?"

His grin froze. "Not from me, Miss Star. I wouldn't give her none without Master John's permission. Miss Emily save the combs to make sealin' wax and smooth the sadirons, you knows, and I ain't got no leave to give 'em away. But Tawn she got some combs, all right."

"How, Dink?"

"Stole 'em, that's how."

"When, Dink? When did you miss them?"

"Couple of weeks ago, Miss Star. Tawn she must be fixin' to conjure somebody agin."

"Again?"

"Lordy, Miss Star! You knows it was Tawn made that image of Mist' Lance. Me and Mauma didn't have nothing to do with it, like we told you, but I knows Tawn the guilty one. She was gonna' put the spell on Mist' Lance, but look like he done put the spell on Tawn."

Star caught her breath. "What are you saying, Dink? What do you know? Tell me everything!"

Dink shifted his weight from one foot to the other, deliberating his accusations before pronouncing them. "Tawn and Mist' Lance gettin' mighty friendly of late, Miss Star. They been puttin' they heads together 'bout something, and I don't like it. Mist' Lance been sneakin' into Tawn's cabin at night, and they been layin' on the bed together. I thinks them two knows full well where Obah be, and they up to some mischief. Miss Star, does you wants my honest 'pinion?"

"Yes, Dink. What is it?"

"Well, I thinks Mist' Lance tired of waitin' for your pa to go to the Promised Land by hisself. He got his mind set on bein' master of Mystic Rose, and he tired of waitin'."

"I've known that for a long time, Dink. But he wouldn't dare harm pa!"

"No'm. Not by hisself. He one big coward, that bucko, and he scared of the gallows. But I don't think Obah scared of nothing, not even evil spirits. Him a wild man, that one, and if Mist' Lance was to get him likkered up, I reckon Obah do most anything. Tawn would help him, too. And maybe some other niggers what wants they freedom."

Star's jaw dropped in horror and disbelief. "But that would be rebellion! Oh, Dink! You honestly believe some of the slaves want their freedom enough to rebel against pa?"

Dink nodded gravely. "I's heard grumblin' in the quarters, specially now the rations is short and not everybody got warm clothes. Yessum, they's grumblin'."

"Oh, but how could they, Dink, when pa is so good to them? Don't they realize what the swamp fever did to us, that even the family is conserving food and clothing and we're doing the best we can?"

"Some of 'em just naturally belongs in the jungles, Miss Star. They was happier there, just huntin' and fishin' and lovin' with the gals. You can't tame every savage, Miss Star, no more'n you can tame every wild animal."

That was simply African logic succinctly expressed. Still, Star was loath to believe another calamity threatened Mystic Rose, one even more horrible than plague or British invasion. Wicked and depraved and rapacious though Lance might be, surely he must realize that he could not possibly succeed in any such fantastic scheme as that! Inciting slave rebellion was a hanging offense. To seal their lips, he would have to eliminate every witness: pa, herself, Dink, Mauma, and even his own mother. Tawn and Obah, too, and any other participants, once they had served their purpose. If this was his intention, his wild fantasy, he must be out of his mind. Demented. Utterly mad.

Tomorrow evening, Star decided, on the way to the ball, she would tell her father everything. About Captain Stewart and herself and Lance's threats and Dink's suspicions. Oh, yes, it would be a relief to tell him!

Chapter 25

MORNING DAWNED GRAY and gloomy, and for the first time in months thunderheads loomed on the horizon. Star noticed them immediately and frowned. Her first ball in two years–naturally it would rain. The streams would rise, the dikes might break, and pa wouldn't leave the plantation for a hundred militia balls.

Mauma had predicted a change of weather several days before, advised by her rheumatic joints which she was treating with a raw potato suspended from a string around her neck.

"Didn't I tell you it goin' rain?" she asked almost triumphantly, proud of her forecasting powers, as Star glumly surveyed the cumulus clouds piled like whipped cream on syllabub. "My old bones never lies. I's got a barometer on each kneecap."

"Well, we do need rain," Star allowed. "But since it waited this long, it could have waited one more day. Oh, why does something always have to spoil my plans!"

Mauma limped painfully to the windows, to reassess her previous prediction. "Might be more'n just rain, honey. Might be a big storm before this day's done."

"Hurricane season is past, Mauma. A squall may be brewing somewhere on the water, but those clouds are mostly in the northeast. The bad gales generally come from the south, you know. The Caribbean. It's probably just the first cold spell of the season blowing in."

"Either that, or I is older than I calculates. This am the worstest misery I is done ever had."

"Sit down, Mauma. I'll dress myself."

"You think you could, missy?"

"Of course! I'm a big girl now."

Star brooded over the sky several moments longer. Then, characteristic of her mercurial nature, her somber mood passed, leaving her gay and hopeful. Amid chemise, petticoats, and hair brushing, she waltzed about the room, admiring herself in the mirror of the dressing table and the full length cheval glass. There was a supple buoyance in her movements, an archness to her smile, and a capricious sparkle in her brilliant eyes. She refused to think of Lance or Troy, the recent plague, the war, or the perverse elements. Maybe it would only be a gentle autumn shower followed by a warm sun and a bright harvest moon.

"What you so happy 'bout, child?"

"I'm going to dance again tonight, Mauma! Oh, I do hope pa won't balk about taking me just because the sky is cloudy! I'm going down to breakfast now and eat a dozen rice cakes with honey—"

But her stepbrother soon dampened her enthusiasm. Lance stood at the foot of the stairway. Leaning against the carved newel post, he grinned up at Star as she descended. "No ball tonight," he greeted her jovially. "Papa already said so. The barometer is falling. Heap big rain coming. Maybe wind, too."

"Well, what are you so pleased about, Chief Yellowface? If so, you can't go, either."

"I had no intention of going."

"Indeed? It would be the first such powwow you ever voluntarily missed."

His amber eyes gleamed with malice and mischief. "Perhaps I have more serious pursuits."

"Gambling and strumpets?"

"Pleasant diversions, both, but hardly serious. I was about to take my morning bracer of sherry. Will Your Highness condescend to join me?"

"I'd sooner join Lucifer."

"And make his life a merry hell as you've made mine?"

Star scowled. "You create your own torment, Lance. Don't you ever give up?"

"Not when I want something badly enough."

Star paused just above him, her vantage height forcing him to look up to her. "Just what is it you want so badly—as if I didn't know!"

"Then why do you ask, little sister?"

"Have you forgotten my warning, Lance?"

"I've forgotten nothing," he muttered. "Nothing that was ever said or done to me by the mighty Lamonts, and the day of reckoning will come. Justice and retribution. Your Dies Irae and my deliverance. So recite your mea culpa, my beautiful and belligerent little gypsy—"

"You sound like a drunken preacher, Lance. And at this hour of the morning, too! Go somewhere and sober up—preferably to the infernal regions where you belong. Where's pa?"

"Sky gazing. Praying for rain and fearing flood. Gad, what a worrywart!"

"Perhaps he has more to worry about than the weather," Star suggested tentatively.

"Perhaps," Lance shrugged. "A man's past sins have a way of catching up with him."

"Sins? Pa? He's a saint!"

"And you're an angel, I suppose?"

Star's hand itched to slap him. Her antipathy for Lance was so great, so encompassing, it flared into open conflict on the slightest provocation. If they were so much as in the same room together, the atmosphere crackled with distrust, antagonism, and barely restrained physical violence.

"Pa never did a wrong thing in his life!"

"That's a matter of opinion, and you're hardly a proper judge, being understandably prejudiced. Others may have a different conception of his character."

"What evil are you contemplating now, Lance?"

His tongue clucked in protest. "What a suspicious Romany mind! You always impute to me the worst possible motives when I'm as innocent as a newborn babe."

"Innocent as Cain!" Star declared. "Just remember, I'm not Abel!"

Lance laughed, his gaze wandering familiarly over her body, lingering on her firm young breasts. "I'm not likely to forget that, my dear."

"You're despicable," Star said, brushing him aside like a fly and proceeding to the breakfast table.

Throughout the day storm clouds gathered in the northeast, forming dark mountains. But a strange calm prevailed at Mystic Rose. The long veils of moss hung motionless on the live oaks. Not a whisper came from the usually murmurous pines. Scarcely a leaf fell from the deciduous trees. All nature seemed suspended in a state of hushed expectancy.

John and the overseer rode the banks of the rice paddies, searching for weak spots and ordering immediate reenforcement. The livestock was herded in from the low-lying pastures, which were frequently flooded, to the shelter of the pens and barns. Doors and shutters and gates were secured. Low Country planters had learned, through bitter experience, to take every possible precaution against high winds and treacherous tides. For, while rare, unseasonal hurricanes were not unknown, an agitated sea could inflict ruinous damage.

Lance occupied himself throwing darts, playing solitaire, and shadowing Star. Emily went about her routine tasks in her usual fashion—brisk, precise, and unperturbed. A bulwark, Star thought, a fortress in herself.

Would she defend her son in any mischief he might be perpetrating? Aid and abet him?

"I'm sorry about the ball, Star," she said with genuine sympathy for her stepdaughter's dashed hopes.

"So am I, Aunt Emily. But thanks, anyway, for making over the gown for me. You did an excellent job. No one could ever have recognized it."

"There'll be other balls, dear."

Star nodded, sighing wistfully. When she could accept life's disappointments and frustrations with Emily's serenity and resignation, then she would have acquired the rudiments and essentials of maturity. But while she admired and even envied her stepmother's poise in a crisis, Star was not sure she desired all of Emily's attributes permanently. For then she would be old. Wasn't that what wisdom and dignity and tranquility were in reality: the mellowness of age? The loss of hopes and dreams, the end of youth?

Dusk fell early. After supper, the family and servants gathered in the dining room for vespers. This practice had begun during the plague. John had read a chapter from the Bible each evening, taking what courage and consolation he could from it and from collective prayer, and now it was an established practice.

This evening, Star tried to concentrate, but her mind kept deviating. She could visualize the armory in Charleston, decorated in patriotic bunting, autumn leaves, and boughs. The handsome militiamen in their dashing blue uniforms, brass buttons gleaming and shining swords swinging, would be leading the grand march. The musicians would be tuning up their instruments about now. Grant would be watching for her arrival, and Lorna would be dreading it. She had passed many pleasant and disturbing hours anticipating the meeting, hers and Grant's, how she would flirt with him, tease and tempt him during the dancing, drive him wild with longing, allow him to lure her to some private place and make desperate love to her. . . .

Glancing up from her irreverent thoughts, she found Lance intent on the mantel clock. It was an exquisite French timepiece, mounted in an ebony case with silver fittings and ivory inlay, but Lance was not admiring its beauty or value. Rather, he seemed to be marking time, counting seconds, minutes, hours. Sensing her eyes on him, he turned and smiled at her, a slow, malevolent smile that chilled her blood.

"Well," John said, closing the Bible after carefully marking his place with a ribbon, "if faith and prayer can bring protection, we need have no fear of the night. Let us retire now. Come, Emily. Good night, all."

"Good night, pa." Star kissed his cheek above his gray beard. "Aunt Emily."

The slaves, except for Mauma and Lance's valet, Bobo, proceeded to their quarters. Star pitied Bobo; he was in for some carping and cuffing if his master's smile was any indication of his mood. She excused Mauma from assisting her, knowing how it pained the poor soul's legs to climb the stairs, and departed without a word to Lance.

But his cruel smile stayed with her, delaying her sleep. She tossed restlessly on the feather mattress, wishing she had found or taken the opportunity to speak to her father about Lance. But John had been busy all day, and Lance had covertly guarded her every move, even when he pretended to be absorbed in other matters, and Star knew he had forced his servant to keep an eye on her when Lance could not. Mauma had had some truck with Bobo on this issue, demanding once, "What you idlin' round for, boy? Ain't you got nothing better to do than watch me and Miss Star? Go on with you!"

The jalousies had been closed earlier against the impending storm, which seemed now to be awaiting a propitious moment to strike, and a stifling darkness enveloped Star when she snuffed the bedside candle. Outside, in the abysmal night, a wind was rising in the tree tops, and a branch scraped the windows, the sound as grating as fingernails on a slate.

She never knew exactly what woke her: the nightmare she was having, the rattle of a loose shutter, the crack of a musket, the jungle yell of a savage, or the pounding on her door and her father's anxious voice.

"Star! Wake up, daughter! Get up and dress! Quickly!"

She threw off the covers and stumbled sleepily to the door. The hall was lit by candles in wall sconces, and John stood there fumbling with the buttons on his shirt. Emily was up, too, hastily grooming herself.

"What is it, pa?"

"Rebellion, I think! Look out the windows. One of the cabins is on fire, and some slaves are dancing around it and shouting. Tawn and Obah are leading them. Star, they're armed! They must have broken into the armory and taken weapons and ammunition."

"Oh, pa! It is rebellion! And I think I know who–"

At that instant Lance strode out of his chambers across the hall, wearing an elegant dressing robe of crimson brocade over his dark wool trousers. He was wide awake. He had not disrobed, he had not retired. "It's rebellion, all right," he agreed, "and I know exactly who incited it. That black devil, Obah! What'll we do, father?"

John took immediate command. "Emily, Star, summon the servants! Take muskets and powder from the gun cabinets and barricade yourselves somewhere in the house. Thank God, you can handle a gun, Emily. I'm going to the south tower and try to speak to them. You might try your luck on the north, Lance."

"Oui, papa," Lance said, using the French words contemptuously, mocking John's first wife and daughter.

Star, still a little dazed with sleep and shock, stared dully as the men started off. Then, suddenly, Lance's vicious smile at vespers and the intent watch he had kept on the clock flashed across her mind, and she cried frantically, "No, pa, no! Don't go! It's a plot! They'll kill you! Pa, wait! Come back, please! There's something I must tell you–"

Shouts from Lance drowned out her voice. Then Emily's skirts rustled past her, hurrying to muster the servants. Star stood alone in the corridor, sick and trembling.

Chapter 26

MYSTIC ROSE was under siege and a reign of terror, and Obah was in his full glory as leader. He was a magnificent black giant, naked except for a loincloth of deer skin, his face and body grotesquely painted with clay stained with the dyes of swamp plants. A chieftain's headgear of egret and flamingo feathers crowned his massive head. A necklace of alligator teeth adorned his throat and bracelets of rattlesnake tail buttons circled his wrists and ankles, rattling dismally as he chanted and did a jungle dance of death around the roaring bonfire. He was Obah, son of Tomba, tribal chief of Zululand! He was a warrior, conqueror, high spirit. He was drunk with power, hatred, vengeance, and alcohol. Death to all who defied him!

Lance, observing the weird spectacle from the comparative safety of the north turret of the mansion, had feared this might happen: that he would not be able to control Obah once he had served his purpose. Already Obah had taken matters into his own hands, disregarding the plans they had so carefully formulated, night after summer night on the edge of the Santee Swamp.

His instructions had been clear and definite. Obah was not to set fire to anything. Lance did not want a burned-out plantation. But many cabins were aflame, and the wind, now that the storm had finally struck, would surely ignite others. The place would be a raging inferno, nothing but rubble and ashes by morning. Obah was not to terrorize the other slaves, but he and a small band of cohorts, secured through Tawn's influence and promises, were driving the nonsupporters from their beds, turning torches on the small frame structures, and killing all who resisted. Women and children were huddled together in nightclothes, crying and screaming in terror or petrified with fright. Some of the men, seeing a possibility of escape, fled across the fields and woods to refuge and long-cherished freedom.

Everything was going wrong, and it had seemed such a perfect plot, such excellent timing. Obah was to sneak into the basement through the tunnel, rob the liquor cellar, dispense alcoholic courage to himself and his followers, break the lock of the armory, and obtain arms and powder. The dogs, barking fiercely now, would be securely confined in the kennels. The militia, charged with quelling civil riot and insurrection, would be pleasantly occupied at the ball in Charleston. Star and her father were to have been ambushed en route to the city and robbed and murdered by supposed brigands, but the weather had negated this grisly plan. Obah could do them in on the plantation, along with Mauma and Dink, and the other house servants. Then he, Lance, would eliminate Obah and Tawn and the other conspirators, and Mystic Rose would have a new master.

Now that Zulu monster had gone berserk. He was a crazed demon with delusions of grandeur, and if not stopped would destroy them all.

John was on the opposite tower, shouting vainly against the howling wind, pleading with the rebels to lay down their arms and peacefully discuss the grievances that had brought them to revolt. "My people," he implored. "My good people, hear me! Listen to your master!"

His anguished voice carried to Star in her chambers below the south tower. She had not gone with Emily and was alone except for Mauma who stood guarding the door with a ready musket, her round black eyes big as saucers. Star's weapon, a loaded dueling pistol, lay on the bed, the long silver barrel glinting in the lamplight. But, remembering the incident with Captain Stewart, she could not bring herself to touch it.

Emily had turned the foyer into a small arsenal, and she, Clem Jones, and the domestic staff had barricaded the lower floor. But the women, chattering hysterically, were of little use; should a rebel enter the manor or manage to set fire to it, they would probably scatter like frightened chickens. The brick and stone walls and slate roof were fairly impervious to flame, but unfortunately the interior was highly vulnerable.

The gale, a freak born out of season, was sweeping down with mounting fury, ripping shutters off windows, hurling them to the ground in splinters, raising blazing cabin roofs and dumping them onto other wood outbuildings. Sparks and flaming boards hissed through the air like rockets and Roman candles, spectacular as an Independence Day fireworks display. Black billows rose from a warehouse of smoldering clothing and blankets. A smokehouse caught, and there was the sickening stench of burning bacon, ham, sausage, chitterlings, and lard.

Soon Star smelled the smoke of precious hay and fodder, and tears rolled down her cheeks. All pa's work gathering feed for the winter! The silos would go, the storehouse of recently harvested rice, and the stables and pens. She wondered vaguely why someone didn't release the frenzied animals—the bellowing cows, whinnying horses, squealing pigs, yelping dogs—before they too were destroyed.

The lurid glare of the flames lit the night as a mighty

torch, illuminating the black forests beyond and the black sky above. Heavy clouds, pregnant with water, hung over Mystic Rose. Lightning, thunder, screeching winds, exploding bullets and the acrid odors of gunpowder and saltpeter, sulphur and brimstone were all combined together. To Star, the end of the world could not have been more ominous or awesome. And maybe it was the end for pa and her? Now she understood what Lance had meant this morning when he had spoken of the day of reckoning for her father as well as his own deliverance. Dies Irae, he had called it, exhorting her to recite her mea culpa. Doomsday!

"Dear God, help us," she prayed aloud. "Sweet Jesus, have mercy on us. Mother in heaven, save and protect us—"

"The house goin' catch next," Mauma predicted dolefully. "We goin' be burned up, roasted like barbecue—"

"If only it would rain! Oh, Mauma, pray for rain!"

"I's prayin', Miss Star. I's prayin' every prayer the preacher and your pa teached me. I only hopes the Almighty ain't deaf or just not listenin'."

Star heard her father's voice again, amplified through cupped hands. "Obah! Mighty son of a mighty chief! Call a truce! Cease fire, and we will negotiate on equal terms! I promise you and your supporters amnesty and—"

A musket cracked, silencing him.

Horror struck Star, knocking her momentarily breathless. Then she gave a terrified scream. "Mauma! It's pa! They've hit him! I've got to go to him!"

Mauma planted herself squarely before the door. "You can't go, Miss Star! They shoot you, too! And worse—you hear?"

"I don't care! Get out of my way, you silly old fool! Pa is hurt and may be dying!"

She pushed Mauma aside, almost unbalancing her, and left the room. But her feet felt numb and strangely leaden, as if they would not carry her to the tower. Mauma dragged after her, limping and puffing up the stone stairs to the battlement.

John was lying on the floor, his head in a pool of blood. The ball had pierced his brain, death was instantaneous.

Star stared at him, the violent wind whipping her hair and clothes. She did not feel or hear the wind. She did not actually see the still, bloody form of her father through her blurred vision. Reality simply would not penetrate her state of shock.

"Oh, Lord!" cried Mauma, clasping her hands and falling to her knees. "Oh, Lord! My master dead!"

"Dead?" Star whispered. "Pa is dead?"

"He gone, honey. Gone Up Yonder. Oh, Jesus, take him to your bosom and give his poor child strength now–"

Her senses still dulled by the opiate of shock and disbelief, Star spoke calmly–so calmly she did not recognize the voice as her own. "Get up, Mauma. There's nothing you can do for him now. Fetch Miss Emily. I'll be in my rooms."

"Yessum."

"And stop crying, Mauma. I can't bear your tears."

The prostrate slave heaved herself off the floor, drying her eyes on her apron, thinking that already her prayer had been answered. The Lord had given her mistress some kind of supernatural strength, for she had not collapsed and disintegrated as Mauma had imagined and feared she would at the death of her father. She appeared in full control of her emotions and faculties, able to understand and think and issue orders. But her tranquility and calmness were deceiving.

They left the tower like figures in a trance.

For Star, tears would not come. There was only a terrible realization of loss and grief and aloneness. Pa was gone, and she was alone. Pa was dead, and Lance had killed him as surely as if he had fired the charge into his brain. And he must pay for it; he must not achieve the goal that had inspired his heinous crime. Lance must never be master of Mystic Rose!

Once reached, the decision was irrevocable.

Star picked up the pistol from the bed, cocked it, and tucked it in the folds of her skirts. She crept out of the room and furtively moved down the hall. Her face was stark white, her features grimly composed and determined. He must not see or hear her until she was upon him, too late for him to escape or fire on her. It was him or her now. For her father's sake, for the sake of all the Lamonts, it must not be Lance!

Absorbed in her grave resolution, her desperate destiny, Star was unaware that the right wing of the manor was afire. One of the rebels had smashed a window and tossed a pine-knot torch into the drawing room. Draperies and carpet were aflame, and clouds of smoke rolled through the maze of hallways.

Cool and deliberate now, intent on a single purpose, Star made her way through the passages leading to the north turret. Entering a guest bedroom adjoining the tower, she paused and listened. She realized that Obah was in the tower with Lance, apparently having scaled the vines on the walls. Lance was shouting angrily at Obah. Star could understand his furious admonishment —and it definitely established Lance as the instigator of the rebellion.

"You crazy gorilla! Didn't I tell you I wanted no fires and no terrorism? You'll destroy everything!"

"Watch your mouth, white man! You is talkin' to Obah, son of Tomba!"

"Son of a bitch!" Lance swore hotly. "You're running amuck! Get those men under control! Put out those fires, or I'll beat you within an inch of your life!"

"You ain't beatin' nobody no more," Obah warned.

"Get out of here, you black bastard!" Lance commanded. "You are not to challenge my orders—you are to obey me! I think you finished off the master. Now get Mauma and Dink and the other one—you know *who*! Did you hear me, Obah?"

"I heard you, white man."

"Then do as you're told! What're you waiting for? Stop looking at me like that, you painted ghoul! Stand away from me now, Obah. Don't come near me! Touch me, and I'll kill you. I'll—"

There was a metallic clatter, the sound of a musket falling on stone, and a scuffling of feet. Violent profanities spewed from Lance's throat, scorching Star's ears. Then came a sputtering, choking guttural sound followed by a heavy scuffling thud, and sudden silence.

Star cracked open the door and peeped in. Lance was sprawled on the stone floor, eyes and tongue popped out of his livid face. Obah stood over him, panting, one bare black foot resting on his trophy, gloating in triumph.

Although Star clamped a hand over her mouth, her gasp attracted Obah's attention. She closed the door swiftly and stood still, stranded in confusion. Dealing with her stepbrother was one thing, with a rebelling slave quite another. While she hesitated, wondering what to do, the door opened, and Obah confronted her.

The instinct of self-preservation guided Star. She retreated a few paces, whipped out the pistol from her skirts, and fired. A wild shot, and there was no time to reload even if she had thought to bring a second charge with her. Obah advanced like an ebony colossus, his jet eyes glittering in the weird painted mask of his face.

His intentions were obvious even to Star's frenzied mind. Rape. Rape and murder. But first, rape.

She flung the weapon at him, missing again, as she screamed in terror and turned to run. In one swift lunge Obah seized her and brought her screaming to the floor. Star struggled against him with the strength born of fear and panic, kicking and biting and scratching, but her efforts were futile.

"You a wild woman," he said, relishing the prospect. "You make much fun for Obah."

"You'll be hanged for this, Obah! Hanged by the neck until you're dead, your corpse left for the buzzards to pick, and your bones left to rattle in the wind!"

He grinned complacently. "First they got to catch me."

"They will, Obah! A posse will hunt you down with

bloodhounds and–" She was stalling with conversation, hoping that someone in the house had heard her cries and would come to her rescue.

"I been in the Santee swamp for months now, and they ain't caught me yet."

"You never raped a white woman before, either! Oh, they'll find you, Obah, no matter how long it takes, and then–"

A roar, not thunder, burst in her ears. A flash, not flame or lightning, illuminated the room. Obah's taunting predictions ceased. With a low animallike groan, he pitched away from his intended victim onto the floor. Blood spurted from a ragged hole in his back, staining the carpet. He heaved and twisted a few moments in moribund convulsions, then finally lay still, eyes and mouth gaping.

Star looked up. Her stepmother stood in the doorway, a smoking musket in her hands. "Filthy beast," she muttered. "Did he succeed?"

Only the stimulant of shattered nerves kept Star from fainting. "No. He delayed too long tormenting me. Oh, Aunt Emily–thank you, thank you! You saved my life."

"I heard your screams, but at first I couldn't make out where you were. I was afraid I might not reach you in time."

Emily removed the heavy green counterpane from the bed and covered the grotesque naked corpse. Then she knelt beside Star, examining the bruises and bloody scratches on her exposed flesh.

"The injuries are superficial, Star. They won't leave physical scars." Emily blotted the wounds with her kerchief, her touch tender and maternal. "Mentally–well, you will just have to try to forget this dreadful experience, Star. Put it completely out of your mind."

The whole night had been strange and weird and unreal to Star. Only the solid presence of her stepmother seemed real, rational, and reassuring, and she was passionately grateful for this one firm pillar, this one impervious and impregnable rampart in a world gone suddenly mad and violent. But then she remembered her father, and her sense of security vanished in sorrow and dismay.

"Aunt Emily, pa is dead."

Emily nodded solemnly. "I know, dear. Cicero and Dink are with him now."

Star hesitated, reluctant to give more bad news. "Lance is dead, too. On the tower outside. Obah killed him."

Pain and grief contorted Emily's face. She rose and went silently to her son. When she returned, minutes later, her taut features were smooth again, though traces of tears remained in her eyes. She took several clean sheets from the linen cabinet. "God give him rest and peace," she said.

Star sat up, clutching the remnants of her gown to her bare and aching breasts. Exhausted and still a little weak and dazed, she began to cough without realizing what was irritating her lungs. Then she saw the gray spectral plumes of smoke, and her heart leaped in horror.

"Aunt Emily, the house is on fire!"

"The right wing," Emily said. "Mr. Jones and the servants are fighting it, but I fear Mystic Rose cannot be saved in this high wind. Only God can help us now, Star."

As she spoke, several large raindrops splashed against the diamond-paned windows. Emily folded her hands in prayer. Star remained on the floor, weeping softly, unable to rise, unable to think of anything but the sound of the blessed rain on the roof.

Chapter 27

A DARK GUTTED SHELL was all that remained of the right wing of the manor. The once glistening diamond-paned windows were cracked or popped out, their molten lead veins solidified now into great dripping tears. Hardly a piece of furniture or decoration had escaped unharmed. The fine old tapestries and paintings, the luxurious carpets and draperies, the exquisite objets d'art were sodden ashes or heaps of unrecognizable debris. This wing had housed the drawing and dining rooms, the ballroom, the parlor and the library. Irreplaceable heirlooms of silver, gold, bronze, porcelain, crystal, ivory, and jade, as well as most of the family portraits, including Angelique's, were destroyed or damaged beyond repair.

How I hated that portrait, Emily thought, coming upon the charred gilt frame. Now it's gone, and he has gone to her, and I'm alone with their daughter. The ways of the Lord are indeed strange and incomprehensible....

Curled black crisps of paper and leather, once rare

old books and manuscripts, which Emily had prized above all other possessions of Mystic Rose, littered the smoked cavern of the library. Poking through them, she found a few good volumes, including some of John's favorite works.

As if by some miracle the St. James Bible, containing the vital statistics of the family back to the first Lord Lamont, had been spared. Its beautiful, gold-stamped moroccan binding and illuminated vellum pages were still intact. It must be preserved for Star. Let her make the entry of her father's passing, the last of her noble ancestors.

The fire had consumed over half of the slave cabins, many outbuildings, a wood silo of grain, two smokehouses, and a warehouse of milled rice. Charred boards and rafters stuck up at crazy angles, still wet with rain. A crew of slaves, silent and grim-faced, carried their murdered brethren to the carpenter shed, once again an emergency morgue, to await burial and then searched the debris for additional victims. And upon this ghastly scene of death and desolation, the sun shone brightly and the autumn skies, rent with fury a few dark hours ago, were blue and placid, never more peaceful.

If Obah's bullet had not killed her father, Star knew the sight of Mystic Rose as it was now would have. Lord Lamont's castle in ruins, the ancestral plantation devastated. Raided by Indians and menaced by pirates, battered by hurricanes and floods, threatened by war and plague, it was finally destroyed in rebellion. She was almost glad he was not there to see it.

"I can't understand it," Emily said, sadly viewing the rubble with Star. "Why did they rebel against John? He was so good to them, and they seemed to love him so much."

"Perhaps," Star sighed, "they loved freedom more."

She lacked the heart to tell Emily about her son's role in the tragedy. Lance was dead; she was at last free of his threat and torment. There was nothing to be gained by adding his sins to his mother's sorrows. But perhaps

Emily knew; she had an uncanny wisdom and perception.

"I've sent Dink for Lorna and Grant," she said. "And Bobo has gone to inform the neighbors. We'll have help soon, Star."

"We needed help last night, Aunt Emily. It's strange that no one saw the flames or heard the shots."

"Not so strange," Emily reasoned. "Many a country place burns late at night without attracting attention, and the storm probably muffled the shots. Then, too, there was the militia ball in town, which presumably most of our neighbors attended. This was well planned, Star. It would almost seem that Obah had allies and assistance."

"It would seem so," Star agreed, but Emily did not pursue the supposition.

Suddenly Star hated the Low Country. It was such a wild, primitive land of jungles and swamps and forests. She hated the torrential rains that swelled the muddy rivers, the furious gales that blew in unexpectedly from the sea, and the swarms of insects that made it necessary to sleep in net cocoons in summer. In her grief and despair, she even hated the plantation; the fevers it bred had taken her mother, and the rebellion it fermented had killed her father. And the sun dared to shine down on her now, mocking her, gleaming on the black skeleton of the house, the scorched gardens, and swelling corpses!

Irrational anger filled her, but she did not vent it. Maybe the plague and drought and rebellion were warnings to show God's displeasure with slavery. Was it the great evil some people believed? Her father seemed to her the very embodiment of goodness and light, yet undeniably his empire was built upon what the evangelists of abolition, including Troy Stewart, called "the dehumanization of man, the trafficking in human flesh as if it were any other commodity on the market." Did the fact that a master treated his slaves with tolerance and mercy justify their enslavement?

She remembered a picture she had once seen of a portly

king in magnificent raiment whose golden throne was supported on the hunched backs of many black men. Was pa like that? Oh, no! Quickly she brushed the disturbing thought away; it was disloyal to her father, the finest man who had ever lived, a desecration of his sacred memory. But even if true, why should God punish only Mystic Rose and the Lamonts? Was this merely a preview, a prelude of things to come? Worse horrors and terrors at some future time?

"Aunt Emily, I'm going to free all the slaves that didn't run away," she said decisively.

"Not many ran away, Star."

"But those who did wanted freedom, and I'll not give their names and descriptions to the law. I don't want them hunted down with hounds and brought back in chains to be hanged on the public square. Nor will I hold the others in bondage."

"How will we work the land if you free the slaves?"

"Why bother? Let it return to wilderness. It's a wild land. Let it remain that way."

"Do you think your father would want that, Star?"

"No. Pa would want me to stay here and fight, hold the land, and uphold the Lamont tradition. But not if it made me unhappy. Pa wouldn't want me to be unhappy. And I could never be happy at Mystic Rose now or ever again."

"My dear, you haven't been happy here for many years. Not since your mother died, and I came."

Shame averted Star's face. "I—I don't feel that way any more, Aunt Emily. I guess maybe I've finally grown up. We've shared so much together—why, I owe my life to you! I'd like to think of us as friends."

"I'd like to think of us that way, too," Emily said, a faint smile penetrating her grief. "And if you'll accept a little friendly advice now, Star, don't make any rash decisions regarding the plantation and your future. You need time to think and plan. And there are more urgent matters at hand. So many burials. Oh, Star! I thought after the plague we were through with funerals for awhile."

Star's eyes brimmed. "Aunt Emily, if you don't mind, I'd like for pa to rest beside my mother."

"That was his will and wish, child." Her voice caught, but she clung to her dignity. "I don't think it would matter to Lance where he lies, so I've chosen a place next to a copse of pines–"

Star merely nodded, unable to muster any sentiment or regrets for Lance, though she understood his mother's bereavement.

"Obah and Tawn and the other rebels must be interred in a separate plot apart from the loyal slaves," Emily said. "What is it, Star? You seem surprised. Don't you agree?"

"Yes, of course. I just didn't know Tawn was dead. I thought she had run away."

"She committed suicide, apparently. I found her in her cabin this morning, an empty vial beside her. She must have swallowed a poison of her own concoction, probably in distress over her loss of Obah." Emily paused, reluctant to impart even more astonishing information. "I found something else in her quarters, Star. Something weird and terrible."

"What?"

"A group of tiny figures, one for every member of the family. Perfect replicas modeled in beeswax, immediately recognizable. Horrifying. I destroyed them."

Over two hundred friends and neighbors attended the funeral of John Lamont. His casket was mahogany, lined in gray satin, with heavy silver handles. His factor had purchased it in Charleston and sent it out by hearse. Emily and Cicero had bathed and dressed the corpse, and the rector of Goose Creek Church conducted the services. The slaves, many of whom had also kept the wake, lined the lane to the cemetery, forming an honor guard as the black hearse drawn by six coal black horses with black head plumes rumbled past, followed on foot by the immediate members of the family.

The pallbearers bore the coffin to the grave and placed it on the leather straps that would lower it into the ground. Standing by the burial site, Star was supported by Grant and Mauma, who kept smelling salts handy. Those of the cortege who could, crowded into the cemetery. The rest stood outside the iron fence, and many wept unrestrainedly. But most disturbing to Star were the mournful tears of poor old Cicero in his black suit and spotless white gloves and the low poignant spirituals of the other loyal slaves.

After the eulogy and Episcopal Prayers for the Dead, the pastor shoveled the first spadeful of sod onto the casket, then passed the spade to Emily, and finally to Star. It was impossible to read the mind behind the solemnly serene face of the widow as she performed the customary ritual. Star's hand trembled as she scooped up the damp earth, and the clods striking the mahogany were hammer blows to her heart. But her eyes remained comparatively dry, for she had spent her tears in Mauma's arms, on Mauma's broad soft bosom, where she had been comforted since childhood. Her floral tribute was a single white bloom from the mystic rose. Tomorrow, she would have Dink plant a cutting on the grave and discuss the tombstone with Mr. Grady. But all she could think of now was that her parents were together again and she was alone.

Throughout the funeral rites, Emily worried that there would not be sufficient food for a proper repast. People ate as heartily at funerals as at weddings and christenings, and Emily did not want them criticizing her hospitality on this final occasion, even if the household must starve for the rest of the week. She did not expect to see many of them again. They were John's friends, John's neighbors, and John was gone. They had never cared much for the second Mrs. Lamont and would probably care even less for her now.

God forgive her for these bitter and selfish thoughts. The wounds should be healed after all these years, the poisons dried up, the pain negligible. Why did it still hurt?

She glanced toward the copse of pines and the new raw mound where her son had been quietly interred only a few hours previously. Lord have mercy on his soul.

In accordance with tradition, the female members of the deceased's family retired to an upstairs parlor in the undamaged left wing of the house, such privacy and seclusion not to be breached by a man except in emergency. The butler and other servants, bent low in grief for the master, prepared a buffet for the guests, supplemented by hams, sausages, cheeses, cakes, and pies which some mourners had thoughtfully brought along with their bouquets of autumn flowers.

Lorna, swathed in elegant mourning for her brother and stepfather, made an incredible gesture. "Mother, you can't possibly go on living here in this dilapidated place! It's unthinkable now. You and Star must come to Charleston until the house is repaired. You can stay with us. We have plenty of room."

Star, wearing one of her old gowns which had been hastily dipped in a black dye bath and a black chiffon veil, was speechless. How dearly that invitation must have cost Lorna! She admired her generosity, though she had no wish to accept it. She was stunned to hear Emily accepting for her.

"That's very kind of you, daughter. And if it won't inconvenience you and Grant, I think Star would benefit greatly by the change. This has been a dreadful ordeal for her. She and Mauma will arrive shortly."

Lorna gasped, as astonished as if her mother had suddenly stuck a knife in her back. Her face, above the black silk of her gown, was chalk white. "That's fine, mother—but the invitation included you, too. Aren't *you* coming?"

To keep an eye on me? Star thought. Oh, Lorna! That's not necessary. Your mother and I are no longer enemies. Haven't you noticed? We're friends!

"Not now, dear. Later, perhaps. There are many things to be done here. Mr. Jones and the slaves and I will manage somehow, until a decision satisfactory to all concerned can be reached. Mr. Grady has the will, of course."

"Oh, the will." Lorna shrugged deprecatingly, secure in her abundant wealth. "You can have my share, mother. It's really a pity, though—"

"What's a pity?" asked Emily, peering through her long black veil.

"Poor Lance. He did so long to be master of Mystic Rose. There was nothing on earth he wanted more."

" 'Man proposes,' " Emily quoted, " 'God disposes.' "

A few days later, as Star was preparing for her stay in Charleston, packing a trunk and some valises (most of her wardrobe had been altered and dyed suitable for mourning), Emily knocked and entered her rooms, a velvet jewel case in her hands. She opened it to reveal a set of gold-and-pearl studs and cuff links, a fine familiar gold watch with chain, and a large diamond stickpin among some other masculine jewelry.

"Take these, Star, in memory of your father."

"Thank you, Aunt Emily. I want them, of course. But I don't need anything tangible to remind me of pa. I could never forget him."

"Nor I," said Emily. "He was a fine man."

Star tucked the case in a leather portmanteau. Her father's precious possessions were mementos to be treasured with her mother's jewels. Then she continued her preparations.

"Aunt Emily, do you think it's wise, my going to Charleston?" Mauma had debated that issue with her several times, contending that it was "just askin' for trouble."

"You mean because of Grant and your former relationship? You told me the other day that you thought you had finally grown up, Star. Well, I think you have, too. The loss of your first love was the initial step along the way. The war and plague and rebellion were all contributing factors to your maturity, and your father's death completed it. Yes, I believe it's safe for you to go to Charleston now, dear. Otherwise, I would not have suggested it. It may provide a challenge to your maturity, but you've experienced others and come through. The city will be good for you. A change of scenery and social aspects are always beneficial in bereavement and have been prescribed in cases of melancholy and doldrums since Hippocrates advised some of his patients to go to the Aegean islands. But you must not seclude yourself in Charleston and brood, Star. Seclusion and meditation are expected of a widow, who would be a scandal and disgrace if she did not conform. But you're single and too young for such drastic mourning. Your friends will comfort you and perhaps help you to decide the course of your future. Then, too, you can watch the sea—"

For the ship that will never come, Star thought wistfully.

"Oh, Aunt Emily! Everything is gone. There's nothing left for me now. Nothing worth living for!"

"Have you ever read any of the philosophers, Star?"

"Only Voltaire and Rousseau," Star admitted, feeling abysmally ignorant. "Miss Christian forced us to read some of their didactics in the original language, not to improve our minds but to polish our French. I've forgotten most of it. Too profound. It wasn't very interesting."

Emily smiled indulgently. "Your father was fond of Epictetus. A lesser philosopher than Plato or Aristotle or Aurelius, to be sure, but often a more practical one. In the first book of his *Discourses,* he writes, 'To a reasonable creature, that alone is unbearable which is unreasonable, but everything reasonable may be borne.' "

"And is this reasonable, Aunt Emily? These horrors that have befallen us? This death and destruction?"

"It's hard to understand and accept, isn't it? But do you know how the Spartans tested the fortitude of their children, Star? They had them publicly whipped at the Altar of Artemis, often so severely that the frail ones died. And those that so perished were not long mourned, for the parents believed they would have been too weak to endure and long survive the trials and tribulations of life. This is a form of public whipping for you, my dear. For both of us. I hope and trust we shall not prove too frail of character and spirit to endure and survive."

So Emily had sustained her in another crisis of her young life and given her the faith and courage to continue when she began to falter and when struggle seemed futile. She was a great lady, Star mused. A fine person. But more than that, and perhaps infinitely more important, Emily was a genuine human being.

Chapter 28

DESPITE EMILY'S confidence and encouragement, it was with hesitancy and misgivings that Star went as a guest to the house of which she had once expected to be mistress. The dream was long gone but not entirely forgotten, and she feared that close contact with Grant might revive it. Emily was so wise in so many ways, but Star hoped that her wisdom and judgment had not erred and perhaps boomeranged in this instance.

The Russell town house, one of a row of distinguished pre-Revolutionary residences on the Battery, was perhaps the showplace of them all. At the time of its construction, in 1750, the Georgian influence prevailed in the architecture of the Carolina provinces, and it was still more handsome and elegantly graceful than anything the new century had thus far produced with the exception of the Greek revival. The cost, a fabulous twelve thousand pounds sterling, and the Italian marble fireplaces, Venetian crystal chandeliers and mirrors, Dresden china doorknobs, Oriental carpets, and exquisite English and French furniture, had created envy in some less prosperous Charlestonians.

Star had always admired the lovely mansion. The pale buff brick walls were so much more cheerful than the mildewed gray stone of Mystic Rose, and the uncluttered windows admitted more light than the leaded panes of the manor. She loved the simple classic lines free of gables and turrets and cupolas, the Ionic pillars supporting the triple piazza, the pink tile roof without gargoyles, and the formal front courtyard with its shirred boxwoods and tall palmettos standing sentinel toward the sea. The mansion had beauty and symmetry and stateliness, but it was not Mystic Rose, and she was not there a week before she was homesick.

Lorna assigned her a commodious bedchamber with attached sitting room on the second floor. The paneled walls were painted a bright jonquil yellow, and robin's-egg blue curtains hung at the corniced windows. The Sheraton furniture was delicate and highly polished.

Star's rooms commanded a broad view of the bay and harbor areas. When company was not present, Star voluntarily immured herself there, against Emily's advice. A telescope and a pair of binoculars were always handy, and only Mauma knew how often she used them. In any attack from the sea, the Battery would be the most likely target, but this possibility did not concern Star as much as it once had. And it was not for battleships that she watched and waited.

But Charleston, as Emily had predicted, was a welcome change for her. Everyone was kind, thoughtful, and solicitous. Afternoon callers were frequent in the Russell parlor. It was obvious that some of the female visitors, familiar with the circumstances of Lorna's marriage, were surprised to find her husband's former sweetheart in residence. But though they might wonder and speculate among themselves, they were tactful and gracious enough in the ladies' presence.

Star, sedate in her dark simple gowns, munched cakes, sipped tea, and tried not to weep when her father's name and attributes were mentioned. But there were no laments or tributes for Lance, and Star knew that Lorna felt keenly this deliberate slighting of her late brother.

"What are your plans now?" the visitors inquired repeatedly of Star, curiosity rivaling interest and sympathy.

Star replied truthfully, "I don't know. I haven't decided yet. It's too soon—"

"Well, the rebellion at Mystic Rose certainly put the Low Country on its toes! The curfew laws had been relaxed somewhat, you know. But they're being rigidly enforced now, and all gatherings of four or more blacks are prohibited. Naturally, the planters are taking extra precautions, too. My dear, you really should offer a reward for the capture of the culprits. How else will you ever get them back?"

Star's answer was always somewhat astonishing and disconcerting to the slaveholders. "There were only eight runaways, and I don't want them back."

"Oh, but you mustn't take that attitude! If they're not caught and punished, others might be encouraged in the same direction. Mercy! We have worries and troubles enough with the British virtually at our throats—"

In addition to the constant threat of invasion and defeat, the war had imposed some hardships, restrictions and many discomforts on once complacent Charleston. The merchants, and hence their customers, were definitely feeling the stringent blockade. Stocks were low, shelves depleted. The tremendous profit on imported goods, which had enabled them to build great mansions and establish an aristocracy of their own, was now cut off and was hampering business to the point of paralysis. A privateer, managing to capture a commercial cargo of either luxuries or necessities and get his prize safely to port, could command his own price privately or reap a fortune in public auction. Some stores and shops had already failed, and others were teetering on bankruptcy. Profiteering had become a lucrative enterprise for the few merchants with hoarded stocks and flexible scruples, and underground contraband markets flourished. Competition was fierce, for agents and representatives from northern cities waited in southern ports—primarily Charleston, Savannah, and Hampton Roads—to bid on whatever merchandise or material arrived.

Inevitably the financial doldrums of the city spread to the country, and the planters and farmers suffered. Fine English agricultural tools were lacking. Wagon trains brought down shipments from New England factories, but they were never quite adequate nor as sturdy as those from Britain. And since the planter must depend largely on foreign trade to buy his products, the blockade also increased his woes. The warehouses and docks were loaded with rice, cotton, grain, tobacco, lumber, and turpentine, but there was only an occasional vessel to ship them, with no guarantee that the goods would reach their destination. The few ships which left harbor generally did so under cover of darkness or fog, and some ran aground or sank within sight of the shore. America had depended for too long on foreign markets and manufacturers and merchant fleets. Perhaps the war would teach her to be more self-reliant and inventive, to employ her own ingenuity and resources to a greater extent, and to form her own independent economy.

Already the crisis was opening up new territories. Pioneers, not content to sit in the East and wait for economic strangulation, cast hopeful eyes toward the unexplored western frontiers beyond the Missouri and Mississippi rivers. Caravans of latter-day Pilgrims in covered wagons called prairie schooners trailed across the Appalachian, Allegheny, and Cumberland mountains toward the great new vistas first glimpsed by Lewis and Clark.

The news that trickled across the Atlantic from Belgium, where the peace commissioners continued to wrangle over a treaty without even a temporary truce, was hardly reassuring. Secretary Albert Gallatin and Representative Henry Clay, heading the United States delegation, were accomplishing nothing because of Gallatin's timidity and Clay's arrogance.

"Mr. Clay is trying to sue for peace the way he plays

at brag," Grant said, tossing the *Courier* aside in disgust.

Business, military maneuvers, and visiting the family plantations for which he acted as attorney and sometimes factor, occupied much of Grant's time, but he and Star met almost every evening at the supper table and later in the parlor. Star made no effort to avoid him, and it was not necessary, for Lorna was never far away. And while her surveillance amused her guest, not so her husband.

Lorna glanced up from the novel she was reading. "What's brag?"

"A kind of poker game with bluffing the main strategy. I understand Clay, like most Kentuckians, excels at it. Trouble is, we have little left to bluff on. And we'll have even less if the Hartford Convention succeeds in its aim. The South can't possibly stand alone if the eastern states secede and form the New England Republic, as they threaten. Britain is undoubtedly aware of our shaky union–we need expect no quarter at Ghent. Unconditional surrender may well be our fate. If so, we have the Yankee traitors to thank!"

"And whom do we thank for bringing us to these straits?" his wife rejoined shortly. "The honorable Messrs. Clay, Calhoun, Cheves, and Williams! Southerners all, and except for Clay, native sons of your beloved South Carolina! Weren't the war hawks in cabal to force war with England, and didn't Mr. Calhoun himself write the bill declaring it? They bragged us into this mess. Now let them bluff us out of it!"

Lorna's knowledge of politics was unseemly in a woman, and she read far too much on the subject; worse still, she comprehended and commented on essentially masculine matters, flaunting her erudition and astuteness, often embarrassing her husband before company.

"You forget, madam, that the New England merchants and ship owners were the original ramrods, demanding federal protection of their commerce and seamen. But now that their vessels are bottled up in harbor or sinking in the ocean, and their ports are idle ghost towns, they want to jump off like rats from a doomed ship. Equally deplorable and treacherous, if not downright treasonable, some of the Judases are engaged in illicit trade with Canada. British army purveyors pay in cash, and your mercenary Yankee would sell his soul to the devil for thirty pounds sterling!"

"I doubt not that a few English sovereigns also lie in your southern banks and tills," Lorna countered, striving to maintain her composure before Star, although the regional differences and conflicts between her and Grant could never be effectively resolved or suppressed. "Despite the blockade, many a cargo of cotton and rice and tobacco is finding its way to British markets."

"Not from Avalon or Edisto!" Grant declared hotly. "Pa would let our crops rot in the fields and warehouses before selling them to England."

Lorna clucked her tongue. "My, my! Such vehemence from the grandson of a Knight of the Garter. Can it be you Charlestonians are not so proud of your English ancestry any more? I never thought I'd live to see the day."

It was like poking a hornet's nest, and Lorna soon felt his angry sting. "In case you've forgotten your history, ma'am, the Revolution severed our ties with Great Britain."

"The political ties, dear. But blood is thicker than politics, and it has taken two bloodlettings at the British sword to convince some of us that we are now Americans. Ah, but I think we might pursue a more pleasant subject for Star's sake. She has never indulged much in such weighty conversation."

"Thank God," Grant muttered. "I only wish you'd learn your proper place and contain your thoughts and tongue before our guests. Don't ever barge into the library again, as you did last evening, and interrupt the men in their discussions."

"Discussions? They were engaged mostly in drinking, smoking, and gambling!" She turned to Star. "Have you heard or read about that arrogant Virginian, John Randolph's conduct in Congress? How he usurps the floor and brings his vicious bitch pointers with him to bark down his opposition? And how Clay once ordered the sergeant-at-arms to eject the dogs because they were *female*? That should give you some idea of what southern gentlemen consider woman's place and the liberty they allow them under the guise of protection! What they really admire is not femininity and delicacy so much as feminine ignorance and subservience to the mighty male. And we pamper them with deference and acquiescence."

"I thought you wanted to pursue more pleasant topics," Grant interrupted. He smiled at their house guest, who was sitting uncomfortably in the tense atmosphere of this domestic quarrel.

"I'm sorry you had to witness this conflict of emotions, my dear. And at the risk of appearing officious, may I suggest that you're confining yourself entirely too much? Your father wouldn't want you to mourn him so tragically, Star. Surely a ride or drive in the country wouldn't be improper or a visit to friends? Perhaps even the theater—"

"It's only been two months, Grant."

"But you can't live like a recluse, Star."

"Let her grieve as she sees fit," Lorna said.

His dark scowl was a reprimand. "We're supposed to help lighten her bereavement, remember?"

"What about *my* bereavement? I lost my only brother, didn't I?"

"You still have your mother. Star has no one."

"She has us, mother and me."

"And you're such a comfort to her," he replied with a sarcastic lift of his brows. "You always have been."

"Please," Star implored, embarrassed. "Don't fret and fuss over me. If you do, I shall return home. I feel guilty, anyway, leaving the burden for Aunt Emily to bear alone."

"She's a strong woman," Grant said. "Much stronger than she looks."

"Yes, indeed!" Lorna proudly agreed. "Mother's a veritable tower of strength. One of the few completely self-sufficient persons I know. She'll manage."

Yes, Star thought. Emily would manage. Lorna would manage. Grant would manage. But what of herself? Never had her future seemed darker and more uncertain. Never had she felt more alone and lonely, less wanted and loved.

She occupied herself with useless fancywork and, driven by boredom and desperation, even spent some time in the library. One afternoon, as she was trying to read *Paradise Lost*, lured by the seemingly apropos title, the Maltese house cat jumped uninvited into her lap, settled herself comfortably and began to purr. Star smiled wryly, lifting a hand to stroke the soft blue gray fur. Cats and books, the old maid's friends and companions. If Troy could see her now, he would not think the prospect so ridiculous or unlikely.

Indeed, all signs pointed to that destiny. There were no unattached male callers at the Russell house. She had refused their attentions so often in the past that they had gradually ceased courting her favor. Some of her old beaus had gone off to the war, and a few had died in battles in places that were only names to her. Others were betrothed or married, many already fathers. The former belle of the Low Country would soon be known as the Lamont spinster. Once at the zenith of her life, she was now at the nadir.

Chapter 29

AS THE WEEKS PASSED Lorna relaxed her vigilance somewhat. She ceased hovering over her husband, marking his every word to Star, his every smile or glance at her. She appeared preoccupied, secure in some secret knowledge that piqued her stepsister's wonder and curiosity.

Star found herself alone with Grant on several occasions, as alone as two people could be with a staff of servants underfoot. One unusually mild January day they sat together in the rear court, while Lorna was shopping. Both of them were aware, however, of the kitchens and slave quarters that enclosed the garden on two sides and of the windows with their shutters open, so they kept their distance and spoke discreetly.

Grant gazed tenderly at Star, but there was anxiety in his eyes. "I'm worried about you," he said. "You're pale and lethargic. My dear, that's not like you. I remember when you had the buoyant energy of a young filly. I fear it's more than grief, Star, and that you're physically ill."

"Just an attack of vapors, Grant. And the rouge pot will cure the pallor."

"You never needed boxed bloom before," he frowned. "Those black weeds don't help much, either. Why don't you go into secondary mourning? Gray is bad enough on a young woman, but black is horrid."

"I'll consider it," Star mused, though by now the sober costumes had become a habit. "Aren't you home early from maneuvers, Grant?"

"Half of my troop didn't appear. There hasn't been a new enlistment in months, despite the efforts of the Drum and Fife Corps." A ponderous pause. "Star, men have lost faith in the cause. Enthusiasm for Madison's War, as it's now called, is waning. And the tragic irony is, I don't think we've ever been nearer to defeat and capitulation."

That stirred Star's apathy, and worry creased her brow. "Why, I thought we were on the road to victory? That's what people said when the British were repulsed at Plattsburgh last fall and the invasion of New York State failed."

"Those were rumors and false hopes built on General Brown's success at Chippewa and strengthened, for a time, by Commodore Macdonough's conquest of Lake Champlain. But the road to victory is often long and rough, and we made some wrong turns along the way. There's been a new development, far from the Canadian border."

Star caught her breath. "Not here, Grant? In South Carolina?"

"No, though I'll never understand why the invasion of Port Royal was so quickly abandoned. We had nothing to stop them. I guess they were interested in bigger stakes. Military headquarters received a dispatch this morning that a British armada landed on the Gulf Coast, at Lake Borgne, two weeks ago. Presumably they intend to join General Sir Edward Pakenham's forces near New Orleans, in a battle for Louisiana."

"Oh, Grant! How awful."

"Yes," he nodded gravely. "If New Orleans falls, we stand to lose the entire Mississippi Valley."

"What then?"

He shrugged. "Surrender, or fight to the last foot of soil and the last man."

"Have we no defenses at New Orleans?"

"General Andrew Jackson and a number of raw recruits—city clerks and frontiersmen turned soldier. I imagine most of the latter are great hunters when it comes to bears and Indians. But the British will likely use seasoned veterans from the Napoleonic Wars, and God knows how well or long our novices will stand against a charge of bayonets."

"Surely a Redcoat is no harder to kill than an Indian or a bear?"

"No. But Indians and bears are generally ambushed or shot at from cover, and the bears at least don't shoot back. Jackson had better have plenty of trees handy for his backwoodsmen, or else dig deep trenches."

Star sighed dismally. "I wonder if the British people are as weary of war as we?"

"Probably, though the fencing at Ghent would not indicate that their leaders are tired of it."

In the ensuing silence Star pondered a personal problem. "Grant, I've been wondering what to do about Mystic Rose? It's a liability now, a white—gray—elephant. Emily and Clem Jones and the loyal slaves are hanging on, and I admire their courage and tenacity, but it seems so futile. I've just about decided to sell it, which Mr. Grady says I can legally do as executrix. I'm sure Lorna would sign off, and I'd split the proceeds with Aunt Emily."

"My dear, who would buy a plantation of that size in these uncertain times? Money is tight, produce almost impossible to market, slaves at a premium, and the British lion is breathing down our necks. You'd have to sacrifice Mystic Rose, Star, virtually give it away. It's valuable land and will be even more so if we win the war.

The demand for our crops abroad will be insatiable, and we'll all be millionaires."

"*If* we win the war, Grant, which you've all but convinced me is already lost! But even if it isn't, I can't go back to Mystic Rose," she said, struggling against tears. "I can't return to fevers and slavery. I loved that land once, but it killed my mother and then my father—and I hate it now."

"You don't mean that, Star. That's grief and despair and bewilderment speaking. You'll feel differently in a few months, when some of the phantoms fade."

"No, Grant. Maybe, deep inside, I still love the place, for it's a part of me, and I do miss it terribly. But I couldn't be happy there now, and I wouldn't be a fit mistress for Mystic Rose or any other plantation. You see, I—I don't believe in slavery any more."

"Hush, Star! That's abolitionist heresy."

"I know, and I reckon I could be lynched for it, or tarred and feathered and ridden out of town on a rail. But I can't help it, Grant. It's how I feel. Oh, I used to defend and advocate the system as strongly as you. Someone once tried to convince me that it was morally wrong and evil and had no place in a democracy, and I put up a fierce argument. Now I know he was right."

"Was that officious crusader by any chance Captain Stewart?"

"Yes."

"You were taken in by a Yankee, Star. Your father must be turning in his grave."

"You forget why pa is in his grave," she said. "I've seen one slave rebellion, Grant, and never want to see another."

"I'm sorry, dear. I did forget. Please forgive me." He longed to take her hand, to press it tenderly. "You stay in your room so much, Star. What do you do there? Meditate? Recant? Pray? Plan?"

"A little of all four," she answered quietly. "I'm going away, Grant. When the war is over, if it ever is, I'm going away."

"Where?"

"I don't know. Just away."

"Alone?"

Her eyes met his levelly. "Alone."

"Forever?"

Star nodded, trying hard to concentrate on a patch of pansies blooming in the winter sun. Suddenly she remembered a garden party here and Grant kissing her under the rose arbor. It was their farewell kiss the night before she had sailed for Boston. How long ago it all seemed now, an eternity during which her girlhood hopes and dreams had died but could not rest in peace. The memory of their courtship still evoked restless fires she had not succeeded in banking. What would happen if he tried to stoke the embers again, if some night after Lorna swallowed the sleeping potion to which she occasionally resorted, he came to her room? Would she admit him to her bed and allow him to make love to her until consummation?

Her face, beautiful in repose, moved him to desire, remorse, and brooding jealousy. "Where will you go, Star? To every port and island in the world? Spend the rest of your life searching for a man you once had to fight off with a gun? My dear, nothing could be more foolish!"

"Nothing," she agreed perceptively, "except what you're thinking, Grant."

His expression mingled surprise and ruefulness. "I never realized my mind was so transparent, nor yours so clairvoyant. Yes, I was going to suggest that we go away together. I don't believe it's possible for either of us ever to be truly happy or content here or anywhere else apart from each other. I love you, Star. I always have and always will. Does that make me a fool?"

She hesitated, reluctant to rebuke him. "It makes you an adulterer, in essence if not fact. Do you honestly imagine we could be 'happy and content' living in adultery?"

"We'll get married."

"How? Bigamy? There's no divorce in this state!"

"I'll get an annulment."

"On what grounds?"

"What difference does it make? With enough money and influence, things can be arranged."

"Well, don't start any proceedings yet!"

"Why not? The sooner the better for us."

"But not for Lorna! Anyway, I'm not so sure I still care that much, Grant. Enough to defy religion and convention and my own conscience."

"That's noble nonsense, and you know it. Delude yourself if you can, Star, but don't try to delude me. I know exactly how you feel."

"Really? Then you know more than I do, Grant."

"You want me to convince you?"

They heard the carriage coming and the stable hands running out to meet it. Grant stood, scowling at the untimely arrival of his wife. "We'll discuss this again, Star. Meanwhile, think about it."

Late that night Star heard him pacing the hall outside her suite. Several times he paused at her door and once even turned the knob. She lay still, listening, uncertain about what she would do if he entered, or how she would react to the idea of an annulment once the act of love was a fait accompli. Something, either fear of discovery or rejection, spared her that dilemma, for he did not proceed.

But a few days later Lorna gave them another opportunity to be alone together, and this time Grant sought her in the parlor. Star glanced at him uneasily. "I was just going up to my room to write a letter to Aunt Emily," she said. "Will you excuse me, Grant?"

"No, and don't try to avoid me with pretexts, Star. You never were much good at fabrication or deceit. Have you thought about our discussion?"

"Some."

"And?"

Her eyes focused on a painting of him as a child, all dressed up in a fancy suit and posed like *The Blue Boy*. "It wouldn't work, Grant."

"Why not?"

"It just wouldn't, that's all."

"Give me at least one reason, Star."

"One? There are dozens, Grant!"

"Religious and legal? I told you, those impediments can be removed."

"And the moral impediments, too?"

"Oh, Christ! What has morality to do with it, Star? You want to live out your life in moral misery?"

"You don't understand," she said.

"No, I don't understand! You'll have to give me a better reason than that, Star."

"Do you think love conquers all, Grant, and makes wrong right? That it gives people a license to do anything and everything, no matter what, to be together?"

"Yes, I do, Star. Because it's the only thing in this goddamned world that makes living worthwhile! And you seem to forget that Lorna didn't consider your feelings or priority on me. Why should you consider hers now?"

"She couldn't jump my claim by herself, Grant. She had a willing partner."

He scowled in embarrassment. "I've explained that to you, Star. Haven't you ever made a mistake?"

She had, of course, and a far greater one than his, for his betrayal with Lorna could hardly equal her shooting of Troy.

"Unfortunately, yes. And this would be another one, Grant." She stabbed about for some plausible, acceptable rationale. "You see, it just isn't there any more—that feeling I used to get when you came to Mystic Rose on your white Arabian charger, and when you and the other knights paraded before the judges' stand on Tilting Day. I was so proud of you, Grant, and so desperately in love with you. You were my paragon, the epitome of everything I wanted in a man. I wanted you above all else on earth, and thought if I could have you, I'd never be sad or lonely or unhappy. And maybe I wouldn't have been. But things didn't work out that way. I didn't get you, and for a long time I thought I would die, Grant. I hoped I would die—"

"Star, don't! Please, darling, don't."

"It's all right, Grant. I don't feel that way any more. I can talk about it now. I want to, in fact." And as she spoke, she realized that she was not dissembling, after all, but telling the truth.

"I've changed, Grant. I think I realized it the other night when you were outside my room trying to decide whether or not to enter. I should have been tense and excited and eager with expectation, but I wasn't. I was wary and uncertain, and sure now that I would have rejected you. Maybe you sensed it, too, and that's what stopped you."

"No," he denied. "Love and respect for you stopped me, Star. I couldn't take you in adultery, no matter how much I wanted you. I determined to wake Lorna and discuss an annulment. But she was heavily sedated, and the next morning she had another of her emotional attacks and summoned her maid before I could broach the subject. I wasn't surprised, for that's how she defeats all my attempts to leave her. She has an uncanny sense of perception and timing. Somehow she perceived my intentions and prevented a confrontation."

"Thank God," Star breathed, "for I couldn't face her if you had succeeded, Grant. And I would expect her to order me out of her house."

"This is my house, Star. I'm master here."

"And your wife is just another domestic chattel?"

"Is that how she appears to you?" A sweep of his hand indicated the wealth and luxury of their surroundings. "With all this and a dozen slaves at her command?"

"I'm sure she'd rather have her husband's love and devotion than anything else," Star said. "Grant, it's over for us. I don't know exactly how or when it happened. Maybe the feeling just wore out or perished of starvation or vanished into thin air like my other illusions. I only know it's gone. I think pa knew it last summer, and I'm sure Aunt Emily did when she suggested that I recuperate in Charleston. Lorna knows it, too. That's why she's away shopping so much lately. She's not afraid of losing you any more, Grant. Not to me, anyway."

"Thank you," he said grimly, "for destroying my last hope and dream. Now I can be a confirmed realist, a sardonic cynic like your great sea captain."

"Don't be bitter, Grant, and don't hate Troy. You may be hating a dead man."

"Should I drink to his resurrection?" he muttered, going to the cellaret.

"Just don't hate him. Hatred is a terrible thing to harbor in one's body, Grant. It's a disease, a malignancy that can make you physically ill. I know. I despised my stepmother for years, resented her so much that I magnified all her faults and belittled her virtues. I was too blind and prejudiced and obstinate to realize that I was hurting myself as much as her. Ironically enough, she proved to be the best friend I ever had. She sustained me through the plague and saved my life in the rebellion. I shall always be grateful and beholden to her."

"A pretty sentiment, my dear, and a fine tribute to my mother-in-law. But I never expect to become Stewart's friend, nor save his life should the occasion arise."

"I only ask that you not take his life should the occasion arise," Star said tentatively.

Grant did not answer. He poured himself a brandy and stood staring into the glass, his broad shoulders slumped. Cynicism played across his somber features, but could not entirely conceal his boyish disappointment and disillusionment.

Chapter 30

LYING IN BED at night, Star could hear the surf pounding the new sea wall under construction. The old one of palmetto logs had been swept away in the violent hurricane of 1804. The engineers assured the citizens of Charleston that this new barrier, built of ballast rocks which had been accumulating from trading vessels over the years and cemented together with tenacious oyster-shell mortar, would withstand any assault from the sea. Out on the islands the yellow lanterns of the lighthouses gleamed and flickered like misty halos in the swirling fog. Star tried to imagine the *Venus* somewhere in that vast ocean, but she could not vest the vision with reality.

Early in the mornings she was awakened by the plaintive cries of the street vendors. In their own inimitable patois, Gullah fish peddlers chanted before dawn:

Ro-ro swimp
Ro-ro swimp
Ro-ro-ro-ro swimp
Come and git your ro-ro swimp!

Big crab
Lil crab
Best of all, the she-crab!

Tuttles, catfish, oysters, too!
They ain't none better in the soup and stew.

Porgy walk, porgy talk
Porgy eat with knife and fork!

Later the vegetable vendors appeared, and the white-turbaned cooks went out to make purchases for their owners, bargaining as shrewdly as if the money were their own, often so aggressively that mistress or master had to be be summoned to settle a boisterous argument or quarrel. And though Charleston was a city of gardens, enterprising old Negro women could always pick up a few extra pennies selling flowers and herbs.

Roses, gardenias, lilac, jasmine,
Help you get and keep your man, Ma'am!

Lavender, rosemary, and mignonette
Make you smell the sweetest yet!

The quaint lyrics and natural musical cadence of their voices were so delightful, Star did not mind the interruption of her sleep. She bought sachets of crushed petals and herbs to scent her lingerie, and a sweetbrier pomander for the armoire.

Now that spices from the Indies were cut off, or, if run through the blockade, priced like precious gems, herbs for seasoning were also hawked in the streets and grown in backyards. Star noticed that even extravagant Lorna had begun to guard and ration her hoard of coffee and tea and spices, and she was supplementing or substituting the traditional refreshment beverages with apple cider, persimmon beer made at Avalon, and scuppernong wine from Edisto. Similar ersatz brews and concoctions were served by other hostesses. Choice liquors were reserved for the male guests and most important occasions.

Star thought a great deal about Mystic Rose, much more than she wanted or had expected to, and looked forward to Emily's long, informative letters. But she tried to remember the plantation as it was before its destruction, and could not bring herself to return lest she spoil the memory. When she explained her reluctance in their correspondence, Emily replied that she understood and advised waiting awhile longer.

Star wanted to remember the good things, not the bad, and the happy experiences, not the sad. Her father riding his big gray gelding over the lush green fields, acres of rice waving golden in the sun, horses romping in the pastures. Wisteria tumbling over the split-rail fences and white honeysuckle covering the meadows. Dawn breaking through the pine woods, blazing sunsets on the horizon, chimney swallows skimming low in the twilight, Negro spirituals around an evening bonfire. Paradisiacal gardens and pools and majestic trees draped with long gray boas of moss. Barbecues, fish fries, balls, and loaded banquet tables. Holiday celebrations and neighborly visiting. Boating on the river and hay rides. Fox-hunts and tilting tournaments.

She wanted to forget the horrors and tragedies that tormented her now: the rows of cots in the infirmary and rows of new graves in the cemeteries; her father dead on the south tower; Obah tearing her clothes off; and the house in flames.

Let Emily have Mystic Rose, if she and Clem Jones could restore it to its former position. And perhaps they could. Emily spoke of planting cotton this spring, and Star noticed that she no longer referred to the overseer as Mr. Jones. He was Mr. Clem now, and sometimes just Clem. Of course, it was much too soon to conceive of a romance between them, but at least they were on friendly terms. And if the plantation could be saved and rebuilt, the combination of a rugged Piedmont mountaineer and a determined Yankee schoolmistress would accomplish the feat. Star wished them luck.

For herself, she longed only for the end of the war and a ship to take her to some distant land, a place which held no past for her, no memories or regrets. Where this haven might be, and what she would do if ever she found it, she had no idea. She had planned her life once, and the sky had fallen on her. Her girlish anticipations had ended in dire disappointments, and her great expectations in tremendous tragedies. If, as Emily counseled, accepting one's lot was the beginning of wisdom and maturity, then she was in the process of achieving sagacious adulthood. But how boring and depressing it could be, how much less fun than frivolous youth and carefree ignorance!

Once, long before, Star had heard her mother tell her father, "Jean, the ennui hangs heavy over our Mystic Rose! We must have a soiree, perhaps a bal masque, or go away on a journey. We must have some pleasure and play, cheri! This is good for Angelique, and then Angelique is good for Jean, n'est-ce pas?"

Star had wondered what she meant. Now she knew, as her father had known when he had smiled and nodded and taken his beautiful young wife upstairs to their suite.

The peace treaty had been signed at Ghent on Christmas Eve, 1814. But the slowness of communications delayed the news for weeks, even months in remote areas. Men died needlessly in the Battle of New Orleans in mid January, although General Jackson's astonishing victory was a much needed boost to the country's morale and unification. It kept New England in the Union and saved Madison's administration. And it proved, to the enemy and the world, the caliber of the American frontiersman.

In his buckskin breeches and coonskin cap, with his rifle and powder horn slung over his back and a wad of tobacco in his cheek, tall and spare of frame and tough of fiber, the frontiersman did not look like a soldier, but he fought like one. He could clear a wilderness, tree a bear, ambush an Indian, or meet a bayonet charge, making up in courage and endurance for what he lacked in skill and equipment. He had followed Andy Jackson through the Creek Indian Wars, on to drive the stubborn Spanish out of Pensacola, and joined him again at New Orleans to repulse the greatest British assault of the entire campaign. He had justified Old Hickory's faith in him, and he was covered with well-deserved glory. With such men as these to lead the way West, the future of America appeared bright and boundless.

The celebrations in Charleston were mild, however, compared to the blatant fanfare that had accompanied the declaration of war. The feeling now was one of gratitude and relief and prayerful thanksgiving. It was good to hear the church bells again and know they were ringing for joy and freedom. There was a military parade, noticeably lacking in pomp and circumstance, in which Grant rode at the head of his troop. Star and Lorna watched the parade, waving tiny flags as the unscarred regiments passed. But, still in mourning, they could not attend the victory ball at the armory that evening.

Accumulated business kept Grant in conference with his father's agents and traveling between Avalon and Edisto, and he was absent from home days at a time. Lorna, pale and frail, kept to her room and avoided callers. But she was pleasant enough to Star and even confided to her about her lassitude and digestive upsets.

Star listened sympathetically, wondering if her maladies were imaginary or affected. "You should see a doctor, Lorna."

"Yes," Lorna agreed, smiling faintly, "I should."

"Would you like me to go with you?"

"Not yet, I'll wait awhile and see what develops. No one takes my complaints seriously any more, not even my physician. I guess I've cried wolf too often."

She glanced down into the courtyard, where a high winter wind clacked the palmettos and scattered the golden fluff balls of the opopanax trees. "I'm glad you're here, Star. It's so lonely with Grant away so much."

"Business occupies him, Lorna. Now that the war is

over and the blockade lifted, he has much to do trying to find some transportation for the family crops."

"Yes, I know. The warehouses of Avalon and Edisto are bulging with rice and cotton. There should be a vast foreign market for these products now. Oh, Star! Mystic Rose will rise again. Mama will make it–I know she will!"

"I'm sure she will, Lorna."

"Then you will go back?" At Star's stricken look, Lorna bit her tongue and instantly apologized. "Forgive me, dear. That was tactless, and I didn't mean it the way it sounded."

Star touched her hand reassuringly. "Of course you didn't. But no, I shan't return to Mystic Rose. Nor shall I ensconce myself here as your permanent guest. I have other plans."

Lorna's relief was apparent. Try as she might, she still harbored some jealousy and resentment of her stepsister. For though she had managed to convince herself that Star no longer loved Grant, she was afraid the feeling was not mutual. Perhaps she had been foolish to give them opportunities to be alone together. Grant was a charming and persuasive man, and old flames could be rekindled as long as a tiny ember remained.

"Well," she said, "I don't want you to think you're not welcome here, dear. For certainly you are. But perhaps you would be happier somewhere else. Have you considered your relatives in Virginia?"

Star smiled. "Yes, and those in Georgia, too. Now you must rest, Lorna. Grant may return today, and you'll want to be fresh as a daisy for him and pretty as a picture."

Lorna gave a forlorn little sigh. Never in her life had she felt fresh as a daisy or pretty as a picture. But this malaise was different and more trying than any she had previously experienced. She simply must consult Doctor Draper. Oh, if only her symptoms and suspicions were true this time!

Chapter 31

By the end of March, Charleston was the busiest port on the Atlantic Coast, surpassing even New York and Boston. World trading vessels arrived daily, and the odors of paint and turpentine and boiling tar tainted the spring air as dry-docked craft made ready for sea. Closed shops reopened, and new ones were built. Mountains of cargo obscured the docks, and idle stevedores and beached sailors were once again gainfully employed. A great wave of prosperity began to roll over the country, and South Carolina was riding the crest of it.

The foundations of a lasting peace seemed strong and impregnable, and Star refused to let herself think of the empire her father might have built on them. The Lamont dynasty was gone now. There was no son to preserve the name, and soon it would be forgotten except in the history of the Carolina Low Country and the annals of the Mystic Rose plantation. Extinct.

She was sitting on the piazza of the Russell town house, lost in this maudlin mood, when Grant joined her. A dull book lay abandoned beside her rattan chair, and she had even tired, temporarily, of her favorite pastime of searching the sea with telescope and binoculars.

"A penny for your thoughts," he said, presenting her a bouquet of fresh wild violets.

Her poignant smile wrung his heart. "They're not worth a penny," she murmured, smelling the nosegay. "How sweet! Thank you, Grant."

"The woods are full of them, especially along the Cooper River Road. We used to pick them together, remember?"

Star nodded but declined to reminisce. "I hope you brought Lorna some, too?"

"Lorna doesn't care much for flowers," he said sheepishly. "She isn't here, anyway. Must be spring shopping. And you should be, too, for something bright and fluffy and frivolous. What were you so serious about a moment ago?"

"Oh, I was just thinking how busy the port is," she said. "Like old times again. Dutch and Portuguese traders put in today, and yesterday there was one all the way from China. An odd vessel, with eerie eyes painted on the bow."

"Chinese superstition," Grant explained, "to help guide it through the perilous seas."

"Have you found someone to ship for your father yet?"

"A couple of prospects, but nothing definite. They want exorbitant fees, and I reckon we'll just have to pay them. Our profits will still be enormous, and eventually we may establish our own commercial fleet, or at least invest in one." He seated himself on the banister, hooking his boots in the ornamental framework. "Are you still going away, Star?"

"I intend to book passage on the first respectable passenger ship that lands," she told him.

"No matter whither bound?'

"No matter."

"Suppose it's around the Horn?"

"That might be interesting. And exciting."

"And fatal," he added. "I wish there were some way to stop you, Star."

"There isn't, Grant."

"Has staying here been so difficult and unpleasant for you?"

"Not at all. You and Lorna have been wonderful to me, and I'm deeply grateful and appreciative."

His mouth gave a wry twist. "Of all the things I never wanted from you–gratitude and appreciation! If you persist in this folly, Star, at least draw enough from your father's estate to secure you financially."

"I've already discussed my finances with Mr. Grady, and I'll have enough for comfort."

"Will you write to me?"

"Not for awhile. I shan't write to anyone until I know where I am and what I want to do with my life."

"Don't you realize you're pursuing a myth, Star? A will-o'-the-wisp? There is no Mecca, no Nirvana, no El Dorado, nor any other such idealistic place of eternal peace, happiness, or abundance! Your quest will be as futile as Ponce de Leon's for the fountain of youth. All he found was Florida, a swampy wilderness of hostile Indians!"

"I'm not seeking and don't expect to find any kind of Utopia, Grant. Nor do I intend to cast myself away on some remote island nor become a nomad in the desert. I shall likely end up in England or on the Continent, in a civilized land among civilized people."

"I'll worry about you, Star. I'll go mad with worry."

"Nonsense! I won't be alone. Mauma will be with me."

"You're taking her as a slave? I thought you didn't believe in slavery any more?"

"I don't. And I offered Mauma her freedom, but she refused it. Says she wouldn't know what to do with it."

"There you are!" Grant exclaimed, quick to defend the system on any principle or pretext. "Mauma's like thousands of other slaves, Star. Offer them their freedom, and they wouldn't take it. They wouldn't even know what to do with it. They'd be like helpless children abandoned in the street and left to starve or beg or steal for a living."

"Some of them, perhaps," Star agreed. "Especially those too long in bondage to understand or imagine anything else. But the young and more ambitious ones would fare better and even prosper. We have freedmen right here in Charleston, you know. Some are useful citizens and gifted artisans. They could go into the professions if any school would admit them to study."

"I won't debate the issue with you, Star. Our viewpoints are too widely divergent now."

"In other matters, too," Star said, picking up the binoculars and focusing them on the sea. "How wonderful the flags look, still waving over the forts!"

"Is it the flags you watch so much, my dear?'

Star glanced at him. Lately his handsome face wore an almost perpetual frown, and he seemed morose and preoccupied. Irritable, too, and quick to anger. "No," she said frankly. "I watch the horizon, too."

"Then you had better look again. Unless my eyes deceive me, those are sails to the far right."

"Yes, I know. I saw them a moment ago."

"Can you make out the ship?"

"Not yet."

"May I use the glasses?"

"Of course. They're yours," she said, handing them to him.

Grant stood and adjusted the lenses to his sight. He gazed at the distant vessel for several minutes. He did not speak, but Star noticed a tenseness about his mouth and jaw, and then his features hardened as if carved in granite.

"The lines are familiar," he said at last, grimly. "I can determine the color. Deep blue. And the United States ensign on the mast."

"Grant–" Star's voice was a tremulous whisper–"it's not–it can't be–"

"It's either the *Venus* or her twin sister," he replied brusquely, thrusting the glasses at her. "Here. Look for yourself."

"I can't, she murmured, refusing to take the binoculars. "I can't look."

"Why not? It should be a momentous occasion for you. A great thrill. Your conquering hero returns. Your lover. Your grand amour. And you tremble at the thought of him! Is it happiness, Star, or fear?"

He watched her, his expression a curious mixture of hope and despair, both challenging and dreading her confirmation. Then, abruptly, he tossed the binoculars into her lap and left without another word.

Star hesitated a moment, then rose and ran after him, grabbing his arm as he reached the stairway landing. "Grant! Where are you going?"

"Three guesses, if you need that many."

"To wait for him?"

"To muster my seconds."

"Oh, you fool! You blind, stubborn fool! You'll be fighting for nothing."

"You call your honor nothing?"

"Troy did not harm me, Grant. On the contrary, it was I who harmed him! I tried to tell you that at Mystic Rose. I even offered to prove it to you–"

"So you did. And now that your champion stud will soon be available, is the offer still good?"

"You're insulting me, Grant. And if you challenge Captain Stewart now, it is you who will destroy my honor and reputation. And yours, too."

"Mine?"

"Yes, yours! and Lorna's. And your child's."

"Child's? What're you talking about, Star?"

"If you paid some attention to your wife, Grant, you'd know what I'm talking about. I–I think Lorna is pregnant." She had not intended to actually say it so bluntly, nor even at all, but this was no time for delicacy and reticence.

"Wishful thinking," he muttered. "Lorna always fancies herself pregnant."

"This time I don't believe it's mere fancy, Grant. According to what I've seen and what her maid tells

Mauma, her physical symptoms are quite real."

Although skeptical, Grant did not deny the possibility of such an event, thereby admitting that he had availed himself of his marital rights and privileges even while pursuing Star. "The servants know. You know—everyone but me, apparently. Why hasn't she told me?"

"Perhaps because she wants to be certain herself first, since she has been mistaken so often before. And perhaps —well, have you given her much opportunity to tell you?"

He stared into the dim stairwell. Above them the crystal pendants and cascades of the chandelier caught and reflected the light from the window. "I guess not."

"A child will make a big difference in your marriage, Grant. Wait and see."

"Sure," he said wryly. "Wait and see."

"I hope it's a boy. Men usually want the first one to be a son in their image, don't they?"

"I suppose so. I haven't thought much about it. I wonder where Lorna is now?"

As if in answer to his question, the front door opened in the hall directly below them, and Lorna entered. Her maid, Sybil, accompanied her. Lorna glanced up at her husband and stepsister on the landing, their strained and guilty expressions suggesting that she had interrupted either a quarrel or intimacy.

She smiled thinly. "Good afternoon."

"Where've you been?" Grant asked.

"She been to the doctor," Sybil announced proudly, fit to burst with her secret. "And the doctor say we goin' have a baby, Mist' Grant!"

A glance from her mistress silenced her. Sybil ducked into the dining room and out to the kitchen, eager to tell the other servants the incredible news that at long last Miss Lorna was in the family way.

Still in her cloak and bonnet, Lorna started up the stairs, proceeding slowly, as if unsure of herself. Grant met her halfway, demanding, "Is it true?"

"If you have a few minutes to spare—" She paused, her hand going to her head.

"What is it, Lorna? Are you ill?"

"Of course she's ill, you big oaf!" cried Star, impatient with his male insensitivity. "Grant, catch her! She's going to faint!"

Lorna's eyes rolled blankly, and her body reeled backward, but Grant prevented her fall.

"Get some smelling salts!" he shouted at no one in particular. "Bring some brandy! Send for the doctor!"

Lorna stirred, found herself in her husband's arms, and relaxed. "It's nothing," she murmured, her head on his shoulder. "I–well, I'm going to have a baby, that's all."

"That's all! You might have told me, Lorna. Or is it the fashion now for the husband to be the last to know?"

"I'm sorry, dear. I wanted to be sure myself, first. It will be sometime in June."

"That's wonderful, Lorna," Star said sincerely. "I'm so happy for you. Both of you," she added.

"Your stays are too tight," Grant admonished. "You've got yourself bound up like a mummy. You'll cripple the child! And what do you mean running around town by yourself? You want to swoon in the street?"

"I wasn't alone. Sybil was with me."

"Just the same–"

He carried her to their chambers, scolding her all the way. Lorna clung tightly to him. Star watched as Grant opened the door and closed it behind them. He seemed to have forgotten, temporarily at least, her presence.

"Congratulations, Mr. Russell," she murmured, then returned to the piazza.

The violets lay wilting on the floor where she had dropped them. The ship was in plain view now. It was the *Venus*, all right. With the glasses she could distinguish some members of the crew. Captain Stewart stood on the quarterdeck.

Suddenly Star began to shiver, first with joy and then with horror. Dear God! Was that an empty sleeve where his left arm should be?

Chapter 32

THE EMPTY SLEEVE of Captain Stewart's uniform tormented Star, for she could not determine if the jacket were just thrown casually over his shoulders, or if his left arm were actually missing. Anxiety and remorse so overwhelmed her she had to grasp a piazza pillar for support. How, even if he would let her, could she ever atone to him for such a loss?

I'll marry him, she decided magnanimously, and be his left arm for the rest of his life!

But suppose he didn't want her any more? It was difficult to convince her now subdued vanity that he had returned to Charleston because of her. The sea was his business, his livelihood. He must have come to deliver a cargo, not to visit her. Certainly not to propose to her again! No man of his pride and egotism would risk another such rebuff.

Then she conceived an idea reminiscent of her former audacity. She went inside and opened the little sandalwood writing box her father had given her when she had gone to the lyceum in Boston. Removing a fresh sheet of scented stationery, she dipped the long green quill into the alabaster inkwell.

Captain Troy Stewart
Merchantship *Venus*
Charleston Harbor

Dear Sir:
I wish to reserve passage for two on the *Venus*, regardless of destination. If you can accommodate us, please inform my traveling companion as to the fare and time of departure.

Cordially,
Star Lamont

She folded the terse note quickly lest she change her mind, slipped it into an envelope, addressed it in her small, neat script, and secured the flap with a blob of sealing wax. The next morning when Mauma came to assist her with her toilette, Star was already up and dressed.

"I want you to take this message to Captain Stewart and bring me his answer. It's a request for passage on his ship for both of us."

Mauma frowned dubiously. "Suppose he say no?"

"Don't argue with him. Just tell him I intend to leave Charleston either on the *Venus* or that Baltimore clipper that arrived this morning. And, Mauma. Be sure to notice his left arm."

"How come?"

"You know how come! It may be missing, or stiff. Just notice. And hurry back. We have lots of packing to do."

"You figure he goin' say yes?"

"I hope so, Mauma. But if not, at least I'll know why he returned, and then I'll seek other passage."

The two hours she waited for his reply, alternating between suspense and despair, seemed interminable to Star. But at last Mauma returned, puffing and grunting from her haste. Star rushed out into the courtyard to meet her, at once eager and fearful, demanding impatiently, "Well, what did he say?"

"Give a old woman time to catch her breath," Mauma said, replenishing her lungs. "Yessum, he goin' take us. He didn't want to, but he will."

"I told you not to argue with him!"

"I didn't arger with him, Miss Star. He just read the note, shake his head, and say, 'I's sorry, but I ain't bookin' no passengers this trip. Try the cap'n of that clipper yonder.' "

"Yes, and then what? Go on!"

"I say, 'Thankee, sir. That just what I'm aimin' to do. My mistress leavin' here if us got to row a dinghy!' Well, he let me get off his boat and walk 'most to the clipper before he send a man to fetch me back. 'I's reconsider,' he say. 'Tell your mistress I'll reserve two berths, as per her request. We sails Saturday if the wind serve, and the fare subject to negotion,' " Mauma finished. "Whatever that mean."

"Negotiation," Star corrected, thinking that *she* knew what it meant. "What's his next port? Is he crossing the Atlantic?"

"I reckon. He goin' take on supplies and a cargo and was bargainin' with chandlers, merchants, and factors."

Star was elated. Maybe this was the silver lining to all the dark clouds she had thought immutable!

"That's wonderful, Mauma. You handled it perfectly. But what about his—his arm?"

"Oh, he got 'em both! But the left one don't look so strong. Leastwise, he don't use it much; it just sort of hung there, like a sausage curin' in the smokehouse."

"Oh," Star murmured, the sun suddenly disappearing behind another black cloud. "Do you think it's paralyzed?"

"I don't know, Miss Star. I ain't no doctor."

"How does he look otherwise?"

"Healthy," Mauma said. "Brown as a roasted coffee bean, and they's a little snow round his temples. But he still 'bout the handsomest white man I ever seen, next to Mist' Grant."

"He didn't say he might call or anything, did he?" Star asked hopefully.

"No'm, he sure didn't. But he kind of grin crooked-like when I told him where us stayin', case he want to get a message to you. He say, 'That mighty convenient, livin' with the Russells, ain't it? Well, if I needs to contact your mistress, I send a messenger.' "

Star suppressed her disappointment. "All right, Mauma. Come inside now and start packing."

For once Star was grateful for the gossipy tongues of the servants, sparing her the ordeal of explanations to Lorna and Grant. Neither of them attempted to dissuade her. Grant's attitude suggested resignation, while Lorna's relief surpassed all her efforts to disguise it.

They drove Star and Mauma to the pier but declined to go aboard the *Venus*. Lorna kissed and hugged her for the first time in all the years they had been stepsisters.

"Bon voyage, dear," she said. "Write to us."

Star nodded, a sudden constriction in her throat, and returned the embrace and kiss with sincerity. "Thank you, Lorna. For everything."

Grant took her hand in a brief hard pressure, a parting as final as the end of a day and as irrevocable as the tide that would soon take her away from him. "Goodbye, Star. God bless and keep you." And to the slave, his voice hoarse, "Take good care of her, Mauma."

"You know I will, Mist' Grant," Mauma sniffed. "Ain't I always took care of her?"

That was all. They waved. The carriage rumbled off. Star watched it out of sight, the metallic echo of the iron-rimmed wheels and shod hoofs on the cobblestones growing fainter and sounding as sad to her as the "gone away" signal of the fox hunt horn or the "lights out" signal of a distant bugle.

The gangplank of the *Venus* formed Star's last tangible link with Charleston and the Low Country, with her friends and her girlhood. Once she crossed it, she would leave twenty-one years of her life behind and hopefully her unhappy memories. She thought she understood now how a pilgrim must feel embarking for a strange new land: nostalgic, regretful, reluctant, uncertain, and perhaps frightened. Yet hopeful; most of all, hopeful. For of all the attributes that sustained the human spirit, hope was surely the main one. Without it, no voyager could set sail for another country, and no pioneer wagon could travel the unchartered and perilous trails West.

She smiled at her philosophy, wondering if she were mellowing or just melancholy. After some moments of wistful hesitation, she turned and mounted the gangway, delicately lifting her black skirts. Mauma followed, carrying a small leather coffer which had not been sent ahead with the trunks.

Although not anticipating a warm welcome, Star was unprepared for such a cold one. A stranger would have been more cordially received. Of course, he was busy with last hour sailing preparations, checking the manifest and the provisions, but he need not have ignored her so elaborately or pointedly. He might have shown some courtesy and awareness, at least before his men. But he only tipped his cap and ordered one of the crew, acting as steward, to escort the passengers to their cabins.

Star noticed some new faces among the sailors and was relieved not to encounter the insolent grin of Finch among the familiar ones. But even Neptune, the ship's mascot, was not present to greet her. The old parrot, glib with the salty vernacular of his tutors, was kept aft when ladies were aboard, lest a slip of his raucous tongue embarrass them.

Expecting no more than cleanliness and reasonable comfort in her cabin, Star was pleasantly surprised to find it luxuriously fitted, indeed sybaritic compared to the usual accommodations of even the finest passenger ships. It even included a private lavatory with all the necessary facilities.

The walls were paneled in polished oak, and gold brocade hangings enclosed the commodious berth, which had the width of a double bed. There was a spacious armoire of tulipwood, an elegant Buhl dressing table with a silver-framed mirror, an ebony screen inlaid with ivory and mother-of-pearl, and several gilt chairs cushioned in jade green velvet with gold tassels. A Persian carpet covered the floor, and the whale oil lamps were mounted in bronze. The heavy musk fragrance left by the last female occupant filled Star's nostrils. She suspected that this intimate boudoir had been furnished with the choicest items of his privateering expeditions and had been designed to please some particular lady's fancy.

"That sure some sweet cologne," Mauma said.

"It's French perfume," Star surmised, recalling some of her mother's imported essence. "Gardenia and ambergris, I think."

"Wonder who wore it?"

Star shrugged. "Who cares?"

"You does, honey. Your face full of care."

"Oh, go to your own quarters!" Star snapped, indicating the small, neat cabin that adjoined.

Star did not go on deck to bid Charleston farewell but stood at her porthole and watched wistfully as the harbor receded and faded from view. Out of sentiment and idleness she had begun a diary after her father's death, and now she removed it from her writing box, turned over a new leaf, and wrote: Today I left South Carolina. Forever? I wonder.

She remained in seclusion for the first few days of the voyage, taking her meals on trays in her cabin, although it was customary for the passengers of any ship to dine with the captain. But not until the fourth day at sea did she receive an invitation from Troy to share a meal with him. The pro tem steward delivered it to her that afternoon.

"Miss Lamont? Cap'n Stewart sends his compliments and requests the pleasure of your company at supper this evening."

"Thank you," she said. "You may tell the captain that I accept his kind invitation. What time?"

"Eight bells, ma'am."

Star wore the same dress in which she had come aboard, a sedate black light woolen one with a simple buttoned bodice, a high white linen collar, and cuffs on the long tight sleeves. She looked trim and puritanical, as serious as a missionary.

Troy greeted her cordially this time, but still with unmistakable reserve. "Good evening, Miss Lamont. Thank you for coming. I trust your accommodations are satisfactory?"

"Quite satisfactory, captain." She glanced at the table, laid with a cloth of heavy Italian lace, hand-painted Bavarian china, delicate Venetian crystal, and ornate Danish silver. More prizes, she thought. "You set a fine table, sir."

"Unfortunately, I fear the food won't do it justice since my cook's culinary arts are limited. It's difficult to store perishables and delicacies at sea, and there are few cordon bleu chefs in merchantman galleys." The chair he pulled back for her was made of Flemish oak, lavishly carved and padded in crimson velvet, one of a massive set of four. "Be my guest."

Silently, Star sat down. The steward lit the tall tapers in the silver candelabra. His performance, smooth and unobtrusive, bespoke considerable practice. Despite herself, she felt a rising jealousy and resentment of the other women Troy had entertained so intimately and especially of the one who had left the lingering scent in her cabin.

"While in Charleston I learned of your father's tragic death and the other misfortunes that befell Mystic Rose last year," he said, sitting opposite her. "The stevedores told me. I meant to offer my sympathy before, but there seemed no propitious moment. I'm sorry, Star. I respected and admired your father even though, as you know, we did not think alike in some respects."

Star dropped her lashes, a sudden mist blurring her eyes. Her loss was still too fresh in her mind and too poignant in her heart. "Thank you," she murmured. "It's hard to speak of it."

"I understand."

"The sailors say we are bound for Marseilles?"

"That's right. Unless perverse elements alter our course. Would you rather land in England?"

"It doesn't matter. Marseilles is fine. But I was surprised to learn that your cargo is rice. Didn't you tell me once that it was against your principles to transport the fruits of slave labor?"

"It is," he said. "But rice is rotting in the warehouses of Charleston while people are starving in the British Isles and on the Continent. This cargo will help feed the dependents of men killed in Napoleon's wars. I'm no crusader. I simply decided to suspend my principles in the interest of suffering humanity."

"The people of France will be grateful."

"A few will be less hungry, that's all."

The food was nourishing and palatable, which was the best Blubber could do in the way of an epicurean feast. A roast stuffed goose, one of several dozen fowl brought aboard alive in cages and slaughtered as needed, was carried in on a large silver platter and set grandly before the skipper. Troy glanced at the bone-handled carving tools, then requested the cook to carve the bird.

Star was tragically conscious of his left arm, noticing that he favored it constantly. She was anxious for supper to be over and for the steward to leave them alone. She ate little, her once vigorous appetite having grown delicate since she had left the plantation. Finally, at his captain's bidding, the steward cleared the table, leaving only the cut glass decanter of Madeira and sterling goblets ornate as cathedral chalices, and departed. Star could contain her curiosity no longer.

"How is your arm, Troy?"

"I still have it," he said, and immediately she could feel tension mounting and a barrier rising between them.

"I can see that. But can you use it?"

He did not answer but merely looked at her coolly.

"You must hate me," she ventured tentatively.

"Wounds heal, Star. I'm lucky you're a poor shot. Otherwise, I would be dead."

"I thought you *were* dead, Troy, and I think I suffered as much as you."

"Afraid of being caught and disgraced before the high tribunal? Finch couldn't have betrayed you; he was killed in an encounter with a British sloop in the Azores a month later."

"Oh? That's too bad."

"Yes. He was a good seaman."

"And you can't forgive me?"

"Forgiveness is only a word, Star. It's easy to say. Without feeling, it's meaningless."

Did he mean he no longer cared for her, or that he did not believe she had ever cared for him? After some reflection, she said, "You once asked me to marry you, Troy. Would it help if I told you that I'm sorry now I didn't?"

He smiled cynically. "What a facile liar you are! And you look so innocent, too, in that garb. So prim and demure and harmless. Quite different from the saucy wench I met at the Russell wedding reception or the violent vixen on my ship that summer night."

"Insult me if you like, Troy. It's true. I regret not accepting your proposal."

"Why, Miss Lamont, ma'am," he affected a credible Southern drawl. "This is so sudden! You can't mean that you would accept me now?"

"Yes," she said softly. "Yes, I would, Troy."

"Why now, Star? I'm no different than I was then. I'm still illegitimate, a Yankee bastard, and you're still a Low Country aristocrat. A high and mighty Lamont, great-grandaughter of a legally wed English lord!"

His expression was impassive, inscrutable, belying his chagrin and restrained anger. Intent on her own dilemma, Star did not realize that he was riding his temper with a curbed bit.

"That's not important any more, Troy. Your background doesn't matter now. Pa is gone, and I never expect to return to Charleston and ancestor worship."

"Has Shintoism gone out of fashion in South Carolina, or have you been exiled as a dissenter?"

"Neither," Star denied, her eyes imploring his chivalry and indulgence. "I left of my own accord and desire." She added, unwittingly, "Don't you understand, Troy? I want to make up to you for what I did."

Something in him seemed to spontaneously explode, scattering fury and sarcasm everywhere. He threw down his napkin and bounded out of his chair, eyes glittering and skin darkly flushed. He was so enraged that she feared he might strike her.

"My dear, you have never been the soul of tact! So your conscience bothers you? You think you crippled me, and you want to make restitution by marrying me? Out of pity and remorse! A burden to be borne in expiation only slightly better than eternal damnation! Is that it? Look at me, Star. Hasn't it occurred to you that I may not want to marry *you* any more?"

Her face turned scarlet. Her hand trembled on the stem of the goblet, spilling some wine onto the table cloth. She gazed at it in acute embarrassment, then rose swiftly from the table. "Thank you for the supper, Captain Stewart. For the remainder of the voyage, however, I prefer my meals in my cabin. Good night, sir!"

But Troy blocked her exit. "One moment, please. You feel that you owe me something. Well, I agree. Not marriage, for that would be a lifetime payment for both of us. I'll let you off easy, Miss Lamont. Depending on the weather, we should reach Marseilles in two or three weeks. I'll settle for that."

A blow from his fist could not have hurt or surprised her more. She stared at him sullenly. "Is that why you agreed to give me passage?"

"It's better than your proposed sacrifice, isn't it?"

Star hesitated, unprepared for the outrage and unable to cope with it immediately. Her mind spun angrily, and her body quivered in indignation. But she would neither swoon nor give him the satisfaction of tears. Emily's lessons in poise and dignity served her well now.

"I assume we are 'negotiating' my fare, captain?"

"In a sense. And I assume you intend to comply, ma'am? No resistance, just suffer in silence? More penance for maiming me? How do you know you're responsible, Star? I've fought with the British and French since then. Maybe I caught one of their bullets—"

"Did you?"

He shrugged, searching her face for something he did not find. "Well, Miss Lamont?"

Suddenly her anger dissolved in acquiescence. She did not care any more; she was indifferent, resigned, compromised. Life had dealt her so many cruel blows, so much pain and disappointment and disillusionment that one more blow couldn't and wouldn't matter.

"My door will be open," she said quietly, and he made no reply but let her pass.

Chapter 33

STAR WAITED for him until the ship's bells told her it was past midnight, but he did not come.

She strolled on deck the next morning, cloaked and mittened against the chilly wind. For though it was spring in the lush Carolina Low Country, the fabulous, formal plantation gardens bursting into glorious bloom, the azaleas and rhododendrons and laurel brightening the deep dark pine woods, and baby lambs, calves, and foals romping in the greening meadows and pastures, the season was not yet full upon the Atlantic Ocean. Still, it was pleasant and invigorating, and Star enjoyed the sun glistening on the lacy water, and even the frequent baptisms of frosty spume on her face. Despite the other irritations, the voyage agreed with her, restoring her vigorous health and vivid beauty. Her eyes began to sparkle again, her cheeks and lips to glow. Soon she could forget the artificiality of cosmetics.

Mauma was not so fortunate, however. At present she was confined in her cabin with a severe attack of mal de mer for which she was sucking lemons and nibbling hardtack, supposedly a sovereign remedy. Star thought she, herself, would have no difficulty as long as the water remained reasonably calm and obliging. She was determined to disprove Troy's contention that females were constitutionally unsuited to the sea and apt to fall apart in any crisis. She only hoped and prayed that no storms or emergencies would arise.

The *Venus* in full sail was an arresting sight, as serene and graceful as a beautiful woman in a white, bouffant ball gown. She did not roll and groan in the heavy troughs, but rocked and swayed and sighed gently, her canvas rustling like crinolines, her well-pitched joints moving with the supple elastic rhythm of youth, not the inhibiting creaking of old age. Her proud young captain, humming a nautical tune at the helm, was her master in every respect: dominating, uncompromising, and nattily attired in full uniform with the elegant decorations of an admiral.

He acts as if he owned the ocean, Star thought, answering his bland smiles with petulant frowns. Still, she could not help admiring his rugged good looks and taking comfort in his competence and self-assurance; with such skillful, confident mastery at the wheel, the *Venus* would surely survive any catastrophe and conquer any challenge of the sea.

Troy was maddeningly suave and courteous, making no reference to the supper or the bargain consummated therein. And when her tray arrived that evening, she found a gorgeous ruby brooch in one of the covered dishes.

"A token of his affection," Mauma said.

"More likely a calling card," Star muttered.

Again she waited for him, and again he failed to appear. Star was angry, frustrated, and puzzled. How dare he tease and humiliate her this way! As if she were a trollop he could take at will or a pet whose antics amused him enough to keep under further observation. Well, she'd fix him, somehow!

Star was hardly civil when next they met. She did not

thank him for the brooch, and he did not mention it. But other gifts, some worth a fortune, accompanied her trays: emerald earrings, an exquisite little lapel watch encrusted in diamonds and opals, a fabulous gold necklace from Delhi, a topaz bracelet, several strands of Oriental pearls, a floral spray of garnets, and a sapphire pendant in Florentine filigree. Lesser presents, too, were delivered to her cabin at all hours of the day: leather gloves and reticules, fans of ostrich plumes and hand-painted silk, fur muffs and capelets, cashmere and Paisley shawls, lace scarves, silver-backed hairbrushes and handmirrors, jeweled vinaigrettes, and bottles of scent with intriguing French names. But no rings.

"I won't accept any of it," Star declared furiously. "I'll fling it all in his face the moment we land!"

"If us ever lands," Mauma moaned, still nursing a queasy stomach. "I fear we goin' sail forever."

"Like the *Flying Dutchman*," Star mused.

"Who that?"

"It's an old legend, Mauma, about a cruel captain doomed to sail the North Sea until Judgment Day, casting lots with the devil for his soul. His phantom ship is supposed to haunt the waters of the Cape of Good Hope in South Africa, and superstitious sailors believe sighting it means stormy weather and possibly a shipwreck or other disaster. But it's only a legend inspired by nautical superstition."

Star had read much sea lore, along with relevant fiction, poetry and ballads, including *The Ancient Mariner*, while sitting on the Russell piazza, waiting and hoping to sight the *Venus*. But it fascinated and even awed Mauma.

"What that captain's name?" she asked.

"Falkenberg, I think. It wasn't Stewart, anyway. So relax, Mauma, and suck your lemons."

The climax came a few mornings later, after Star's regular promenade. She was leaning against the port bulwark and gazing wistfully over the ocean, longing passionately for a glimpse of land, when Captain Stewart, having turned the wheel over to his highly capable first officer, joined her.

"I don't like the clothes you are wearing," he greeted her critically.

Star glanced at him, astonished at this new effrontery and criticism. "May I ask what's wrong with them?"

"They depress me. The color, the style—everything. I've seen religious habits with more flair and appeal."

"Well, I've nothing against religion, captain! If I were Catholic, I might consider the convent."

"France is full of convents, my dear; so are Italy and Spain. Perhaps you can change your faith. But until you do, I wish you wouldn't dress like a nun."

"I'm sorry my garb displeases you, sir, but I happen to be mourning my father."

"Mourn him in your heart," Troy said. "That's where true sentiment belongs, not on the back or sleeve."

"I have no other clothes with me, captain. I'm afraid my wardrobe is both limited and dated."

"I can remedy that, Miss Lamont. I have several trunks of rather recent fashions. Many would fit you, I'm sure."

"Indeed? Do you keep clothes and jewelry handy for your female passengers?"

Her indignation amused him. "Do you object to a little preliminary courtship?"

"I resent being toyed with like a plaything! I made a bargain with you, and I intend to keep it. But you don't have to woo me with trinkets!"

His dark brows arched in surprise. "Trinkets? Those are quite valuable gifts, my dear, and could see you through lean days in the future."

Star affected a nonchalant shrug, as if she still regarded them as trifles. "Nevertheless, they make me feel cheap and common. And the longer you delay, the more you cheat yourself."

"Anticipation is half the pleasure, my pet. And there'll be time enough. I'll see to that."

"How? By sailing in circles? I suspect we already are, to some extent. Do with me as you please, Captain Kidd, but don't torture me in the process."

"Your idea of torture seems to differ somewhat from the average woman's," he said. "However, I don't differ much from the average man. I enjoy seeing a lovely lady appropriately dressed, and selfish ulterior motives inspire my generosity. Come with me now. I have some more things for you. Dispose of them as you wish when we reach port but use them aboard my ship. That's an order, Miss Lamont."

Seething in silent rage, Star followed him to the strongroom below. The padlocked door was opened, and the splendors within suggested the mythical dens of Ali Baba and the forty thieves. The glitter of gold, the sparkle of crystal, and the luster of silk and satin were dazzling. There were Venetian mirrors in ornate gilt frames; lavish pieces of porcelain and china; repoussé silver; priceless cloisonné, vermeil, jade, ivory, and enamel objets d'art; Oriental tapestries and carpets; master paintings and marble sculptures; silks from Damascus, velvets from Genoa, French brocades, Spanish laces, and Irish linens; two heavily laden sea chests of gold bullion and jewels; and several embossed leather trunks containing some of the most stunning feminine apparel Star had ever seen.

Star caught her breath, staring in wide-eyed fascination. "Oh, they were right! Lance and Grant were right about you all along. You *are* a pirate!"

"Privateer," he corrected, affronted. "There's a difference, regardless of what you or anyone else might believe. Most of this booty was taken from English and French vessels that proved inferior to mine. Those I couldn't whip, I outsailed. My warrant was an American marque from President Madison, and if I had not been stronger or more clever than my opponents, my cargoes would have been lifted with no more qualms than I lifted theirs. All this is forfeit, Star, the spoils of war—and I might add that I enjoyed, even relished, some of my victories immensely. Those gowns, for instance, were bound for the ladies of the Court of St. James." His eyes gleamed with malicious mischief, as if he had scored a personal triumph over his noble mother. "I disappointed them."

In spite of her mood, Star felt compassion for him. His bastardy would haunt and frustrate him all his life. It was the root out of which grew his bitter cynicism and his skeptical suspicion and distrust of all women. Unless she or someone else helped him overcome his obsession, he would end up a lonely old stoic with a withered, wasted heart.

Now he reached into one of the trunks and brought out a ball gown of turquoise satin embroidered in crystals and silver beads, as elegant and modish as any that might be found in the grand salons of the Tuileries or Versailles. "I should like to see you in this at supper this evening."

Star accepted the puff of simmering cloth coolly. "Any other orders, captain?"

From one of the coffers he took a small case of traced and gilded leather. A diamond necklace, bracelet and earrings blazed against the black velvet interior. "These, I understand, were part of the crown jewels of Marie Antoinette. Some London jeweler bought them at auction but, unfortunately, the duchess who had commissioned him to bid for her never received them. They were on the same schooner with the gowns. They're yours now, Miss Lamont. Wear them tonight."

"Aye, aye, sir!" Star retorted, though aware of their tremendous value and the joy with which a duchess or even a queen would welcome them. "I hope I shall not meet with the same fate as their original owner."

His eyes raked her, a roguish grin on his mouth as he withdrew some boudoir lingerie, a white velvet negligee with a slight train and flowing bishop's sleeves edged in lace, a wispy white chiffon nightgown, and lace shift. Intimate, seductive, mortifying.

"For whom was that intended?" she asked tremulously. "One of the prince regent's mistresses?"

"Probably." He placed the heap of fluff in her arms, atop the gown and the jewel box, and added some silver evening slippers and a pair of white velvet mules with marabou pompons. "Tonight they are your chamber robes. You may expect me."

Her equanimity began to give way slightly at that, but at least the suspense was almost over. "May I go now, please? I can't possibly carry any more."

"Of course, my dear. You're not a prisoner."

"Not in the brig, no. But since I can't swim to shore, I might as well be. Good day, captain. I'll be at your—your service this evening."

Mauma's eyes popped as Star dumped the luxuries on her berth. "Glory be! That white man has found the Promised Land!"

"He's buying me with baubles and bangles as he would any strumpet," Star said, giving an angry kick at the bunk. "And he's not giving me anything, Mauma. He expects to take it all out in trade."

"Honey, them gems ain't just gewgaws. They got a wicked gleam that look mighty real to me. Why, he could get hisself a harem with that kind of treasure."

"I don't doubt his collection of harbor wenches would constitute a harem! This cabin still reeks of potent perfume, and it's not mine. He hasn't forgiven me, Mauma. He's mean and spiteful and plans to use me until we reach Marseilles and then unload me with the rest of the baggage. In a few months I'll likely be puffed up like a pompano, and he'll be in Timbuktu! And to think I once thought he loved me. I worried about him and waited so long. Oh, how could I have such foul luck with men! I must have been born under an evil sign."

"Well, I still don't think he goin' to force you to be bad with him, missy. But if you needs any help tonight, jest holler. You know I ain't far away."

Chapter 34

THE SUPPER was much the same as it had been on the first occasion—the appointments excellent, and the food something less. The wine was a vintage champagne from one of his confiscated cargos intended for the British royal cellars. Star found it delightful, simultaneously relaxing and exhilarating. After her second glass, she ceased fretting over her predicament and almost forgave Troy for the unfair advantage he was taking.

The candlelight cast a bluish sheen over her jet black hair and made her dark, provocative eyes even more compelling in the lacy shadows of her long curved lashes. The gown fit as if it had been designed for her, and the lustrous blue green hues enhanced her vivid coloring. Above the deep décolletage, her shoulders and bosom had a creamy opalescence, the many-faceted diamonds striking radiant fire at her throat, ears, and wrists, so that every scintillating movement attracted attention. There was admiration in Troy's intense gaze and desire, and something else she could not quite fathom.

"How lovely you are," he said softly, "exceeding all my dreams of fair ladies."

Star regarded the flattery as part of his technique, his prelude to seduction. She was annoyed that he considered it necessary at this stage, for she was as much his captive and chattel as a slave or indentured servant.

"Your glib tongue bespeaks much practice at spurious affection, captain, and don't delude me or yourself. It's only an illusion due to the candlelight and wine."

He shook his head, chagrined. "It's you, Star, and my compliments are sincere, so don't deny me the pleasure of paying them. A man would have to be blind and feeble to ignore your beauty and charms. Frankly, I was surprised to find you still single."

"Why? I told you once I'd never marry."

"Yes, I remember that discussion quite well, and I thought then that a certain Carolina cavalier was responsible for your drastic decision. Is he still?"

"Grant Russell is a memory," she said, averting her eyes as he replenished her glass. "I left him in the Low Country with the rest of my memories."

"That's encouraging, if not quite convincing."

"I wouldn't attempt to convince you of anything, captain, and I didn't think you needed encouragement."

He smiled, then drank. "The boldest suitor does, on occasion."

"Suitor? I'm afraid I wouldn't put you in that category, sir. Where I come from a man who forces himself on a lady is something else."

"Oh, I'm a terrible cad, but rarely without provocation."

"I'll try not to provoke you," she said sullenly.

"Have you ever seen a full moon at sea?"

"I've watched it on the bays of Charleston and Boston, but it's probably not the same."

"Not quite. Shall we go on deck?"

Star wanted to ask if she had any choice, but she refrained. They had fought enough already to last the remainder of the journey, which she hoped now would end tomorrow.

"It's cold out there," she hedged, reluctant to leave the brazier of glowing coals in his quarters and the warmth of the wine. "I don't have a wrap with me."

"There may be one in my cabinet."

"Left over from your last liaison and rendezvous?"

Wordlessly, he produced a regal ermine cape and slipped it over her bare shoulders, his hands lingering long enough to make her conscious of the pressure. Was his arm not totally disabled, after all? Had he just been pretending and forgotten himself? Surely he could not be that cruel and vengeful! She must be mistaken, possibly even a bit tipsy, or her imagination must be playing tricks on her.

The night was vast, infinite. The moon never appeared so great and luminous on land, the heavens so near, the universe so encompassing. How could any mere mortal comprehend the vastness and grandeur of the creation, the significance of eternity? Star felt very small, lost, apprehensive—an insignificant speck in time and space.

"It's beautiful," she said. "But awesome, too. Like being on a floating island."

"That's what every ship is, Star. But people can and do live on them, just as they do on land. I did, with my father, and ever since. And I know captains whose wives and families go to sea with them. Of course, they usually have a homestead somewhere, too. For respite and retirement."

"I've been in boats before, on the Cooper and Ashley rivers," Star reflected. "I made my first ocean voyage at sixteen, to Boston, and was terrified when the shore of my familiar world disappeared from sight. Once the sea was becalmed, and we barely moved for three days. The ship seemed anchored in the middle of nowhere, and some of the passengers panicked."

"That happens," Troy nodded. "Not often, but enough to foul up schedules. And tempers. According to Colonial history, the Pilgrims encountered several windless weeks on the Atlantic, driving some of them insane."

They fell silent then, watching the phosphorescent waves, each of them pursuing an abstraction. Preoccupied, Star did not notice Troy's brooding countenance, nor his hand straining on the bulwark, as if to steady and control himself.

Somewhere on the *Venus* a crewman played a concertina and another scraped away on a fiddle. A mournful, repetitious tune reminding Star of the Negro songs. Unexpectedly, she began to cry, quietly, hoping he would ignore her tears.

"What's the matter, Star?"

"Nostalgia, I guess. I was thinking of home. The plantation and my parents." She could almost smell the mystic rose in the cemetery, see the dew on the white petals, and hear the wind whispering in the trees.

"Why did you leave?"

"Because I couldn't bear it alone."

"You weren't alone, Star. You had many friends and a stepfamily there. But you will be alone in Europe. What will you do, where and how will you live? Or haven't you considered such common problems?"

"Please, Troy," she sobbed wretchedly, abashed at her lost composure. "I don't want to discuss it."

"Very well. But I've sailed that course, Star, and I think you'll discover that you can neither jettison your past nor chart your future. When nostalgic memory fogs you in, you'll be lucky not to founder before it clears up and enables you to get your bearings again." His voice was compassionate and somehow reassuring. He passed her a large clean white cambric kerchief. "Come, my dear. I'll take you to your cabin."

At the door Star paused, blotted her eyes, and looked at him questioningly.

"Later," he said. "And I won't knock."

"I didn't expect you would, captain! Apparently you're accustomed to entering this cabin without signal. Who occupied it before me? Some French courtesan?"

In the dim, smoky light of a whale oil sconce, his face

was impassive and inscrutable. "Monette was French, yes, but not a cocotte off the streets. She was a young widow whose husband had been killed at Waterloo, and her morals were not my concern. She approached me in desperation, seeking a chance at a new life in America. I gave her passage to New York and staked her adventure."

"In return for certain favors?"

He grinned. "Jealous?"

"Curious!" Star snapped and went inside, accompanied by his low resonant laughter.

Damn him! she thought furiously. If I weren't on this ship, I'd pull the seacocks and scuttle it! And I just might do it, anyway, after tonight....

Star was sitting at the dressing table, pensively brushing her hair, when Troy returned. He had replaced his uniform jacket with a handsome lounging sack of hunter's green jacquard probably destined for Beau Brummell or some other courtier, if not the prince regent himself, since it was contraband being smuggled to England on a French ship captured off Gibraltar. Their eyes met in the mirror, his lighting with quick passion as he observed her dishabille. Star felt wanton and naked and knew that too much of her breasts were on display. Scandalized, Mauma hovered protectively in the cabin until her mistress ordered her out. She left reluctantly, muttering, "Your pa and Miss Angel ain't goin' rest easy tonight."

"So you wore it?" Troy said.

"Yes, I wore it."

"Why, Star?"

"Orders, captain."

"You could have disobeyed."

"And walk the plank? Besides, I'm not a welsher."

"Well, you look lovely. Like a bride."

"I don't feel like one."

"How do you feel?"

"Like a ship about to be plundered."

He suppressed a smile. "A ship on her maiden voyage?"

Star nodded, distressed by her virginity, wishing now that Grant had entered her room that restless night and taken her.

Troy touched her hair, fondling a long silky tendril, curling it around his fingers. A tremor ran through her flesh, and he asked, "Is it fear or revulsion?"

"Fear, I guess."

And yet it wasn't pain she feared as much as desertion upon landing, abandonment in a strange country carrying his seed, watching it grow helplessly inside her—a poor nameless little bastard of a bastard father. But at least Mauma had some knowledge and practice of midwifery, having assisted at Star's own birth. Not as much as Tawn or Granny Mae, who had delivered numerous slave women, but Mauma could manage. She might even know some secrets or black magic to relieve her burden before it became a bulging reality and devastating dilemma.

Troy's hand under her elbow urged Star to her feet. "Don't be afraid, darling. I won't hurt you or let anything happen."

He kissed her, and her mouth yielded with patient coaxing. Star relaxed, submitted, and gradually responded to his artistry. If only love, not lust, had brought him to her! If only love and respect inspired his tenderness, his finesse, and his promises. But it didn't matter why he had come, what had brought him, what strange circumstances or perverse fate threw them together now. He was here, and she wanted him passionately, and as desperately as she had that other long-ago night on the *Venus* when she had denied her natural instincts and impulses and shot him for pursuing his.

It took her several minutes to realize that he was holding her with both arms, and both were strong and virile. So he had deceived and beguiled her, tormented her with the insinuation and appearance of a disability that she had inflicted. Instantly, she broke the embrace and pushed him away, her eyes blazing.

"There's nothing wrong with your arm!"

"I never said there was."

"But you let me think—oh, you despicable rogue! You tricked me! I ought to shoot you again!"

"Calm down, Star, and listen to me."

"I won't calm down! Of all the low, vile, sneaky sea serpents!" She lashed out at him, but he dodged her blow. "Get out of here, damn you, or I'll scream for Mauma!"

Her rage seemed to please and even gratify him. "It was just a test to see how far you would go on a pang of conscience. I think you'd have gone all the way, meek and humble as a penitent sinner to the sacrificial altar. Did you honestly believe I would want and take you on those terms, Star? My God, I hope I'm not *that* kind of bastard! But it was worth it to discover that you still have some fire and spirit. I was afraid your emotions had frozen solid, that you were incapable of feeling or caring about anything any more. And I should find marriage with an apathetic wife extremely dull."

"Marriage?" she asked weakly.

"Yes, my little gypsy! Marriage. You're ready for it—the volcano is still highly active under the affected icecap. As a captain at sea, I could perform the ceremony myself. But if you prefer to have a third party officiate, we'll find someone in Marseilles. A Protestant minister, if there are any left in France. If not, we might persuade a priest to accommodate us if we threaten to live in sin."

"Oh, Troy! If you hadn't said that, I—I think I'd have jumped overboard. You really want to marry me?"

"I just proposed, Miss Lamont. Would you be more convinced if I got on my knees?"

"Maybe. And you do still love me?"

"Enough to sail into Charleston with a cargo mostly of ballast merely to see you again, hoping all the way that you were still unattached. But I anticipated more difficulty. Your note made it incredibly easy—and saved my pride."

"But you sent Mauma away, at first?"

"Not for long. I'd have blasted that Baltimore clipper out of the water before letting you take passage on it."

"You villain." Star slipped her arms about his neck, standing on tiptoe to kiss him. "How am I ever to trust you at sea? I'll need a lot of little anchors, I reckon, to bring you home to me. We'll raise them in Nantucket and give your father something to do besides polish shells and build ships in jugs."

"From which he first drains the liquor," Troy frowned. "I've worried that he would drink himself to death out of loneliness and despair. This might give him a new perspective and reason for living. Yes, I think the old skipper would like a whole raft of youngsters."

"And the young skipper?"

The prospect obviously intrigued him. "Sure. A small crew, anyway. And I want them all to be legitimate, so don't use this velvet-and-lace bait again until everything is legal. It's like dangling fresh meat before a hungry shark."

"It's all right, now, isn't it?" she offered tentatively, astonished at her boldness. "I mean, if we're betrothed?—"

"Don't tempt me, Star. I'm no monk, and I've waited for you about as long as I can. That's mostly what love is about, you know. And life, too. Lock your door and keep it locked every night until we make port."

"Why, since you can marry us yourself?"

"Would you like that, Star?"

"I think it would be wonderful, Troy! Beautiful."

He pondered it seriously. "Different, certainly. Few men officiate at their own weddings, and while I've performed several at sea, never mine. This takes some concentration, love."

Expecting immediate action, Star was disappointed. "Then it won't be now, tonight?"

"Anxious?" he teased.

"Aren't you?"

"Hell, yes! But it has to be something special, Star,

not the usual proscribed and parroted exchange of vows. We'll make a ceremony of it tomorrow, at sunset, with the crew as our witnesses, and I'll hang Blubber from the yardarm it he doesn't provide a reasonable feast for the reception. I'm positive he has some goodies stashed in the galley and elsewhere, which he saves for himself and barters with other cooks in port."

"And you still want me to lock my door, captain?"

"No, but those are orders, Miss Lamont, and you'd better obey. Besides, I want to give you a little more time to consider it, to be sure, because it's for keeps, Star. Once I get you, I'll never let you go. Never! Understand?"

"Aye, sir."

"You're going to live on the ship with me and bear our children at sea–I'll sign on a doctor, and tutor when necessary. Eventually, of course, I'll retire. I'll use some of my privateering fortune to buy a small fleet of merchant vessels, promote myself to commodore or even admiral, and build us a fine house close to the sea. On an island or coastal bluff. There're many suitable locations. Nantucket, Martha's Vineyard, Long Island. The coasts of Maine, Massachusetts, Connecticut, New Jersey. Or further south, if you prefer, as long as it's near salt water."

"It sounds perfect," Star visualized dreamily. "We'll be together while we're young, and I'll get to see the whole world! Oh, Troy, I'm so happy! And do you know something else? If you hadn't returned to Charleston for me, I'd probably have sailed from port to port searching for you."

He kissed her again, quick and hard. "We were meant for each other, Star. What else could explain all that's happened to us since we met? The long separations and calamities, the waiting and yearning, and the hoping that neither of us would find another mate. I knew I wanted you the first time I saw you, and it angered me to realize that you loved Russell."

Her fingers worked in the long hair at the back of his

head, soothing his tense neck muscles. "I loved Grant with the naive, innocent love of a young girl, Troy. But I don't think I was ever *in love* with him. If so, I wouldn't have cared about his marriage or anything else, would I? I'd have given myself to him freely. That's what every mature woman wants to do when she's truly and deeply in love with a man—commit herself to him totally, in every respect, no matter what the consequences. The way I want to do with you now. But you're the stronger of us, Troy."

"For a damned good reason," he said grimly, "and you know what it is, Star. I want that total commitment, that complete relationship, desperately now, and I'm fighting temptation like the devil. Because I want our offspring conceived in wedlock; no known child of mine will ever bear that wretched stigma. So concentrate on the ritual that'll make it right, Star. Sacred. Irrevocable."

She nodded, adding wistfully, "I've always wanted to wear a bridal costume. You wouldn't by any chance have something appropriate aboard?"

Troy grinned. "Oh, I might. I'll look and see." He turned to go, his hand hesitating on the knob.

"Well, before you leave, I have a confession to make, darling. I knew my poor aim didn't cripple you. You forgot yourself when you put the cape on me earlier this evening and used both hands."

"That was intentional, Star. I was hoping you'd notice. And being aware of my pretense, why did you let me in here?"

"Oh," she smiled archly, "maybe I just wanted to see how far you'd go on a bluff."

Troy was amused, enjoying the ancient male-female game they were playing. "God, what a scheming wench! But suppose your scheme had backfired, and I was less than a gentleman?"

Shrugging, peering at him coyly, she said, "In that unfortunate event, sir, I'd have promptly developed 'certain symptoms' to give you a guilty conscience."

"And when land was in sight, Mauma would have

shyly confided your 'little secret' to me, eh?" Troy laughed, shaking his head. "Well, my charming and adorable pet, as I once said, life with you could never be dull."

"Good night, captain."

"Until tomorrow," he said, departing swiftly.

Chapter 35

WHEN HE HAD GONE, Star opened the connecting door to Mauma's cabin, not surprised to find her eavesdropping.

"Didn't I tell you Cap'n Stewart wouldn't make you be bad with him?" she crowed triumphantly. "We's goin' have a weddin', ain't we?"

Star was too happy to scold her. "So it seems, Mauma, and he's going to do the honors himself! Isn't that thrilling? I've never known a girl to have such an experience before!"

"I knows, honey, I hear. And what you bet he got a bridal outfit jest your size tucked away somewhere on this boat? Ain't no figurin' that man! He kind of sneaky in some ways."

"Well, so what? Didn't I scheme to get aboard his ship?"

"Yessum, you guilty of that, all right. And while I think most of your marriage goin' be smooth sailin', they's goin' be some rough seas, too. You is both stubborn as a couple of field mules."

"And we both have English blood, Mauma. You know he's the son of a British noblewoman–and don't deny it, because you listen at the keyhole every chance you get."

"I ain't denyin' it," Mauma shrugged, not reminding her mistress that spying on her stepbrother had once proved very useful. "But who goin' be your bridesmaid, sugar?"

"You," Star said emphatically.

"Me? A black slave that's been with you since you was birthed? It ain't proper."

Star hugged her. "I can't think of anything more proper, Mauma, and don't argue with me! Go to bed and get some sleep. We have much to do tomorrow." Tears of joy glistened in her dark eyes, beading her long lashes with iridescence. "Oh, Mauma, it's going to be the happiest day of my life!"

"Lawd, give us calm seas," Mauma prayed. "Is I goin' live on the boat with you from now on, like the cap'n say?"

"That's right. You'll help deliver and tend our children. You know I couldn't do without you, Mauma."

"Yessum, and I reckon it's sort of mutual."

Star was too excited to rest well that night. Once she rose and crept toward the master cabin, turning back when she heard the watch changing. Back in her bunk, she wondered curiously about the women who had occupied it before her: had Troy loved any of them or had he merely used them out of loneliness and male necessity? What would her first sexual experience with him be like? Maybe Mauma could enlighten her; she'd find some way to broach the subject tomorrow. Was Troy awake too, tossing restlessly, longing to come to her but restrained by the inveterate willpower and determination so ingrained in his character? Oh, would daylight never dawn!

Her breakfast arrived on a silver tray: fresh scrambled eggs from the laying hens kept aft in cages, biscuits which only made her hungry for the big fluffy ones served at Mystic Rose, and a pot of hot tea with wedges of precious lemon. Troy maintained a good supply of staples under guard, and the cook was required to list whatever he removed. Pilfering was punishable by a sentence in the brig, with a threat of worse, which the crew did not care to challenge. For while Captain Stewart was considerably more tolerant and lenient than the average ship's master, he demanded discipline and rigidly enforced all rules and regulations on the high seas. His intrepid exploits and prowess as a privateer had earned him an enviable reputation among his peers, the praise of President Madison, the commendation of Congress and gratitude of the country, as well as the awe and respect of every seaman from Maine to the Mediterranean. And though it was the nature of sailors to grumble and complain of conditions on even the finest vessels, Troy Stewart had a long list of applicants eager to sign on the *Venus*.

Orders from the captain kept the crew busy all morning. The deck was swabbed with lye soap and pails of water drawn up from the sea. Even the sails and rigging, washed by recent rains and bleached by the sun, looked clean and fresh, the varnished masts and booms glossy. Exceptionally large for its class, the *Venus* had many stores of which Star, who had never explored it, was unaware. From the spare timber, the ship's carpenter improvised a small altar and arched trellis. A long white linen-and-lace tablecloth covered the crude wood, and a pair of elaborate silver candelabrum from the vault of captured treasure provided adornment. Potted greenery appeared from the miniature conservatory. A heavy net holding wine and champagne was lowered into the cold Atlantic to be effectively chilled, and Blubber remained in the galley planning and preparing the wedding feast.

Along with Star's luncheon, the acting steward, Hawkins, brought a message from Captain Stewart requesting Mauma's presence in his quarters. She gazed at him questioningly. "Ain't you mistaken, man? Don't he mean he want to see Miss Star?"

Annoyed at his assignment to attend the women,

Hawkins answered brusquely, "He said you, so come along now, I ain't got all day! Jesus Christ, you'd think we was gonna pipe the president aboard, with all the hustle and bustle here today! That bird in the crow's nest better keep a sharp watch, cause it don't seem like the captain's payin' much attention to his business today." He gestured impatiently. "Come on, I say!"

Nodding, wanting to cuff him for his insolence and disregard of her age, Mauma followed Hawkins to the master stateroom. She found the prospective bridegroom in a state of restless anxiety that she would not have believed possible. "Hello, Mauma. Thank you for coming."

"Hawkins didn't give me no choice, sir." Mauma glanced at the huge box on his sea chest. "What is it you want, cap'n?"

"I think you know, you sly old lynx!"

A wide, almost toothless grin creased her black face. "I expect I do, sir. In that box yonder is her weddin' duds, right?"

"Correct, and if you dare tell her I had it made in London with her measurements in mind, I'll throw you to the sharks! Understand?"

Still grinning, she said, "Yessuh."

"I want you to steam the creases out of the gown, I'm sure you know how, and make any necessary adjustments. Remember, all I had to go on was memory when I gave the seamstress the specifications. There'll also be something new and nice for you to wear, Mauma. You can't attend your mistress in a calico rag."

"Who say I goin' attend her?"

"I do, and I'm master of this ship!" Troy paced the floor, pausing to study a chart, twirl the globe, flip a few pages of the log on his desk. "After the rites and reception, you're to come here and get my quarters ready for us. Here's a list of things to be done."

"Lawdy, Mist' Troy, I cain't read!"

"Hawkins will help you, Mauma. Her slippers are size four and a half, but if they're too large or small, we'll find a perfect pair."

"You got the right size," Mauma told him, "though how she keep her feets so tiny I don't know, since she always wantin' to run barefoot. One time I chase her all mornin' through a clover field, with her laughin' and darin' me to catch her, and her pa and Aunt Emily, Cicero and the rest of the house niggers watchin' and hootin' at how slow I was. I's warnin' you, cap'n, that lil gal ain't the easiest person to manage. And you might jest as well leave out that 'obey' part in the ceremony, cause she most probly goin' honor you most of the time, but she ain't goin' obey you all the time. When she want to do something, she goin' do it—be it tearin' off on a horse or shuckin' herself to the buff and dippin' in a moonlit fountain. Lawd, what I done went through with Miss Angel's lil pixie, 'tis a wonder I ain't in my grave by now!"

At Troy's smile, Mauma cautioned, "You ain't goin' find it so funny, sir, when you be the one chasin' after her!"

"Mauma, I've been doing that since I met her—and if you betray my secret, I'll confine you to your cabin on bread and water for the remainder of the voyage."

"Before you throws me to the sharks?" Mauma quipped. "They ain't gone like it if I's dwindled down to skin and bones."

Troy laughed, opening the door to summon Hawkins. "You know your chores for the day, Mauma. Go perform them."

The servant waddled off, the sullen attendant toting the bundles behind her. Neither frightened nor intimidated by Captain Stewart's bluffs, Mauma rather enjoyed bandying wits with him. He was certainly a different master from John Lamont, and Mauma was certain of one thing: life in the Stewart domain, be it on shipboard or land, would never be dull. Her mistress was more than a handful for any man, and she herself was not exactly docile and retiring.

"Well," she declared, as Hawkins deposited the load in Star's cabin and was dismissed, "here 'tis!"

Star had washed her hair in rainwater with castile soap and was now drying it with a Turkish towel. "Here what is?"

"Your marryin' clothes, like I told you! And I think they goin' fit you, from head to toes."

Unable to contain her curiosity, Star immediately opened and scrambled through the boxes, delighted with the contents. The bridal ensemble consisted of an exquisite gown of heavy white French satin and Chantilly lace, and a small crown of diamonds and pearls with a veil of illusion attached. Included also were some delicate convent-made lingerie, long silk gloves, and a pair of white satin slippers with Baby Louis heels. "Oh," she sighed wistfully, "how beautiful everything is and how expensive! Do you suppose it was part of a captured cargo, like the other gifts he gave me?"

"Don't ask no questions," Mauma advised succinctly, "less you wants me tossed overboard."

"Did he have this gown made just for me?" Star persisted. "Tell me, Mauma, or I'll put you in a dinghy and let you drift at sea!"

Mauma chuckled. "Well, that better than his threats, anyway. And I's plum scared to see what kind of outfit he goin' send me! First off, I got to make sure it all fits you, then smooth out the wrinkles over a pot of boilin' water and press it with the sadirons. 'Pears we goin' have a evenin' weddin'. Other folks gets married in the mornin' or at high noon, but that man got ideas of his own."

"Oh, he's different, thank heaven! I'm glad it's at sundown, when the horizon seems limitless."

"I jest hope the water's calm, so's I don't have to suck lemons the whole time. One thing sure, we ain't goin' need no cradles to rock the babies to sleep—and they's goin' be babies, Miss Star. One every year, I calculate."

Star sat on the berth, applying the big fluffy towel to her curls again, rubbing vigorously. "Mauma, what's going to happen tonight? I mean, when we retire?"

Mauma frowned pensively. "You should've ask Tawn

or some of them other loose nigger gals what was foolin' with the bucks, honey. Or Miss Emily or Miss Lorna. How a woman know what a man do in bed, if she never laid with one? But he goin' take you, that much I know. He goin' get a part of him into a part of you, what the law call consummatin', I think. Have you ever seen a man naked down yonder?"

"Only the little boys around Mystic Rose."

"I ain't talkin' 'bout lil sprouts, missy. Ain't you never felt a full-growed man hard up against you when he was holdin' and kissin' you?"

Star nodded, blushing as she remembered several such occasions with Grant, Troy, and other aggressive beaus. There had been Obah, too, but she had shut her eyes against that grotesque sight.

"Well, then you knows somethin' 'bout it. And I knows you seen animals matin', cause Mist' Lance used to coax you to the kennels and barns and pastures every chance he got. Jest use your imagination, child, and Cap'n Stewart'll do the rest. I reckon he done had his share, and more, of females in bed, and probly some was whores what didn't need no coachin'. You's a virgin, so you goin' bleed some, and it might hurt a mite, too. But I don't think the cap'n goin' be rough or impatient with you, more likely kind and gentle as a lamb."

"I saw some rams that weren't so gentle."

"I said lamb, honey, not ram."

"Oh. Well, take care of my clothes. Then see that I get some fresh warm water in here for a bath."

"The men all fussin' cause they got to spruce up for the weddin'," Mauma confided, relaying some of Hawkin's scuttlebutt. "The cap'n ordered everyone of 'em to wash, and they can't use none of the fresh water in the storage tanks or the rainwater caught from the sky, neither. He give me a long list of orders 'bout preparin' the nuptial chamber, too, which Hawkins goin' explain to me, account of I can't read."

"Only because you didn't care to learn, Mauma, while my governesses, including Miss Emily, were teaching me," Star reminded. Suddenly that time seemed like another age and Mystic Rose another world.

Would Emily eventually marry the overseer, Clem Jones, and be welcomed socially in the Low Country? Together they could probably restore Mystic Rose to its former grandeur and position as one of the finest plantations in the South, and somehow Star felt it wouldn't matter to either of them whether or not they were received in the drawing rooms of the proper Charlestonians. Lorna Wilson had been accepted because of her marital alliance with Grant Russell, grandson of a Knight of the Garter, and her children would be accepted, too, because the blood of the father was more important than that of the mother to Carolina gentility. But what of it? John Lamont was dead, and his daughter was marrying a Yankee sea captain, who had been received and entertained at the executive mansion in Washington, and hailed and honored as one of the great privateering heroes without whose courageous assistance the American navy could not have survived the war and without whom the nation's commerce would have been seriously jeopardized, if not driven off the seas.

Pensively mulling the past, Star had an innate conviction that her father would have approved of her marriage to Captain Troy Stewart despite his background; that John would have given them his blessings and best wishes for a new and happy life wherever destiny took them.

And there would be no more "fancy ladies" in this fancy cabin, either! Star had already determined that it should be the future nursery, with Mauma in close attendance next door. Within a month or two, she hoped, the ship's carpenter would be building a crib and other appropriate furniture, while she and Mauma redecorated it and stitched a layette.

Wooden pails of hot and cold water were brought from the galley by two crewmen, and Mauma prepared her mistress's bath in a little porcelain tub painted with cupids and flowers, which matched the chamber pot in the marble-topped commode. A jar of sweet salts and a vial of precious attar of jasmine from his cache had also been delivered, and Star enjoyed the luxury and relaxation, feeling like Cleopatra being prepared by her handmaidens to meet Marc Antony, except that she had only one assistant, an aging, graying, beloved black slave whose rheumatic joints creaked so loudly that Star ordered her off her knees immediately after the first sponging. And since fresh water was too dear at sea ever to waste, Mauma would later use it for her own ablutions.

Chapter 36

THE CREW was somewhat less elated over the prospect that would, in their estimation, forever alter the lifestyle aboard the merchantman *Venus.* They carped and cursed throughout the preparations, casting lots for the order of the saltwater baths in the dipping vat, which also decided the sequence of the rinse in the barrel of rainwater, the losers aware that the fresh water would be as briny as the deep by the time their turns came.

Shaving at sea was always a personal preference, never a requisite. Now, they were barbering one another's hair, scraping off beards, trimming mustaches, cleaning and pressing their dress uniforms, which conformed to those in the regular navy: blue jackets, white trousers, and round tarpaulin hats. When distinguished visitors were expected or aboard, no vessel afloat could put on a more impressive exhibition, and they were the envy of every privateer in the war when Captain Stewart sailed across the Chesapeake Bay and up the Potomac River to the capital, to receive congratulations from the president of the United States and attend one of the first lady's famous balls.

Perhaps action was what they missed most now: the sound and fury of their naval engagements, the victorious encounters with an equal or superior hostile brig or schooner or sloop, the dangerous escapes from more powerful cruisers or battleships, or the thrill of an enemy's surrender, allowing them to board with cutlasses, spikes and other weapons in hand, disarm the officers and men, and seize a valuable cargo in which they shared. They never tired of reliving and recounting these exciting adventures, elaborating on them to strangers, until it seemed the *Venus* must surely have been the menace and scourge of the sea, her flag striking terror and signaling defeat to all foes, her captures more important and rewarding than all other privateers combined.

"You tars can forget your shipboard freedoms," Boatswain Briggs drawled disgruntedly. "No more cussin' or spittin' whenever you please, and no more pissin' over the rail when you get the urge, either, unless it's pitch-dark on deck and damn quiet in the master cabin. And you go to the head to shit, regardless. Goddamn, I can't imagine nothin' worse than havin' a petticoat aboard all the time!"

"We had women aboard before," Carl Bull reminded, picking his teeth. "But now we got a 'lady' who'll soon be the skipper's wife! There's a helluva big difference."

"Yeah, I can jest see her now, considerin' herself mistress of the ship like it was a house, puttin' up fancy curtains on the portholes and rearrangin' everything that ain't screwed or nailed down. Jesus Christ, the *Venus*'ll probably be the laughingstock of the seven seas!"

"Naw, I doubt that," Hammer disagreed for the sake of disagreement. "Troy'll pamper her, all right, cause he's done caught tight in her tentacles. But he'll always be master of his ship and keep the missus in her place. I'll lay two to one she spawns before their first anniversary and be too busy in the nursery to interfere much elsewhere. I remember my pa sayin' the only way to keep a wife in line was to keep her pregnant, and that's what he done, too. Ma had fifteen kids, and Lord only knows how many miscarriages. Some of 'em was stillborn, some died in infancy, only about three or four of us growed up. By then ma was dead, and pa got him a real young bride and started the whole process over again. I don't know how many brats he had with her, cause I'd done left home and ain't never been back. I'll stay with the *Venus* even if she's crawlin' with youngsters like monkeys in the riggin', cause Troy's a great skipper, and seamanship is the only thing I know or want to know."

"Ditto," Briggs nodded. "I'd die like a beached fish on dry land."

"Fish is right," said the sailor washing his back. "I don't know if this is dirt or scales I'm scrapin' off your hide, but a scaler would be better than a brush."

"Ah, shut up and scrub, or I'll piss in the rinse water," Briggs threatened, roaring with laughter, "and it's your turn in the barrel next."

The lowering sun suffused the western sky in brilliant shades of rose, cerise, saffron, and magenta, and the Atlantic was as serene as Star had ever seen it since their departure from Charleston. The weather seemed a good omen, and she knew even without Mauma's exuberant exclamations that she made a beautiful bride. Excitement flushed her skin and flashed in her dark eyes, and her white costume contrasted strikingly with her vivid coloring and blueblack hair now adorned with the jeweled crown and misty veil.

While in Charleston harbor, potted camellias and gardenias had been added to the small plant collection of the *Venus*, and Mauma fashioned a bridal bouquet of these flowers in a cone of stiff white satin and lace with ribbon streamers.

"Cap'n Stewart goin' go plum wild when he see you," Mauma predicted. "I declare you is even prettier than Miss Angel in her youth and glory! If only her and your pa could behold their beloved daughter now! You should be comin' down the great stairway at Mystic Rose, with hundreds of folks admirin' you!"

Gazing at her mirrored reflection, Star sighed wistfully, wishing Mauma had not mentioned her parents or Mystic Rose. She murmured, "Thank you, Mauma. Now you'd better get yourself ready. Do you need any help?"

"I been dressin' myself more'n fifty years, Miss Star, and I reckon I can manage one more time."

"Well, hurry, then! I don't want to be late for my own wedding."

"Don't worry, he'll wait."

Some minutes later Star heard laughter in the adjacent cabin. It began as an amused chuckle, increasing in crescendo until it verged on cackling hysteria. Opening the door curiously, she saw Mauma standing before the cheval glass in a pale blue moire gown with clusters of silk roses at the neckline and scattered over the draped skirt, a gorgeous garment elegant enough for a state reception.

"Lawd a mercy!" cried Mauma, giggling convulsively. "Will you look at this old nigger all done up in these fine trappings! The black gals at the plantation would be pea green with envy! I feels like I's goin' to a ball at the president's palace. That be the day, won't it, when a nigger go to a president's party?"

"You look very nice, Mauma," Star complimented. "But you must stop giggling like a silly schoolgirl, lest Captain Stewart think you don't appreciate his gift. That's a most expensive creation, probably designed for some royal or noble lady to wear to a court affair."

"Black poplin uniform with white apron be more proper and comfortable," Mauma surmised, "and maybe a fresh starched white tignon, 'stead of this fancy head gear."

"It's just egret feathers dyed to match the costume, Mauma, and perfect with it. Hurry and finish now. We're due on deck in ten minutes!"

"Who goin' give the bride away?"

"The first officer, and he'll also be the best man."

"Not in the cap'n's presence, he won't."

"Oh, Mauma–will you stop this chatter and get on with it? I'm too nervous to go out there alone!"

The first officer, waiting at the head of the stairs to escort her, was agog when Star appeared, as if he were seeing a vision. Star smiled graciously as Mr. Sims took her arm but scarcely noticed him, for her eyes were on Troy, standing tall and erect and exceptionally handsome in a magnificent white uniform with gold buttons, gold braid and fringed epaulettes, and holding a Bible in his gloved hands. He removed his billed and decorated cap as she approached the altar, where tall cathedral candles flamed in the breeze, and for a few quivering moments Star feared her tumultuous emotions might capsize her. How could she ever have believed that she loved Grant Russell above all else on earth and could not live without him? The memory was dim now, vague, fading into nothingness. Behind her, she could visualize Mauma's expression, sense her realization of Star's own feelings, but she was barely aware of the neatly dressed and assembled crew, gawking at attention, and the watch gaping down from the crow's nest.

Being both magistrate and groom, Troy faced his bride rather than standing beside her and began the official ceremony with a prayerful intercession in a voice so clear and sincere that a deep, reverent silence fell upon the ship, leaving only the sounds of the sails and the sea.

"O Lord, we implore Thee, let Thy inspiration precede our actions and Thy help further them, so that all our prayers and deeds may ever take their beginning from Thee and, so begun, may through Thee reach completion. Through Christ our Lord. Amen."

"Amen," the crew murmured, clearing throats.

"Praise the Lawd!" Mauma cried in a high soprano.

Troy continued: "Dear friends, you are about to witness a most sacred and serious union, established by God Himself, to give man a share in the greatest work of creation, that of the continuation of the human race. In this way, He sanctified human love and enabled man and woman to help each other live in His good graces, by sharing a common life under His fatherly care. Thus, marriage is a holy institution, binding together those who enter into it for life, in a relationship so close and intimate that it will profoundly influence their whole future, and requiring complete and unreserved giving of self. For we know not what hopes and disappointments, successes and failures, pleasures and pains, joys and sorrows may lie ahead. And yet, not knowing, we wish to join ourselves together in wedded life, and henceforth belong entirely to each other, becoming one in mind, in heart, and in spirit, to share generously the bountiful gifts we may enjoy, along with whatever sacrifices may be required of us.

"No greater blessing can come to married life than pure conjugal love, loyal and true to the end. May, then, this love with which we join our hands and hearts today, never fail, but grow deeper and stronger as the years pass. Amen."

The crew bowed heads, and Mauma sniffed and again praised the Lord.

Before pursuing the rite, Troy waited for Star to raise her eyes, which glistened mistily beneath the wispy tulle veil. "Will you, Star Lamont, take me, Troy Stewart, for your lawful husband, to have and to hold, from this day forward, for better, for worse, for richer, for poorer, in sickness and in health, forsaking all others, until death do us part?"

"I will," Star said, her expressive features and consent portraying eternal love.

"I, Troy Stewart, take you, Star Lamont, for my lawful wife, to have and to hold, from this day forward, for better, for worse, for richer, for poorer, in sickness and in health, forsaking all others, until death do us part."

Mr. Sims produced the rings. Troy slipped the symbolic gold band on Star's finger, and she, fumbling slightly, placed a larger one on his. Then they joined hands, still facing each other, and Troy declared, "We

Hawkins had been doing the past hour, preparing the bridal chamber according to the master's instructions! And he had thought of everything, including the exotic incense emanating from the Oriental jade-and-bronze burner.

Star was pleasantly surprised and pleased. "It's grand, Troy! You have excellent taste."

"If you want anything changed, or more space?–"

"No, darling. It's quite adequate–it's perfect. We're going to be very happy and cozy here."

"Traditionally, the groom is supposed to leave now," he said tentatively. "Disappear for awhile to smoke or drink, giving the bride some privacy."

Star smiled. "Do you want to bow to tradition?"

"No, I had in mind something else. Let me show you?"

At her nod, he went to the table, popped the cork from the champagne, partially filled the goblets, and handed her one. "To us, Star, and our future together."

"Always," she whispered, sipping a Versailles' vintage intended for Buckingham Palace– "Forever."

At Troy's eloquent gaze, a tingling warmth invaded Star's flesh, and she felt as if she would melt into malleable wax. He urged her to drink more wine, and soon she began to relax, her tensions and apprehensions easing, at which point he took the goblet from her and set it aside. Then, with slow, gentle expertise, he proceeded to disrobe her, from the symbolic crown and veil to the chaste bridal gown and undergarments, until she wore only the white silk stockings and satin slippers.

Glimpsing her nudity in a mirrored wardrobe door, Star wondered at her immodesty and dissolving inhibitions. Virtues she had believed instinctive did not prevail, as she allowed him a long full view of her lovely figure, with its slender waist, supple hips, and virginal breasts now with taut pink nipples inviting his hands and mouth, his touch and taste. As she awaited his approach, her tremors were excitement, anticipation, desire, and eagerness. She craved consummation, even ravishment, and the sudden revelation of such intense, secret, and vital emotions astonished her.

Without haste, Troy removed his uniform and other clothing and stood unashamedly before her, as if for inspection. Her eyes drifted from his serious, sea-bronzed face to his massive shoulders and dark-haired chest, downward over his lean flat belly and muscular legs. Swollen in passion, his genitals seemed enormous. She gasped slightly, fearful that she could never accommodate him without considerable pain and suffering, for she knew this was the part of him, as Mauma had said, that would have to enter her, and she trembled for other reasons now.

Sensing her reaction, Troy embraced her reassuringly. "No, Star, it won't be like that, I promise you. Tell me if I hurt you, and I'll stop immediately. It doesn't have to happen all the way tonight, darling, unless you say so. We can just play with each other—that's fun, too. You'll see."

As he spoke he urged Star toward the berth, sat down with her, and began to kiss and caress and soothe her, until she was ready to lie with him. And through preliminary fondling and intimate conversation, Star learned that there was much more to lovemaking than the actual coital act. His skillful exploration of her body's erogenous zones evoked ecstatic and even gratifying sensations, such as she had never dared pursue with anyone else. A few times she reached out for him, groping his groin, indicating her willingness for further, total experience.

"There's no hurry, darling," he whispered against her lips. "We have the rest of our lives." His fingers probed a particularly sensitive area, and she moaned in pleasure. "You like that?"

"Mmmm."

His fingers gently probed again, and she felt extreme, almost unbearable, rapture. "And this?" he asked.

"Yes . . . oh, yes!"

"You're ready, darling." Spreading her legs gently, he

moved between her thighs and over her. "Help me, Star."

"How?"

"Relax and take me into you."

"I can't, I can't!"

"Yes, you can, love. Not all at once. Gradually. Try." His voice was tense, husky, supplicating. "Please, try."

"I'm trying but—oh, it hurts! Stop!"

"You're tense again, darling. Let yourself go limp as if lolling in a warm bath and concentrate on pleasure. Yes, that's right. Now kiss me—"

His mouth stifled her cry, and Star inadvertently rebelled and attempted to push him away, but Troy would not be denied now. Persisting, he succeeded in complete penetration, proceeding leisurely for awhile, before a few swift and violent thrusts forced his climax. Heaving, his muscles twitching in the aftermath, his head still on her breast, he apologized sheepishly. "I'm sorry, darling—I couldn't stop. It was too late, we had gone too far. Forgive me for raping you like a brute."

"It's all right," Star consoled him. "You weren't brutal, and you didn't rape me."

"Technically," he insisted. "And I know that wasn't very good for you, darling—the first time rarely is for a girl. But it'll improve with time and practice. Sex is a fine and wonderful thing between a man and woman, especially if they're in love. There's always some lust involved—that's what overwhelmed me a moment ago—but it only intensifies the pleasure. And it's right in marriage, never wrong or evil or sinful, no matter what some Puritans might preach. Nothing could be more proper than giving and sharing our bodies in this sensual intimacy. You believe that, don't you?"

"Yes, Troy, I believe it."

"And you do love me, as much now as you thought before?"

"More, darling, more."

"Oh, Star." A strong emotion ran through his body, reverberating in his pulse. "My love, my wife, that's what I wanted to hear. Are you tired, sleepy?"

Star would not admit fatigue, nor the unfamiliar aching in her lower anatomy. "Not especially. Are you?"

"No, wide awake. I think I'll have a nightcap. Would you like some more champagne?"

"A little, so you won't have to drink alone."

"In that case, share some of Napoleon's favorite cognac with me. It'll have a sedative effect later."

"Ladies are not supposed to drink strong liquor," Star said demurely, "but I'll make an exception on my wedding night."

Troy laughed, tousling her dark curls, and rose to pour the drinks. Watching him, Star exclaimed, "Dear God, we forgot to snuff the candles!"

"I didn't forget, Star. I wanted to see you and have you see me." He grinned. "Notice any physical change in your husband now, Mrs. Stewart?"

"Some, captain."

"A man doesn't look nearly so frightening in this deflated state, does he? Not quite like a little boy, but certainly not terrifying."

Star shook her head negatively, thinking what an unusual creature the male of the species was, even miraculous in his sexual transformation. She wanted to know more, everything, about his body, and knew that Troy would encourage her interest and curiosity, and gladly teach her. She sat up, ignoring the red stain on the sheet, leaving her breasts bare as she plumped the pillows against the headboard of the berth. Beyond the portholes, the heavens glimmered with starlight and a late-rising moon made the waves seem luminous. She accepted the snifter of cognac and, as Troy returned to his place beside her, asked. "When do you expect to reach Marseilles?"

"In a week or so, if the wind serves."

"Can we stay awhile in port? Visit Paris?"

"We'll spend part of our honeymoon there."

"Part?"

"You might like to see London, too."

"Oh, yes, very much! I have English ancestors, you

Also in Hamlyn Paperbacks

Johanna Lindsey
CAPTIVE BRIDE

Desert Stars

On a night made for love, there was only terror for beautiful Christina Wakefield. She who had recklessly followed her brother from London to Cairo on a whim was now made prisoner by an unknown abductor who carried her off to his hidden encampment.

Soon she would share his bed, know his touch, growing ever closer to the man who owned her as a slave.

And soon she would learn to want him as he wanted her – to share his soul, his being – her body aching to be his alone in the trembling ecstasy of everlasting rapture.

Shifting Sands